The Tale of
The Next Great War,
1871–1914

The Tale of the Next Great War, 1871–1914

*Fictions of Future Warfare and
of Battles Still-to-come*

EDITED BY
I. F. CLARKE

SYRACUSE UNIVERSITY PRESS

First Edition 1995

95 96 97 98 99 00   6 5 4 3 2 1

Published in the United States by Syracuse
University Press,
Syracuse, New York 13244-5160,
by arrangement with Liverpool University Press,
Liverpool, United Kingdom

Library of Congress
Cataloging-in-Publication Data
CIP data available from the
publisher upon request

ISBN 0-8156-2672-X *cloth*
0-8156-0358-4 *paper*

Text set in 10½/12½ Meridien
by Action Typesetting Limited, Gloucester

Printed and bound in the European Community
by Bell & Bain Limited, Glasgow

For
Julian and Elaine

Contents

Acknowledgements

This anthology owes much to the advice and assistance of many people; and I now take this opportunity to thank all those who have helped me in the selection and preparation of the various entries.

I am greatly indebted to the knowledge and professional skills of librarians, and especially to: the Librarian, Imperial War Museum, London; Service Historique, Ministère des Armées, Paris; Katalogabteilung, Deutsche Staatsbibliothek; Storage and Delivery Branch, British Library. The staff of the London Library were of great assistance, and I owe a special debt to the Bodleian Library, especially to Ms Rosemary McMcarthy of the Quick-Copy Service who supplied perfect xerographic copies of many extracts and short stories. In some ways my greatest debt is to the staff of the Department of Manuscripts, National Library of Scotland. They guided me through the abundant correspondence and many files in the Blackwood Papers; and in particular I thank Mr Kenneth Dunn for the advice and information he gave me. The various extracts from the Blackwood Papers are published with the permission of the Keeper of Manuscripts and the Trustees of the National Library of Scotland.

M. Guy Costes of Quetigny, France, proved a true bibliophile and a good friend, when he sent me at short notice two missing pages that had vanished from a photocopy of Robida's *La Guerre au XXme siècle*. The translation of Robida's marvellous story owed everything to the extensive knowledge and careful work of Mrs Penny Bath. Invaluable information on those eminent Royal Engineers—Chesney, Swinton, and Vickers—came from Captain Arnold, Librarian, RE Corps Library. Another expert, Commander Jeff Tall, Director of the Royal Navy Submarine Museum, Gosport, looked at the specifications of the submarines in *Danger!*; and he gave Conan Doyle top marks for intelligent anticipation. Neil Barron, librarian and bibliographer in seemingly remote California, worked through several internet systems to discover information on Hugh Grattan Donnelly, a writer who seems to have vanished almost without trace.

In the end all things fell into place and were put into good order by Mrs Sue Hughes. I thank her for the great care she took in the editing of this collection. Finally, and most of all, I am greatly indebted to my wife, my best and kindest critic. She has lived through the evolution of this book and she has survived.

I.F. Clarke
Milton under Wychwood

Illustrations

Introduction: The Paper Warriors and their Fights of Fantasy

I. F. CLARKE

This selection of short stories offers a return journey through the future as it used to be. Time speeds backward to the 1870s, to the alpha point of modern futuristic fiction, when a new college of prophets and predictors first began to describe the new machines, the new societies, and the new wars that would follow in the next decade or the next century. The 1870s were the opening years of that enchanted period before the First World War when Jules Verne, H. G. Wells, and many able writers delighted readers from Sydney to Seattle with their most original revelations of things-to-come. In all their anticipations, the dominant factor, and the prime source of their material, was the recognition that the new industrial societies would continue to evolve in obedience to the rate of change. One major event that caused all to think furiously about the future was the Franco-German War of 1870. The new weapons and the new methods of army organization had shown that the conduct of warfare was changing; and, in response to that perception of change, a new form of fiction took on the task of describing the conduct of the war-to-come.

The 1870s saw the beginning of a profitable and ever-expanding publishing industry, dedicated exclusively to presenting decidedly partisan versions of the *Zukunftskrieg, La Guerre de demain,* and *The Next Great War.* Ever since the unprecedented uproar that followed on the publication of the anonymous tale of the *Battle of Dorking* in May 1871, the projections of the war-to-come have earned their reputation as a dedicated, instant response form of fiction. From time to time, these anticipations of the course and consequences of future wars have done much to shape public opinion. On notable occasions they have caused national commotions, international recriminations, even worldwide astonishment. These tales of the next great war, like divisional artillery, go from one sudden bombardment to another. Their characteristic reactions to targets of opportunity are immediately recognizable nowadays in the high seriousness of so many recent accounts of the Cold War period. There is, for example, the final conflict in *The Third World War: A Future History* (1978) by General Sir John Hackett and associates; the end of all human life in Stanley Kramer's film *On the Beach* (1959); and in *Russian Hide and Seek* (1980) an ingenious variation on the Russian occupation theme by Sir Kingsley Amis.

The imaginary wars in this collection are powerful remembrances of dominant expectations as these were perceived and projected during a fateful period of European history. Old antagonisms and once flourishing alliances are here restored to the full life of fiction. They are venerable echoes from the last age of innocence, before the military technologies of the First World War demonstrated in the most brutal ways that the unexpected can make nonsense of assumptions about the future. In this fiction, after a century of occasional alarms and sporadic projections, fire for effect began in 1871 with the sudden appearance of the perfect archetype—Chesney's account of *The Battle of Dorking*. That prodigiously successful short story about a rapid German conquest of the United Kingdom was the first tale of the future to attract immediate attention throughout the world. After Chesney, the rolling barrage of the future war stories moved forward year by year. As the major industrial nations advanced from ironclad warships to the first dreadnoughts, a succession of paper warriors—British, French, German, and some Americans—made it their business to describe the most likely shape of the war-to-come in many tales of glorious victories and salutary defeats. And then in July 1914, as time suddenly ran out for this anticipatory fiction, the *Strand Magazine* published *Danger*, an unusually prescient tale of submarine warfare and one of the last of these stories to appear before the real war broke out. The author was Arthur Conan Doyle, who had already tried his hand at an end-of-civilization fantasy with *The Poisoned Cloud* in 1913. Later on, in 1918, he said that he had written his account of the coming end to British naval superiority in order to put the case for a Channel Tunnel.[1]

The short stories in this collection are all prime examples of the first main phase in brain warfare. This powerful and popular form of futuristic fiction is one of several crucial literary inventions that have taken their themes from the range of contemporary possibilities—social, political, technological—and they have used time-to-come as the most apt means of projecting the worst or the best that could be. Ideal worlds, police states, the everlasting nuclear winter, interplanetary conflicts and marvellous adventures in distant galaxies, devastating wars and the end of humankind—these are all familiar topics in the immense outpouring of futuristic fiction in modern times. In their different ways, they show that the tale of the future has been the most favoured means of mediating between the reader and tomorrow's world ever since the appearance of Jules Verne's *De la terre à la lune* in 1865, J. F. Maguire's *The Next Generation* in 1871, and Edward Maitland's *By and By* in 1873.

The old-style battle, with both sides in full view, the generals following every move, as observed at Marengo, on 14 June 1800

Today, in marked contrast to those imaginative projections, a new profession of calculators and predictors has sought to bring order and greater rigour to the old business of prophecy. Since the 1950s innumerable down-to-earth experts—social analysts, statisticians, demographers, forecasters and futurologists, experts from the think-tanks and the commissions for the twenty-first century—have laboured to deliver the most up-to-date news about the state of the world in the next millennium. These latest refinements in detecting patterns of probabilities are a practical recognition of the process of change forever at work in any advanced technological society. They are, however, no more than the most recent entries in the great book of future-think.

The modern stage in the never-ending search for the true shape of coming things began in the seventeenth century with the writings of Francis Bacon, Baron Verulam, first Viscount St Albans and Lord

Chancellor of England. In the *De Augmentis* of 1605, and more particularly in the *Novum Organum* of 1620, Bacon set out to show Europe
how to achieve the Kingdom of Man over nature. 'No book ever
made so great a revolution in the mode of thinking'—so Lord
Macaulay wrote of the *Novum Organum* in a famous essay. What the
historian admired most was 'the vast capacity of that intellect which,
without effort, takes in at once all the domains of science, all the
past, the present, and the future, all the errors of two thousand
years, all the encouraging signs of the passing times, all the bright
hopes of the coming age'.[2]

Macaulay had in mind Bacon's future-directed proposition that
the end of scientific knowledge must be 'the endowment of human
life with new inventions and riches'. In the *Novum Organum* Bacon
had outlined a method for exploiting nature to the advantage of
mankind; and in his *New Atlantis*, which he finished in 1623, this
remarkable man evolved a most appropriate mode for presenting his
vision of a scientific community toiling away at the frontiers of
knowledge. In the other-world of Bensalem, far beyond the utmost
reach of navigation, Bacon revealed a working model of the future
as it might be, if the world attended to what he had to say about the
sciences. Although his College of the Six Days' Work existed in an
everlasting there-and-now at the edge of the known world, 'this
glorious prophecy', as Macaulay called it, was the manifest and true
bill of the wonders that would follow from the division of scientific
labour. The objective of all research in Bensalem is to empower
humankind. All their operations aim at 'the knowledge of causes
and secret motions of things, and the enlarging of the bounds of
human empire to the effecting of all things possible'. With that celebrated phrase, the source of true wisdom for his devoted followers,
Bacon separated the moral from the material, and thereby left a
time-bomb ticking away in his earthly paradise. The earnest,
complacent calculator could not foresee the consequences of his
projected military inventions—of making weapons 'stronger and
more violent than yours are, exceeding your greatest cannons and
basilisks'.

Bacon's propositions had no direct influence on the development
of the sciences, but his ideas continued to signal the coming break-
through in the great campaign for the mastery of nature. In
November 1750, when Diderot issued the first prospectus for the
Encyclopédie, that most Baconian compilation of knowledge, he
saluted the author of the *Novum Organum* as 'the greatest, the most
universal and the most eloquent of philosophers'. That was the time

when ideas about human progress had begun to circulate throughout Europe. An early and emphatic statement of the new doctrine of bigger–better–wiser came from Anne Robert Jacques Turgot, a student of the Sorbonne at the time and later Contrôleur Général des Finances. On 11 December 1750 Turgot presented a paper entitled 'A Philosophical Review of the Successive Advances of the Human Mind'. History, he said, was the record of the long advance from barbarism to the fullness of civilization. One of the first lessons from history showed that 'the whole human race, through alternate periods of rest and unrest, of weal and woe, goes on advancing, although at a slow pace, towards greater perfection'.[3] Mankind was entering on a new age of increasing knowledge: 'Already Bacon has traced out for posterity the road which it must follow.' Although Turgot was confident that the great advance would continue, he could not foresee the way ahead. For an aspirant cleric, as Turgot was at that time, the future was best left to prayer: 'May men continually make new steps along the road of truth! Rather still, may they continually become better and happier!'

The French army established the first balloon company in history on 2 April 1794. It consisted of one hydrogen balloon and a crew of two. The company saw service in the French victory at Fleurus on 26 June 1794

As the road to the future opened up in the second half of the eighteenth century, a process of convergence started between the limitless possibilities of fiction and the ever more confident hopes of the greater changes still to come. The new and the potential were matters that demanded their proper form. So, in a hesitant and experimental way, the tale of the future began as a marriage of convenience between old styles and new opportunities.

The first major English example of this transformation is the anonymous *Reign of George VI, 1900–1925* of 1763. Like so many of his successors in the business of constructing future worlds, the author built with borrowed material. The score for this first hymn to an ideal future was programme music from a bygone age; for the author had taken his principal ideas from the archaic scheme of monarchical government that had appeared in Bolingbroke's *Idea of a Patriot King* of 1749. Nevertheless, the form of the story is truly original. The author has the distinction of inaugurating the tale of coming things with a double-take; for he combines two of the most effective modes in futuristic fiction in his account of the great wars-to-come and of an ideal Britain in the early twentieth century. The alien geography and the other-world chronologies of the terrestrial utopias vanish. The long voyage to Bensalem and Lilliput becomes an instant time-journey through the future-imperfect of the United Kingdom during the troubled reigns of George IV and George V. Then comes the virtual reality of a better age, when King George VI succeeds to the throne on 16 February 1900. Happy days have come again. It was the beginning of 'a period the most remarkable, and abounding in the most astonishing events, that have ever been recorded in modern history'.

This devoted Hanoverian fantasy displays for the first time the essential mechanism of the imaginary war story: the assessment of those contemporary enemies, coalitions, and alliances that can be expected to decide the future of any nation; the application of approved theories—political, military, technological—that will come together in a convincing demonstration of cause and effect; and the future victories, or the disasters and defeats, that will present the exemplary verdicts of a triumphant or a despairing posterity. True to his eighteenth-century assumptions, however, the author puts the future George VI in his rightful place—at the source of all power, as the prime mover in the affairs of state, and as the wise, prudent paragon of a warrior king. His chief service to his country will be twenty years of constant and most profitable warfare. Six of the ten chapters in *The Reign of George VI* are devoted to the many successful campaigns that make the British monarch ruler of Europe, King of France, and master of a vast empire overseas. This empire extends from the Philippines to Mexico and—note well—to 'the British American dominions in North America'. The global scale of the narrative is in marked contrast to the old-style convictions, which create a static, ever-lasting Hanoverian world of the future. The only conceivable changes in this *sicut erit* history are the territorial gains that come from successful campaigns. Technology has not begun to affect the conditions of warfare on land or at sea. Ships-of-the-line, cavalry, and musketeers continue the practices of the eighteenth-century drill books. War is not yet a matter for citizens: it remains the favoured argument of kings. The European monarchs—Austrian, British, French, Russian, Spanish—maintain their own armies, recruit their own mercenaries, and plan their campaigns as they will; they select their senior officers from the aristocracy; and they never fail to lead their troops into battle. All the engagements in *The Reign of George VI*, for example, are action replays of eighteenth-century warfare—one-day affairs fought during the campaigning season from April to September. Here is the British monarch in his role as commander-in-chief at the Battle of Alençon on 5 July 1925:[4]

> The French army was posted in the most advantageous manner. In their front was a rivulet, behind which were nine redoubts mounted with cannon; their wings were defended in the same manner, and every approach guarded with artillery.
>
> The King, having reconnoitred the enemy's position, drew up his troops on the same plain at some distance in their front. As the French army outspread his, he disposed his cannon in his wings, in such a manner as to prevent his being surrounded; himself commanded the centre, the Duke of Devonshire the right, and the Earl of Bury the left. Everything being prepared for the engagement, the King ordered the signal to be made for beginning it, and about nine in the morning the battle began which was at once to decide the fate of two mighty kingdoms. The French army was the most numerous; and commanded by their King. The Monarch of the English also headed them, and they were eager to engage, and obliterate by their bravery the memory of their late defeat. The fire of the artillery was the beginning of this great action; as the British troops advanced under cover of their

own cannon, that of the enemy played on them with great fury, and some effect. But the skill of the English engineers so well directed their fire, that several batteries of the enemy were thrown into confusion. The King however soon brought on warmer work; at the head of the first line of his centre, he began the attack, which was received with firmness.

If the author lived on to the end of the century, he must have noted how the very different conditions of a revolutionary age had brought about distinct changes in the representation of the war-to-come. During the Napoleonic period, the desire for the greatest possible realism had made eager patriots turn to print-making and play-writing in order to portray their versions of the future as they hoped it would be. On the French side, the battles of tomorrow opened with highly dramatic presentations of the coming conquest of the United Kingdom in *Les Prisonniers français en Angleterre* in 1797, and *La Descente en Angleterre: Prophétie en deux actes* in 1798. The British response began in 1803, the year of greatest danger, when Napoleon's invasion forces were encamped at Boulogne, waiting for the crucial six hours of good weather that would permit them to cross the Channel. In London happy British audiences applauded the end of French ambitions in *The Invasion of England: A Farce in Three Acts* and the equally desirable calamities in *The Armed Briton; or, the Invaders Vanquished*.

These British and French plays reveal the first signs of a shift in both attitudes and expectations which would come to dominate all future-war fiction from 1871 onwards. Monarchs and their dynasties vanish from these dramas. The whole nation—soldiers, sailors, volunteers, and citizens—become the principal actors in the battle-to-come; and, even more indicative of a change in perceptions, there are the earliest anticipations of new means of warfare. These appear at their most menacing in the many prints of the great invasion craft, powered by windmills, that were supposed to be waiting for GB Day in Boulogne harbour. The most original were French prints of an invasion by way of a secret Channel Tunnel, or by vast troop-landing balloons speeding through the clouds on their way to Dover.

When Nelson died in the action off Cape Trafalgar on 21 October 1805, it seemed that the British command of the sea was secure for generations to come. Within forty years, however, the technologies of the new iron age had begun to change the conduct of warfare. The sail navies changed to steamships, and then to ironclads in response to the first shell-guns. The armies abandoned the old

Print warfare in Year XI of the Republic: a French projection of an air-landing brigade
(3,000 men), transported by Montgolfier balloon across the Channel

muzzle-loading musket for the far more accurate rifle, and the
artillery regiments greatly increased the rate and accuracy of their
fire with the breech-loading gun. Although admirals and generals
debated the effects of these changes at great length in many tracts

about the application of the new weaponry, the tales of the war-to-come had little to say about the future.[5] One reason was the prevailing belief in the idea of progress—the conviction that, as the Prince Consort put it in 1850, the British people were fortunate enough to be 'living at a period of most wonderful transition'. If all things were manifestly improving, it followed that the military technologies would advance the cause of universal peace as surely as the steamship and the railway had already done so much for the improvement of mankind. In 1841, it was fast forward and progress in all directions. That thought was written into the exultant verse of Tennyson's 'Locksley Hall':

> Men, my brothers, men the workers, ever reaping
>   something new:
> That which they have done but earnest of the things
>   that they shall do:
>
>
> For I dipt into the future, far as human eye could see,
> Saw the Vision of the world, and all the wonder that
>   would be;
>
>
> Saw the heavens fill with commerce, argosies of magic sails,
> Pilots of the purple twilight, dropping down with costly
>   bales;
>
>
> Heard the heavens fill with shouting, and there rain'd
>   a ghastly dew
> From the nations' airy navies grappling in the central
>   blue;
>
>
> Far along the world-wide whisper of the south-wind
>   rushing warm,
> With the standards of the people plunging thro' the
>   thunder-storm;
>
>
> Till the war-drum throbb'd no longer, and the battle-
>   flags were furl'd
> In the Parliament of man, the Federation of the world.

A French anticipation of the day when Napoleon would arrive in Boulogne for
La Descente en Angleterre

Artist's impression of vast French landing craft, powered by wind-mills, supposed to be
ready for the invasion of Britain

In the new age of steam navies, only a major enemy—possessed of a great army and a large fleet—could disrupt the dream of peace. That unlikely combination made for a relaxed attitude. Even in 1841, when the Prince de Joinville caused some alarm by his proposals for a large French navy, the British press took matters calmly on the whole. A typical response appeared in an editorial in the *Illustrated London News*. It began with the sensible observation: 'The landing of a French army on the sea coast is an event not very probable; but, as there have been invasions in times past, there is at least a possibility of it—quite enough to throw timid people into a sense of mild terror.'[6] There was, however, a momentary tremor of alarm in 1851, when Louis Napoleon staged the coup that made him ruler of France. The combination of a French steam navy and the memory of the first Napoleon was enough to set the alarm bells ringing in the press. And yet, the response in fiction to the antici-pated dangers was one short story, *The History of the Sudden and Terrible Invasion of England by the French*—a tale of French treachery and the most conspicuous British incompetence. Louis Napoleon is a villain: 'Vain, dissipated and insignificant, during his exile in England he associated only with the wildest spirits of the aristocracy; but under the cloak of gaiety he concealed an undying hatred to the British name.' The British government does not understand that 'it was no longer possible to guard the long line of coast against the sudden attacks of steamers; and that, in fact, we are now become a *Continental* nation, and, like the rest, would be compelled to keep up a large and powerful standing army to preserve our firesides from invasion'. For the French army, well prepared and well armed, the invasion is little more than annual manoeuvres. London surrenders, and the Londoners pay £20 million to be saved from the looters. Or so they hoped. But:[7]

> In levying this heavy contribution some disputes arose between the citizens and the conquerors, which led to blows, and the ruthless soldiers of Bonaparte immediately commenced an indiscriminate massacre and pillage which continued for three days, till the Algerian warriors were forced to show mercy, because, through sheer exhaustion, they could no longer continue their barbarities. With the concentrated vengeance of three days they effaced the bitter recollections of centuries: Cressy, Agincourt, Salamanca, and Waterloo, were all dust in the balance with the sacking of London. The destruction of life was enormous, especially in

the City; and few of the public buildings escaped the ruthless violence of the enemy. The *Punch* office and Printing-house Square were made especial bonfires of, and all was conflagration and dismay. The parapets of Waterloo-bridge were hurled into the Thames, and Waterloo-place with a considerable part of Regent-street was utterly destroyed by fire. Even the wild animals of the Zoological-gardens were let loose, and, like the tigers of Tippoo at the storming of Seringapatam, added confusion and terror to the scene.

Twenty years later, the rapid and totally unexpected German victories in the War of 1870 astounded the world and caused great alarm in the United Kingdom. Newspapers were filled with articles about the new kind of warfare, as editors sought to take full advantage of the national nervousness. Naval historians, admirals, and generals presented their views on 'Future Naval Battles', 'Are we Ready?', 'Our Naval Supremacy', and 'National Armies and Modern Warfare'. They wrote at length on the importance of railway systems in concentrating and transporting troops, the new means of control and rapid communication in the electric telegraph, the new rifles and the new artillery which 'have effected a complete revolution in the methods of combat, the organisation of the troops, and their instruction'. Throughout 1870 and well into 1871, the comments varied from statements of stupefaction to forecasts of the consequences for Europe.

So, what did the future hold? In a lecture delivered on 25 April 1871, the eminent historian, Lord Acton, told his audience that the future was beyond the calculation of historians: 'To exhibit a coherent chain of causes in the revolution of the last nine months, which has shifted the landmarks of European politics, and has given new leaders to the world, is still an impossible task.'[8] A week later another historian, Edward Augustus Freeman, told the readers of *Macmillan's Magazine* that they had every reason to rejoice in the defeat of the French. As for their anxieties about invasion, it was all a fit of the vapours: 'We have been passing through, perhaps we have not yet fully come out of, one of those curious fits of panic which seem ever and anon to seize upon the English nation, and which, after exciting everybody for a while, die away and are forgotten.'[9]

Lord Acton and Edward Freeman were not to know that the greatest literary explosion of the nineteenth century was already in train, as the typesetters completed work on No. 667 of *Blackwood's Edinburgh Magazine*. When the May issue burst upon the nation, the

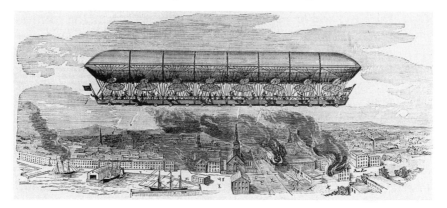

With the beginnings of the illustrated press in the 1840s, the look-into-the-future
became a popular feature of the new magazines

first entry proved so startling that by the end of the month readers
throughout the world had learnt the message of *The Battle of Dorking:
Reminiscences of a Volunteer*. The anonymous author was a distinguished officer of Engineers, Lieutenant-Colonel at the time, later
General Sir George Tomkyns Chesney. His intention in writing was
to warn his fellow-countrymen that the War of 1870 could easily be
repeated on their home ground, if the nation did not accept the need
for a reorganization of the army and for conscription.

The extraordinary success of *The Battle of Dorking* derived for the
most part from a well-told story which compelled readers to partic-
ipate in the imagined defeat and humiliation of their country.
Chesney had three advantages: he knew how to write about
warfare; he had the good sense to base his narrative on the episodic
I-was-there style of the then popular Erckmann–Chatrian stories;
and he went into print at a time when there was great debate and
some anxiety about the shape of wars-to-come. The result was a
fast-moving tale of total disaster and the most damning incompetence, told by the Volunteer who observes and explains those sins of
omission in manpower and of commission in strategy that led to the
final lamentation: 'Truly the nation was ripe for a fall; but when I
reflect how a little firmness and self-denial, or political courage and
foresight, might have averted the disaster I feel that the judgement
must have really been deserved.'

By the end of May *Blackwood's Magazine* had gone through six
reprints, and still the demand was for more. In June, when John
Blackwood started to publish *The Dorking* as a sixpenny pamphlet,
the sales went up and up at the rate of 20,000 a week to reach the

grand total of 110,000 in July. And then, on 2 September, the British Prime Minister, William Ewart Gladstone, attacked the 'alarmism' of the Chesney story in a speech at Whitby. On 5 September William Blackwood wrote to his uncle and partner, John Blackwood: 'Gladstone's speech is contemptible but it will do "The Dorking" good and introduce it to quite a new class of people. We will soon have to think of a people's edition. I think at 1*d* or 2*d*.'[10] It was a sign that the times were changing. War had become the concern of all citizens. A short story for the middle-class readers of *Blackwood's Magazine* had caught the attention of 'a new class of people' throughout the world. As populations had gone on increasing during the great forward movement of the nineteenth century, and as the levels of literacy continued to rise in the major industrial nations, more and more publications were able to meet the demand for information about coming things. So, there were translations of the *Blackwood's* story into Danish, Dutch, French, German, Italian, Portuguese, and Swedish; and there were instant reprints in New Zealand, Canada, and the United States. By the end of 1871 there had been some eighteen British variations and counter-blasts on the lines of *The Battle of Dorking: A Myth*, and, in final proof of an unprecedented notoriety, there were two music-hall songs on the invasion theme and a fictitious edition of *The Official Despatches and Correspondence relative to the Battle of Dorking, as moved for in the House of Commons, 21st July 1920.*

The 'Dorking' episode was the beginning of the great flood of future war stories that continued right up to the summer of 1914. The new wave of writers learnt the basics of their trade from Chesney. His name and reputation lived on in faithful imitations and occasional reprints. In fact, the recollection of his invasion story was powerful enough to lend support to Colonel Maude's account of *The New Battle of Dorking* in 1900. A more sinister occasion was the reappearance of *The Dorking* in 1940, published by the Nazi propaganda machine with the apposite title of *Was England erwartet!*

From 1871 to 1914, the tale of the next great war was a staple of the European press. Year by year, patriotism and profit worked happily together to produce more and more of these stories to satisfy the ever-growing interest in coming things. It was the first great age of the future—that primal time when the potential found appropriate shape in ideal states like Edward Bellamy's *Looking Backward, 2000–1887*, in the heroic enterprise fiction of Jules Verne, and in the earliest essays in future-think that appear in David Goodman Croly's collection of speculations, *Glimpses of the Future: Suggestions as to the*

Drift of Things (1888). They were all fantasies of the conscious mind; they made the seemingly logical connections between today and tomorrow.

The first patent application (No. 747) for an armoured fighting vehicle was presented on 3 April 1855 by James Cowen and James Sweetlong. 'This invention consists of an improved locomotive battery to be used in the field of battle, and is so constructed as to exert a most destructive force against the enemy, while protected from damage in return'

This may-be fiction opened up two main lines into the future. First, the political account in the Chesney mode described how catastrophe—or victory—would surely follow, because the nation had—or had not—adopted whatever safeguards the authors considered essential in any future conflict. Later on, when the technological narratives began in the 1880s, they broke new ground by combining entertainment with instruction in exciting tales about 'what it will be like' in the new kind of war at sea or in the air. In 1888, for instance, Hugh Arnold-Forster, an MP at the time and later Secretary of the Admiralty, wrote *In a Conning Tower: A Story of Modern Ironclad Warfare* in order to give the readers of *Murray's Magazine* 'a faithful idea of the possible course of an action between two modern ironclads availing themselves of all the weapons of offence and defence which an armoured ship at the present day possesses'. Ironclads, then submarines, destroyers, and aeroplanes—there was no end to speculation. In 1900, for example, the American inventor,

J. P. Holland, delivered the first effective submarine to the US Navy; and in 1901 George Griffith wrote *The Raid of Le Vengeur*, an ingenious tale of anti-submarine warfare. On 25 July 1909 Louis Blériot made the first aeroplane crossing of the English Channel, and at once the new versions of the war-in-the-air began to multiply. The Swedish writer Gustaf Janson considered the inhumanity of air warfare in his *Vision of the Future* (1912); and the British writer Frederick Britten Austin described an air attack on infantry and the breakdown of morale in *"Planes!"* (1913).

Thus, the future war story is at all times a specific response, both in form and in content, to the perceived potential in contemporary society. For two decades after 1871, the tales of the next great war kept close to the Chesney model. Most of them began as short stories in the principal middle-class magazines; and most of their authors were eminent Victorians who wrote their tales of the war-to-come in order to give the public the benefit of their views on military or naval matters. For example, General Sir William Francis Butler, a distinguished soldier, wrote *The Invasion of England* (1882) to call attention to the materialism that could endanger the nation. In 1887 Sir William Laird Clowes and Alan Hughes Burgoyne brought out *The Great Naval War in 1887*, in which they presented a French conquest of the United Kingdom as 'the natural result of years of indifference, mismanagement, and parsimony'. The guiding principle in these stories was: tomorrow's wars begin today. In 1882, for instance, the proposals for a Channel Tunnel led to a sudden flurry of I-told-you-so stories—*How John Bull lost London, The Story of the Channel Tunnel, The Seizure of the Channel Tunnel*. The dastardly French invaders come secretly by train to Dover. They leap from the carriages—Zouaves disguised as tourists—and depart at the double to seize Dover Castle. The enemy in these stories know nothing of chivalry and the rules of war. In *The Taking of Dover* there is an early example of the fifth column at work, for Horace Francis Lester makes a feature of the despicable behaviour of the French and Russians agents as they assemble a secret assault group for the capture of Dover. In fact, the primary law in this fiction is: the more political the story, the greater the uniformity in the telling. A secondary law holds that the end will always justify the means.

Change the circumstances, and the narrative style of the invasion-of-England story reappears in *The Stricken Nation*, an anti-British projection from across the Atlantic. This tale of the great American disaster, like the Channel Tunnel stories, was a product of the times. In the 1880s a debate had opened in the United States about the need for a large navy; and in 1889, when Congress began to consider a naval construction programme, Henry Grattan Donnelly decided to put the case for a great American navy in the Chesney manner. His test to destruction was a tale of terror in which naval superiority leads to the conquest of the United States. In his story the British are as vile as the French in *The Taking of Dover*: 'There were British spies on our ships, British spies in our arsenals, and British influences had for years been powerful enough to defeat every attempt that was made to get appropriations for defence.'

The attention Donnelly gave to British armaments was one sign of a growing interest in the seemingly limitless possibilities of ever more lethal weaponry. The most striking example of this new direction in fiction is undoubtedly the magnificently illustrated album of *La Guerre au vingtième siècle* ('War in the Twentieth Century') of 1887. The author and the illustrator was Albert Robida, a gifted caricaturist with a sharp eye for the grotesque. This most original artist took the idea of the future as his theme, and in a series of illustrated stories in the weekly *La Caricature* he created his own iconography of daily life in the twentieth century—many varieties of mechanical transportation, submarine pleasure boats, video-phones, television news, trips to the moon for 80,000 francs, even synthetic foods. The stories later appeared as books, of which the most remarkable are *La Vie électrique*, *La Vie au vingtième siècle*, and most of all *La Guerre au vingtième siècle*. The images of the world war of 1945 in that book—chemical warfare battalions, bombing planes, submarines, and armoured fighting vehicles—are an ironic commentary on the assumptions of a technological epoch. No matter what the weapons might be, the citizens of the great industrial nations thought that future wars would continue to be like the limited and relatively humane engagements of the old days. New weapons and old ideas—that fatal combination would make nonsense of all their anticipations of coming wars. They failed to scale up the casualty lists, and they could not even begin to guess at the changes for the worse to be expected in the great technological war of the future. Experience had deceived them. The future very rarely turns out to be what was expected, as so many Kremlin-watchers discovered not so long ago.

The nineteenth-century prophets could contemplate the possibility of future wars with equanimity. Like Tennyson, they had looked into the future and they had seen 'the Vision of the world, and all the wonder that would be'. The diffusion of knowledge, the constant improvement in education, the increasing wealth of nations, the convenience and security of life in the great new urban centres, the application of world-changing technologies and the benign discoveries of the medical sciences, the spreading European empires and the growing interdependence of nations—all those familiar phrases from the non-stop discourse on progress encouraged a positivist, optimistic attitude to the future. The data persuaded some world-changers, like Josiah Strong, that all the signs pointed to a decisive conflict for the domination of the planet. The time was coming when the world would 'enter upon a new stage of its history—the final competition of races, for which the Anglo-Saxon race is being schooled—this powerful race will move down upon Mexico, down upon Central and Southern America, out upon the islands of the sea, over upon Africa and beyond. And can anyone doubt that the result of this competition of races will be the "survival of the fittest?" '.[11]

From the same data there came a very different set of assumptions, which looked forward to peace and worldwide co-operation. They promised that the meek would find their heaven in any of the characteristic nineteenth-century ideal worlds of the future. Indeed, in the most popular of them all, *Looking Backward*, Edward Bellamy noted in a postscript that his description of the peaceful and co-operative world-state in the year 2000 was intended 'in all seriousness, as a forecast, in accordance with the principles of evolution, of the next stage in the social and industrial development of humanity'. Destiny was the bell-ringer of the coming age. These prophets knew where they were going; for it was written that the social and technological achievements of the nineteenth century were the marvellous prologue to the growing harmony and increasing happiness of all humankind.

No one put that conviction better than H. G. Wells in 1901, when he welcomed the twentieth century with his forecasts of coming things in *Anticipations of the Reaction of Mechanical and Scientific Progress upon Human Life and Thought*. The future was, he declared, in the safe hands of the New Republicans. They are 'the new class of modern efficients', those educated and rational minds that 'will already be consciously and pretty freely controlling the general affairs of humanity before this century closes'. The fortunate peoples of planet Earth will go on for ever and ever in the good hands of these prudent managers; for their 'broad principles and opinions must necessarily shape and determine that still ampler future of which the coming hundred years is but the opening phase'.

Optimism came easily to Wells and his contemporaries. Their forecasts of things-to-come had no entries for global warming, shrinking

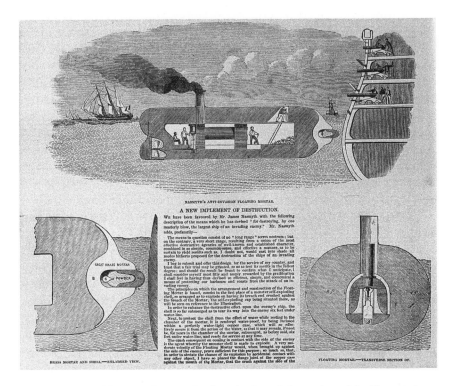

Possibilities of future military technology fascinated the readers of the illustrated magazines, as is apparent in the proposal by James Nasmyth for a 'floating mortar ... for destroying, by one masterly blow, the largest ship of an invading army'

tropical forests, the nuclear winter, future-shock, or ecological catastrophes such as the desolation of the Aral Sea. In their speculations about time-to-come, they assumed that their successors would manage change, even in warfare, as well as their predecessors had controlled the development of the great industrial societies. As new armaments appeared, the imagination raced ahead to the limits of the possible. Dynamite cruisers, electric rifles, giant submarines, vast flying machines—these appeared regularly in the many popular accounts that began in the 1890s.

The perfection of this new style is apparent in the remarkable sequence of full-length stories from H. G. Wells. In *The War of the Worlds* of 1898, he took weaponry as far as he could imagine in the Martian fighting machines, the Black Smoke, and the Heat Ray; in 1908 he came closer to the possible in the air bombardments described in *The War in the Air*; and in 1913 he produced the most fateful anticipation of all these stories in his account of the atomic war in *The World Set Free*. Out of that great evil, Wells plucked the blessings of universal peace and the union of all nations in the World Republic.

From 1890 onwards, the tales of the war-to-come multiplied and diversified in various ways. The armed forces and their role in any future war had become matters of absorbing interest for readers at all levels throughout Europe. Everywhere, writers met the demand for more exciting and more chauvinistic fiction with full-length stories that gave their versions of the expected war against France, or Russia, or Germany. In 1892, for example, *The Times* naval correspondent and historian of the Royal Navy, Sir William Laird Clowes, dedicated the 308 pages of *The Captain of the 'Mary Rose'* to answering the question, 'What will the sea-fighting of tomorrow be like?' In France, from 1889 to 1910 there was a succession of twelve books, some 12,000 pages in all, about *La Guerre qui vient* from Capitaine Danrit, the *nom de guerre* of the distinguished officer of Chasseurs, Commandant Émile Auguste Driant. And there were illustrated stories in French magazines. For example, *La Guerre Anglo-Franco-Russe*, Henri De Nousanne's account of the total defeat of the British, was published as a special supplement to *Le Monde Illustré* for 10 March 1900. In Germany, tales of *Der Krieg gegen England* first began to affect opinion from the time of the Navy Bill of 1900. An opening shot in the *Zukunftskrieg* against the British had the apt title of *Die Abrechnung mit England* (1901). Indeed, the German tales of the next great war had the most uncompromising titles: August Niemann, *Der Weltkrieg—Deutsche Träume* (1904); Karl Bleibtreu, *Die 'Offensiv-Invasion' gegen England* (1907); and so on to the most inflammatory of them all: Paul Georg Münch, *Hindenburgs Einmarsch in London* (1915).

Although the short story continued to hold its own in *Blackwood's, The Strand,* and the other major British journals, the immutable laws of supply and demand gave the best of the trade to the new popular press and to the book publishers. Astute newspaper proprietors, entrepreneurs like Pearson and Harmsworth, sought to increase sales by giving their readers long, lurid accounts of the next great war against the French in the 1890s and against the Germans after 1903. These serial stories became the norm in the popular press and in the more expensive weekly illustrated magazines. The first of the new serials appeared in January 1891. This was the fully illustrated projection of *The Great War of 1892*, which the editor of *Black and White* had commissioned from Admiral Colomb and his eminent associates. The experts gave their readers what they wanted: a professional analysis of the expected European war to be fought by Germany and the United Kingdom against France and Russia. Their forecast proved so popular, especially in the book edition, that journalists—George Griffith, Robert Cromie, F. T. Jane, and Louis Tracy, for example—took to writing future war stories.

The most successful, and certainly the most notorious, of them all was William Le Queux. In 1894 he entered on his long collaboration with Alfred Harmsworth when he wrote *The Great War in England in 1897* for *Answers*, the new Harmsworth weekly. It did wonders for the circulation figures, and Le Queux followed up that success with another war story, *England's Peril* (1899). Then, in 1906 he did better than ever for Alfred Harmsworth (Baron Northcliffe by that time) with his sensational account of German victories and British disasters in *The Invasion of 1910*. Again, there was alarm and anger when the ridiculous story began to appear in the *Daily Mail*; and once again, a British prime minister felt it was necessary to denounce yet another tale of the great German invasion. Le Queux was a scaremonger, said Sir Henry Campbell-Bannerman, and his story was 'calculated to inflame public opinion abroad and alarm the more ignorant public at home'. Nevertheless, *The Invasion of 1910* proved to be a greater commercial success than Chesney's *Battle of Dorking*. For six months it was the talk of the nation, and it enjoyed close scrutiny in the French and German press. The final balance sheet showed twenty-seven translations, and sales of the book at over one million copies.

Between 1903 and 1914, every stage of the coming war against Germany was related for British readers in a literature of extraordinary contrasts. There were the inflammatory serial stories, and there were stories of great originality and high quality. In 1903, for example, Erskine Childers described the rehearsal for a German invasion in his admirable *Riddle of the Sands*. In 1909, a bumper year, good patriots could choose to see Guy du Maurier's play *An Englishman's Home* at Wyndham's Theatre; and, if they made the effort, they could read a poetic version of the German invasion story in Charles Doughty's *The Clouds*. If they wanted to be amused, they had a brief piece in *Punch*, *The Secret of the Army Aeroplane*, in which the promising young humorist A. A. Milne made fun of Le Queux's *Spies of the Kaiser Plotting the Downfall of England*. Two months later another young humorist, P. G. Wodehouse, added to the merriment with his comic deflation of the future war story in *The Swoop! or, How Clarence saved England*.

At the same time, the short story made an evolutionary advance to new themes. Out went the political and moral demonstrations that had once shaped and animated the old Chesney-style fiction, and in came more generalized stories. These concentrated on one or other aspect of warfare, and not on the known enemies and the expected wars of the serials. No doubt this retreat from the popular consensus on the next great war was the decision of the magazine editors. They must have realized that they could not compete with the serials in length, exciting episodes, and conspicuous chauvinism.

An early and classic example of this new direction appeared in the *Strand Magazine* for December 1903. It was Wells's famous account of *The Land Ironclads,* and a favourite entry in the anthologies of the last forty years. Like Conan Doyle's study of submarine warfare in *Danger,* it was as near an essay in abstractions as these war stories can be. All the particularities of nations and alliances, all the linear projections of contemporary governments and military systems, all the customary bric-a-brac of would-be realistic stories such as *The Invasion of 1910* have vanished. Wells develops his parable of possibilities by giving his entire attention to the fighting vehicles and to the rift in thinking and expectations between the two cultures of the mechanical and lamentably unmechanical. There are the young engineers—'alert, intelligent, quiet'—in their land ironclads. Opposed to them are the miserable foot-slogging enemy, the unmechanized, whom the victors despise as 'some inferior kind of native'.

A comparable concentration on essentials is apparent in the twenty stories that Lieutenant-Colonel Swinton, as he was then, wrote between 1906 and 1914 for *Blackwood's Magazine, The Strand,*

From 1890 onwards the illustrated magazines gave their readers tales of the next great war as these were expected to develop

and *The Cornhill*. The best of these is undoubtedly *The Green Curve*, a clever tale of the life-and-death choices that have to be made in time of war. And here fact begins to come close to fiction, for the land ironclads of the Wells story of 1903 became the reality of the Swinton proposal to the Committee of Imperial Defence in October 1914. As the opposing armies dug themselves in for the trench warfare the military had not expected, Swinton argued that the answer to barbed wire, trenches, and machine-guns was a bespoke weapon. Let them invent the tank! Major-General Sir Ernest Swinton, KBE, CB, deserved his promotion and his honours. He had shown the world how to invent the secret weapon.

Indeed, invention is the mother of futuristic fiction. All these tales of tomorrow—future wars, utopias and dystopias, space adventures and final holocausts—are the acknowledgement that imagination pays to the rate of change. This fact is most apparent in the tales of the next great war during the first main period of their development between 1871 and 1914. As will be apparent in this anthology, these stories are not the unfettered speculations of minds set free to consider every conceivable possibility: they are shaped by the dominant expectations and assumptions of their day. Despite the startling originality of the stories from Wells and Conan Doyle, these tales of the war-to-come can never tell the whole story of what will be. They are solitary planets, moving through the eternal silence of a history that will never be written.

In the beginning, in the circumscribed world of 1763, the author of *The Reign of George VI* had imagined that in 1915 his ever-victorious British monarch would be building a magnificent new city on classical lines near Uppingham in Rutlandshire. He could not conceive how the world would have changed within a century and a half. By 1915, the American colonies had become a great nation and the small German principalities of the eighteenth century had been welded into a powerful Reich. Millions of combatants, employing weapons beyond all conjecture in 1763, were engaged in trench warfare along the Western Front. When Americans like the publisher George H. Putnam looked into the future, they foresaw the dangers that faced their country. Putnam was a great admirer of Chesney's *Battle of Dorking*; and on a visit to England in 1915 he 'spent some time in tramping over the Dorking region with the book in my hand to find how closely he had in his narrative followed the topography'.[12] He applied the Chesney formula to the situation of the United States, and in 1915 he published *America Fallen* by J. Bernard Walker. It was an invasion story, designed to show 'that unless Americans are prepared to take active measures for the protection of their coasts, the United States is exposed to the risk of invasion'.

By 1915, however, as the New World was preparing to play its part in the first great technological war in history, the tales of the

By 1916 American writers had taken to relating their own tales of the German invasion of the United States

future had dwindled to a trickle. The last tale of the war-to-come was in German: *Hindenburgs Einmarsch in London,* an Old World account of rapid victories and a final glorious triumph that brings down the curtain in the shadow theatre of the next great war. The wars that began with Chesney's *Battle of Dorking* now end with the spectacle of Hindenburg addressing the victorious German troops outside Buckingham Palace. They were to write down all they had seen and experienced, 'so that in the future, if in the course of the next centuries a war-like feeling arise again in Europe, your children's children shall say, to your honour and to the confusion of our enemies: "One of my forefathers once bivouacked before Buckingham Palace after helping to subdue a whole world of enemies." Good night, comrades!'

Notes

1. Sir Arthur Conan Doyle, *Danger and Other Stories* (1918), v–vii.

2. Lord Macauley, 'Lord Bacon', in *Literary Essays Contributed to the Edinburgh Review* (1932), 408.

3. Ronald L. Meek, (ed.), *Turgot on Progress, Sociology and Economics* (1973), 41.

4. I. F. Clarke (ed.), *The Reign of George VI* (1972), pp. 56–7.

5. A full account will be found in I. F. Clarke. *Voices Prophesying War,* (1992).

6. *Illustrated London News,* 18 December, 1847, p. 1.

7. Anonymous, *The History of the Sudden and Terrible Invasion of England by the French ... in May, 1852* (1851), pp. 18–19.

8. Lord Acton, 'The War of 1870: A Lecture delivered at the Bridgnorth Literary and Scientific Institution on the 25th of April, 1871' (1871), p. 3.

9. Edward A. Freeman, 'The Panic and its Lessons', *Macmillan's Magazine,* May 1871, pp. 1–14.

10. National Library of Scotland, *Blackwood MSS.* 1871, Ms. 4271, no. 81.

11. Josiah Strong, *Our Country: Its Possible Future and its Present Crisis* (1891), p. 175.

12. George H. Putnam, *Memories of a Publisher* (1915), p. 67.

The Battle of Dorking: Reminiscences of a Volunteer

GENERAL SIR GEORGE TOMKYNS CHESNEY

You ask me to tell you, my grandchildren, something about my own share in the great events that happened fifty years ago. 'Tis sad work turning back to that bitter page in our history, but you may perhaps take profit in your new homes from the lesson it teaches. For us in England it came too late. And yet we had plenty of warnings, if we had only made use of them. The danger did not come on us suddenly unawares. It burst on us suddenly, 'tis true, but its coming was foreshadowed plainly enough to open our eyes, if we had not been wilfully blind. We English have only ourselves to blame for the humiliation which has been brought on the land. Venerable old age! Dishonourable old age, I say, when it follows a manhood dishonoured as ours has been. I declare, even now, though fifty years have passed, I can hardly look a young man in the face when I think I am one of those in whose youth happened this degradation of Old England—one of those who betrayed the trust handed down to us unstained by our forefathers.

What a proud and happy country was this fifty years ago! Free trade had been working for more than a quarter of a century, and there seemed to be no end to the riches it was bringing us. London was growing bigger and bigger; you could not build houses fast enough for the rich people who wanted to live in them, the merchants who made the money and came from all parts of the world to settle there, and the lawyers and doctors and engineers and others, and trades-people who got their share out of the profits. The streets reached down to Croydon and Wimbledon, which my father could remember as quite country places; and people used to say that Kingston and Reigate would soon be joined to London. We thought we could go on building and multiplying for ever. 'Tis true that even then there was no lack of poverty; the people who had no money went on increasing as fast as the rich, and pauperism was already beginning to be a difficulty; but if the rates were high, there was plenty of money to pay them with; and as for what were called the middle classes, there really seemed no limit to their increase and prosperity. People in those days thought it quite a matter of course to bring a dozen children into the world—or, as it used to be said, Providence sent them that number of babies; and if they couldn't always marry off all the daughters, they used to manage to provide for the sons, for there were new openings to be found in all the professions, or in the government offices, which went on steadily getting larger. Besides, in those days young men could be sent out to India, or into the army or navy; and even then emigration was not uncommon, although not the regular custom it is now. Schoolmasters, like all other professional classes, drove a capital trade. They did not teach very much, to be sure, but new schools with their four or five hundred boys were springing up all over the country.

Fools that we were! We thought that all this wealth and prosperity were sent us by Providence, and could not stop coming. In our blindness we did not see that we were merely a big workshop, making up the things which came from all parts of the world; and that if other nations stopped sending us raw goods to work up, we could not produce them ourselves. True, we had in those days an advantage in our cheap coal and iron; and had we taken care not to waste the fuel, it might have lasted us longer. But even then there were signs that coal and iron would soon become cheaper in foreign parts; while as to food and other things, England was not better off than it is now. We were so rich simply because other nations from all parts of the world were in the habit of sending their goods to us to be sold or manufactured; and we thought that this would last for ever. And so, perhaps, it might have lasted, if we had only taken proper means to keep it; but, in our folly, we were too careless even to insure our prosperity, and after the course of trade was turned away it would not come back again.

And yet, if ever a nation had a plain warning, we had. If we were the greatest trading country, our neighbours were the leading military power in Europe. They were driving a good trade, too, for this was before their foolish communism (about which you will hear when you are older) had ruined the rich without benefiting the poor, and they were in many respects the first nation in Europe; but it was on their army that they prided themselves most. And with reason. They had beaten the Russians and the Austrians, and the Prussians too, in bygone years, and they thought they were invincible. Well do I remember the great review held at Paris by the Emperor Napoleon during the great Exhibition,[1] and how proud he looked showing off his splendid Guards to the assembled

In 1871 Charles Yriarte translated the *Battle of Dorking* into French. In the preface he asked: '...if such a book, published here in 1869, might not have had an influence on our future'

kings and princes. Yet, three years afterwards, the force so long
deemed the first in Europe was ignominiously beaten, and the
whole army taken prisoners. Such a defeat had never happened
before in the world's history; and, with this proof before us of the
folly of disbelieving in the possibility of disaster merely because it
had never happened before, it might have been supposed that we
should have the sense to take the lesson to heart. And the country
was certainly roused for a time, and a cry was raised that the army
ought to be reorganized, and our defences strengthened against the
enormous power for sudden attacks which it was seen other
nations were able to put forth. But our Government had come into
office on a cry of retrenchment, and could not bring themselves to
eat their own pledges.[2] There was a Radical section of their party,
too, whose votes had to be secured by conciliation, and which
blindly demanded a reduction of armaments as the price of alle-
giance. This party always decried military establishments as part of
a fixed policy for reducing the influence of the Crown and the aristocracy. They could not understand that the times had altogether
changed, that the Crown had really no power, and that the Government merely existed at the pleasure of the House of Commons, and
that even Parliament-rule was beginning to give way to mob-law.
At any rate, the Ministry were only too glad of this excuse to give
up all the strong points of a scheme which they were not really in
earnest about. The fleet and the Channel, they said, were sufficient
protection. So the army was kept down, and the militia and volunteers were left untrained as before, because to call them out for
drill would 'interfere with the industry of the country'. We could
have given up some of the industry of those days, forsooth, and
yet be busier than we are now.

But why tell you a tale you have so often heard already? The
nation, although uneasy, was misled by the false security its leaders
professed to feel; the warning given by the disaster that overtook
France was allowed to pass by unheeded. The French trusted in their
army and its great reputation, we in our fleet; and in each case the
result of this blind confidence was disaster, such as our forefathers in
their hardest struggles could not have even imagined.

I need hardly tell you how the crash came about. First, the rising
in India drew away a part of our small army; then came the difficulty with America, which had been threatening for years, and we
sent ten thousand men to defend Canada[3]—a handful which did not
go far to strengthen the real defences of that country, but formed
an irresistible temptation to the Americans to try and take them

prisoners, especially as the contingent included three battalions of the Guards. Thus the regular army at home was even smaller than usual, and nearly half of it was in Ireland to check the talked-of Fenian invasion fitting out in the West. Worse still—though I do not know it would really have mattered as things turned out—the fleet was scattered abroad: some ships to guard the West Indies, others to check privateering in the China Seas, and a large part to try and protect our colonies on the Northern Pacific shore of America, where, with incredible folly, we continued to retain possessions which we could not possibly defend. America was not the great power forty years ago that it is now; but for us to try and hold territory on her shores which could only be reached by sailing round the Horn, was as absurd as if she had attempted to take the Isle of Man before the independence of Ireland. We see this plainly enough now, but were all blind then.

It was while we were in this state, with our ships all over the world, and our little bit of an army cut up into detachments, that the Secret Treaty was published, and Holland and Denmark were annexed. People say now that we might have escaped the troubles which came on us if we had at any rate kept quiet till our other difficulties were settled; but the English were always an impulsive lot: the whole country was boiling over with indignation, and the Government, egged on by the press, and going with the stream, declared war. We had always got out of our scrapes before, and we believed our old luck and pluck would somehow pull us through.

Then, of course, there was bustle and hurry all over the land. Not that the calling up of the army reserve caused much stir, for I think there were only about 5,000 altogether, and a good many of these were not to be found when the time came; but recruiting was going on all over the country, with a tremendous high bounty, 50,000 more men having been voted for the army. Then there was a Ballot Bill passed for adding 55,500 men to the militia; why a round number was not fixed on I don't know, but the Prime Minister said that this was the exact quota wanted to put the defences of the country on a sound footing. Then the shipbuilding that began! Iron-clads, despatch-boats, gunboats, monitors—every building-yard in the country got its job, and they were offering ten shillings a day wages for anybody who could drive a rivet. This didn't improve the recruiting, you may suppose. I remember, too, there was a squabble in the House of Commons about whether artisans should be drawn for the ballot, as they were so much wanted, and I think they got an exemption. This sent numbers to the yards; and if we had had a couple of years to prepare instead of a couple of weeks, I daresay we should have done very well.

It was on a Monday that the declaration of war was announced, and in a few hours we got our first inkling of the sort of preparation the enemy had made for the event which they had really brought about, although the actual declaration was made by us. A pious appeal to the God of battles, whom it was said we had aroused, was telegraphed back; and from that moment all communication with the north of Europe was cut off. Our embassies and legations were packed off at an hour's notice, and it was as if we had suddenly come back to the Middle Ages. The dumb astonishment visible all over London the next morning, when the papers came out void of news, merely hinting at what had happened, was one of the most startling things in this war of surprises. But everything had been arranged beforehand; nor ought we to have been surprised, for we had seen the same power, only a few months before, move down half a million men on a few days' notice, to conquer the greatest military nation in Europe, with no more fuss than our War Office used to make over the transport of a brigade from Aldershot to Brighton—and this, too, without the allies it had now. What happened now was not a bit more wonderful in reality; but people of this country could not bring themselves to believe that what had never occurred before to England could ever possibly happen. Like our neighbours, we became wise when it was too late.

Of course the papers were not long in getting news—even the mighty organization set at work could not shut out a special correspondent; and in a very few days, although the telegraphs and railways were intercepted right across Europe, the main facts oozed out. An embargo had been laid on all shipping in every port from the Baltic to Ostend; the fleets of the two great powers had moved out, and it was supposed were assembled in the great northern harbour, and troops were hurrying on board all the steamers detained in those places, most of which were British vessels. It was clear that invasion was intended.

Even then we might have been saved, if the fleet had been ready. The forts which guarded the flotilla were perhaps too strong for shipping to attempt; but an ironclad or two, handled as British sailors knew how to use them, might have destroyed or damaged a part of the transports, and delayed the expedition, giving us what we wanted, time.[4] But then the best part of the fleet had been decoyed down to the Dardanelles, and what remained of the Channel squadron was looking after Fenian filibusters off the west of Ireland; so it was ten days before the fleet was got together, and by that time it was plain the enemy's preparations were too far advanced to be stopped by a *coup-de-main*. Information, which came chiefly through Italy, came slowly, and was more or less vague and uncertain; but this much was known, that at least a couple of hundred thousand men were embarked or ready to be put on board ships, and that the flotilla was guarded by more ironclads than we could then muster. I suppose it was the uncertainty as to the point the enemy would aim at for landing, and the fear lest he should give us the go-by, that kept the fleet for several days in the Downs; but it was not until the Tuesday fortnight after the declaration of war that it weighed anchor and steamed away for the North Sea.

Of course you have read about the Queen's visit to the fleet the day before, and how she sailed around the ships in her yacht and went on board the flag-ship to take leave of the admiral; how, overcome with emotion, she told him that the safety of the country was committed to his keeping. You remember, too, the gallant old officer's reply, and how all the ships' yards were manned, and how lustily the tars cheered as her Majesty was rowed off. The account was of course telegraphed to London, and the high spirits of the fleet infected the whole town. I was outside the Charing Cross Station when the Queen's special train from Dover arrived, and from the cheering and shouting which greeted her as she drove away, you might have supposed we had already won a great victory. The leading journal, which had gone in strongly for the army reduction carried out during the session, and had been nervous and desponding in tone during the past fortnight, suggesting all sorts of compromises as a way of getting out of the war, came out in a very jubilant form next morning. 'Panic-stricken inquirers,' they said, 'ask now, where are the means of meeting the invasion? We reply that the invasion will never take place. A British fleet, manned by British sailors whose courage and enthusiasm are reflected in the people of this country, is already on the way to meet the presumptuous foe. The issue of a contest between British ships and those of any other country, under anything like equal odds, can never be doubtful. England awaits with calm confidence the issue of the impending action.'

Such were the words of the leading article, and so we all felt. It was on Tuesday, the 10th of August, that the fleet sailed from the Downs. It took with it a submarine cable to lay down as it advanced, so that continuous communication was kept up, and the papers were publishing special editions every few minutes with the latest news. This was the first time such a thing had been done, and the feat was accepted as a good omen. Whether it is true that the Admiralty made use of the cable to keep on sending contradictory orders, which took the command out of the admiral's hands, I can't say; but all that the admiral sent in return was a few messages of the briefest kind, which neither the Admiralty nor any one else could have made any use of. Such a ship had gone off reconnoitring; such another had rejoined—fleet was in latitude so and so. This went on till the Thursday morning. I had just come up to town by train as usual, and was walking to my office, when the newboys began to cry, 'New edition—enemy's fleet in sight!'

You may imagine the scene in London! Business still went on at the banks, for bills matured although the independence of the country was being fought out under our own eyes, so to say; and the speculators were active enough. But even with the people who were making or losing their fortunes, the interest in the fleet overcame everything else; men who went to pay in or draw out their money stopped to show the last bulletin to the cashier. As for the street, you could hardly get along for the crowd stopping to buy and read the papers; while at every house or office the members sat restlessly in the common room, as if to keep together for company, sending out some one of their number every few minutes to get the latest edition. At least this is what happened at our office; but to sit still was as impossible as to do anything, and most of us went out and wandered about among the crowd, under a sort of feeling that the news was got quicker at in this way.

Bad as were the times coming, I think the sickening suspense of that day, and the shock which followed, was almost the worst that we underwent. It was about ten o'clock that the first telegram came; an hour later the wire announced that the admiral had signalled to form line of battle, and shortly afterwards that the order was given to bear down on the enemy and engage. At twelve came the announcement, 'Fleet opened fire about three miles to leeward of us'—that is, the ship with the cable. So far all had been expectancy; then came the first token of calamity. 'An ironclad has been blown up'—'the enemy's torpedoes are doing great damage'—'the flagship is laid aboard the enemy'—'the flagship appears to be sinking'—'the vice-admiral has signalled'—there the cable became silent, and, as you know, we heard no more till two days afterwards, when the solitary ironclad which escaped the disaster steamed into Portsmouth.

Then the whole story came out—how our sailors, gallant as ever, had tried to close with the enemy; how the latter evaded the conflict at close quarters, and, sheering off, left behind them the fatal engines which sent our ships, one after the other, to the bottom; how all this happened almost in a few minutes.[5] The Government, it appears, had received warnings of this invention; but to the nation this stunning blow was utterly unexpected. That Thursday I had to go home early for regimental drill, but it was impossible to remain doing nothing, so when that was over I went up to town again, and, after waiting in expectation of news which never came, and missing the midnight train, I walked home. It was a hot sultry night, and I did not arrive till near sunrise. The whole town was quite still—the lull before the storm; and as I let myself in with my latch-key, and went softly up-stairs to my room to avoid waking the sleeping household, I could not but contrast the peacefulness of the morning—no sound breaking the silence but the singing of birds in the garden—with the passionate remorse and indignation that would break out with the day. Perhaps the inmates of the house were as wakeful as myself; but the house in its stillness was just as it used to be when I came home alone from balls or parties in the happy days gone by. Tired though I was, I could not sleep, so I went down to the river and had a swim; and on returning found the household was assembling for early breakfast. A sorrowful household it was, although the burden pressing on each was partly an unseen one. My father, doubting whether his firm could last through the day; my mother, her distress about my brother, now with his regiment on the coast, already exceeding that which she felt for the public misfortune, had come down, although hardly fit to leave her room. My sister Clara was worst of all, for she could not but try to disguise her special interest in the fleet; and though we had all guessed that her heart was given to the young lieutenant in the flagship—the first vessel to go down—a love unclaimed could not be told, nor could we express the sympathy we felt for the poor girl. That breakfast, the last meal we ever had together, was soon ended, and my father and I went up to town by an early train, and got there just as the fatal announcement of the loss of the fleet was telegraphed from Portsmouth.

The panic and excitement of that day—how the funds went down to 35; the run upon the bank and its stoppage; the fall of half the houses in the city; how the Government issued a notification suspending specie payment and the tendering of bills—this last precaution too late for most firms, Carter & Co. among the number, which stopped payment as soon as my father got to the office; the call to arms, and the unanimous response of the country—all this is history which I need not repeat. You wish to hear about my own share in the business of the time. Well, volunteering had increased immensely from the day war was proclaimed, and our regiment went up in a day or two from its usual strength of 600 to nearly 1,000. But the stock of rifles was deficient. We were promised a further supply in a few days, which, however, we never received; and while waiting for them the regiment had to be divided into two parts, the recruits drilling with the rifles in the morning, and we old hands in the evening. The failures and stoppage of work on this black Friday threw an immense number of young men out of employment and we recruited up to 1,400 strong by the next day; but what was the use of all these men without arms? On the Saturday it was announced that a lot of smooth-bore muskets in store at the Tower would be served out to regiments applying for them, and a regular scramble took place among the volunteers for them, and our people got hold of a couple of hundred. But you might almost as well have tried to learn rifle-drill with a broom-stick as with old Brown Bess; besides, there was no smooth-bore ammunition in the country. A national subscription was opened up for the manufacture of rifles at Birmingham, which ran up to a couple of millions in two days, but, like everything else, this came too late.

To return to the volunteers: camps had been formed a fortnight before at Dover, Brighton, Harwich, and other places, of regulars and militia, and the headquarters of most of the volunteer regiments were attached to one or other of them, and the volunteers used to go down for drill from day to day, as they could spare time, and on Friday an order went out that they should be permanently embodied; but the metropolitan volunteers were still kept about London as a sort of reserve, till it could be seen at what point the invasion would take place.[6] We were all told off to brigades and divisions. Our brigade consisted of the 4th Royal Surrey Militia, the 1st Surrey Administrative Battalion, as it was called, at Clapham, the 7th Surrey Volunteers at Southwark, and ourselves; but only our battalion and the militia were quartered in the same place, and the whole brigade had merely two or three afternoons together at brigade exercise in Bushey Park before the march took place. Our brigadier belonged to a line regiment in Ireland, and did not join till the very morning the order came. Meanwhile, during the preliminary fortnight, the militia colonel commanded. But though we volunteers were busy with our drill and preparations, those of us who, like myself, belonged to government offices had more than enough of office work to do, as you may suppose. The volunteer clerks were allowed to leave office at four o'clock, but the rest were kept hard at the desk far into the night. Orders to the lord-lieutenants, to the magistrates, notifications, all the arrangements for cleaning out the workhouses for hospitals—these and a hundred other things had to be managed in our office, and there was as much bustle indoors as out. Fortunate we were to be so busy—the people to be pitied were those who had nothing to do. And on Sunday (that was the 15th of August) work went on just as usual. We had an early parade and drill, and I went up to town by the nine o'clock train in my uniform, taking my rifle with me in case of accidents and, luckily too, as it turned out, a mackintosh overcoat.

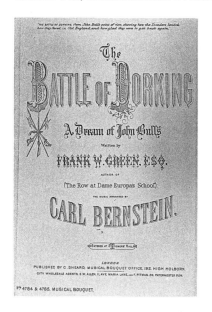 

Chesney's story soon became part of the national folklore. 'England invaded, what a strange idea', they sang in the music-halls. 'She, the invincible, has nought to fear'

When I got to Waterloo there were all sorts of rumour afloat. A fleet had been seen off the Downs, and some of the despatch-boats which were hovering about the coasts brought news that there was a large flotilla off Harwich, but nothing could be seen from the shore, as the weather was hazy. The enemy's light ships had taken and sunk all the fishing-boats they could catch, to prevent the news of their whereabouts reaching us; but a few escaped during the night and reported that the *Inconstant* frigate coming home from North America, without any knowledge of what had taken place, had sailed right into the enemy's fleet and been captured. In town the

troops were all getting ready for a move; the Guards in the Welling-
ton Barracks were under arms, and their baggage-waggons packed
and drawn up in the Bird Cage Walk. The usual guard at the Horse
Guards had been withdrawn, and orderlies and staff officers were
going to and fro. All this I saw on the way to my office, where I
worked away till twelve o'clock, and then, feeling hungry after my
early breakfast, I went across Parliament Street to my club to get
some luncheon. There were about half-a-dozen men in the coffee
room, none of whom I knew; but in a minute or two Danvers of the
Treasury entered in a tremendous hurry. From him I got the first bit
of authentic news I had had that day. The enemy had landed in force
near Harwich, and the metropolitan regiments were ordered down
there to reinforce the troops already collected in that neighbourhood; his regiment was to parade at one o'clock, and he had come to
get something to eat before starting. We bolted a hurried lunch, and
were just leaving the club when a messenger from the Treasury
came running into the hall.

'Oh, Mr Danvers,' said he, 'I've come to look for you, sir; the
secretary says that all the gentlemen are wanted at the office, and
that you must please not one of you go with the regiments.'

'The devil!' cried Danvers.

'Do you know if that order extends to all the public offices?' I
asked.

'I don't know,' said the man, 'but I believe it do. I know there's
messengers gone round to all the clubs and luncheon-bars to look
for the gentlemen; the secretary says it's quite impossible any one
can be spared just now, there's so much work to do; there's orders
just come to send off our records to Birmingham tonight.'

I did not wait to condole with Danvers, but, just glancing up
Whitehall to see if any of our messengers were in pursuit, I ran off as
hard as I could for Westminster Bridge, and so to the Waterloo
Station.

The place had quite changed its aspect since the morning. The
regular service of trains had ceased, and the station and approaches
were full of troops, among them the Guards and artillery. Everything was very orderly; the men had piled arms, and were standing
about in groups. There was no sign of high spirits or enthusiasm.
Matters had become too serious. Every man's face reflected the
general feeling that we had neglected the warnings given us, and
that now the danger so long derided as impossible and absurd had
really come and found us unprepared. But the soldiers, if grave,
looked determined, like men who meant to do their duty whatever

might happen. A train full of guardsmen was just starting for Guild-ford. I was told it would stop at Surbiton, and, with several other volunteers, hurrying like myself to join our regiment, got a place in it. We did not arrive a moment too soon, for the regiment was marching from Kingston down to the station. The destination of our brigade was the east coast. Empty carriages were drawn up in the siding, and our regiment was to go first. A large crowd was assembled to see it off, including the recruits who had joined during the last fortnight, and who formed by far the largest part of our strength. They were to stay behind, and were certainly very much in the way already; for as all the officers and sergeants belonged to the active part, there was no one to keep discipline among them, and they came crowding around us, breaking the ranks and making it difficult to get into the train. Here I saw our new brigadier for the first time. He was a soldier-like man, and no doubt knew his duty, but he appeared new to volunteers, and did not seem to know how to deal with gentlemen privates. I wanted very much to run home and get my greatcoat and knapsack, which I had bought a few days ago, but feared to be left behind; a good-natured recruit volunteered to fetch them for me, but he had not returned before we started, and I began the campaign with a kit consisting of a mackintosh and a small pouch of tobacco.

It was a tremendous squeeze in the train; for, besides the ten men sitting down, there were three or four standing up in every compartment, and the afternoon was close and sultry, and there were so many stoppages on the way that we took nearly an hour and a half crawling up to Waterloo. It was between five and six in the afternoon when we arrived there, and it was nearly seven before we marched up to the Shoreditch station. The whole place was filled up with stores and ammunition, to be sent off to the east, so we piled arms in the street and scattered about to get food and drink, of which most of us stood in need, especially the latter, for some were already feeling the worse for the heat and crush. I was just stepping into a public-house with Travers, when who should drive up but his pretty wife? Most of our friends had paid their adieus at the Surbiton station, but she had driven up by the road in his brougham, bringing their little boy to have a last look at papa. She had also brought his knapsack and greatcoat, and, what was still more acceptable, a basket containing fowls, tongue, bread-and-butter, and biscuits, and a couple of bottles of claret—which priceless luxuries they insisted on my sharing.

Meanwhile the hours went on. The 4th Surrey Militia, which had

marched all the way from Kingston, had come up, as well as the
other volunteer corps; the station had been partly cleared of the
stores that encumbered it; some artillery, two militia regiments, and
a battalion of the line had been despatched, and our turn to start had
come, and long lines of carriages were drawn up ready for us; but
still we remained in the street. You may fancy the scene. There
seemed to be as many people as ever in London, and we could
hardly move for the crowds of spectators—fellows hawking fruits
and volunteers' comforts, newsboys, and so forth, to say nothing of
the cabs and omnibuses; while orderlies and staff-officers were
constantly riding up with messages. A good many of the militiamen,
and some of our people too, had taken more than enough to drink;
perhaps a hot sun had told on empty stomachs; anyhow, they
became very noisy. The din, dirt, and heat were indescribable.

So the evening wore on, and all the information our officers could
get from the brigadier, who appeared to be acting under another
general, was that orders had come to stand fast for the present.
Gradually the street became quieter and cooler. The brigadier, who,
by way of setting an example, had remained for some hours without
leaving his saddle, had got a chair out of a shop, and sat nodding in
it; most of the men were lying down or sitting on the pavement—
some sleeping, some smoking. In vain had Travers begged his wife to
go home. She declared that, having come so far, she would stay and
see the last of us. The brougham had been sent away to a by-street,
as it blocked up the road; so he sat on a doorstep, she by him on the
knapsack. Little Arthur, who had been delighted at the bustle and
the uniforms, and in high spirits, became at last very cross, and
eventually cried himself to sleep in his father's arms, his golden hair
and one little dimpled arm hanging over his shoulder. Thus went on
the weary hours, till suddenly the assembly sounded, and we all
started up. We were to return to Waterloo. The landing on the east
was only a feint—so ran the rumour—the real attack was on the
south. Anything seemed better than indecision and delay, and, tired
though we were, the march back was gladly hailed. Mrs Travers,
who made us take the remains of the luncheon with us, we left to
look for her carriage; little Arthur, who was awake again, but very
good and quiet, in her arms.

We did not reach Waterloo till nearly midnight, and there was
some delay in starting again. Several volunteer and militia regiments
had arrived from the north; the station and all its approaches were
jammed up with men, and trains were being despatched away as fast
as they could be made up. All this time no news had reached us

since the first announcement; but the excitement then aroused had now passed away under the influence of fatigue and want of sleep, and most of us dozed off as soon as we got under way. I did, at any rate, and was awoke by the train stopping at Leatherhead. There was an up-train returning to town, and some persons in it were bringing up news from the coast. We could not, from our part of the train, hear what they said, but the rumour was passed up from one carriage to another. The enemy had landed in force at Worthing.[7] Their position had been attacked by the troops from the camp near Brighton, and the action would be renewed in the morning. The volunteers had behaved very well. This was all the information we could get. So, then, the invasion had come at last. It was clear, at any rate, from what was said, that the enemy had not been driven back yet, and we should be in time most likely to take a share in the defence.

It was sunrise when the train crawled into Dorking, for there had been numerous stoppages on the way; and here it was pulled up for a long time, and we were told to get out and stretch ourselves—an order gladly responded to, for we had been very closely packed all night. Most of us, too, took the opportunity to make an early breakfast off the food we had brought from Shoreditch. I had the remains of Mrs Travers's fowl and some bread wrapped up in my waterproof, which I shared with one or two less provident comrades. We could see from our halting-place that the line was blocked with trains beyond and behind. It must have been about eight o'clock when we got orders to take our seats again, and the train began to move slowly on towards Horsham. Horsham Junction was the point to be occupied—so the rumour went; but about ten o'clock, when halting at a small station a few miles short of it, the order came to leave the train, and our brigade formed in column on the high road. Beyond us was some field-artillery; and further on, so we were told by a staff-officer, another brigade, which was to make up a division with ours.

After more delays the line began to move, but not forwards; our route was towards the north-west, and a sort of suspicion of the state of affairs flashed across my mind. Horsham was already occupied by the enemy's advanced-guard, and we were to fall back on Leith Common, and take up a position threatening his flank, should he advance either to Guildford or Dorking. This was soon confirmed by what the colonel was told by the brigadier and passed down the ranks; and just now, for the first time, the boom of artillery came up on the light south breeze. In about an hour the firing ceased. What

In 1870 the illustrated magazines were filled with artists' impressions of German military efficiency. Reserve troops of *Landwehr* on the move

did it mean? We could not tell. Meanwhile our march continued. The day was very close and sultry, and the clouds of dust stirred up by our feet almost suffocated us. I had saved a soda-water-bottleful of yesterday's claret; but this went only a short way, for there were many mouths to share it with, and the thirst soon became as bad as ever. Several of the regiment fell out from faintness, and we made frequent halts to rest and let the stragglers come up.

At last we reached the top of Leith Hill. It is a striking spot, being the highest point in the south of England. The view from it was splendid, and most lovely did the country look this summer day, although the grass was brown from the long drought. It was a great relief to get from the dusty road on to the common, and at the top of the hill there was a refreshing breeze. We could see now, for the first time, the whole of our division. Our own regiment did not muster more than 500, for it contained a large number of government office men who had been detained, like Danvers, for duty in town, and others were not much larger; but the militia regiment was very strong, and the whole division, I was told, mustered nearly 5,000 rank and file. We could see other troops also in extension of our division, and could count a couple of field-batteries of Royal Artillery, besides some heavy guns, belonging to the volunteers apparently, drawn by cart-horses. The cooler air, the sense of numbers, and the evident strength of the position we held raised our spirits, which, I am not ashamed to say, had all the morning been depressed. It was not that we were not eager to close with the enemy, but that the counter-marching and halting ominously be-tokened a vacillation of purpose in those who had the guidance of affairs. Here in two days the invaders had got more than twenty miles inland, and nothing effectual had been done to stop them. And the ignorance in which we volunteers, from the colonel down-wards, were kept of their movements filled us with uneasiness. We could not but depict to ourselves the enemy as carrying out all the while firmly his well-considered scheme of attack, and contrasting it with our own uncertainty of purpose. The very silence with which his advance appeared to be conducted filled us with mysterious awe.

Meanwhile the day wore on, and we became faint with hunger, for we had eaten nothing since daybreak. No provisions came up, and there were no signs of any commissariat officers. It seems that when we were at the Waterloo station a whole trainful of provisions was drawn up there, and our colonel proposed that one of the trucks should be taken off and attached to our train, so that we might have some food at hand; but the officer in charge, an assistant-controller I think they called him—this control department was a newfangled affair which did us almost as much harm as the enemy in the long-run—said his orders were to keep all the stores together, and that he couldn't issue any without authority from the head of his department. So, we had to go without. Those who had tobacco smoked—indeed, there is no solace like a pipe under such circumstances. The militia regiment, I heard afterwards, had two days' provisions in their haversacks; it was we volunteers who had no haversacks, and nothing to put in them. All this time, I should tell you, while we were lying on the grass with our arms piled, the general, with the brigadiers and staff, was riding about slowly from point to point of the edge of the common, looking out with his glass towards the south valley. Orderlies and staff-officers were constantly coming, and about three o'clock there arrived up a road that led towards Horsham a small body of lancers and a regiment of yeomanry, who had, it appears, been out in advance, and now drew up a short way in front of us in column facing to the south. Whether they could see anything in their front I could not tell, for we were behind the crest of the hill ourselves, and so could not look into the valley below; but shortly afterwards the assembly sounded. Commanding officers were called out by the general, and received some brief instructions; and the column began to march again towards London, the militia this time coming last in our brigade.

A rumour regarding the object of this counter-march soon spread through the ranks. The enemy was not going to attack us here, but was trying to turn the position on both sides, one column pointing to Reigate, the other to Aldershot; and so we must fall back and take up a position at Dorking. The line of the great chalk-range was to be defended. A large force was concentrating at Guildford, another at Reigate, and we should find supports at Dorking. The enemy would be awaited in these positions. Such, so far as we privates could get at the facts, was to be the plan of operations. Down the hill, therefore, we marched. From one or two points we could catch a brief sight of the railway in the valley below running from Dorking to Horsham. Men in red were working upon it here and there. They were the Royal Engineers, someone said, breaking up the line. On we marched. The dust seemed worse than ever. In one village through which we passed—I forget the name now—there was a pump on the green. Here we stopped and had a good drink; and passing by a large farm, the farmer's wife and two or three of her maids stood at the gate and handed us hunches of bread and cheese out of some baskets. I got the share of a bit, but the bottom of the baskets must soon have been reached. Not a thing else was to be had till we got to Dorking about six o'clock; indeed, most of the farmhouses appeared deserted already.

On arriving there we were drawn up in the street, and just opposite was a baker's shop. Our fellows asked leave at first by twos and threes to go in and buy some loaves, but soon others began to break off and crowd into the shop, and at last a regular scramble took place. If there had been any order preserved, and a regular distribution arranged, they would no doubt have been steady enough, but hunger makes men selfish: each man felt that his stopping behind would do no good—he would simply lose his share; so it ended by almost the whole regiment joining in the scrimmage, and the shop was cleared out in a couple of minutes; while as for paying, you could not get your hand into your pocket for the crush. The colonel tried in vain to stop the row; some of the officers were as bad as the men. Just then a staff-officer rode by; he could scarcely make way for the crowd, and was pushed against rather rudely, and in a passion he called out to us to behave properly, like soldiers, and not like a parcel of roughs. 'Oh, blow it, governor,' says Dick Wake, 'you arn't agoing to come between a poor cove and his grub.' Wake was an articled attorney, and, as we used to say in those days, a cheeky young chap, although a good-natured fellow enough. At this speech, which was followed by some more remarks of the sort from those about him, the staff-officer became angrier still. 'Orderly,' cried he to the lancer riding behind him, 'take that man to the provost-marshal. As for you, sir,' he said, turning to our colonel, who sat on his horse silent with astonishment, 'if you don't want some of your men shot before their time, you and your precious officers had better keep this rabble in a little better order'; and poor Dick, who looked crest-fallen enough, would certainly have been led off at the tail of the sergeant's horse, if the brigadier had not come up and arranged matters, and marched us off to the hill beyond the town. This incident made us both angry and crest-fallen. We were annoyed at being so roughly spoken to: at the same time we felt we had deserved it, and were ashamed of the misconduct. Then, too, we had lost confidence in our colonel, after the poor figure he cut in the affair. He was a good fellow, the colonel, and showed himself a brave one next day; but he aimed too much at being popular, and didn't understand a bit how to command.

To resume: we had scarcely reached the hill above the town, which we were told was to be our bivouac for the night, when the welcome news came that a food-train had arrived at the station; but

there were no carts to bring the things up, so a fatigue-party went
down and carried back a supply to us in their arms—loaves, a barrel
of rum, packets of tea, and joints of meat—abundance for all; but
there was not a kettle or a cooking-pot in the regiment, and we
could not eat the meat raw. The colonel and officers were no better
off. They had arranged to have a regular mess, with crockery,
steward, and all complete, but the establishment never turned up,
and what had become of it no one knew. Some of us were sent back
into the town to see what we could procure in the way of cooking
utensils. We found the street full of artillery, baggage-waggons, and
mounted officers, and volunteers shopping like ourselves; and all
the houses appeared to be occupied by troops. We succeeded in
getting a few kettles and saucepans, and I obtained for myself a
leather bag, with a strap to go over the shoulder, which proved very
handy afterwards; and thus laden, we trudged back to our camp on
the hill, filling the kettles with dirty water from a little stream which
runs between the hill and the town, for there was none to be had
above. It was nearly a couple of miles each way; and, exhausted as
we were with marching and want of rest, we were almost too tired
to eat. The cooking was of the roughest, as you may suppose; all we
could do was to cut off slices of the meat and boil them in saucepans,
using our fingers for forks. The tea, however, was very refreshing;
and, thirsty as we were, we drank it by the gallon.

Just before it grew dark, the brigade-major came round, and, with
the adjutant, showed our colonel how to set a picket in advance of
our line a little way down the face of the hill. It was not necessary to
place one, I suppose, because the town in our front was still occupied with troops; but no doubt the practice would be useful. We had
also a quarter-guard, and a line of sentries in front and rear of our
line, communicating with those of the regiments on our flanks. Fire-
wood was plentiful, for the hill was covered with beautiful wood;
but it took some time to collect it, for we had nothing but our
pocket-knives to cut down the branches with.

So we lay down to sleep. My company had no duty, and we had
the night undisturbed to ourselves; but, tired though I was, the
excitement and the novelty of the situation made sleep difficult. And
although the night was still and warm, and we were sheltered by the
woods, I soon found it chilly with no better covering than my thin
dust-coat, the more so as my clothes, saturated with perspiration
during the day, had never dried; and before daylight I woke from a
short nap, shivering with cold, and was glad to get warm with others
by a fire. I then noticed that the opposite hills on the south were

Chesney was undoubtedly aware of the image of the German army in the illustrated
magazines, when he contrasted the evident competence of the German troops with the
incompetence of the half-trained Volunteers

dotted with fires; and we thought at first they must belong to the
enemy, but we were told that the ground up there was still held by a
strong rear-guard of regulars, and that there need be no fear of a
surprise.

At the first sign of dawn the bugles of the regiments sounded the
reveillé, and we were ordered to fall in, and the roll was called. About
twenty men were absent, who had fallen out sick the day before;
they had been sent up to London by train during the night, I believe.
After standing in column for about half an hour, the brigade-major
came down with orders to pile arms and stand easy; and perhaps
half an hour afterwards we were told to get breakfast as quickly as
possible, and to cook a day's food at the same time. This operation
was managed pretty much in the same way as the evening before,
except that we had our cooking pots and kettles ready. Meantime

there was leisure to look around, and from where we stood there was a commanding view of one of the most beautiful scenes in England.

Our regiment was drawn up on the extremity of the ridge which runs from Guildford to Dorking. This is indeed merely a part of the great chalk-range which extends from beyond Aldershot east to the Medway; but there is a gap in the ridge just here where the little stream that runs past Dorking turns suddenly to the north, to find its way to the Thames. We stood on the slope of the hill, as it trends down eastward towards this gap, and had passed our bivouac in what appeared to be a gentleman's park. A little way above us, and to our right, was a very fine country-seat to which the park was attached, now occupied by the headquarters of our division. From this house the hill sloped steeply down southward to the valley below, which runs nearly east and west parallel to the ridge, and carries the railway and the road from Guildford to Reigate; and in which valley immediately in front of the chateau, and perhaps a mile and a half distant from it, was the little town of Dorking, nestled in the trees, and rising up the foot of the slopes on the other side of the valley which stretched away to Leith Common, the scene of yesterday's march. Thus, the main part of the town of Dorking was on our right front, but the suburbs stretched away eastward nearly to our proper front, culminating in a small railway station, from which the grassy slopes of the park rose up dotted with shrubs and trees to where we were standing.[8] Round this railway station was a cluster of villas and one or two mills, of whose gardens we thus had a bird's-eye view, their little ornamental ponds glistening like looking glasses in the morning sun. Immediately on our left the park sloped steeply down to the gap before mentioned, through which ran the little stream, as well as the railway from Epsom to Brighton, nearly due north and south, meeting the Guildford and Reigate line at right angles. Close to the point of intersection and the little station already mentioned was the station of the former line where we had stopped the day before. Beyond the gap on the east (our left), and in continuation of our ridge, rose the chalk-hill again. The shoulder of this ridge overlooking the gap is called Box Hill, from the shrubbery of box-wood with which it was covered. Its sides were very steep, and the top of the ridge was covered with troops.

The natural strength of our position was manifested at a glance; a high grassy ridge steep to the south, with a stream in front, and but little cover up the sides. It seemed made for a battle-field. The weak point was the gap; the ground at the junction of the railways and the roads immediately at the entrance of the gap formed a little valley, dotted, as I have said, with buildings and gardens. This, in one sense, was the key of the position; for although it would not be tenable while we held the ridge commanding it, the enemy by carrying this point and advancing through the gap would cut our line in two. But you must not suppose I scanned the ground thus critically at the time. Anybody, indeed, might have been struck with the natural advantages of our position; but what, as I remember, most impressed me, was the peaceful beauty of the scene—the little town with the outline of the houses obscured by a blue mist, the massive crispness of the foliage, the outlines of the great trees, lighted up by the sun, and relieved by deep blue shade. So thick was the timber here, rising up the southern slopes of the valley, that it looked almost as if it might have been a primeval forest. The quiet of the scene was the more impressive because contrasted in the mind with the scenes we expected to follow; and I can remember, as if it were yesterday, the sensation of bitter regret that it should now be too late to avert this coming desecration of our country, which might so easily have been prevented. A little firmness, a little prevision on the part of our rulers, even a little common-sense, and this great calamity would have been rendered utterly impossible. Too late, alas! We were like the foolish virgins in the parable.

But you must not suppose the scene immediately around was gloomy; the camp was brisk and bustling enough. We had got over the stress of weariness; our stomachs were full; we felt a natural enthusiasm at the prospect of having so soon to take a part as the real defenders of the country, and we were inspirited at the sight of the large force that was now assembled. Along the slopes which trended off to the rear of our ridge, troops came marching up—volunteers, militia, cavalry, and guns; these, I heard, had come down from the north as far as Leatherhead the night before, and had marched over at daybreak. Long trains, too, began to arrive by the rail through the gap, one after another, containing militia and volunteers, who moved up to the ridge to the right and left, and took up their position, massed for the most part on the slopes which ran up from, and in rear of, where we stood. We now formed part of an army corps, we were told, consisting of three divisions, but what regiments composed the other two divisions I never heard.

All this movement we could distinctly see from our position, for we had hurried over our breakfast, expecting every minute that the battle would begin, and now stood or sat about on the ground near our piled arms. Early in the morning, too, we saw a very long train

come along the valley from the direction of Guildford, full of
redcoats. It halted at the little station at our feet, and the troops
alighted. We could soon make out their bear-skins. They were the
Guards, coming to reinforce this part of the line. Leaving a detachment of skirmishers to hold the line of the railway embankment, the
main body marched up with a springy step and with the band
playing, and drew up across the gap on our left, in prolongation of
our line. There appeared to be three battalions of them, for they
formed up in that number of columns at short intervals.

Shortly after this I was sent over to Box Hill with a message from
our colonel to the colonel of a volunteer regiment stationed there, to
know whether an ambulance-cart was obtainable, as it was reported
this regiment was well supplied with carriage, whereas we were
without any: my mission, however, was futile. Crossing the valley, I
found a scene of great confusion at the railway station. Trains were
still coming in with stores, ammunition, guns, and appliances of all
sorts, which were being unloaded as fast as possible; but there were
scarcely any means of getting the things off. There were plenty of
waggons of all sorts, but hardly any horses to draw them, and the
whole place was blocked up; while, to add to the confusion, a
regular exodus had taken place of the people from the town, who
had been warned that it was likely to be the scene of fighting. Ladies
and women of all sorts and ages, and children, some with bundles,
some empty-handed, were seeking places in the train, but there
appeared no one on the spot authorized to grant them, and these
poor creatures were pushing their way up and down, vainly asking
for information and permission to get away. In the crowd I observed
our surgeon, who likewise was in search of an ambulance of some
sort: his whole professional apparatus, he said, consisted of a case of
instruments.

Also in the crowd I stumbled upon Wood, Travers's old coachman.
He had been sent down by his mistress to Guildford, because it was
supposed our regiment had gone there, riding the horse, and laden
with a supply of things—food, blankets, and, of course, a letter. He
had also brought my knapsack; but at Guildford the horse was
pressed for artillery work, and a receipt for it given him in exchange,
so he had been obliged to leave all the heavy packages there, including my knapsack; but the faithful old man had brought on as many
things as he could carry, and, hearing that we should be found in
this part, had walked over thus laden from Guildford. He said that
place was crowded with troops and that the heights were lined with
them the whole way between the two towns; also, that some trains

with wounded had passed up from the coast in the night, through Guildford. I led him off to where our regiment was, relieving the old man from part of the load he was staggering under. The food sent was not now so much needed, but the plates, knives, etc., and drinking-vessels promised to be handy—and Travers, you may be sure, was delighted to get his letter; while a couple of newspapers the old man had brought were eagerly competed for by all, even at this critical moment, for we had heard no authentic news since we left London on Sunday. And even at this distance of time, although I only glanced down the paper, I can remember almost the very words I read there. They were both copies of the same paper: the first, published on Sunday evening, when the news had arrived of the successful landing at three points, was written in a tone of despair. The country must confess that it had been taken by surprise. The conqueror would be satisfied with the humiliation inflicted by a peace dictated on our own shores; it was the clear duty of the Government to accept the best terms obtainable, and to avoid further bloodshed and disaster, and avert the fall of our tottering mercantile credit. The next morning's issue was in quite a different tone. Apparently the enemy had received a check, for we were here exhorted to resistance. An impregnable position was to be taken up along the Downs, a force was concentrating there far outnumbering the rash invaders, who, with an invincible line before them, and the sea behind, had no choice between destruction or surrender. Let there be no pusillanimous talk of negotiation: the fight must be fought out, and there could be but one issue. England, expectant but calm, awaited with confidence the result of the attack on its unconquerable volunteers. The writing appeared to me eloquent, but rather inconsistent. The same paper said the Government had sent off 500 workmen from Woolwich, to open a branch arsenal at Birmingham.

All this time we had nothing to do, except to change our position, which we did every few minutes, now moving up the hill farther to our right, now taking ground lower down to our left, as one order after another was brought down the line; but the staff-officers were galloping about perpetually with orders, while the rumble of the artillery as they moved about from one part of the field to another went on almost incessantly. At last the whole line stood to arms, the bands struck up, and the general commanding our army corps came riding down with his staff. We had seen him several times before, as we had been moving frequently about the position during the morning; but he now made a sort of formal inspection. He was a tall thin man, with long light hair, very well mounted, and as he sat his horse with an erect seat, and came prancing down the line, at a little distance he looked as if he might be five-and-twenty; but I believe he had served more than fifty years, and had been made a peer for services performed when quite an old man. I remember that he had more decorations than there was room for on the breast of his coat, and wore them suspended like a necklace round his neck. Like all the other generals, he was dressed in blue, with a cocked-hat and feathers—a bad plan, I thought, for it made them very conspicuous. The general halted before our battalion, and after looking at us a while made a short address: We had a post of honour next her Majesty's Guards, and would show ourselves worthy of it, and of the name of Englishmen. It did not need, he said, to be a general to see the strength of our position; it was impregnable, if properly held. Let us wait till the enemy was well pounded, and then the word would be given to go at him. Above everything, we must be steady. He then shook hands with our colonel, we gave him a cheer, and he rode on to where the Guards were drawn up.

Now then, we thought, the battle will begin. But still there were no signs of the enemy; and the air, though hot and sultry, began to be very hazy, so that you could scarcely see the town below, and the hills opposite were merely a confused blur, in which no features could be distinctly made out. After a while, the tension of feeling which followed the general's address relaxed, and we began to feel less as if everything depended on keeping our rifles firmly grasped: we were told to pile arms again, and got leave to go down by tens and twenties to the stream below to drink. This stream, and all the hedges and banks on our side of it, were held by our skirmishers, but the town had been abandoned. The position appeared an excellent one, except that the enemy, when they came, would have almost better cover than our men. While I was down at the brook, a column emerged from the town, making for our position. We thought for a moment it was the enemy, and you could not make out the colour of the uniforms for the dust; but it turned out to be our rear-guard, falling back from the opposite hills which they had occupied the previous night. One battalion of rifles halted for a few minutes at the stream to let the men drink, and I had a minute's talk with a couple of the officers. They had formed part of the force which had attacked the enemy on their first landing. They had it all their own way, they said, at first, and could have beaten the enemy back easily if they had been properly supported; but the whole thing was mismanaged. The volunteers came on very pluckily, they said, but they got into confusion, and so did the militia, and the attack failed with serious loss. It was the wounded of this force which had passed through Guildford in the night. The officers asked us eagerly about the arrangements for the battle, and when we said that the Guards were the only regular troops in this part of the field, shook their heads ominously.

While we were talking a third officer came up; he was a dark man with a smooth face and a curious excited manner. 'You are volunteers, I suppose,' he said, quickly, his eyes flashing the while. 'Well, now, look here; mind I don't want to hurt your feelings, or to say anything unpleasant, but I'll tell you what; if all you gentlemen were just to go back, and leave us to fight it out alone, it would be a devilish good thing. We could do it a precious deal better without you, I assure you. We don't want your help, I can tell you. We would much rather be left alone, I assure you. Mind I don't want to say anything rude, but that's a fact.' Having blurted out this passionately, he strode away before any one could reply, or the other officers could stop him. They apologized for his rudeness, saying that his brother, also in the regiment, had been killed on Sunday, and that this, and the sun, and marching, had affected his head. The officers told us that the enemy's advanced-guard was close behind, but that he had apparently been waiting for reinforcements, and would probably not attack in force until noon. It was, however, nearly three o'clock before the battle began. We had almost worn out the feeling of expectancy. For twelve hours had we been waiting for the coming struggle, till at last it seemed almost as if the invasion were but a bad dream, and the enemy, as yet unseen by us, had no real existence. So far things had not been very different, but for the numbers and for what we had been told, from a Volunteer review on Brighton Downs.

I remember that these thoughts were passing through my mind as we lay down in groups on the grass, some smoking, some nibbling at their bread, some even asleep, when the listless state we had fallen into was suddenly disturbed by a gunshot fired from the top of the hill on our right, close by the big house. It was the first time I had ever heard a shotted gun fired, and although it is fifty years ago, the angry whistle of the shot as it left the gun is in my ears now. The sound was soon to become common enough. We all jumped up at the report, and fell in almost without the word being given, grasping our rifles tightly, and the leading files peering forward to look for the approaching enemy. This gun was apparently the signal to begin, for now our batteries opened fire all along the line. What they were firing at I could not see, and I am sure the gunners could not see much themselves. I have told you what a haze had come over the air since the morning, and now the smoke from the guns settled like a pall over the hill, and soon we could see little but the men in our ranks, and the outline of some gunners in the battery drawn up next us on the slope on our right. This firing went on, I should think, for nearly a couple of hours, and still there was no reply. We could see the gunners—it was a troop of horse-artillery—working away like fury, ramming, loading, and running up with cartridges, the officer in command riding slowly up and down just behind his guns, and peering out with his fieldglass into the mist. Once or twice they ceased firing to let their smoke clear away, but this did not do much good.[9] For nearly two hours did this go on, and not a shot came in reply. If a battle is like this, said Dick Wake, who was my next-hand file, it's mild work, to say the least.

The words were hardly uttered when a rattle of musketry was heard in front; our skirmishers were at it, and very soon the bullets began to sing over our heads, and some struck the ground at our feet. Up to this time we had been in column; we were now deployed into line on the ground assigned to us. From the valley or gap on our left there ran a lane right up the hill almost due west, or along our front. This lane had a thick bank about four feet high, and the greater part of the regiment was drawn up behind it; but a little way up the hill the lane trended back out of the line, so the right of the regiment here left it and occupied the open grass-land of the park. The bank had been cut away at this point to admit of our going in and out. We had been told in the morning to cut down the bushes on the top of the bank, so as to make the space clear for firing over, but we had no tools to work with; however, a party of sappers had come down and finished the job. My company was on the right, and was thus beyond the shelter of the friendly bank. On our right again was the battery of artillery already mentioned; then came a battalion of the line, then more guns, then a great mass of militia and volunteers and a few lined up to the big house. At least this was the order before the firing began; after that I do not know what changes took place.

And now the enemy's artillery began to open; where their guns were posted we could not see, but we began to hear the rush of the shells over our heads, and the bang as they burst just beyond. And now what took place I can really hardly tell you. Sometimes when I try and recall the scene, it seems as if it lasted for only a few minutes; yet I know, as we lay on the ground, I thought the hours would never pass away, as we watched the gunners still plying their task, firing at the invisible enemy, never stopping for a moment except when now and again a dull blow would be heard and a man fall down, then three or four of his comrades would carry him to the rear. The captain no longer rode up and down; what had become of him I do not know. Two of the guns ceased firing for a time; they had got injured in some way, and up rode an artillery general. I think I see him now, a very handsome man, with straight features and a dark moustache, his breast covered with medals. He appeared in a great rage at the guns stopping fire.

'Who commands this battery?' he cried.

'I do, Sir Henry,' said an officer, riding forward, whom I had not noticed before.

The group is before me at this moment, standing out clear against the background of smoke, Sir Henry erect on his splendid charger, his flashing eye, his left arm pointing towards the enemy to enforce something he was going to say, the young officer reining in his horse just beside him, and saluting with his right hand raised to his busby. This for a moment, then a dull thud, and both horses and riders are prostrate on the ground. A round shot had struck all four at the saddle line. Some of the gunners ran up to help, but neither officer could have lived many minutes. This was not the first I saw killed. Some time before this, almost immediately on the enemy's artillery opening, as we were lying, I heard something like the sound of steel striking steel, and at the same moment Dick Wake, who was next me in the ranks, leaning on his elbows, sank forward on his face. I looked round and saw what had happened; a shot fired at a high elevation, passing over his head, had struck the ground behind, nearly cutting his thigh off. It must have been the ball striking his sheathed bayonet which made the noise. Three of us carried the poor fellow to the rear, with difficulty for the shattered limb; but he was nearly dead from loss of blood when we got to the doctor, who was waiting in a sheltered hollow about two hundred yards in rear, with two other doctors in plain clothes, who had come up to help. We deposited our burden and returned to the front. Poor Wake was sensible when we left him, but apparently too shaken by the shock to be able to speak. Wood was there helping the doctors. I paid more visits to the rear of the same sort before the evening was over.

All this time we were lying there to be fired at without returning a shot, for our skirmishers were holding the line of walls and enclosures below. However, the bank protected most of us, and the brigadier now ordered our right company, which was in the open, to

get behind it also; and there we lay about four deep, the shells crashing and bullets whistling over our heads, but hardly a man being
touched. Our colonel was, indeed, the only one exposed, for he rode
up and down the lane at a foot-pace as steady as a rock; but he made
the major and adjutant dismount and take shelter behind the hedge,
holding their horses. We were all pleased to see him so cool, and it
restored our confidence in him, which had been shaken yesterday.

'An Impregnable Iron Fortress for the Coast and River Defence of the United Kingdom.'
From the 1860s onwards the illustrated magazines made a regular feature of proposals
for the defence of the country

The time seemed interminable while we lay thus inactive. We
could not, of course, help peering over the bank to try and see what
was going on; but there was nothing to be made out, for now a
tremendous thunderstorm, which had been gathering all day, burst
on us, and a torrent of almost blinding rain came down, which
obscured the view even more than the smoke, while the crashing of
the thunder and the glare of the lightning could be heard and seen
even above the roar and flashing of the artillery. Once the mist
lifted, and I saw for a minute an attack on Box Hill, on the other side
of the gap on our left. It was like the scene at a theatre—a curtain of
smoke all round and a clear gap in the centre, with a sudden gleam
of evening sunshine lighting it up. The steep smooth slope of the hill
was crowded with the dark-blue figures of the enemy, whom I now
saw for the first time—an irregular outline in front, but very solid in
rear: the whole body was moving forward by fits and starts, the men
firing and advancing, the officers waving their swords, the columns
closing up and gradually making way. Our people were almost

concealed by the bushes at the top, whence the smoke and their fire could be seen proceeding; presently from these bushes on the crest came out a red line, and dashed down the brow of the hill, a flame of fire belching out from the front as it advanced. The enemy hesitated, gave way, and finally ran back in a confused crowd down the hill. Then the mist covered the scene, but the glimpse of this splendid charge was inspiriting, and I hoped we should show the same coolness when it came to our turn.

It was about this time that our skirmishers fell back, a good many wounded, some limping along by themselves, others helped. The main body retired in very fair order, halting to turn round and fire; we could see a mounted officer of the Guards riding up and down encouraging them to be steady. Now came our turn. For a few minutes we saw nothing, but a rattle of bullets came through the rain and mist, mostly, however, passing over the bank. We began to fire in reply, stepping up against the bank to fire, and stooping down to load; but our brigade-major rode up with an order, and the word was passed through the men to reserve our fire. In a very few moments it must have been that, when ordered to stand, we could see the helmet-spikes and then the figures of the skirmishers as they came on: a lot of them there appeared to be, five or six deep I should say, but in loose order, each man stopping to aim and fire, and then coming forward a little. Just then the brigadier clattered on horseback up the lane. 'Now, then, gentlemen, give it them hot,' he cried; and fire away we did, as fast as ever we were able. A perfect storm of bullets seemed to be flying about us too, and I thought each moment must be the last; escape seemed impossible, but I saw no one fall, for I was too busy, and so were we all, to look to the right or left, but loaded and fired as fast as I could. How long this went on I know not—it could not have been long; neither side could have lasted many minutes under such a fire, but it ended by the enemy gradually falling back, and as soon as we saw this we raised a tremendous shout, and some of us jumped up on the bank to give them our parting shots. Suddenly the order was passed down the line to cease firing, and we soon discovered the cause; a battalion of the Guards was charging obliquely across from our left across our front. It was, I expect, their flank attack as much as our fire which had turned back the enemy; and it was a splendid sight to see their steady line as they advanced slowly across the smooth lawn below us, firing as they went, but as steady as if on parade. We felt a great elation at this moment; it seemed as if the battle was won.

Just then somebody called out to look to the wounded, and for the first time I turned to glance down the rank along the lane. Then I saw that we had not beaten back the attack without loss. Immediately before me lay Lawford of my office, dead on his back from a bullet through his forehead, his hand still grasping his rifle. At every step was some friend or acquaintance killed or wounded, and a few paces down the lane I found Travers, sitting with his back against the bank. A ball had gone through his lungs, and blood was coming from his mouth. I was lifting him up, but the cry of agony he gave stopped me. I then saw that this was not his only wound; his thigh was smashed by a bullet (which must have hit him when standing on the bank), and the blood streaming down mixed in a muddy puddle with the rain-water under him. Still he could not be left here, so, lifting him up as well as I could, I carried him through the gate which led out of the lane at the back to where our camp hospital was in the rear. The movement must have caused him awful agony, for I could not support the broken thigh, and he could not restrain his groans, brave fellow though he was; but how I carried him at all I cannot make out, for he was a much bigger man than myself. But I had not gone far, one of a stream of our fellows, all on the same errand, when a bandsman and Wood met me, bringing a hurdle as a stretcher, and on this we placed him. Wood had just time to tell me that he had got a cart down in the hollow, and would endeavour to take off his master at once to Kingston, when a staff-officer rode up to call us to the ranks. 'You really must not straggle in this way, gentlemen,' he said; 'pray keep your ranks.'

'But we can't leave our wounded to be trodden down and die,' cried one of our fellows.

'Beat off the enemy first, sir,' he replied. 'Gentlemen, do, pray, join your regiments, or we shall be a regular mob.' And no doubt he did not speak too soon; for besides our fellows straggling to the rear, lots of volunteers from the regiments in reserve were running forward to help, till the whole ground was dotted with groups of men. I hastened back to my post, but I had just time to notice that all the ground in our rear was occupied by a thick mass of troops, much more numerous than in the morning, and a column was moving down to the left of our line, to the ground before held by the Guards.

All this time, although the musketry had slackened, the artillery-fire seemed heavier than ever; the shells screamed overhead or burst around; and I confess to feeling quite a relief at getting back to the friendly shelter of the lane. Looking over the bank, I noticed for the first time the frightful execution our fire had created. The space in front was thickly strewed with dead and badly wounded, and beyond the bodies of the fallen enemy could just be seen—for it was now getting dusk—the bear-skins and red coats of our own gallant Guards scattered over the slope, and marking the line of their victorious advance. But hardly a minute could have passed in thus looking over the field, when our brigade-major came moving up the lane on foot (I suppose his horse had been shot) crying, 'Stand to your arms, Volunteers! they're coming on again!' and we found ourselves a second time engaged in a hot musketry fire. How long it went on I cannot now remember, but we could distinguish clearly the thick line of skirmishers about sixty paces off, and mounted officers among them; and we seemed to be keeping them well in check, for they were quite exposed to our fire, while we were protected nearly up to our shoulders, when—I know not how—I became sensible that something had gone wrong. 'We are taken in flank!' called out some one; and looking along the left, sure enough there were dark figures jumping over the bank into the lane and firing up along our line. The volunteers in reserve, who had come down to take the place of the Guards, must have given way at this point; the enemy's skirmishers had got through our line, and turned our left flank.

How the next move came about I cannot recollect, or whether it was without orders, but in a short time we found ourselves out of the lane and drawn up in a straggling line about thirty yards in rear of it—at our end, that is; the other flank had fallen back a good deal more—and the enemy were lining the hedge, and numbers of them passing over and forming up on our side. Beyond our left a confused mass were retreating, firing as they went, followed by the advancing line of the enemy. We stood in this way for a short space, firing at random as fast as we could. Our colonel and major must have been shot, for there was no one to give an order, when somebody on horseback called out from behind—I think it must have been the brigadier—'Now, then, Volunteers! give a British cheer, and go at them—charge!' and, with a shout, we rushed at the enemy. Some of them ran, some stopped to meet us, and for a moment it was a real hand-to-hand fight. I felt a sharp sting in my leg, as I drove my bayonet right through the man in front of me. I confess I shut my eyes, for I just got a glimpse of the poor wretch as he fell back, his eyes starting out of his head, and, savage though we were, the sight was almost too horrible to look at. But the struggle was over in a second, and we had cleared the ground again right up to the rear hedge of the lane. Had we gone on, I believe we might have recovered the lane too, but we were now all out of order; there was no one to say what to do; the enemy began to line the hedge and open fire, and they were streaming past our left; and how it came about I know not, but we found ourselves falling back towards our right rear, scarce any semblance of a line remaining, and the volunteers who had given way on our left mixed up with us, and adding to the confusion.

It was now nearly dark. On the slopes which we were retreating to was a large mass of reserves drawn up in columns. Some of the leading files of these, mistaking us for the enemy, began firing at us; our fellows, crying out to them to stop, ran towards their ranks, and in a few moments the whole slope of the hill became a scene of confusion that I cannot attempt to describe, regiments and detachments mixed up in hopeless disorder. Most of us, I believe, turned towards the enemy and fired away our few remaining cartridges; but it was too late to take aim, fortunately for us, or the guns which the enemy had brought up through the gap, and were firing point-blank, would have done more damage. As it was, we could see little more than the bright flashes of their fire. In our confusion we had jammed up a line regiment immediately behind us, and its colonel and some staff-officers were in vain trying to make a passage for it, and their shouts to us to march to the rear and clear a road could be heard above the roar of the guns and the confused babel of sound. At last a mounted officer pushed his way through, followed by a company in sections, the men brushing past with firm-set faces, as if on a desperate task; and the battalion, when it got clear, appeared to deploy and advance down the slope. I have also a dim recollection of seeing the Life Guards trot past the front, and push on towards the town—a last desperate attempt to save the day—before we left the field.

Our adjutant, who had got separated from our flank of the regiment in the confusion, now came up, and managed to lead us, or at any rate some of us, up to the crest of the hill in the rear, to re-form, as he said; but there we met a vast crowd of volunteers, militia, and waggons, all hurrying rearward from the direction of the big house, and we were borne in the stream for a mile at least before it was possible to stop. At last the adjutant led us to an open space a little off the line of fugitives, and there we re-formed the remains of the companies. Telling us to halt, he rode off to try and obtain orders, and find out where the rest of our brigade was. From this point, a spur of high ground running off from the main plateau, we looked down through the dim twilight into the battle-field below. Artillery fire was still going on. We could see the flashes from the guns on both sides, and now and then a stray shell came screaming up and burst near us, but we were beyond the sound of musketry.

This halt first gave us time to think about what had happened. The long day of expectancy had been succeeded by the excitement of battle; and when each minute may be your last, you do not think much about other people, nor when you are facing another man with a rifle have you time to consider whether he or you are the invader, or that you are fighting for your home and hearths. All fighting is pretty much alike, I suspect, as to sentiment, when once it begins. But now we had time for reflection; and although we did not yet quite understand how far the day had gone against us, an uneasy feeling of self-condemnation must have come up in the minds of most of us; while, above all, we now began to realize what the loss of this battle meant to the country. Then, too, we knew not what had become of all our wounded comrades. Reaction, too, set in after the fatigue and excitement. For myself, I had found out for the first time that, besides the bayonet-wound in my leg, a bullet had gone through my left arm, just below the shoulder, and outside the bone. I remember feeling something like a blow just when we lost the lane, but the wound passed unnoticed till now, when the bleeding had stopped and the shirt was sticking to the wound.

This half-hour seemed an age, and while we stood on this knoll the endless tramp of men and rumbling of carts along the downs beside us told their own tale. The whole army was falling back. At last we could discern the adjutant riding up to us out of the dark. The army was to retreat, and take up and take up a position on Epsom Downs, he said: we should join in the march, and try and find our brigade in the morning; and so we turned into the throng again, and made our way on as best we could. A few scraps of news he gave us as he rode alongside of our leading section; the army had held its position well for a time, but the enemy had at last broken through the line between us and Guildford, as well as in our front, and had poured his men through the point gained, throwing the line into confusion, and the first army corps near Guildford were also falling back to avoid being outflanked. The regular troops were holding the rear; we were to push on as fast as possible to get out of their way, and allow them to make an orderly retreat in the morning. The gallant old lord commanding our corps had been badly wounded early in the day, he heard, and carried off the field. The Guards had suffered dreadfully; the household cavalry had ridden down the Cuirassiers, but had got into broken ground and had been awfully cut up. Such were the scraps of news passed down our weary column. What had become of our wounded no one knew, and no one liked to ask. So we trudged on. It must have been midnight when we reached Leatherhead. Here we left the open ground and took to the road, and the block became greater. We pushed our way painfully along; several trains passed slowly ahead along the railway by the roadside, containing the wounded, we supposed—such of them, at least, as were lucky enough to be picked up.

It was daylight when we got to Epsom. The night had been bright and clear after the storm, with a cool air, which, blowing through my soaking clothes, chilled me to the bone. My wounded leg was stiff and sore, and I was ready to drop with exhaustion and hunger. Nor were my comrades in much better case; we had eaten nothing since breakfast the day before, and the bread we had put by had been washed away by the storm; only a little pulp remained at the bottom of my bag. The tobacco was all too wet to smoke. In this plight we were creeping along, when the adjutant guided us into a field by the roadside to rest awhile, and we lay down exhausted on the sloppy grass. The roll was here taken, and only 180 answered out of nearly 500 present on the morning of the battle. How many of these were killed and wounded no one could tell; but it was certain many must have got separated in the confusion of the evening. While resting here, we saw pass by, in the crowd of vehicles and men, a cart laden with commissariat stores, driven by a man in uniform. 'Food!' cried some one, and a dozen volunteers jumped up and surrounded the cart. The driver tried to whip them off; but he was pulled off his seat, and the contents of the cart thrown out in an instant. They were preserved meats in tins, which we tore open with our bayonets. The meat had been cooked before, I think; at any rate we devoured it. Shortly after this a general came by with three or four staff-officers. He stopped and spoke to our adjutant, and then rode into the field.

'My lads,' said he, 'you shall join my division for the present: fall in, and follow the regiment that is now passing.'

We rose up, fell in by companies, each about twenty strong, and turned once more into the stream moving along the road—regiments, detachments, single volunteers or militiamen, country people making off, some with bundles, some without, a few in carts, but most on foot; here and there waggons of stores, with men sitting wherever there was room, others crammed with wounded soldiers. Many blocks occurred from horses falling, or carts breaking down and filling up the road.

In the town the confusion was even worse, for all the houses seemed full of volunteers and militiamen, wounded or resting, or trying to find food, and the streets were almost choked up. Some officers were in vain trying to restore order, but the task seemed a hopeless one. One or two volunteer regiments which had arrived from the north the previous night, and had been halted here for orders, were drawn up along the roadside steadily enough, and some of the retreating regiments, including ours, may have preserved the semblance of discipline; but for the most part the mass pushing to the rear was a mere mob. The regulars, or what remained of them, were now, I believe, all in the rear, to hold the advancing enemy in check. A few officers among such a crowd could do nothing. To add to the confusion, several houses were being emptied of the wounded brought here the night before, to prevent their falling into the hands off the enemy, some in carts, some being carried to the railway by men. The groans of these poor fellows as they were jostled through the street went to our hearts, selfish though fatigue and suffering had made us.

At last, following the guidance of a staff-officer who was standing to show the way, we turned off from the main London road and took that towards Kingston. Here the crush was less, and we managed to move along pretty steadily. The air had been cooled by the storm, and there was no dust. We passed through a village where our new general had seized all the public-houses, and taken possession of the liquor; and each regiment as it came up was halted, and each man got a drink of beer, served out by companies. Whether the owner got paid, I know not, but it was like nectar.

It must have been about one o'clock in the afternoon that we came in sight of Kingston. We had been on our legs sixteen hours, and had got over about twelve miles of ground. There is a hill a little south of the Surbiton station, covered then mostly with villas, but open at the western extremity, where there was a clump of trees on the summit. We had diverged from the road towards this, and here the general halted us and disposed the line of the division along his front, facing to the south-west, the right of the line reaching down to the Thames, the left extending along the southern slope of the hill, in the direction of the Epsom road by which we had come. We were nearly in the centre, occupying the knoll just in front of the general, who dismounted on the top and tied his horse to a tree. It is not much of a hill, but commands an extensive view over the flat country around; and as we lay wearily on the ground we could see the Thames glistening like a silver field in the bright sunshine, the palace at Hampton Court, the bridge at Kingston, and the old church tower rising above the haze of the town, with the woods of Richmond Park behind it.

To most of us the scene could not but call up their associations of happy days of peace—days now ended and peace destroyed through national infatuation. We did not say this to each other, but a deep depression had come upon us, partly due to weakness and fatigue, no doubt, but we saw that another stand was going to be made, and we had no longer any confidence in ourselves. If we could not hold our own when stationary in line, on a good position, but had been broken up into a rabble at the first shock, what chance had we now of manoeuvring against a victorious enemy in this open ground? A feeling of desperation came over us, a determination to struggle on against hope; but anxiety for the future of the country, and our friends, and all dear to us, filled our thoughts now that we had time for reflection. We had had no news of any kind since Wood joined us the day before—we knew not what was doing in London, or what the Government was about, or anything else; and, exhausted though we were, we felt an intense craving to know what was happening in other parts of the country.

Our general had expected to find a supply of food and ammunition here, but nothing turned up. Most of us had hardly a cartridge left, so he ordered the regiment next to us, which came from the north and had not been engaged, to give us enough to make up twenty rounds a man, and he sent off a fatigue-party to Kingston to try and get provisions, while a detachment of our fellows was allowed to go foraging among the villas in our rear; and in about an hour they brought back some bread and meat, which gave us a slender meal all round. They said most of the houses were empty, and that many had been stripped of all eatables, and a good deal damaged already.

It must have been between three and four o'clock when the sound of cannonading began to be heard in the front, and we could see the smoke of guns rising above the woods of Esher and Claremont, and soon afterwards some troops emerged from the fields below us. It was the rear-guard of regular troops. There were some guns also, which were driven up the slope and took up their position round the knoll. There were three batteries, but they only counted eight guns amongst them. Behind them was posted the line; it was a brigade apparently of four regiments, but the whole did not look to be more than eight or nine hundred men. Our regiment and another had been moved a little to the rear to make way for them, and presently we were ordered down to occupy the railway station on our right rear. My leg was now so stiff I could no longer march with the rest, and my left arm was very swollen and sore, and almost useless; but anything seemed better than being left behind, so I limped after the battalion as best I could down to the station. There was a goods shed a little in advance of it down the line, a strong brick building, and here my company was posted. The rest of our men lined the wall of the enclosure. A staff-officer came with us to arrange the distribution; we should be supported by line troops, he said; and in a few minutes a train full of them came slowly up from Guildford way. It was the last; the men got out, the train passed on, and a party began to tear up the rails, while the rest were distributed among the houses on each side. A sergeant's party joined us in our shed, and an engineer officer with sappers came to knock holes in the wall for us to fire from; but there were only half-a-dozen of them, so progress was not rapid, and as we had no tools we could not help.

It was while we were watching this job that the adjutant, who was as active as ever, looked in, and told us to muster in the yard. The fatigue-party had come back from Kingston, and a small baker's hand-cart of food was made over to us as our share. It contained loaves, flour, and some joints of meat. The meat and the flour we had not time or means to cook. The loaves we devoured; and there was a tap of water in the yard, so we felt refreshed by the meal. I should have liked to wash my wounds, which were becoming very offensive, but I dare not take off my coat, feeling sure I should not be able to get it on again. It was while we were eating our bread that the rumour first reached us of another disaster, even greater than that we had witnessed ourselves. Whence it came I know not; but a whisper went down the ranks that Woolwich had been captured. We all knew that it was our only arsenal, and understood the significance of the blow. No hope, if this were true, of saving the country. Thinking over this, we went back to the shed.

Although this was only our second day of war, I think we were already old soldiers so far that we had come to be careless about fire, and the shot and shell that now began to open on us made no sensation. We felt, indeed, our need of discipline, and we saw plainly enough the slender chance of success coming out of such a rabble as we were; but I think we were all determined to fight on as long as we could. Our gallant adjutant gave his spirit to everybody; and the staff-officer commanding was a very cheery fellow, and went about as if we were certain of victory. Just as the firing began he looked in to say that we were as safe as in a church, that we must be sure and pepper the enemy well, and that more cartridges would soon arrive. There were some steps and benches in the shed, and on these a part of our men were standing, to fire through the upper loop-holes, while the line soldiers and others stood on the ground, guarding the second row. I sat on the floor, for I could not now use my rifle, and besides, there were more men than loop-holes.

Although changes were expected in naval warfare, the general view of land warfare expected that the cavalry would continue to make final, decisive charges

The artillery fire which had opened now on our position was from a longish range; and occupation for the riflemen had hardly begun, when there was a crash in the shed, and I was knocked down by a blow on the head. I was almost stunned for a time, and could not make out what had happened. A shot or shell had hit the shed without quite penetrating the wall, but the blow had upset the steps resting against it, and the men standing on them, bringing down a cloud of plaster and brickbats, one of which had struck me. I felt now past being of use. I could not use my rifle, and could barely stand; and after a time I thought I would make for my own house, on the chance of finding some one still there. I got up therefore, and staggered homewards. Musketry fire had now commenced, and our side were blazing away from the windows of the houses, and from behind walls, and from the shelter of some trucks still standing in the station. A couple of field-pieces in the yard were firing, and in the open space in rear a reserve was drawn up. There, too, was the staff-officer on horseback, watching the fight through his field-glass. I remember having still enough sense to feel that the position was a hopeless one. That straggling line of houses and gardens would surely be broken through at some point, and then the line must give way like a rope of sand. It was about a mile to our house, and I was thinking how I could possibly drag myself so far when I suddenly recollected that I was passing Travers's house—one of the first of a row of villas then leading from the station to Kingston. Had he been brought home, I wondered, as his faithful old servant promised, and was his wife still here? I remember to this day the sensation of shame I felt, when I recollected that I had not once given him—my greatest friend—a thought since I carried him off the field the day before. But war and suffering make men selfish. I would go in now at any rate and rest awhile, and see if I could be of use.

The little garden before the house was as trim as ever—I used to pass it every day on my way to the train, and knew every shrub in it—and a blaze of flowers, but the hall-door stood ajar. I stepped in and saw little Arthur standing in the hall. He had been dressed as neatly as ever that day, and as he stood there in his pretty blue frock and white trousers and socks showing his chubby little legs, with his golden locks, fair face, and large dark eyes, the picture of childish beauty, in the quiet hall, just as it used to look—the vases of flowers, the hat and coats hanging up, the familiar pictures on the walls— this vision of peace in the midst of war made me wonder for a moment, faint and giddy as I was, if the pandemonium outside had any real existence, and was not merely a hideous dream. But the roar of the guns making the house shake, and the rushing of the shot, gave a ready answer. The little fellow appeared almost unconscious of the scene around him, and was walking up the stairs holding by the railing, one step at a time, as I had seen him do a hundred times before, but turned round as I came in. My appearance frightened him, and staggering as I did into the hall, my face and clothes covered with blood and dirt, I must have looked an awful object to the child, for he gave a cry and turned to run toward the basement stairs. But he stopped on hearing my voice calling him back to his god-papa, and after a while came timidly up to me. Papa had been to the battle, he said, and was very ill; mamma was with papa; Wood was out; Lucy was in the cellar, and had taken him there, but he wanted to go to mamma.

Telling him to stay in the hall for a minute till I called him, I climbed up-stairs and opened the bedroom-door. My poor friend lay there, his body resting on the bed, his head supported on his wife's shoulder as she sat by the bedside. He breathed heavily, but the pallor of his face, the closed eyes, the prostrate arms, the clammy foam she was wiping from his mouth, all spoke of approaching death. The good old servant had done his duty, at least—he had brought his master home to die in his wife's arms. The poor woman was too intent on her charge to notice the opening of the door, and as the child would be better away, I closed it gently and went down to the hall to take little Arthur to the shelter below, where the maid was hiding. Too late! He lay at the foot of the stairs on his face, his little arms stretched out, his hair dabbled in blood. I had not noticed the crash among the other noises, but a splinter of a shell must have come through the open doorway; it had carried away the back of his head. The poor child's death must have been instantaneous. I tried to lift up the little corpse with my one arm, but even this load was too much for me, and while stooping down I fainted away.

When I came to my senses again it was quite dark, and for some time I could not make out where I was; I lay indeed for some time like one half asleep, feeling no inclination to move. By degrees I became aware that I was on the carpeted floor of a room. All noise of battle had ceased, but there was a sound as of many people close by. At last I sat up and gradually got to my feet. The movement gave me intense pain, for my wounds were now highly inflamed, and my clothes sticking to them made them dreadfully sore. At last I got up and groped my way to the door, and opening it at once saw where I was, for the pain had brought back my senses. I had been lying in Travers's little writing-room at the end of the passage, into which I made my way. There was no gas, and the drawing-room door was closed; but from the open dining-room the glimmer of a candle feebly lighted up the hall, in which half-a-dozen sleeping figures could be discerned, while the room itself was crowded with men. The table was covered with plates, glasses, and bottles; but most of the men were asleep in the chairs or on the floor, a few were smoking cigars, and one or two with their helmets on were still engaged at supper, occasionally grunting out an observation between the mouthfuls.

'*Sind wackere Soldaten, diese Englischen Freiwilligen,*' said a broad-shouldered brute, stuffing a great hunch of beef into his mouth with a silver fork, an implement I should think he must have been using for the first time in his life.

'*Ja, ja,*' replied a comrade, who was lolling back in his chair with a pair of very dirty legs on the table, and one of poor Travers's best cigars in his mouth, '*Sie so gut laufen können.*'

'*Ja wohl,*' responded the first speaker, '*aber sind nicht eben so schnell wie die Französischen Mobloten.*'

'*Gewiss,*' grunted a hulking lout from the floor, leaning on his elbow, and sending out a cloud of smoke from his ugly jaws, '*und da sind hier etwa gute Schützen.*'

'*Hast recht, lange Peter,*' answered number one, '*wenn die Schurken so gut exerciren wie schützen könnten, so wären wir heute nicht hier!*'

'*Recht! Recht!*' said the second, '*das exerciren macht den guten Soldaten.*'

What more criticisms on the shortcomings of our unfortunate volunteers might have passed I did not stop to hear, being interrupted by a sound on the stairs. Mrs Travers was standing on the landing-place; I limped up the stairs to meet her. Among the many pictures of those fatal days engraven on my memory, I remember none more clearly than the mournful aspect of my poor friend, widowed and childless within a few moments, as she stood there in her white dress, coming forth like a ghost from the chamber of the dead, the candle she held lighting up her face, and contrasting its pallor with the dark hair that fell disordered round it, its beauty radiant even through features worn with fatigue and sorrow. She was calm and even tearless, though the trembling lip told of the effort to restrain the emotion she felt.

'Dear friend,' she said, taking my hand, 'I was coming to seek you; forgive my selfishness in neglecting you so long; but you will understand'—glancing at the door above—'how occupied I have been.'

'Where', I began, 'is'—

'my boy?' she answered, anticipating my question. 'I have laid him by his father. But now your wounds must be cared for; how pale and faint you look!—rest here for a moment'—and, descending to the dining-room, she returned with some wine, which I gratefully drank, and then, making me sit down on the top step of the stairs, she brought water and linen, and, cutting off the sleeve of my coat, bathed and bandaged my wounds. 'Twas I who felt selfish for thus adding to her troubles; but in truth I was too weak to have much will left, and stood in need of the help which she forced me to accept; and the dressing of my wounds afforded indescribable relief. While thus tending me, she explained in broken sentences how matters stood. Every room but her own, and the little parlour into which she with Wood's help had carried me, was full of soldiers. Wood had been taken away to work at repairing the railroad, and Lucy had run off from fright; but the cook had stopped at her post, and had served up supper and had opened the cellar for the soldiers' use; she did not understand what they said, and they were rough and boorish, but not uncivil. I should now go, she said, when my wounds were dressed, to look after my own home, where I might be wanted; for herself, she wished only to be allowed to remain watching there—pointing to the room where lay the bodies of her husband and child—where she would not be molested. I felt that her advice was good. I could be of no use as protection, and I had an anxious longing to know what had become of my sick mother and sister; besides, some arrangement must be made for the burial. I therefore limped away. There was no need to express thanks on either side, and the grief was too deep to be reached by any outward show of sympathy.

Outside the house there was a good deal of movement and bustle; many carts going along, the waggoners, from Sussex and Surrey, evidently impressed and guarded by soldiers; and although no gas was burning, the road towards Kingston was well lighted by torches held by persons standing at short intervals in line, who had been seized for the duty, some of them the tenants of neighbouring villas. Almost the first of these torch-bearers I came to was an old gentleman whose face I was well acquainted with, from having frequently travelled up and down in the same train with him. He was a senior clerk in a government office, I believe, and was a mild-looking old man with a prim face and a long neck, which he used to wrap in a wide double neckcloth, a thing even in those days seldom seen. Even in that moment of bitterness I could not help being amused by the absurd figure this poor old fellow presented, with his solemn face and long cravat doing penance with a torch in front of his own door, to light up the path of our conquerors.

But a more serious object now presented itself, a corporal's guard passing by, with two English volunteers in charge, their hands tied behind their backs. They cast an imploring glance at me, and I stepped into the road to ask the corporal what was the matter, and even ventured, as he was passing on, to lay my hand on his sleeve. '*Auf dem Wege, Spitzbube!*' cried the brute, lifting his rifle as if to knock me down. 'Must one prisoners who fire at us let shoot,' he went on to add; and shot the poor fellows would have been, I suppose, if I had not interceded with an officer who happened to be riding by. '*Herr*

Hauptmann,' I cried, as loud as I could, 'is this your discipline, to let unarmed prisoners be shot without orders?' The officer, thus appealed to, reined in his horse, and halted the guard till he heard what I had to say. My knowledge of other languages here stood me in good stead, for the prisoners, north-country factory hands apparently, were of course utterly unable to make themselves understood, and did not even know in what they had offended. I therefore interpreted their explanation: they had been left behind while skirmishing near Ditton, in a barn, and coming out of their hiding-place in the midst of a party of the enemy, with their rifles in their hands, the latter thought they were going to fire at them from behind. It was a wonder they were not shot down on the spot.

The captain heard the tale, and then told the guard to let them go, and they slunk off at once into a by-road. He was a fine soldier-like man, but nothing could exceed the insolence of his manner, which was perhaps all the greater because it seemed not intentional, but to arise from a sense of immeasurable superiority. Between lame *Freiwilliger* pleading for his comrades and the captain of the conquering army, there was, in his view, an infinite gulf. Had the two men been dogs, their fate could not have been decided more contemptuously. They were let go simply because they were not worth keeping as prisoners, and perhaps to kill any living thing without cause went against the *Hauptmann's* sense of justice. But why speak of this insult in particular? Had not every man who lived then his tale to tell of humiliation and degradation? For it was the same story everywhere. After the first stand in line, and when once they had got us on the march, the enemy laughed at us. Our handful of regular troops was sacrificed almost to a man in a vain conflict with numbers; our volunteers and militia, with officers who did not know their work, without ammunition or equipment, or staff to superintend, starving in the midst of plenty, we had soon become a helpless mob, fighting desperately here and there, but with whom, as a manoeuvring army, the disciplined invaders did just what they pleased. Happy those whose bones whitened the fields of Surrey; they at least were spared the disgrace we lived to endure. Even you, who have never known what it is to live otherwise than on sufferance, even your cheeks burn when we talk of these days; think, then, what those endured who, like your grandfather, had been citizens of the proudest nation on earth, which had never known disgrace or defeat, and whose boast it used to be that they bore a flag on which the sun never set! We had heard of generosity in war; we found none: the war was made by us, it was said, and we must take the consequences.

London and our only arsenal captured, we were at the mercy of our captors, and right heavily did they tread on our necks.

Need I tell you the rest?—of the ransom we had to pay, and the taxes raised to cover it, which keep us paupers to this day?—the brutal frankness that announced we must give place to a new naval Power, and be made harmless for revenge?—the victorious troops living at free quarters, the yoke they put on us made the more galling that their requisitions had a semblance of method and legality? Better have been robbed at first hand by the soldiery themselves, than through our own magistrates made the instruments for extortion. How we lived through the degradation we daily and hourly underwent, I hardly even now understand. And what was there left to us to live for? Stripped of our colonies; Canada and the West Indies gone to America; Australia forced to separate; India lost for ever, after the English there had all been destroyed, vainly trying to hold the country when cut off from aid by their countrymen; Gibraltar and Malta ceded to the new naval Power; Ireland independent and in perpetual anarchy and revolution. When I look at my country as it is now—its trade gone, its factories silent, its harbours empty, a prey to pauperism and decay—when I see all this, and think what Great Britain was in my youth, I ask myself whether I have really a heart or any sense of patriotism that I should have witnessed such degradation and still care to live!

France was different. There, too, they had to eat the bread of tribulation under the yoke of the conqueror; their fall was hardly more sudden or violent than ours; but war could not take away their rich soil; they had no colonies to lose; their broad lands, which made their wealth, remained to them; and they rose again from the blow. But our people could not be got to see how artificial our prosperity was—that it all rested on foreign trade and financial credit; that the course of trade once turned away from us, even for a time, it might never return; and that our credit once shaken might never be restored. To hear men talk in those days, you would have thought that Providence had ordained that our Government should always borrow at three per cent, and that trade came to us because we lived in a foggy little island set in a boisterous sea. They could not be got to see that the wealth heaped up on every side was not created in the country, but in India and China, and other parts of the world; and that it would be quite possible for the people who made money by buying and selling the natural treasures of the earth, to go and live in other places, and take their profits with them. Nor would men believe that there could ever be an end to our coal and iron, or that they would get to be so much dearer than the coal and iron of America that it would no longer be worth while to work them, and that therefore we ought to insure against the loss of our artificial position as the great centre of trade, by making ourselves secure and strong and respected.

We thought we were living in a commercial millennium, which must last for a thousand years at least. After all, the bitterest part of our reflection is that all this misery and decay might have been so easily prevented, and that we brought it about ourselves by our own shortsighted recklessness. There, across the narrow Straits, was the writing on the wall; but we would not choose to read it. The warnings of the few were drowned in the voice of the multitude. Power was then passing away from the class which had been used to rule, and to face political dangers, and which had brought the nation with honour unsullied through former struggles, into the hands of the lower classes, uneducated, untrained to the use of political rights, and swayed by demagogues; and the few who were wise in their generation were denounced as alarmists, or as aristocrats who sought their own aggrandizement by wasting public money on bloated armaments. The rich were idle and luxurious; the poor grudged the cost of defence. Politics had become a mere bidding for Radical votes, and those who should have led the nation stooped rather to pander to the selfishness of the day, and humoured the popular cry which denounced those who would secure the defence of the nation by enforced arming of its manhood, as interfering with the liberties of the people.

Truly the nation was ripe for a fall; but when I reflect how a little firmness and self-denial, or political courage and foresight, might have averted the disaster, I feel that the judgement must have really been deserved. A nation too selfish to defend its liberty could not have been fit to retain it. To you, my grandchildren, who are now going to seek a new home in a more prosperous land, let not this bitter lesson be lost upon you in the country of your adoption. For me, I am too old to begin life again in a strange country; and, hard and evil as have been my days, it is not much to await in solitude the time which cannot now be far off, when my old bones will be laid to rest in the soil I have loved so well, and whose happiness and honour I have so long survived.

The Battle of Dorking

ANONYMOUS

There's a Tory alarmist article in *Blackwood's Magazine*;
It's called the 'Battle of Dorking', and has made a great sensation;
It's put in the mouth of a Grandfather, who describes what he has seen,
When England was invaded, and ceased to be a nation.

It tells how a German army landed, somewhere 'twixt Deal and Dover—
Our fleet, at the time, being, most of it, just where it should not have been;
How the few ships that were in the Channel were sunk, smashed, and sailed over;
How our Line, Volunteers, and Militia by the foe were chawed up clean:

How, about Leith Hill and Dorking, we got an an awful thrashing,
And a second somewhere near Richmond; then further resistance was idle;
How through our suburban roofs and walls the German shells came crashing;
Till BISMARCK put his hook in our nose, and in our jaws his bridle

By our bungling defence on land and sea shows us utter noodles and silly asses;
Paints our parlours and pantries made free with the High and Low German fellers
And harrows up the best feelings of *pater-* and *mater-familiases*,
By describing British ratepayers shot down in their own cellars,

While their fair-haired little darlings—which a horror even
  worser is
Than gen'ral *bouleversement*, bombardment, beating, and
  bobbery—
Are having their dear little brains dashed out at the doors of
  their own nurseries,
Till Old England is given up helpless to organized German
  robbery.

Her colonies rent from her, her dependencies independent;
Her youth deserting her stagnant shores, no longer a land of
  Goshen;
Her manufactures gone with the coal, the basis of her ascen-
  dant;
And BRITANNIA a rotten hulk upon an idle ocean.

So easy it is for the foe to invade this Mammon-worshipping
  island—
So easy to prove the foundations we build our hopes on,
  vapour—
So easy to turn a Channel of twenty miles' sea to dry land—
So easy, in fact, to crumple up Old England—upon paper!

There's a fable, how once in ÆSOP'S days a Man with a Lion
  beside him,
Was admiring a group—say in Ebony—where some artist of
  the day
Had carved a Lion on the ground, and a hunter triumphant
  astride him:
'Behold,' said the Man, 'how human brains bring brute force
  under sway.'

The Lion smiled—as one that smiles when treated to
  pompous platitudes—
'Ah,' said he, 'my friend, if the sculptor had been Lion instead
  of Man,
How easy it would have been for him to have reversed the
  attitudes,
And, instead of the Man the Lion, made the Lion bestride the
  Man.'

So Ebony's[1] Article-writer might have shifted colours and
  figures—
Have given England the Lion's part and Germany that of the
  mouse,
Made *our* fleet floor *their* transports, *our* Enfields *their* needle-
  triggers,
Had he but hailed from GLADSTONE'S, 'stead of DIZZY'S,[2]
  side of the House.

The 'Battle of Dorking' he calls his fight—'tis clear he's no
  game chicken—
In fact, I believe, that fighting fowls your Dorkings never
  are—
Though they take kindly to cramming, and when roasted are
  pretty picking—
But *this* Dorking bird seems to be a cross between Dung-hill
  Cock and *Canard*.

War-Office and Admiralty may have their share of bungle and
  blunder;
But JOHN BULL is not yet the brainless ass that *Blackwood's*
  prophet would make him;
We may grudge the cost of our Army's strength, and of our
  Navy's thunder,
But if the British Lion's asleep, 'twill prove no joke to wake
  him.

Der Ruhm:
or, The Wreck of German Unity
The Narrative of a Brandenburger *Hauptmann*
ANONYMOUS

He was grinding the dusty gravel on the sidewalk of a Strasse near the Potsdam Bahnhoff—a tall, lean old man with a snow-white beard. His step was feeble and tottering, and his shoulders were bent; yet in the carriage of the old man was something that told he had been a soldier. As he came short right about and mechanically straightened himself when I spoke to him, it seemed possible for me to believe what the drosky driver had said, as I yesterday drove past the gaunt old promenader: 'Old white-beard there is Hauptmann von Scharzhoff, the first man into Flavigny the day of the Schlacht bei Vionville in the old war of eighteen hundred and seventy.'[1]

The methodically courteous *Hauptmann* was ready with his *'Ich habe die Ehre'* when I handed him the card which was my letter of introduction; and we fell easily into talk. He was *Hauptmann* no longer, he said, and he would rather not be thus addressed. 'Yes, Potsdam was a pleasant town, and there was the drill-ground close by, no doubt; but he did not care to see drilling now, and the pavements were very bad.' Such was his talk—of trivialities with a dash of regretful sadness through it; but of the past the old man was very wary. The ice in that direction seemed very thin, and he could not find it in his heart to trust himself on it.

Now and then his eye brightened and a light came into his sad face as a boy or a girl came romping out of the house with a cheery salute for *'der Grossvater'*.

'Carl,' he cried to a bright boy of fourteen who came out holding in the palm of his hand something at which he was gazing curiously; 'Carl, dear boy, what hast thou there?'

'I know not, *Grossvater*; I found it in the bottom of your old chest—it is a little black cross edged with white, and in the middle has the letter W, with 1870 below it. See; tell me, I pray you, what the little thing is.'

PUNCH, OR THE LONDON CHARIVARI.—August 12, 1871.

CARDWELL'S COLLAPSE.

Our War Minister (*to* H.I.H. "Fritz"). "NOW THAT YOUR IMPERIAL HIGHNESS IS HERE, P'RAPS YOU'LL KINDLY TELL US *HOW* TO MOVE 30,000 MEN *THIRTY MILES.*'

In the eyes of *Punch* the newly elected German Emperor, Wilhelm I, represents military efficiency and the Secretary of War, one of the great military reformers, represents *Battle of Dorking* incompetence

It was painful to see the old man. The red blood rushed into his withered face, as with flashing eye he reared his head and threw back his shoulders. From between the parted lips came as if involuntary the words '*Gott im Himmel—das eiserne Kreuz!*'[2] He clutched it from the boy, and gazed on it with a look of such proud wistfulness; and then his face broke and the tears began to drop on the bit of iron. Just then a grandchild-girl in the garden began to sing an old nearly forgotten *Lied*, '*Was ist des Deutschen Vaterland?*'

'*Ach mein Gott, mein Gott*, will you tear me to pieces, then, my children? You are stabbing me to the quick with worse than knives.' And then in his extremity the old warrior took to swearing quaint passionate oaths of the Lager and the bivouac; for in truth he was deeply moved, and emotion in military men has a trick of working itself off in such language as that to which our troops were addicted in Flanders.

His grandchildren hung about him in penitent, bewildered concern. I put in a word where there seemed an opportune chance, and at length the old man became comparatively calm. Curious to say, garrulity succeeded the spasm of emotion, and the old soldier seemed eager to speak on the very topics which he had disappointed me by shunning. The sluice-gate of reticence was raised. The grandchildren and myself followed him into the arbour at the bottom of the garden, where we all seated ourselves; and then the *Grossvater Hauptmann*, having taken his pipe from Carl in token of reconciliation, began a long and surely not uneventful history.

'No wonder,' said he, 'that the sight of that Iron Cross moved me. It reached me on the very day of the culmination of German ascendancy and unity; on the very day on which Wilhelm—you have heard of Kaiser Wilhelm, my children—accepted the dignity of Emperor of Germany.[3] The old man stood there in the Salle des Glaces in the Schloss at Versailles, the successor of *der alter Barbarossa*, with Prussians, Bavarians, Saxons, Würtemburgers, with representatives of all Germany cheering for him and for German unity.

'Presently the war was finished and the real work of unification was commenced. Ah, what a man was that Bismarck—the first, and the last but one, Chancellor of the German Empire! A pitiless, clever, plotting, daring, bluff man, with a mind like a vice, a will like a sledge-hammer, a heart like a flintstone. And Bismarck was honest, too; he had no self-seeking; he was the most capable of administrators; and the meaning and aim of his life was to achieve and consummate German unity.

'For my part I wished for peace, and for lasting peace, for what more could war bring me than the Iron Cross; and had I not a wife and children? It gladdened me, then, that, when on his way home from war Bismarck, in reply to a Frankfort citizen, said in his bluff off-hand way, that Germany would make no more war while he and the citizen lived.

'Then came the triumphal entry into Berlin, of which you may read in Treskow's or Wickede's histories. It was a gallant spectacle truly, and there were emblems of peace; and all the people, while hailing the war victors, seemed so joyous because there was once more peace, that when I returned at night to my bivouac on the Kreuzberg, my heart was serene within me, to think of years to come when, with your grandmother in our happy home, I should till those acres of which you may have heard your father speak. I laughed at that croaking foreboder *Feldwebel* Schmidt, who had been gloomy ever since he buried his last brother under the garden wall at Artenay. In the gladness of my heart, I bade him drink a glass to the future of Germany. Schmidt tossed off the Branntwein—he never refused drink—but as he put down the glass, his sententious words were, "*Ach, Herr Hauptmann, zum Teufel! der Ruhm* is getting into the head of Germania."[4] I thought the cognac had got into Schmidt's head, and bade him go to the devil for an old raven.

'We left the Kreuzberg and went into quarters here in Potsdam. There seemed an universal breathing of peace and prosperity. Old Kaiser Wilhelm was bluff, fresh, and hearty as if he had taken a fresh lease of life. I went into the Reserve and took to farming, never thinking that I should have to buckle on sabre more. Miraculous Bismarck, appointed by the Reichstag to a seemingly irresponsible dictatorship over Alsace and Lorraine, was reported to be regenerating these provinces into a Germanhood which was almost enthusiastic. Alexander of Russia, stirred from his misanthropical apathy by the intensity of his admiration for his uncle Kaiser Wilhelm, almost lived in Germany, drinking the waters at Ems, attending reviews at Berlin, Königsberg, or Breslau, and striving to have everything in Russia moulded after the German pattern. King Ludwig of Bavaria, King Johann of Saxony, stupid Karl of Würtemburg, were all in Berlin at one time, and the Court festivities were the talk of Europe. Bismarck stalked along the alleys of the Thiergarten, making the leaves quiver with his stentorian laugh; to see and hear him, you would think him a man whose life was a holiday.

'But somehow events seemed to ripen toward his consummation of a Pan-Germanic union. One morning it was quietly announced that Luxemburg was now a portion of the German Empire. France was too much in the mire to do more than make a plaintive remonstrance, to which Bismarck did not take the trouble to reply. I remember England talked rather big on the subject. The *National Zeitung* quoted a bullying article from the *Times*, which was, as it is still, I suppose, the leading journal in England, and followed the quotation with a truculent comment (reported to be inspired), reviving the dormant cry for an immediate cession of Heligoland, and asking England how she would like to see a couple of German army corps marching on London.

'Somehow the bother died out. England's chief Minister in those days was one Gladstone—I heard he was afterwards made a Lord—a man whose measure was taken in Germany as one whose turn for economy was so strong as to blind him to the fact that to fight is sometimes the cheapest thing that a nation can do.

'So we had Luxemburg without a drop of blood; and then there came first hints, and then outspoken assertions in the press and elsewhere, that Holland was as much German as Luxemburg, and that the German Empire must have an eligible sea-board. And we were not allowed to forget that elsewhere there were Germans who were not of the German unity, nor under the sway of the *Deutsches Kaiserreich*. The newspapers never ceased writing of the nine million Germans in Cisleithan Austria, who panted to be incorporated in the German unity; and some of the journals were so free in their reproaches against Bismarck for not having emancipated these our brethren in the settlement of 'six-and-sixty', that men not behind the scenes wondered at the licence accorded to them.[5]

'Meanwhile, the military organization of the Empire was continually being strengthened and improved. Moltke—you have all heard of Moltke, surely—was getting very feeble, but he still worked hard; and his right-hand man was a General Göben, who was said to have distinguished himself much in the Amiens campaign of the 1870 war. I met Schmidt at one of the annual trainings to which all the German troops were subjected in those days; and I jeered him about his forebodings respecting *"der Ruhm"*. *"Herr Hauptmann,"* replied Schmidt, with a wag of his bullet-head, "the air is thick with clamours for more *Ruhm*; be sure you have a good *Vogt.*"

'Croaking Schmidt was a true prophet, with a murrain to him. Gortschakoff—that was misanthropically apathetic Alexander of Russia's right-hand man—and our Bismarck had not been gossiping together for nothing in the shady walks of the Kursaal garden at Ems. Gortschakoff in his master's name suddenly picked a quarrel with Turkey, a territory in those days nominally Mahommedan and ruled over by a certain Sultan Abdul Aziz—he and his have long disappeared from history into infinite space. The Sclavonic element was, however, strong in Turkey and in its nominal or quasi-nominal dependencies; and Russia, the Pan-Sclavonic champion, made Pan-Sclavism one of her pretexts for the aggression. Turkey fought, for, though sick nigh unto death, there was fight in the Moslem to the last gasp; and he cried aloud unto Western Europe for succour, basing his demands on the articles of the "Treaty of Paris" which constituted the settlement after the Crimean War.[6]

'But it seemed there had been a certain "London Conference" in 1871, the terms agreed to at which left Western Europe a hole through which to creep out of the obligations of the "Treaty of Paris". France had no power to succour, had she been ever so inclined. The nation of Britain was very pugnacious in print and at public meetings. A well-known diplomatist of those days, one Odo Russell, declared point-blank that England must fight Russia in this quarrel, if she fought single-handed; and his single-sighted bluntness drove him for a time out of the public service. Gladstone, who was still England's Prime Minister, had no fight in him. It was not his line. He avoided fighting on various pretexts: all Europe, he contended, was equally with England bound to fight; and if none of the rest of Europe regarded the treaty obligations, why should they be binding on England? But the London Conference had weakened the treaty obligations, so that they were only binding in certain contingencies which had not arisen. Treaty obligations, as he finally expressed himself with much periphrase, had come in those days to be things of expediency, to be held binding or not binding as best suited the exigency of statesmanship.

'In short, England would not make nor meddle in the *mêlée*. It was said at the time that England had the cue from Prussia that it was best to leave this chestnut to toast on the hob, and it was left accordingly. But Austria could not keep out of the fray, if she were to exist at all. The essence of her being had come to be Sclavonic. From Saxony after six-and-sixty there came to Austria one Beust—a clear-sighted, yet not penetrating statesman.[7] He, accepting as inevitable the consummation of German unity, had accepted as equally inevitable the loss to Austria of her nine million German subjects in Cisleithania, and had thenceforward concentrated himself on conciliating Hungary to the Habsburgs—Hungary the Sclavonic. But Russia's Pan-Sclavonic assertions manifestly threatened Sclavonic Hungary, and Austria had to fight for even a fragmentary existence.

'It was when Austria was buying horses fiercely and calling out her Landwehr, that Schmidt's warning came home to me among my corn-fields. An order came out from Göben—Moltke by this time, although still alive, was a *kindische Greis*—for the reserve to be called up quietly, and everything to be put in readiness for war at an hour's notice. Then there was a scene between Kaiser Wilhelm and the Austrian ambassador at Berlin; the Berliners afterwards spoke familiarly of the Austrian ambassador as *"Bennedettig"*—and next morning the German Empire declared war against Austria.

'The war lasted longer than was at first expected. Austria made a gallant fight of it with us; but the chief retardment of victory was caused by the obstinate resistance of the Turks. The Russians had hard work with them, and Kaiser Wilhelm had to march an army to Constantinople. The old man died there—I may say in his boots, for he had not two days' illness.

'Of the military operations in this war I can tell you but little, for I had the charge of an Etappen Commando in one of our own frontier towns and saw none of the fighting. But I saw the *cortége* pass homeward with old Wilhelm's body, and his son Fritz, very mournful, with little Blumenthal by his side. Although there was no triumphal entry this time, on account of the national mourning, there was universal exultation over our victories, and *"der Ruhm"* was in everybody's mouth.

'I remember well the day that Bismarck announced to the Reichstag the grand consummation of German unity. The nine millions of Cisleithan Germans were now in the *Deutsches Kaiserreich*. Bismarck shed tears as he concluded his speech with an adaptation of Simeon's words— "Germania, now lettest thou thy servant depart in peace; for mine eyes have seen thy Unity." The same day he resigned all his offices; and Berlin saw the bluff set face of him no more. It was said that he and the new Emperor had never become reconciled after their quarrel in the Prefecture at Versailles.

'Emperor Fritz was not as Kaiser Wilhelm had been. Germany expected much of him, and with confidence: he disappointed her. There never was a more amiable man, and we had thought he had force of character too; but if he had this once, the scenes of earlier *Ruhm* through which he had passed had broken it down. He leant on Blumenthal—a waspish, rat-faced, keen little general, who had been the chief of his staff—with something approaching positive childishness. He was idling in the Schloss garden with his wife and children when old Wilhelm would have been in the saddle, or at the council board. An historian has drawn a parallel between him and Louis XVI of France; but Louis was a man exclusively of peace, whereas Fritz, although he did not like war, had no objection to gratify the natural craving for *"der Ruhm"*.

'Blumenthal superseded Göben, the selected of Moltke. And who was to succeed Bismarck? One party supported a certain Herr Buchner, who had been in his early days a pro-unity man when the cry of "German Unity" was proscribed. He had been a refugee in England till Bismarck, with his intuitive appreciation of capable men who could wear muzzles, made him his secretary. Some men said that Bismarck in his later days was really Buchner; anyhow, Buchner came to the front after Bismarck retired, and was supported by most of the Kaiser Wilhelm party. But Fritz and Blumenthal carried their dislike of Bismarck to Buchner; and the new chancellor was one George von Bunsen, a son of that Baron Bunsen who was once so well known. He was a man of capacity, honesty, and enthusiasm, yet a dreamer in a mystic way; a man of the same gentle, dependent type as Emperor Fritz; a crony of his in garden-lounging, and an abstract lover of *"der Ruhm"*.

'And there was another death about this time, that of the misanthropically apathetic Kaiser Alexander of Russia, in whose stead ruled his son, also an Alexander, a man of a quite different character. Alexander III was a Pan-Sclavist of the Pan-Sclavists, it is true; but he was a confirmed anti-German, and full of the recognition that German ascendancy in Europe was antagonistic to the modified Russian dominance which he desired.

'One of the new Alexander's first steps was to re-establish in Warsaw the Council of State for Russian Poland, abolished in 1867. He set himself assiduously to conciliate the Sclavism of Poland, promising the resuscitation of the constitution abolished in 1830, and telling the Poles he wished to see their country not the Ireland but the Scotland of Russia. There was a wondrous stir and awakening throughout all Poland. Even in the Prussian annexes of the once great kingdom, men began to mutter and to talk of a resuscitated Poland.

'The rulers of Germany did not recognize this stir among the dry bones, or if they did, they did not think it worth heeding. The German newspapers, doubtless not without a hint, began to write about the non-consummation of German unity so long as the German-speaking middle and upper classes in Courland and Livonia still obeyed the Czar. There was nothing Russian at all, they contended, in these provinces; for, while the better classes were chiefly German, the peasants were Letts, a race with no affinity to the Russ.

'From Russia, on the other hand, came startling arguments in favour of the re-establishment of Polish unity under the Czar's august auspices. "Polish unity!" retorted the German press, "Why, what was at one long-forgotten time Prussian Poland is now more German than Germany herself!" "Fine reasoning," came grimly back from Muscovy—"fine reasoning truly, when Polish is the language of the people right to the borders of Brandenburg; and when, spite of your earnest Germanizing, it is still Poznau, Gnezna, Gdansk, Grudzia, and Cholmn, instead of Posen, Gnesen, Dantzic, Grandenz, and Culm. Then as to long-forgotten time, you had not a scrap of Poland before 1772; and just bethink yourselves, O scrupulously logical Germans, that France had Alsace and Lorraine a century before that date!"

'So the battle of words, and very hard words, went on; not indeed between officialisms, but with officialisms plainly, although with a pretext of covertly standing behind the arguers.

'"*Der Ruhm*" by this time had come to be the watchword and the key-note of Germany. Emperor Fritz dallied in the Schloss garden with his wife and children, or looked over books and pictures with von Bunsen. Blumenthal, the fighting man with the rat-face, ruled Kriegs-Ministerium, Army and Empire. While Russia and Germany were exchanging their cantankerous despatches, a clamour rose for explanations with England. England had been putting, it seemed, a row of new coping-stones round the edge of an old battery on the bluff of Heligoland. England had been building a couple of ironclads for Russia. Prince George of England, married to a Danish bride, had been on a visit to Copenhagen, and rumour went that he had expressed an opinion in favour of strengthening the military forces of Denmark. "*Der Ruhm*" demanded that England should take off the coping-stones, and say something diplomatic about the Prince's remarks. Nobody in Germany thought for a moment that England would refuse; she had been so complaisant, not to say obsequious, for ever so long, that it was taken for granted, if she were asked to send the coping-stones to the Arsenal in Unter-den-Linden, she would not only comply, but pay the carriage.

'I remember how it was that I first heard of England's reply. There lived in Potsdam a young Englishman who got the *Times* regularly, and with whom I was very friendly. He was from Oxford, fellow of a collegium there. One morning he rushed into my chamber, and in his pleasant English way cried, "Take down that old bread-knife of yours, *Hauptmann*, for there is to be another try for more '*Ruhm*'"— he and I often talked about the future of Germany. "England says she will see Germany d—d before she takes down the coping-stones." He went off the same afternoon to be "in luck's way", he said, if there was to be any fighting, for he belonged to the English *Freiwilligen*.

'Gladstone, the economic-peaceful man, was no longer, I must tell you, the Minister of England. He had been succeeded by a man of, I have heard, his own selection, but a man for all that of a very different stamp. Herr Goschen was a German by race and German too in character, after a fashion. Of a Dresden family—the house is still in good repute there—he had none of the rugged bluntness of the North German, and not a tittle of the ardour which is commoner in South Germany. But he was a man of quiet unemotional efficiency, with a rare talent for planning and executing combinations which somehow were not talked of till the right time; and, although his closeness both of mouth and of deed was un-English, yet he so understood the English character that he had brought the nation whose destinies he practically swayed into the belief that it was the wisest course not to bother and badger him with inopportune questionings. He had served in more than one subordinate position before he became Chief Minister, and knew of his own knowledge when things were right or wrong in the departments.

'I learnt all this afterwards, and was, I remember, particularly struck with the details of Herr Goschen's attention to the Navy. He had been himself Minister of Marine, and when he became Chief Minister he had entrusted his old office to a certain Herr Baxter, of whose capacities he had had experience. Goschen was not an aristocrat either by birth or leanings.

'The general opinion in Germany was that England's refusal to take down the Heligoland coping-stones was a *casus belli*, and an opening for more *Ruhm*. Blumenthal, to do him justice, had not driven Moltke's system out of gear, and war preparations went on quietly but rapidly, while an ultimatum was on the road to England giving her a week to choose between the removal of the coping-stones and war. Meanwhile there were some unpleasant rumours current as to the designs of Russia, which hardly anybody heeded, unless to hint at more *Ruhm* being obtainable from that source when a proper quantum had been exacted from England.

'But a really serious blow to German unity was dealt from the South. Discontent and caballing in that quarter had been vaguely hinted at for some time. King Albert of Saxony, who had succeeded John his father, was, although a Catholic, very popular, both in his own Protestant kingdom and in Würtemburg, Protestant also. His Catholicism gave him consideration in Cisleithania and Bavaria, and it had been talked of how he was the head secretly of a not-yet-perfectly-formal South German Confederacy opposed to Prussian dominance in Pan-Germanic matters. These rumoured intestine troubles took shape and form in an ominous moment, and yet in a curiously constitutional manner.

'The ultimatum I have spoken of was despatched to England by Emperor Fritz through the Foreign Minister, without any communication with the Federal Council of the Empire. But it came to be remembered that, although the Imperial Constitution vested it in the Emperor to declare war, he required the consent of the Federal Council of the Empire for the exercise of the right. The question was accordingly submitted by Chancellor von Bunsen. Judge of the horror of North Germany when the Federal Council, by a majority of two, withheld its consent. It consisted of 58 votes, of which the Southern Confederacy held 26. It had only to secure four of the single-vote States to give it the clear majority, and intrigue managed that. So Emperor Fritz, Blumenthal and *"der Ruhm"* were outvoted.

'Here was a pretty fix. If England should reject the ultimatum, now that the Federal Council had negatived resort to the alternative, what a humiliation, what a sacrifice of *"der Ruhm"*! How everybody prayed that England, if she did not knuckle down, should be hotly outspoken, and, resenting the affront by a declaration of war on her part, so cut the knot and re-consolidate Germany into resistance. But Goschen was too astute for this. He simply said "No" to the ultimatum, and serenely went to the opera the same night.

'We could not eat dirt, spite of the Southern Confederacy's machinations; so Emperor Fritz and Blumenthal declared war according to threat, having available for fighting purposes the military forces of Prussia, and determined to leave it to chance and the effects of another dose of *"der Ruhm"* to settle for the violation of the Constitution and the use of the Federal fleet. Prussian tactics, since six-and-sixty and before, had been those of invasion, never of waiting to repel invasion.

'Britain is an island, and to invade it shipping had to be resorted to, a novelty in our warfare. The German fleet, the nucleus of which was formed by Prussia before the establishment of the Confederation, had been largely increased since the great war with France. A great slice of the war indemnity exacted from that country was spent in building ironclad ships of war of the newest and most formidable construction. At first it had been resolved to take out a portion of the indemnity in the picked vessels of the French ironclad fleet, but this design was departed from in consequence of reports from naval architects, chiefly British, that the French ironclads were so faulty in principle and construction as not to be worth making a bother to secure. When the war was over the German Government sent skilled men, with *carte blanche* as to cost, into the private building-yards of England, Scotland, and America. A great English naval architect, who had been disgusted out of the service of England, was enticed to Germany to take the superintendence of Germany's home naval dockyards; and by the time of which I am speaking, the Imperial fleet comprised upwards of twenty-five first-class ironclads. Owing, however, to the awkwardness of our seaboard, the fleet had a difficulty in concentrating. Some of the ships were in the Baltic, at Dantzic, Kiel, and Stralsund, while the larger vessels were for the most part in Kaiser Wilhelm's pet naval harbour of Wilhelmshafen, on the Bay of Jade, on the North Sea. The Kiel Canal did not admit of the passage of large ironclad ships between the Baltic and the North Sea: it had not been deepened in proportion to the increased draught of water of the new ships.

'By the day that war was formally declared, our Army Corps (the 3rd) had the bulk of it concentrated in and around Wilhelmshafen. The 10th (Hanoverian) Corps was at Bremerhafen; the Garde Corps at Hamburg; the 9th Corps (Schleswig-Holstein) in and around Altona. These were the corps constituting the army of invasion, which after all deductions was to number 110,000 men. While we waited to embark, news came that that impudent little Denmark had suddenly declared war, and that her fleet was blockading Kiel and holding the Sound passage. A division of the 9th Corps, supported by another of the 7th (Westphalian) Corps, was sent up through Schleswig to chastize Denmark, and the other division of the 7th Corps supplied the place of the former in the army of invasion.

'Our means of transport consisted, first, of the ships of war; secondly, of the large North-German-Lloyd's ocean-steamers in port at Hamburg and Bremerhafen (built, as you may have heard, with a special aptitude for transport services); and thirdly, of the merchant vessels found in these two ports, requisitioned, no matter of what nationality, for the service. With the latter there was much trouble and difficulty. The burghers of the old Hanse towns were neither fond of the Empire nor of war; the shipowners were discontented because they had not got the compensation they sought out of the French war indemnity; the sailors ran away and disguised themselves; the foreign sailors, when their craft were requisitioned, struck point-blank, and Blumenthal had to order a little shooting to bring them to reason.

'Strange to say, not an English ship of war was visible all this time in the North Sea waters. Reports had been industriously circulated that the bulk of the German war navy was in the Baltic, and that it was from Dantzic that the invading expedition was to set forth. Large English ships had been reported passing the Sound, and a great fleet, Danish and English combined, had been signalled off Dars Point. We were glad then to believe that England had been led off on the false scent, and looked forward to experiencing but trifling opposition before sighting Harwich, which was to be the landing-point of ourselves and the Guards. The other moiety of the invading army was to land on the coast of Kent.

'Our rendezvous was off the island of Nordeney. My battalion was on board the *König Wilhelm*, one of the finest of our ironclads, but a slow sailer, for her bottom was said to be very foul. Her crew looked very landsmen-like. They wore campaigning boots, like my men, and seemed stiff and clumsy. Before I got sea-sick myself—and I was dreadfully bad—I noticed that many of them were sick too. We had an admiral on board; he wore spurs, and was one of the first sick.

'What a vast miscellaneous convoy there was! The big merchant steamers—most of them with half-a-dozen sailing vessels in tow, for the wind was not good—the sailing vessels bumping and splintering one upon another; the great ironclads yawing about like badly-bitted horses, now crashing into an unfortunate sailing ship, now in collision one with another; English-requisitioned captains unable or refusing to understand German orders and signals, and so complicating the blundering; horses, guns, and waggons on deck, between decks, and in holds, all adrift together in a chaos of confusion; the men, of whom the vast majority had never seen the sea before, in speechless agonies of sea-sickness. I thought, with a shudder, what our fate would have been if a sea-accustomed enemy had swooped down upon us when in this plight. But the proverbial good fortune of Germania was with us: no enemy appeared.

'By next morning we were in rather better trim. A ship or two was reported sunk by collisions, which operated as a salutary caution to the others. The great fleet got slowly under way, each steam-vessel towing strenuously, for the wind was still unfavourable. The delays were incessant; ropes broke, ships went adrift; some steamers were too weak to tow, and had enough to do to propel themselves; and the diabolical confusion inside every ship still continued. By nightfall it was estimated that we had not made eighty miles on our way to England. At night, as the weather became worse and grew very foggy, the order was issued to lie-to till daylight, while the frigates and corvettes scouted round the fleet.

'Just before daylight, when the fog was densest, there came booming out of it the report of a single gun. Then there was a crash of artillery, and huge shells came splintering among the confused mass of shipping. The ironclads steamed straight into the fog, seeking an enemy. Dimly from the forecastle of the *König Wilhelm* was discerned a vessel, evidently a war-ship, half enveloped in smoke. The admiral, pale from sea-sickness, was full of daring. From our fore batteries in the bulkheads aft the bow, the ship's gunners opened fire on the foe, while the big ship put on steam and rushed through the water to ram her antagonist. Crash! everybody was thrown on his back; the ship staggered and strained to her remotest corner. The surface of the water was clothed with fragments and splinters, spars and general wreckage. The enemy was almost literally cut in two, and rapidly sinking; I heard the water pouring like a mill-race into her.

'Great God, it was no enemy! These were our own men around us in the water; it was our own *Arminius* that we had thus cruelly brained! Men sickened at the sight and thought—not this time with sea-sickness. The cry rose for succour, but succour could be only piecemeal. The shattered ship lurched and heeled, and then with a final heave, as in protest, went down like a stone. That morning old General Stülpnagel shot himself in his cabin.

'We steamed slowly back in our discomfiture to the fleet, to learn of more mischief. The *Hansa*, an ironclad corvette, was gone utterly away in the fog that was now drifting off to leeward. An enemy's steam ram had come crashing in from the starboard side—we had been away to larboard—came crashing in among the merchant sailing vessels, ramming through them as a ploughshare goes through lea land. The *Elisabeth*, one of the finest of our older frigates, had a cargo of torpedoes on board with which it was expected wonders were to be done. By placing them round the mouths of British harbours, it was anticipated that all the purposes that could be served by a blockading squadron would be fulfilled. Another use for which the torpedoes were destined was to encircle a fleet when lying at anchor with a girdle much like the *Feldwachen* of a land force, only differing in this; that, whereas a *Feldwache* when attacked falls back, the torpedo was to blow up and annihilate everything around it. This morning had indeed furnished evidence that the torpedoes would blow up with extreme zealous readiness, but had not only weakened their reputation for discretional explosion, but rendered it necessary to speak in the past tense of them and of the *Elisabeth*, freighted with the mischievous cargo. A shell had struck and pierced the *Elisabeth's* side; whereupon, as eye-witnesses told, she suddenly blew into fragments. The torpedoes had exploded simultaneously, and the violence of the explosion had been fearfully destructive. The *Rhein*, one of the largest of the North-German-Lloyd steamers–a whole cavalry regiment on board—had been struck with a huge shell, punctured between wind and water, and was now on fire. And, strangest thing of all, not an enemy was visible. The fog away to leeward had a black density in it that seemed to tell of steamer-smoke; that was the only index we had to the whereabouts of the workers of our disasters.

'There was a council of generals and admirals in the flagship. Somehow all our admirals were of the type of generals, and all our sailors looked like soldiers. It was decided to go on after repairing damages. The *Rhein* had burned almost to the water's edge. It was afternoon before we got under way again, and I heard nobody now talking of "*der Ruhm*". We were unmolested. Perhaps, after all, the British ships, ghostly in their coming, ghostly in their going, had got nearly as good as they had given, and were in no present humour for more fighting. The setting sun gilded the green waves of the now calm water, and as we recovered from our sea-sickness our spirits rose in a measure. Ha! what is that coming up out of the eye of the setting sun? The black smoke from a steamer's funnel. In the name of God, how many smoke-clouds are there on that golden horizon? They blend into one dense bank, ever advancing toward us, obscuring the golden evening as with a pall. It is the British fleet!

'Out to the front with the ironclads and men-of-war, and form line of battle! Now we can see the enemy, and out of that smoke-bank we shall snatch more of "*der Ruhm*". Back with the transports, tugged by all available steam power; steam power that does not propel ships armed with the cannon of Krupp. Ha! there is the *bonne bouche* from England, heavier rather than a Heligoland coping-stone! How the huge projectile crashes into the half-protected bow of the *Spicheren-Berg*—making her recoil as a horse checked with the wrench of a powerful bit is thrown on his haunches. Now they round to, those castle-sided monsters, and give us a broadside, while the low black ships with the gun-towers rising up out of them hold straight on, firing as they come. But neither are our gunners idle. There speaks Krupp in that yelling shell—another and another; Krupp can hold his own on sea as on land!

'The cannonade is deafening, furious; incomparable to it that French din from the beset heights of Amanvilliers. We soldiers, what can we do? Would God that that heaving sea were dry land, so that

with the old shout of *"Immer vorwarts"* we could get to hand-grips
with these Britons so fond of long bowls! Here is one at least steering
straight out of the smoke, that has a soul above long bowls. A stately,
swanlike boat, with broadside batteries like our own; surely she has
picked us out on the principle of "like to like". She rounds to for a
broadside, and we give her a greeting of the same character. Sacra-
ment! We are both so strong in our armour-casing that the shells
drop off the sides as if they were musket bullets. Now she is alongside, armour-plate grinding against armour-plate, and we can have
it out in fair fight, where we soldiers can do something. Never mind
those fellows in dark green in the tops, deadly marksmen though
they are. *Englische Freiwilligen* are they? Herr Lieutenant, dress the
left flank there! One *schnell Feuer*, and then over the side and into
the *Englander* with the bayonets.

'Who is that *Schweinhund* there that has leaped up, sword in hand,
and is standing on the *Englander's* bulwarks, holding on by the
shroud? Pick him off, Fusilier Müller! With a wave of his sword he
bellows "Boarders away!" *Donnerwetter*! The avalanche of hell is
upon us. Like wild cats, like monkeys, like raving lions, the bearded,
open-throated sailors of Britain throw themselves into the *König
Wilhelm*, cutlass in one hand, revolver in the other! Stand fast,
Fusiliers, give them the bayonet! But how can you give a man the
bayonet when he jumps with the force of a catapult bolt into your
face, lays your head open, shoots the man next you, is up before he
is down, and laying about him as if five hundred fighting devils were
in his single arm? We might not conquer against a rush of fighting
prowess similar to none of which we had any experience, but we
could at least die. The scuppers of the *König Wilhelm* ran blood. Her
sailors (in their boots) and our Fusiliers fought with the wooden
doggedness of good Prussians, and when we got a chance we went at
the cutlass-devils as we had gone at the Spicheren-Holz. But they
took us front, rear, and flank, and crunched us up so that we could
get neither formation nor the use of our weapons.

'Why need I dwell on the scene? It was in the starboard battery,
where, having been hustled and driven I know not how, I took the
quarter which an officer tendered me, and gave up my sword. From
the main truck of the *König Wilhelm* the German flag had disappeared; the Union Jack waved there in its room. As I looked from
the quarter-deck through the lurid smoke of the battle, I seemed to
see everywhere that fluttering Union Jack. Away behind us there
was dismal confusion in the defenceless convoy. Steamers had cast
off their towage and were steering out of the press; the sailing

vessels, too, on its verges were getting out their canvas and making off; till the convoy looked like nothing more than a great flock of ducks in a pond suddenly scared by a stone falling in their midst.

'I can tell you no more of the battle, for, wounded and bruised, I had to go below and find somehow a doctor and a berth. The *König Wilhelm*, with ten more German war-ships, were sent as prizes into the Thames; we, the wounded prisoners, to the number of some three thousand, were accommodated in Greenwich Hospital, near London.

'What came afterwards I learnt chiefly from English newspapers during my captivity. The English ships seen in the Baltic with the Danish fleet had been dummy men-of-war, large merchant steamers disguised to deceive us. What fragments of our expedition effected an escape met with diverse fate. Some of the ships ran into Dutch ports, where the Hollanders, as scrupulous neutrals, interned the soldiers till the war was over. Others got back to Wilhelmshafen to find it besieged by the Hanoverian *Landwehr*. The older soldiery had not forgotten King George, and the King of Saxony had artfully sent among them their old officers who, when Hanover was annexed to Prussia in six-and-sixty, had to the number of over a hundred joined the Saxon army rather than take service under the Prussian flag. These had stirred the old leaven, and Hanover was in insurrection. The mouth of the Elbe was blockaded, and some ships, frustrated in making this refuge, steered for the bay of Tonning instead, to find Schleswig up as well as Hanover, and commanding the Kiel Canal from the old line of the Daneverk.

'Nor were those all the intestine troubles. The Southern Confederacy, in angry assertion that Prussia had violated the Imperial Germanic Constitution, had massed armies on their frontiers next us—armies full of the bitter recollections of six-and-sixty. At a word these were ready to cross the frontier, but it seemed as if South Germany preferred that North Germany should have the lesson taught her by the foreigner.

'The foreigner was not slow by any means with his lesson. The truth is, Goschen and Gortschakoff had engineered an European compact against "*der Ruhm*". Russia—all Poland now her friend— was over the Vistula, with her legions marching straight on Berlin by Bromberg. An English army had landed at Gluckstadt, and, strengthened by Danes and Hanoverians, had given fortified Hamburg the go-bye, and was steadily pushing up the valley of the Elbe. The French, with a great spasm of revengeful joy, had hurried troops to the frontier, had regained Alsace and Lorraine, half glad, half sorry; and, regardless of Metz and Strasburg still hostile, had swarmed over the Saar and down the Moselle on to the Rhine.

'Ah, children, I am getting tired, and my heart is very sore. Those who don't know it already too well may read of what a fight Prussia made—no more for *"der Ruhm"*, but for very life—and how the Treaty of Copenhagen muzzled and mangled her. Thank God, you never hear of *"der Ruhm"* now.'

La Guerre au Vingtième Siècle

ALBERT ROBIDA

The first half of the year 1945 had been particularly peaceful. Apart from the usual goings-on—that is, apart from a small three-month civil war in the Danubian Empire, apart from an American offensive against our coast which was repulsed by our submarine fleet, and apart from a Chinese expedition which was smashed to pieces on the rocks of Corsica—life in Europe continued in total calm.

On June 25, 1945, my friend Fabius Molinas from Toulouse, a charming fellow of independent means, was reclining in great content with a cigarette between his lips. The large windows were opened on to the garden to let in the scent from the flowers and the breezes from the Pyrenees. Fabius was tired. For two days he had been packing for the summer bathing season which he intended to spend on the Norwegian beaches. Molinas was so taken up with his preparations that he had hardly any time to listen to the telephone news. So, on June 25 he was surprised to learn from the Midday Bulletin that a threat of war had been growing over the last two days, and that the fairly rosy political outlook had suddenly become very black indeed. What seemed serious was the purely financial nature of the clash. It was a matter of tariffs that went to the heart of national interests. Business is business! Nowadays, in civilized countries, commercial treaties are imposed by gunfire. 'Well, well!' Molinas thought, 'I only hope that it will not ruin my bathing holiday.' As he was finishing his cigarette, an announcement came through on the telephonograph.

Mobilization Orders,

M. Molinas Fabius is assigned as Gunner, 2nd Class, to the Territorial Section, 6th Squadron. Today, at five o'clock, he will rejoin the aircraft *Épervier* at 3,200 metres over Pontoise.

'Damn it!' exclaimed Molinas, as he leapt to his feet. 'It's almost 1.00 pm! … I've only just got time! … I won't be going to the sea-side this year!' Accustomed to these sudden departures, Molinas quickly telephoned his farewells, put away his papers, and then, opening his drawers, found all his kit in order. Forty-five minutes later—

squeezed into his leggings, buttoned into his jacket, his cloak rolled
up, with his automatic revolver and his sabre by his side, his oxygen
cylinder slung over his shoulder—Molinas was one of the many
arriving at the tube station. A special train rushed them to Paris. At
ten past four, a little numbed, they got out at the city's central tube
station. Aircraft were waiting for them, and, at five o'clock exactly
the party of airmen assigned to the *Épervier* began climbing on to the
balloon platform.

The commander of the *Épervier* called his men together and told
them, in words full of patriotic fervour, that war would be declared
at midnight precisely. The crew hurried off to their battle stations.
From time to time the commander took out his watch. Suddenly, on
a signal from below, the lieutenant pressed a button. The electric
propeller began to turn and the *Épervier* leapt forward, setting my
friend Molinas on a path to glory.

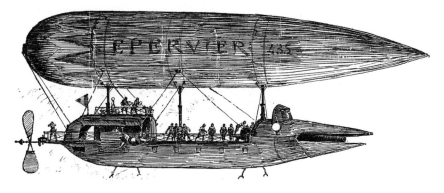

'The electric propeller began to turn and the *Épervier* leapt forward'

At dawn a nauseating smell roused Molinas from his hammock,
and he went to the bridge of the *Épervier* which was making its way
through a thick fog. The squadron was passing over a division of
flying mist-makers which were engaged in spreading a dense fog
over the frontier in order to conceal military operations.

Les Blockhaus Roulants

There was Fabius in a day-dream, leaning on the guard-rail of the
Épervier. Still dazed by the speed of events, he thought vaguely that
he was on his way to the sea-side. 'Have I brought my bathing

costumes! Damn! Only the made-to-measure swim-suits have any style!'

A gun went off almost in his ear and brought him back with a jolt to the real world. He opened his eyes and beheld, at a distance of 600 metres, a group of the enemy *Blockhaus Roulants* stopped in their tracks by the fog. A whistle from the Engineer sent the crew of the *Épervier* to action stations. The squadron deployed rapidly. The balloon section formed into line with the intention of attacking the flank and the rear of the enemy, who were pushing their engines to the limit by going at full speed in an attempt to break through. The *Épervier* with five other aircraft went into action head-on and at close quarters.

Fabius, who was the port-side No. 2 Gun Number, passed the cartridges to the loader without seeing anything of the action. Suddenly a burst of shrapnel penetrated the gun-port and knocked out the No. 1 and all the other gunners with the exception of Fabius. Our hero immediately leapt to the loaded gun, aligned it with the most complete sang-froid, and fired. A tremendous explosion followed on his shot, and the *Blockhaus Roulant*, which he'd had in his sights, was blown to pieces.

The fog slowly dispersed and the battle then appeared in all its horror. A dozen *Blockhaus Roulants* had been destroyed: the rest were offering little resistance, and two aircraft were lying in smoking ruins on the ground. The *Épervier*, which had been badly damaged, dived straight down on a group of the enemy machines and decimated their crews who were obliged to surrender. It was all over. Only a few of the enemy machines had managed to escape and find safety in a forest where the planes could not attack them. The crews of the *Épervier* and of those aircraft that had been knocked out were distributed amongst the captured *Blockhaus* and sent on forward. And Fabius, promoted sub-engineer for distinguished service, was given command of the leading *Blockhaus Roulant*.

Full speed ahead! Towards nine o'clock in the morning the *Blockhaus*, hurtling along as if it were pursued, had no trouble in bursting through the outer defences of a strong-point guarded by a female foe—a women's territorial brigade. They had been called up to take over from the 1st and 2nd line troops, all men between 17 and 50 years of age. What a dreadful surprise for those inexperienced Amazons. In the twinkling of an eye they were disarmed and the town taken. Alas! The occupation of the town was not to be of long duration. It had not been possible to cut all the telephone lines in

Le commandant de l'Épervier réunit ses hommes et leur annonça en quelques mots vibrants de patriotisme que la guerre devait être déclarée à minuit juste. L'équipage s'installa hâtivement. De temps en temps le commandant tirait sa montre. Soudain sur un signal d'en bas, le lieutenant toucha un bouton, le propulseur électrique entra en action et l'Épervier s'élança en avant emportant mon ami Molinas vers la gloire. Au jour levant, une odeur nauséabonde réveilla Molinas dans son hamac, il monta sur le pont de l'Épervier qui filait à travers un brouillard épais.

L'escadre croisait une division de brouillardiers volants en train de couvrir la frontière d'un brouillard opaque destiné à dissimuler les opérations.

'Over enemy lines! The aircraft make their bombing runs'

time; and so the enemy, who had been forewarned, prepared to wipe out the daring little band that had ventured so far.

Towards the middle of the night an enemy battalion, escorted by armoured vehicles to within a few kilometres of the town, made its way into a suburb without being detected. One by one, men dressed as for chemical warfare glided through the streets, aprons over their tunics, leather helmets enclosing head and neck. Silently they assembled strange and unusual equipment on the terrace of a garden; bits of equipment were coupled up and tubes connected. In ten minutes they had set up a field chemical battery. The men lowered their chinpieces to seal off their helmets. They then went to their action stations, and waited for their commander's order—Fire! One after another four gas bombs traced a short curve through the sky.

The Town Surprised

Fabius and his companions were grouped round their camp fires. A sentry, who had seen something suspicious in the dark, was about to give the alarm when the first bomb exploded in a greenish cloud. There was a loud cry, and a puff of smoke. Three more bombs followed; and then there was total silence. The camp fires had been extinguished, and a pall of death covered all, even the wretched inhabitants who had stayed on in the town. They were all instantaneously suffocated in their homes. These things are the accidents of war to which the recent advances of science have accustomed all of us.

By great good fortune Fabius, who was starving and thirsty, had gone down into the cellars to get his rations. At the moment of the explosion he had entered a vault which was completely sealed off from the outside air. Fabius was the only one of his companions to escape suffocation, and he remained unconscious and without food or drink for thirty-six hours. During that time, when news arrived that the enemy had retaken the town, the Army Commander-in-Chief sent off a detachment of long-range Model 1944 attack aircraft. The bombers, which were lying up, hidden in the cirrus and the nimbus clouds at a height of 3,000 metres, waited for the first shades of evening to fall upon the town. Then they started their engines and dropped down from the sky. As they came into range, they launched their dreadful bombs. Suddenly the town, sundered from its foundations, was torn apart and disintegrated.

By great good luck, the still unconscious Molinas, together with a number of light objects, whizzed through space fast enough to escape the fire-blast. He suddenly regained consciousness, a trifle scorched, and borne—as it were—on a pillar of smoke. He clung feverishly to something his hand had touched: it was a weather-cock that had been blown up along with him. As the upward movement ended, Molinas felt the descent that was about to begin. A distinctly uneasy moment. Thirty seconds later a sudden feeling of coolness came over him.

The Medical Assault Corps

After lying for a few seconds unconscious beneath the water, Molinas came round to find himself, dazed and bewildered, going through the motions of swimming to the surface of a river. He made straight for the bank where he was able to hide in a clump of reeds. Towards evening a party of the enemy chemical troops came by to enjoy a dip. Molinas emerged from the river, helped himself to one of their uniforms, and attached himself to a patrol that was return-

ing to a strong-point. An NCO put him on guard in a large hall
where the Medical Assault Corps–chemical engineers, doctors,
chemists—were discussing the final stages of their plan to lay explosive charges in the path of the French army: a dozen mines packed
with poison gas, malignant fever bacilli, glanders, dysentery,
measles, and other maladies.

Aircraft engage the enemy armour, the *Blockhaus roulants*

The bombs were made ready; and the ammunition wagons were
being prepared to transport the zinc shells which had been loaded
with the gases and with the containers of bacteria. Fabius, however,
thanks to his knowledge of the language, understands everything.
Burning with the most sublime resolution, he dedicates himself to
saving the army. Fabius quickly takes aim with his magazine rifle
and fires off every round into the large gas and chemical tank. An
appalling, terrifying explosion follows on the shots from our hero
Molinas!!! Everything goes up—the gas tank, the wagons, the shells.
The concentrated gases explode with unheard-of force. Dense
columns of vapour swirl and billow upwards. Escaping through
every opening, they spread across the open country and rise up into
the atmosphere, bringing with them nameless odours and the germs
of innumerable diseases. Nothing remains of the operations centre.
Generals, officers, chemical engineers, doctors, soldiers—all have
been struck down in the blast, and all are writhing on the ground,

afflicted by all the diseases which Molinas had let loose. Instant epidemics ravage the enemy army, and in five minutes they are doing their worst within a radius of fifteen leagues. Fabius had offered up his life; but, thanks to his gas-proof helmet, he got away with a raging toothache.

Fortunately the French army escaped all the contagions. A microbiological engineer in the French Medical Assault Corps, who was on watch in the front line, correctly interpreted the distant rumbling of the explosion and realized what had happened to the enemy. He telephoned the General, and the General ordered all his available chemical batteries to go forward and cover the army front with a protective fog. So, having got rid of the enemy who threatened his left, and under cover of the fog, the General abandoned the contaminated zone. In a sudden semi-circular movement, he fell back on the enemy corps that was operating on his right. Molinas, who was still suffering from the toothache, rejoined the army at this point and reported to the General. Overwhelmed with congratulations from the General, embraced by the entire General Staff, decorated, mentioned in despatches, Molinas felt that his toothache was at last getting better. However, the trouble remained and a little later he had to have a complete set of false teeth.

And here we hasten to report that the enemy hospitals had to look after 179,549 casualties, both civilian and military. The combination of all the toxic vapours gave rise to an absolutely new and extraordinary disease. It was taken up by all the doctors in Europe, and it is now known as Molinas Fever, after the name of the man who brought it into the world. The point of origin has remained a most unhealthy place.

Siege Operations: Pompistes and Médiums

As a reward for his outstanding conduct, Molinas was appointed second-lieutenant in the *Pompistes* brigade. This was a new formation, a kind of very fast mobile artillery which could go anywhere at high speed and bring down instant, concentrated fire to bear on positions that the normal artillery could not cover.

To begin with, Molinas had four *Pompes* under his command, each operated by five men. In the first engagement, which was a fierce encounter, Molinas and his *Pompistes* were crammed into the ruins of a house. They sustained four successive attacks; the men were replaced on three occasions; and Molinas was the only one to come away without a scratch from the slaughter. That same evening he was promoted lieutenant.

Lines of mines, linked by wires, ran through the army operational area; and both the mines and the artillery gun-platforms had been carefully concealed. Everyone moved cautiously: the electrical engineers and the *Médiums* went on ahead in order to defuse the mines and blow up the enemy gun positions.[1] Because the air division was engaged on another part of the front, it was not possible to attack the gun-platforms from above. So, siege warfare was the order of the day. Lieutenant Molinas and his *Pompistes* took part in the assault on a group of forts. After the heavy artillery had succeeded in disabling or destroying the turning mechanism of the gun-turrets with a series of lucky shots, the assault columns went into the attack and penetrated the gun positions through breeches in the defences.

Bicycle troops speed past immobilized armoured fighting vehicles

When the army had taken out the first-line barbettes, preparations went ahead for the assault on an important strong-point. After a feint against another section, one dark night the General brought up a squad of Reserve *Médiums* who had been placed under his orders by the Minister of Science. These *Médiums*—the most powerful mesmerizers and mind-benders in Paris, according to the scientists—moved forward slowly towards the enemy lines, and with their energetic passes they released torrents of fluid.[2] A moment of dreadful anxiety! Are the enemy forward posts going to open fire, or will the fluid subdue them so that they let the *Médiums* pass?

The profound silence continues unbroken ... the *Médiums* go on advancing ... they have crossed the front line. A column of troops follows them; and they find, first, a number of sentries and outposts in a completely paralytic state and, next, all the combat troops of a redoubt stretched out on the ground, rigid in a magnetic sleep. A telephone call gave the General the news. He sent the troops forward and hastened to occupy the strong-point without striking a blow.

The *Médiums*, who had collapsed in total exhaustion, simply had to have two hours' rest. Alert! Danger! The enemy could saturate the redoubt with poison gas before it could be put in a state of defence. But the enemy suspected nothing and their guns remained silent. And then at first light, their energy restored, the *Médiums* began their passes once more. After immense efforts of will, and after losing three hypnotists to brain-storms, the chief *Médium* succeeded in using magnetic suggestion to persuade the commander of the fortresses to the south of the town to surrender.

The Fearless Chemical Battery

All was not yet finished. After a well-earned rest, the *Médiums* had to direct their efforts against the main enemy defensive position; and that same evening they commenced operations. Unfortunately, in their haste to advance, they had failed to defuse the mines the enemy had scattered throughout the terrain; and the entire squad was blown to pieces by a booby trap which their magnetic passes had caused to explode.

It was necessary to revert to conventional operations. During the night, covered by a storm of shot and shell from every type of gun, the General assembled a large chemical siege battery. It was a scene of immense horror! The sky was ablaze with flares—red, green, violet, yellow, or blue. Sudden flashes and great flaming jets of fire streaked across, as thousands of shells and chemical canisters passed over to explode in multi-coloured bursts of gas and smoke. The enemy chemists were on the job as well; it was an epic duel between the two scientific corps. When day came they unmasked two batteries which showered our troops with paralysing gas bombs; they collapsed on their guns, rigid or struck down with a lethal paralysis.

In response, we sent up gas shells that caused fearful epileptic attacks. But their gas shells continued to fall like hail on our positions, as well as canisters of scabies, that superb invention of an illustrious enemy scientist. Our chemists suffered dreadfully until one of our engineers finally invented the corrosive dewdrop—airborne sulphuric acid, for which he was awarded the medal of the Academy of Sciences— and that destroyed the enemy batteries in a single night.

Biological warfare companies in action, firing off gas shells and canisters of scabies

While all this was going on, news came that the enemy submarine fleet was making ready to leave its home port for an unknown destination with the intention of either attacking our ports or making a landing at some point on our coast. A reconnaissance vessel, which had made the risky passage through enemy waters, had been able to observe the magnificent submarine monitors of the enemy fleet, high-speed armoured raiders, and torpedo-craft moving and manoeuvring with remarkable speed beneath the waves. The French fleet—just as big and no less impressive—was on the high seas operating together with the submarine infantry and a landing corps. The Engineer Admiral planned to attack and destroy the enemy fleet as a preliminary to moving against the enemy ports.

Orders came for Fabius Molinas to join the French fleet. In consideration of his brilliant service, he had been attached to the navy as a torpedo-engineer, with strong recommendations to the Admiral. He made Fabius commandant of the *Potassium Cyanide*, a submarine torpedo vessel of entirely new construction. Fabius lost no time in getting to his base port where he took command of his ship. The *Potassium Cyanide*, a very small craft which carried only six men, was one of those small, slender fish-shaped vessels, built for fast actions and for dangerous reconnaissance. It was one of those fearful ocean hounds, the midgets that slip unseen through the water and come up from below to plant their torpedoes on the hull of the big battleships.[3]

Submarine Torpedo-craft *Potassium Cyanide*

'You are a regular land animal,' the Admiral had said to Molinas, when he handed over his torpedo-craft. 'See to it that you are just as good at sea.'

'Hell's teeth! You'll see, and the enemy as well!' That was the modest reply from Molinas.

The *Potassium Cyanide* pushed on ahead, almost scraping the sea floor, blending in with the seaweed-covered rocks. After two days' sailing, they entered hostile waters and arrived almost bang up against the line of mines that protected the coast. For seventy-two hours they all toiled away, without any of them taking a second's break, and in that time Molinas succeeded in disconnecting three lines of mines which covered twenty leagues or more. Molinas was careful to leave the cables uncut so that the enemy would go on thinking that their defences were still intact; and then he emptied all the mines without accident.

One line of mines remained, anchored at the end of the roadstead where the enemy fleet was in the habit of charging its electric batteries. The *Potassium Cyanide* was able to approach close to them without being seen, and on this occasion Molinas did not empty the mines: he had another plan. He cut the enemy cable and attached the line of mines to his electric battery. Meanwhile, hidden in a hole in the rocks, taking in air by a tube, the *Cyanide* waited for the moment when the enemy fleet would at last pass through the narrows to get to the open sea.

'Go! Go!' Molinas said to the master electrician.

The mines went off. Seven enemy battleships were blown to

smithereens, vanishing in a gigantic column of water, and another
five or six were wrecked and flung ashore in a badly damaged condition. As soon as the leading vessels had gone past, the heroic
Potassium Cyanide shot forward out of hiding and fixed a torpedo to
the side of a big battleship. That was the last of the *Cyanide*'s exploits.
The forward section of the battleship fell on the submarine, broke
the torpedo-launching tube, and badly damaged the propellers. At
the precise moment when the *Cyanide* was being put out of action,
Molinas spotted all the enemy reconnaissance vessels and torpedo
craft rushing on them at full speed. 'Time for a little deception!' said
Molinas to himself; and, instead of taking flight towards the open
sea, he made for the coast and kept close inshore, taking cover
among the rocks.

Submarine warfare: underwater troops take on the French submarines

The *Cyanide* slipped among the rocks and shot through the larger
open spaces; but behind them, and drawing ever closer, the enemy
torpedo-craft kept on following them. As night fell, the *Cyanide* ran
aground near the mouth of a river; and two enemy scouting craft,
which had come on too rapidly, collided and were smashed to
pieces. Molinas took advantage of the disaster to make his men put
on their diving suits and take one last chance. They were just in
time: the enemy divers were already attacking the *Cyanide* with axes.
Molinas and his men made off along the sea-bed into the unknown;
and after a momentary hesitation the enemy divers set off in pursuit
of them. They slipped past slimy rocks, stopping at times to let the
enemy have a round from their compressed air carbines. Then,

diverging of a sudden into a creek, Molinas was able to push ahead into a river.

For nine days they pressed on in this way, sometimes hugging the shore and sometimes going mid-stream through towns, pursued, lost, and again pursued by the cavalry sent to seek them out. And then one day Molinas heard the dull sound of gunfire. Now, since water is a good conductor of sound, there could be no doubt that there was a battle going on some twenty-five leagues away. So, it followed that they would come upon the French army again!

'Forward! Hell's teeth!'

Another three days of forced marches followed; they took every precaution, and passed without mishap through several of the enemy army corps. At last Molinas recognized the uniforms. There was a fire-fight going on, and at the height of the exchange between troops on the river banks, Molinas and his divers appeared before the astonished soldiers.

'Who are these men?' said the General who was busy telephoning through his orders. 'Bravo!' said the General after Molinas had explained how they had got there. 'But before you get in the ambulance, I still have a job for you.'

'At your service!' Molinas replied.

'Get back into the water!' And the answer came from Molinas: 'I'm on my way!'

'You will go down river with your men; a league from here you will find the enemy forward positions; you will cross them. Further on the enemy have a battery of their great *Blockhaus Roulants*: they will fire at you but you will carry on ... Still further on you will find the telephone lines that keep communications going between the left flank of the enemy, where I will create a considerable diversion, and their right flank, which I am going to annihilate. You will cut the telephone wires, and then you will return again under fire from the enemy's fighting vehicles. When you are back, you will report to me on the operation. Get moving!' Molinas, however, was already on his way.

Air Torpedo-Ship No. 39

After successfully completing his mission, Molinas reappeared with two more wounds. He got straight into the ambulance and was whisked off to the French hospital area. Three weeks later, his convalescence over, orders came for him to rejoin the air squadron and take command of *Voltigeur 39*. In keeping with the orders he had from the Chief Engineer, Molinas made a long detour to reach the northern provinces of the enemy. Here and there he made sudden, random attacks in order to wreck services, cut telephone lines, exact war levies from towns, and blow up enemy strong-points whenever he could.

Voltigeur 39, which Molinas now commanded, caused the enemy unbelievable trouble what with his swift forays, his sudden descents, and his unexpected attacks. The enemy planes wasted their time in fruitless missions in one sector, when Molinas was causing ruin and havoc in some other area fifty leagues away. In the end, the enemy in their despair committed an entire fleet together with some sections of small, independent planes to the chase after Molinas. Then a reconnaissance aircraft spotted *Voltigeur 39*. Innumerable planes, big and little, with crews of two or even six men, came up and surrounded the *Voltigeur*. Molinas knew full well that only daring could save him. So he went in on his own, risking everything by charging right through the enemy planes and racing off ahead of their squadron.

'Hell's teeth!' said Molinas. 'If there's nothing more to do here, I'll go and give their colonies a surprise!' With the help of a sudden squall, he pushed off at once for the south. He was pursued by a few dedicated *Torpédistes* who had guessed his intentions and did their best to overtake him. However, Molinas never let them overtake him or catch him off guard. By crafty dodges, he succeeded in knocking them down one after the other. But in a desperate attempt, the last of the *Torpédistes* damaged the propeller shaft and shattered the rudder of *Voltigeur 39*. The enemy colonies were saved. The damage obliged Molinas to come down to a wooded area on the bank of a river; and, on checking his bearings, he found it was the White Nile, some hundreds of leagues from the Belgian territories, from the area of the lakes, the French Congo, and the American colonies.

Molinas was toiling away at repairs to *Voltigeur 39*, when all of a sudden wild animals, attracted by the smell of fresh meat, came along, to the great inconvenience of the workers. It was an unpleasant encounter! There was a family of lions, a rhinoceros and his mate, various snakes, and a whole tribe of alligators.

'These animals are too much of a good thing!' Molinas exclaimed, as he beat a hasty retreat to the stern of his craft. Since the propeller was for the time being down for repairs, *Voltigeur 39* was in no condition to move. The invasion went on unchecked, as the lions and crocodiles redoubled their tactless attentions.

'Take your pick. You are spoilt for choice!' said the second-in-command who had a line in black humour. 'What do you prefer: a lion's stomach or the belly of a crocodile?'

'Come on!' yelled Molinas. 'I've told you that they are only animals! Haven't we still got a supply of sulphuric acid? Get down to the stores!'

One of Robida's more extreme fantasies was the role of female troops in the Revolution of 1953

After some considerable difficulty they succeeded in placing an acid container with a hand-pump on the stern gun-platform. And so, with the defence organized, Molinas began by giving a blast to the witless rhinoceros that was threatening to do more damage to *Voltigeur 39*. The stiff dose caused him to burst into fifteen bits, to the immense astonishment of his lady wife. 'Would you like one as well, madame?' asked Molinas in his gracious way.

At that precise moment when the lions, snakes, and crocodiles were advancing on the refuge of Molinas and his men, the pump went into action. The jet of sulphuric acid had great effect on the attackers, as it scored direct hits—first on the majestic face of Mr Lion and then on the crawling swarm of alligators. How they leapt, and wriggled, and roared. 'Keep up the pumping!' said Molinas. 'Gently, gently, and we'll get the lot of them!' They handled the pump with skill and went on spraying with sulphuric acid, whilst two men quickly set the propeller to rights. All of a sudden the *Voltigeur* took off with a make-shift rudder and soared upwards. Lions, snakes, and crocodiles—roasted, toasted, and burning—flung themselves overboard and were smashed to bits on the rocks.

The Air Battles

Over the Mediterranean, *Voltigeur 39* rejoined the air fleet. Since time was of the essence, the Admiral congratulated Molinas and straightway posted him to the vanguard. In keeping with instructions, the advanced scouts were to report on the enemy fleet without engaging them in combat. Nevertheless, during the second night on patrol, and whilst they were flying at a high altitude in banks of cloud, the *Voltigeur* surprised and captured a large enemy plane. After Molinas had brought his prize to the air arsenal at Antibes, he departed at full speed. The hostile air fleet had been reported, and one of the greatest air battles of the century was about to take place. The *Voltigeur* took up battle stations at the far end of the left wing. Molinas, with his finger on the electric buttons, scanned the sky for an enemy worthy of him. What a battle! What close engagements; planes ripped apart, planes falling out of the sky down to the depths of the sea! What heroic deeds on both sides! For a long time the outcome was uncertain; and then, as our side came closer to victory, the long-threatening thunder clouds burst into a fearful storm. The tempest snatched up the two fleets and in its fury swept them, still fighting, past Gibraltar and out over the Atlantic.

For three days the surviving aircraft were carried forward on the wings of the storm. Through gaps in the clouds they caught sight of one another; they fired on one another, and then they were lost to view. Suddenly the wind fell, and between the blue of the sky and the green of the sea the coast of America appeared.

'It's Mexico!' said Molinas as he got his bearings. He looked behind him. A single enemy plane was still in sight. The two planes, battered in battle and in the storm, were handling very badly. It was imperative for the two of them to land in order to repair damages, but more than anything else both of them wanted to go on fighting. Molinas aimed the gun himself, and he had the good luck to land his first shot right on the hull of the enemy aircraft. The guns rumbled on without stopping. The two planes turned and banked; they climbed and then they dived to catch each other out with their feints and manoeuvres. The engagement had taken them over a large Mexican town where the inhabitants anxiously watched the ups and downs of the struggle. A few rounds had already hit the town; there had been some deplorable accidents, and three houses had been blown up. Finally, a well-aimed shot went straight through the hostile aircraft from stem to stern; it lost control and dropped down slowly. Throwing caution to the winds, the enemy loosed off a dozen rounds at *Voltigeur 39*. At that a tremendous cry of horror arose from the ground. The two planes appeared in a vast cloud of smoke twisting and turning down towards the town.

The fall was frightening, terrifying, annihilating. With a noise like thunder, the enemy plane dived straight down on to a monument and vanished in the ruins, whilst the *Voltigeur* reduced its rate of descent and, spiralling down, drove its nose into a block of smart houses. Everything fell apart. The roof split open. After the fore-part of the *Voltigeur* had gone through three ceilings and had shattered all the walls, it finally came to rest on the ground floor of a handsome looking property. There, on the furniture, covered in glory and in bruises, Molinas passed out.

The lady of the house was a charming highly born Mexican señorita; and, having fainted away with fear, she lay next to Molinas, who was half dead. She was the first to recover. Then help came. Dolores, the young Mexican lady, had no desire to let anyone else look after the hero who had broken into her room … and probably into her heart as well. Fifteen days later, Molinas was the talk of the town and was on the mend. Then the father of Dolores appeared, dressed in his smartest suit; and he invited Molinas to enter his family in the way he had entered their house. The commandant of *Voltigeur 39* was at liberty. The telephonograph told all four corners of the world that a glorious peace had been signed ...

And so, that was how, some time later, my friend Fabius Molinas, now well and wedded, set off rejoicing in the direction of France, on board his *Voltigeur 39*—repaired, revictualled, and with all flags flying.

The Taking of Dover

(Translated from the French)

HORACE FRANCIS LESTER

London, June 1898

My beloved Son,

Your last welcome letter informed me of the pleasant fact that you are making progress in your military studies. You tell me that the authorities at St Cyr have chosen for the subject of the annual essay on some military topic a discussion, to be carried on between two or more interlocutors, on 'The best means to gain possession of a strongly fortified position in a neighbouring country'. You will readily understand that I shall take the greatest interest in your efforts to gain the prize, and shall rejoice if you succeed in obtaining that high distinction.

My own labours in this country, so recently occupied, continue to be immense and unceasing. Believe me, I feel the burden of the administration exceedingly heavy, and, but for the sense of duty in serving His Gracious Majesty the Emperor to the best of my ability, even this renowned and responsible office might cease to tempt me for any length of time.

Yet I feel bound to find the opportunity, my beloved child, to write to you an account of that great and celebrated exploit in which I took a part—the surprise and capture of the town and castle of Dover—although I must have narrated parts of the tale to you already by word of mouth. Since you request it, I will willingly give you a more exact and detailed description of the event. Your pen, more skilful than mine, will be able to shape my words into the form required by so able and exacting a tribunal as the Committee of Examination at the Academy of St Cyr.

You know well, my dear son—I have often told you—that in many ways I retain an admiration for the people of this country, although now a conquered people. They have genius, courage, patriotism. But they are slow, lazy, credulous, and confiding to a ridiculous extent. I ask you, as a young officer trained in the science of warfare, whether any other European or barbarous power would have permitted foreign nations to become acquainted with almost every detail of the defensive capabilities of such a port as Dover? Supposing that we had been fools enough to practically throw open to the world the armaments, the construction, and the extent of the garrisons of the Fort de Querqueville, or the Fort des Flamands at Cherbourg; or that we had permitted foreigners, after a few formalities had been gone through, to wander at will over our dockyards at Toulon, to inspect the defences of Boulogne, or had invited them to visit La Malgue or Valérien—should we not have been taken for lunatics? Yet this nation was guilty of that incredible folly. Nor need I mention Dover alone. Was not the same the case with Chatham, Woolwich, Portsmouth, and Plymouth, and all the depots of artillery and garrison towns and forts throughout the whole province? They were harmless as doves, these English, then, but they were by no means 'wise as serpents'.

The Channel Tunnel proposals of 1882 raised the spectre of a French invasion

Yet once more, at the risk of wearying you, and before I enter on the account which I have promised you, I will tell you to what I attribute the fall of this once great and powerful nation. Five years ago, if you walked through the streets of this capital, you would have seen in many shop windows belonging to *'papetiers'* (what they call 'stationers') a sight of much interest. What was that? A map of the world, with the portions held by Great Britain, her colonies and dependencies, coloured in red. Ah, my son, half the world, I assure you, looked red then! The colour was that of blood when it is dry. Perhaps it expressed their thought. They fancied themselves secure—that never again would they be obliged to shed blood in their own defence. You see no such maps now. The stationers no longer sell them. It would be too humiliating; for the English are a proud race, even in their decline and national degradation. Where are India, Canada, Australia, and New Zealand now? But I need hardly ask you, who have studied the history of the events of the past few years and the Partition Treaty of Moscow line by line, I doubt not, under the guidance of your able professors and tutors.

Well, then, to what do I attribute England's fall? Entirely to one cause. It was the prevalence in every branch of human life of the commercial spirit, of which they were so proud. This made them conceited, and all Europe hated them. When they talked of making a Channel Tunnel, which would have helped to render their ruin certain, what were the great arguments used? Commerce would profit. What are called 'calico shirtings' would be more easily exported. That was the Manchester doctrine, the doctrine of Cobden and others. Military men protested, but the tunnel went on. By the end of this century I doubt not it would have been actually in use; but as your are aware, it has never been completed.

Some day I hope, when you are older than you are now, to show you this great city of London. Believe me, my son, I feel deeply, as does your dear mother, the separation from you and our other children. But my resolution is inexorable never to allow one of my sons to be brought up on this side of the Straits of Calais. The pedlar spirit pervades everything here still, in spite of all their misfortunes. Poor England, with what it considers the worse than Egyptian plague of a Franco-Russian occupying army! As you know, Liverpool and Manchester, Birmingham, Edinburgh, and Glasgow are all garrisoned by our joint troops, and are the seats of separate military governors, all of whom, however, are answerable to General Count Ignatieff and myself.[1] I think the people have learned a lesson, but we will take care they have no opportunity of profiting by it to regain their independence. The sole cloud on our horizon is the trouble with the United States of America regarding the occupation of Dublin. But those Transatlantics, they too are shop-keepers, and shop-keepers without a navy. Let them take Ireland from us if they can! Meanwhile, at your renowned military school you, my son, are being brought up as befits a man of honour and a Frenchman. Courage, chivalry, the rules of war, the science of offence and defence, are your *'sujets d'instruction* [educational subjects]; not the ignoble toil of book-keeping clerks or pettifogging lawyers and *literateurs.'*

Well, to my tale. Expect not the arts of an accomplished narrator. I can only plainly and simply tell you the facts. The date of the capture of Dover was December 26th, 1894, or four years ago. You will, perhaps, recollect what was the state of politics in France and in Europe at that period. Here let me bestow on you a hint. It is absolutely necessary to make mention of this point in your essay; for had Europe not been disturbed, and had there not existed the possibility of moving large bodies of troops to our coast, and of collecting the *'matériel'* of war, without exciting the suspicion of the English, our task would have been doubly difficult. We were besides much helped by the astuteness of our Russian allies, who are famous strategists in international diplomacy.[2]

Upon the defeat of Germany in 1892 by the allied armies of France and Russia (shortly after the deaths of Bismarck and von Moltke) at the great and decisive struggle of Coblentz, his Gracious Majesty our Emperor's 'Grand Design'—as he has often called it in my hearing— was ready to be accomplished. This was the simultaneous capture of Belgium and Great Britain. I was entrusted with one branch of the latter enterprise, the most important of all. This was the surprise of Dover, where, as you know, the strongest fortress on the South-East coast is to be found. Dover may really be called the gate of London.

Well, we were much aided by the International Comedy—I can call it nothing else—got up for the purpose of throwing England off her guard. France and Russia, the joint conquerors of Austro-Germany, agreed to quarrel; the subject of the fictitious dispute was to be the garrisoning of the Eastern fortresses of Germany. France, through our Gracious Emperor, claimed a share in the work. Russia, through the Czar Alexander the Sixth, refused the claim, and international relations were of the worst kind.[3] England was delighted with the prospect of a quarrel between Russia and France. She had just before promised to defend Belgium at all hazards if it were attacked. Well, we knew she could not have done so effectually, so small was her standing army; but we were aware of the dogged character of the British, and they might have given us much trouble, even after we had made ourselves masters of the Belgian towns.

Just at the point when a real rupture between the Emperor and

THE INVADER IN THE TUNNEL.

Here's the portrait,
  true as nature,
Both in figure and
  in *fayture*
(So the Irish all pro-
  nounce it),
Of the Frenchman
  who will "bounce"
  it
And come march-
  ing through the
  funnel
Called "Sir Ed-
  ward Watkin's
  Tunnel,"
With intention to
  invade us,
Cut our throats and
  cannonade us !
Though his eyes
  look rather foggy,
And his legs are somewhat "groggy,"
Not to say a little bandy,
Still he has a rifle handy ;
Well he knows, too, how to cock it ;
Dynamite is in his pocket !
Therefore when he makes for Dover,
Under sea instead of over,
Let us run away like muttons
From a tiger. Dash my buttons !
We must not with strife o'ertax him,
Sauve qui peut ! shall be our maxim.

"Jumbo's March."—March, 1882.

One comic artist believed that the 'Sir Edward Watkins' Tunnel' would prove to be an invitation for the French to invade

the Czar appeared certain, the quarrel was patched up by an agreement which allowed French soldiers to share in garrisoning Breslau, Lemberg, and Krakow, on the Russian frontier, provided Russian troops were allowed at Metz, Strasburg, Toulon, and Cherbourg. If this arrangement had been come to amicably, England would have been suspicious of a joint design on her coasts. As it was, her public men all declared that the 'compromise'—so they called it—between France and Russia could not last long, and that a bloody war would soon be fought between the two Empires, which would give another impetus to British trade. So much for statesmanship guided by commercial ideas!

Previous to our grand *coup*, our agents had been indefatigable. We knew every detail of the forces which would oppose us. I myself, whose knowledge of English is almost unrivalled among foreigners, had been working at Dover for months. I knew by heart every rock, every passage, every magazine and sentinel's box in the old Castle, and also in the fortifications of the 'Heights', as they were called.[4]

The Dover garrison then consisted of about 2,500 men and four companies of artillery. The infantry was a battalion of the East Kent regiment, or the 'Buffs', as they used to be termed, two battalions of Scotch Fusiliers, and a third battalion of the 55th Foot. The whole was commanded by Lieutenant-Colonel the Honourable Charles Fitzroy, with whom I became intimately acquainted. This was part of our plan. I have told you that I was specially appointed by the wish of his Gracious Majesty the Emperor to prepare the way in front of our troops. I was wonderfully assisted in all that I did by Mirakoff, the Russian colonel. For cunning I never met with any man or any animal to match him. But he was courageous too, and full of loyalty to his Czar, and of a wild kind of enthusiasm. He said England was the hereditary enemy of the Slav race, to which he belonged; and he burned with a sacred madness for the time when the Muscovite Colossus, one foot on London and the other on Calcutta, should 'bestride the ruins of the British Empire'.

Well, we reported to our respective governments that all would be ready for the attempt on December 26th, 1894. That day was chosen because it was the day after Christmas, when the English make it a point of religion to indulge in inordinate eating and drinking. Then would be the time, if ever, for finding them off their guard.

As for Mirakoff, he was not so presentable in society as myself, owing to his imperfect knowledge of English; also, the cloven hoof of the Tartar peeped out suspiciously if he became at all excited. So I had to keep him in the background in public, and pass him off as a distinguished Polish refugee. The Colonel commanding Dover Castle never suspected him to be, as he was, the most thorough liar in Europe—or, rather, the most accomplished diplomatist; for, my dear child, in such a case as ours, deceit became excusable, inasmuch as it was absolutely necessary.

We took apartments in the most expensive and fashionable hotel in Dover. I passed as the Vicomte d'Yverne, and Mirakoff was M. Schulzitska. Knowing English perfectly, and being fond of 'sport' and a good rider, you can understand that I soon accomplished my object of obtaining an entrance into Dover military society. We met the Lieutenant-Colonel and the officers of the garrison constantly. Hospitable gentlemen, every one of them: Mirakoff and I used to go up to the Castle to 'mess' with them often, and to play whist and *écarté* afterwards. We lost a good deal of money to our entertainers on purpose, but the information we gained was invaluable. Our eyes and ears were constantly open; over most part of the fortifications we were allowed to perambulate at will. But a special order from the colonel in command was necessary before we could be shown the underground galleries in the Castle cliff, or the works which commanded the entrance to the harbour. From what I have said, you will readily gather that we met with no difficulty in getting the required permit from our friend Colonel Fitzroy.

To understand what follows, you must above all things have a correct idea in your mind of the 'lay of the land', and the position of each and all of the fortresses. I strongly advise you to include a well executed map of the Dover fortifications, as they existed four years ago, before our occupation, in your essay. If you apply, in my name, to 'Monsieur le Colonel Commandant, Douvre, Préfecture Maritime de Kent', you will be supplied with an excellent one, I feel sure.

You know, I think, that Dover is a most remarkably situated town; it is in a deep hollow between a line of chalk hills. On the left, as you advance down the High Street to the harbour and shore, rises the Castle Hill, with the Castle and its picturesque tower. The Castle was the residence of Colonel Fitzroy (though, according to the rules of the military art, he certainly ought to have lived at the most important of the fortresses—which unquestionably is that overlooking the entrance to the harbour). It is a magnificent specimen, this Dover Castle, of an old Norman citadel, with 'keep', inner and outer courts, gates, and watch-towers, still much as they were when first made. The Castle Hill lay on the left, or north side, and on the right rose another line of hills, divided by nature into 'the Heights', a little distance from the sea and skirting the Folkestone Road, and Hay Hill, or Shakespeare's Cliff, abutting right upon the shore.

Let me describe to you Dover by an illustration. You have seen the billows of the ocean alternately rising and falling, leaving a deep hollow between them. The town of Dover lies in that hollow, and the billows on each side are the Castle Hill and the 'Heights' with Hay Hill. The High Street of the town runs along the trough of the waves. Imagine too, if you can, the billows suddenly broken off at the end, so as to form a precipice of water. These are the cliffs of Dover, so well known to every Frenchman who has ever beheld them looming white across the Straits of Calais.

They were very proud of their fortifications. Indeed, they were splendidly constructed. The only fault was that they were insufficiently guarded, and that everyone who cared to do so might know the exact position of the armouries, the magazines, and the barrack-rooms. Before the new harbour was completed, the 'Heights' was the strongest fortress in Dover. But on that great engineering feat being accomplished, the English Government constructed a still more magnificent series of works on Shakespeare's Cliff or Hay Hill,

The Germans found British anxieties over the Channel Tunnel a matter for fun

directly commanding the entrance of the port. All English military authorities acknowledged this to be the key of England. Yet—can you credit the stupidity of these islanders?—Mirakoff and I were allowed, because we were inoffensive foreign citizens forsooth, to examine all the ins and outs of the fort, every ward, to keep up the metaphor, of that key, as much as we pleased.

Any false step, any appearance of anxiety to pry into the defences of Dover, would—I knew—be dangerous and perhaps ruinous.

Consequently I was excessively cautious, and you may imagine my horror when, over a game of cards in the Castle, Mirakoff one night got into a conversation—as well as he could in his broken English—about the possibility of taking the place by a *coup de main*. Positively my hair stood on end, and the perspiration came out on my face and hands, as I heard him arguing away excitedly, and maintaining that 'with a force of five thousand men he could take the place to-morrow—that day—that very night'.

If he had been a Frenchman, the Colonel would probably have become angry. As it was, however, fortunately for us, he and all the

English officers laughed at Mirakoff, and I joined in the laugh too. Everyone was exclaiming:

'Our friend thinks he could take Dover! Ha! Ha! Ha!'

'Well, let him try!'

'Monsieur the Pole would find it a hard nut to crack.'

'We could sink his transports in an instant.'

Such was the talk of our entertainers, but none of them treated Mirakoff's boast as anything more than a joke. For myself, I was at a perfect loss to know why he had been so indiscreet. But he was a good strategist, for in the course of the argument which followed the British officers let out a vast amount of details as to the defensive precautions taken. The Colonel himself obligingly went so far as to tell Mirakoff, in rather a scornful tone, exactly what he would do 'if any of you foreign gentlemen were thinking of breaking your heads against our stone walls'. As a fruit of the argument, we left the Castle late that night, having—I fancy—given the English the idea that Mirakoff was a lunatic, but also with valuable information, and an invitation to inspect the most secret parts of the fortifications the very next day.

Perhaps I ought here to mention a singular hallucination which possessed the mind of the amiable Commandant. Colonel Fitzroy believed implicitly in war balloons, not simply for spying purposes, but for actual offensive operations. They had lately invented a new type of these at Woolwich, which—it was announced—by becoming stationary in the air over an army could destroy a whole battalion at a time! A shell, or other explosive weapon, was to be dropped. The explosive itself was a new discovery, as also was the shape of the balloon and the mode of steering it. And the English War Office believed that the whole idea was a complete secret, utterly unknown to any foreign power.

This famous balloon was called the Jenkinson Autopropeller, after its inventor. I remember the Colonel on this particular evening waxing warm on the terrors of the machine.

'Take Dover!' he exclaimed. 'Are you aware' (sinking his voice to a mysterious whisper) 'that we have *no less than four autopropellers* at Dover now—at this moment?' Then he stared at Mirakoff to see what effect the announcement would have. The Russian snorted his disdain.

'Four *Jenkinson* autopropellers!' insisted the Colonel. He thought the name must stagger us. Well, neither of us were greatly staggered, as you may surmise. We knew that nearly every power had autopropellers of its own, or that if it had not it was due to its voluntary abstention, not to any difficulty in learning all about how Mr Jenkinson made his. As far as new discoveries went, Woolwich laboured and Toulon entered into its labour immediately afterwards. Also, we did not intend to give the English much time for getting their balloons ready when we attacked in earnest.

The next day Mirakoff changed front. His device was to hold at first to the opinion he had expressed the night before; then bit by bit to change it, as we were shown the real strength of the defensive works; then to profess himself at last thoroughly convinced that Dover was impregnable. This, we knew, would flatter the English officers; and so it turned out.

We got our duly-signed official 'permit' from the Colonel, and first were shown the underground galleries on the Castle Cliff, of which I have already spoken. The Castle is guarded by a deep moat, and a strong earthwork on the other side of the moat. The whole Cliff inside the wall is honeycombed with underground passages and chambers, which had been ingeniously constructed, at an immense cost. As we were popular with the officers, in our characters of distinguished foreigners, we had quite an escort of them to show us over the place. Men with torches preceded us, as is usually done. In this way we went over the armoury, and the splendid artillery barracks, and the subterraneous casemates capable of containing two thousand men, and the immense magazines. Suddenly, after traversing the galleries, we came to a strong door; through this we caught a ray of daylight. It was opened, and on the other side was a sentry's box, and a winding path down the Cliff, leading directly into one of the streets of the town, called East Cliff Terrace. Mirakoff and I looked at each other. I could see he understood the importance of this discovery on our part perfectly.

'What do you think now, Monsieur?' asked one of the young officers, jestingly.

Mirakoff appeared to be almost dumb. He hesitated and stammered. Oh, he was a capital actor, was Mirakoff! The English were delighted to see him tongue-tied with admiration, as they thought. To increase the effect, we were shown all the other forts as well.

The fortifications on the 'Heights' were ascended by steps, constructed in a tall military shaft of brickwork. At the bottom of this shaft was a door, guarded by a sentry, opening into Snargate Street. Then there were three spiral flights of steps, 420 steps in all, winding round and round till a plateau was reached at the top, which communicated at once with the interior of the fort and the barrack-rooms. Would you believe it, my dear son? I speak the truth when I say that *one sentinel* was placed guarding the door at the top of this flight of steps which admitted into the fortress!

Mirakoff looked at me again.

'Ah! It is stronger than I thought,' he said to our guides.

For me, I contented myself with taking the whole matter indifferently, as if it was of no great interest; indeed, rather as if I were bored with the inspection.

Next, we proceeded to the new fort on Shakespeare's Cliff. Here it was that two battalions of troops were kept. They had constructed a subterraneous road from the fortress on the 'Heights' to this other and stronger citadel, and we were conducted along this vault-like passage. It was dark as night, except for our flambeaux. As usual, the only protection at the other end was a heavy door. On the further side—strange increase of precaution!—there were placed *two* sentries instead of one. That was how the 'Key of England' was guarded, and that was the sole defence that it possessed in case of the 'Heights' being taken by an enemy.

Inside, no doubt, the Harbour or Shakespeare's Cliff Fort was marvellously strong. On the sea-front we at once confessed, both of us, that it would be impossible to scale its walls. The main entrance was by a moat and bridge leading on to the shore-road. This was most carefully safeguarded. Moreover, there were double gates. Had we captured the first by stratagem, the second would have opposed us still. But we did not contemplate entering the Fort in that way.

Colonel Fitzroy had joined me by this time; and, after showing us all over the works, he turned triumphantly to the Russian, with 'What do you say now, eh?'

'Oh!' said Mirakoff, with a sigh, as if unburdening his soul of a confession, 'I repent. It is *impregnable*.'

'I thought you would say as much,' the Colonel replied, in high good humour.

Mirakoff, I remember, still further flattered insular prejudices by praising the appearance of the soldiers in the Fort. Scotchmen, really fine handsome men, in their scarlet uniforms, faced with blue, which render them excellent targets. But when he got back to the hotel, then these 'noble fellows' were 'heavy swine', 'fat English beef-eaters', 'stupid sheep', and other uncomplimentary epithets.

Positively, he used to hug himself with joy at the thought of how we were tricking these Englishmen, and how little they suspected our real designs. Every saint in his Greek calendar was invoked to afford us continued assistance in our enterprise.

It is impossible to recount to you all the precautions we took, in other places as well as Dover. Our emissaries were doing in Chatham, Woolwich, at Shorncliffe camp, at Canterbury, and other places, something of what we effected in Dover. But your own task, my son, will be merely to describe the taking of Dover itself, as an example of the manner in which similar enterprises should always be conducted; therefore, in my opinion, it becomes unnecessary for you to dilate at length on our general preparations for the invasion of this country.

In all such adventures, however, be sure of one thing—there are certain to be *contretemps* of one kind or another. Human prudence is apt to fail at some points; and, you know, it is the unexpected which always happens. I will assert, however, that we laid our plans for taking Dover so as to leave the minimum of possibility of any hitch occurring to mar the perfect success of the undertaking. But it is a fact that all Englishmen are not credulous and stupid, like most of them. One or two officers from the very first appeared to have a lurking distrust of Mirakoff, and perhaps of myself too. The worst of it was that we knew not at that time, and could not know, how far this distrust went: whether it was not, after all, merely the race instinct of suspicion of foreigners, which is a common prejudice enough in England. A young Lieutenant Cameron, one of the officers of the Royal Scots Fusiliers, quartered at the Harbour Fort, appeared to be the most dangerous. Mirakoff fixed his attention on this stripling, and also on the surgeon of the East Kent regiment. These two always seemed to be asking us questions about our families and our position abroad. Mirakoff could sometimes put them off by his convenient pretence of not understanding; for myself, I did as best I could, and I fancy that I satisfied them tolerably well. We were obliged, however, to tread cautiously. We kept no compromising letters, or, indeed, papers of any kind. Our rule was, never to allow any of our numerous spies to communicate with us, except by word of mouth alone. This was tedious and expensive; but it was the only safe plan. Had we been arrested on suspicion, nothing to compromise us would have been found, either on our persons, or at our hotel.

So the time drew near to the English Christmas. Thus, my son, had we prepared the invasion on *this* side of the Channel.

Now, what had been happening on *your* side, meanwhile?

The following was the disposition of the various regiments within striking distance of England. The troops to be used were those forming the *corps d'armée*, stationed, both in time of peace and war, in the 'regions' of the Pas de Calais and La Manche. Reserves were to be drawn from Paris and from Chalons. At Cherbourg, for conveyance across by sea (and transports had been secretly collected), were five regiments of French infantry, one of Cuirassiers, one of Dragoons, five batteries of artillery, besides some companies of the artillery train, and one company of Pontoniers. At the same place was an equal number of Russian troops, divided in almost similar proportions into infantry, cavalry, and artillery. This Cherbourg force was intended to land on the South Coast, whence we calculated that all available troops would have been withdrawn on the first news of the capture of Dover. The invasion being successful, they would occupy the Southern and South-Western districts of the island. Then at Rouen we had concentrated almost another *corps d'armée*, consisting entirely of French soldiers. These were to be among the first troops to come across the Channel when the Dover forts were taken. There was no cavalry in this force; but in artillery it was exceedingly strong. There were two whole regiments of this branch of the service; that would mean, as you know, twenty-six batteries. Besides these were two companies of Ouvriers d'Artillerie, and some companies of the artillery train, and more Pontoniers. Ah! I have made an error as to cavalry above. One regiment of Chasseurs was to accompany this Rouen force, as I now recollect. Two entire *corps d'armée* were in reserve at Paris, ready to start for the North at a moment's notice; and General Regnier, the celebrated hero of the Battle of Coblentz, was commanding another half *corps d'armée* (or four regiments) at Amiens.

Curiously enough (you know, my son, I told you that *contretemps* are almost certain to happen in a grave affair of this nature), it was this force of General Regnier's which aroused British suspicions. This was unfortunate. But, after all, what was it they suspected? An attack on Dover? An invasion of the free soil of England? Nothing of the kind. It was for Belgium and Brussels that they were all anxious. The force, so close to the Belgian frontier, disquieted a certain portion of the English people and the English newspapers. What if France should suddenly launch her thunderbolts at the independence of Belgium, which England had sworn to protect? Was there to be another Waterloo, with Russian troops helping ours, and no Germans to interfere?

You would be astonished if you read the English newspapers of that day, as Mirakoff and I did, line by line, to view the incredible complacence of this nation under the danger which was gathering round it. You know the Latin proverb—*Quem Deus vult perdere, prius dementat*. The same is true of peoples, my son. It was considered what the English call 'alarmist' to be nervous of French troops in the vicinity of Belgium. The French were their 'allies'. So were the Belgians. So were the Russians, even. 'Come,' said the English, 'let us flood Europe, as usual, with our Birmingham guns and our Manchester cotton, and don't let us be frightened by shadows!'

I have preserved, as curious historical relics of that time, copies of two English newspapers. One is of the date the 10th day of December, 1894; the second is the 23rd of the same month—three days before the capture of Dover! Listen to these sapient journalists. This is the extract from the earlier paper:

> We believe that some uneasiness has been caused in certain quarters by the presence, at Amiens, close to the Belgian frontier, and again at Rouen and Chalons, as well as at Paris itself, of large and imposing bodies of French troops. By some persons this is represented to be a menace to Belgium, and through her to England. Nothing could be more absurd than these apprehensions. We are confident that the English people entertain no suspicion whatever of their French allies, and we would point out the undignified nature of the alarm which is every now and then attempted to be created by certain confirmed Franco-phobists. Since the battle of Coblentz these periodical scares have become too common, and for the reputation of Great Britain it is time that they should stop. The country ought to recognize once and for all that France can have no possible interest in entering on the hazardous task of conquering Belgium. She and Russia have sufficient work on their hands in organizing the wreck of the Austro-German administration, and guarding against German revolt. To further embroil herself with this country would be suicide on the part of the French Emperor.

Then, on the 23rd, this was written in another journal:

> At this season of the year, marked by peace on earth and goodwill, the wild screams of terror, of hatred, and of suspicion, which emanate from certain organs of the Press and certain politicians towards allied and friendly nations, are peculiarly inappropriate. It is said that the French are organizing a raid on Belgium. Next we shall probably hear of the Channel being unsafe, and of Portsmouth or Dover being in danger. There is no limit to the gullibility of some mortals. We

called attention yesterday to the exceedingly gratifying returns, so far as can be at present estimated, of this year's trade with France, both in exports and imports. The fact is, that the French are pouring wine and other goods into our markets at the rate of an increase of 25 per cent over last year's returns, and are receiving our products to an amount of over 38 per cent of increase. And yet we are told that there is some secret danger—that the French are busying themselves with ideas of conquering Belgium, instead of (as the returns conclusively prove) with a revival of commerce and the new era of trade prosperity which seems opening. We can quite understand the desire of military men for battles, for promotion, and the sort of 'glory' that can be got out of bloodshed; but at least at this Christmastide our professional alarmists ought, out of mere shame, to be silent, and not interrupt with their distracting war-whoops the sacredness of a season which even they must respect.

After these quotations, you will understand, my son, that we were not very anxious as to the suspiciousness of the English press. Their government was just the same. They appeared really to be afraid to be afraid. But other circumstances caused as much discussion in private. For instance, one night I was to meet two of our spies, who had been at work at Shorncliffe, at a lonely part of the Folkestone Road. While engaged in conversation, a man passed us; I was startled to recognize the features of the Lieutenant I have spoken of.

'Holla, Count!' he cried. 'What are *you* doing out now at this cutthroat sort of place?'

'Ah, my dear Lieutenant!' I answered. 'Two foreign friends; I am conducting them part of their way—they wish to reach Folkestone to-night.'

'Folkestone!' said the Lieutenant. 'I am going there; if they like to accompany me—'

And so my couple of emissaries—two Russians, as it happened, who spoke English excellently—had to accept the escort of this officer, who plied them with questions all the six miles or so to Folkestone. They pretended not to know English, so he got little information out of his accursed inquisitiveness. But why was he going to Folkestone at all this evening—especially on foot? Mirakoff made enquiries, and discovered that he returned to Dover by train a quarter of an hour after quitting our spies. This and other incidents forced us to be very cautious.

But you will tell me that I have mentioned the *reserves* prepared for the invasion of England, and that I have not yet disclosed the number or nature of the troops to whom the actual capture of Dover was entrusted. In this we were obliged to use the utmost care. Several plans had suggested themselves. We thought first of landing a couple of thousand men on a dark night on the coast towards Deal, where it is flat. Then we abandoned that design, and, thanks greatly to Mirakoff, hit upon the device which succeeded so admirably. This was, to send picked men by small instalments to Dover, to Folkestone, to Canterbury, and indeed all the neighbouring towns, *as civilians*, with their arms, revolvers mostly, concealed in their baggage. In this way we had two thousand foreigners scattered about the hotels and lodging-houses of Dover, and quite two thousand more in the other towns, ready to concentrate at any signal given by me.

The soldiers had to be most carefully selected out of the whole French and Russian army. There were numerous necessary qualifications. One was zeal and courage (that is common enough); another was discretion; and, besides, a knowledge of English was desirable, and perfect obedience to orders, and thorough soberness. Also we took incredible trouble to choose out such men as resembled Englishmen—or at all events to exclude such soldiers as could have been taken for Russians at a glance. The English are peculiar in their discrimination between nationalities. They would never have suspected a pleasant Frenchman, but a Muscovite in England appeared an anomaly, worthy of distrust. That was the only fault about Mirakoff. People who had travelled much abroad would have been inclined to entertain considerable doubts as to his Polish origin.

Very possibly you will enquire how, after taking Dover, we were going to keep it. This point will not require much consideration in your forthcoming composition, seeing what are the terms employed by the Examining Committee in fixing the subject of the essay. Yet it would be a foolhardy thing to plant a few thousand devoted men in a hostile country if there were no prospect of continuing the *coup de main* by a regular invasion. England possessed a very powerful navy, and the methods by which most of her ships were engaged in the Baltic and the Mediterranean, just at the moment when they ought to have been guarding the Pas de Calais, are worthy of attentive examination. Fortunately, as you know, within a week of the capture of Dover the naval power of England had ceased to exist; but that thrilling story I must leave you to learn from the pens of naval writers, more conversant than I am with the science of maritime warfare.

It is enough if I tell you that the transports set out from Cherbourg and other ports so as to land our troops soon after the Dover capture was effected, and that a French fleet, collected with the same secrecy and consummate skill which marked all the operations under the Emperor's supreme direction, was easily able to protect the ships, carrying over more and more soldiers, which started each day from our ports. The English always counted on their 'silver streak' to protect them. It failed them however, at the last.

As the eventful day approached, I became nervous and depressed; Mirakoff was proportionately elated. We had left nothing at all undone. We knew the exact strength of the guards at each gate. Our men were told off for their respective duties, and knew them well. If all went properly, there ought to be no struggle at all, or at best but a trifling spurt of opposition here and there. The design was so carefully mapped out beforehand that, in the absence of unforeseen eventualities, Dover would fall into our hands without a drop of blood being shed.

That which was the foundation of our plan was to separate the bulk of the officers in the different forts from the soldiers, so that at the moment of our attempt the latter should be left as far as possible without guidance. I had the honour to suggest the means of securing this result. We resolved to give a ball to the *élite* of Dover society, both military and civil, on the night of December 26th. It was to be on a grand scale, this entertainment of ours. Our invitations had been issued weeks before, the largest hall in the place hired, bands secured, and everything done to add *éclât* to the occasion. Of course the Colonel was to be one of our guests. In addition, fifty officers were invited, and all but three had accepted the invitation.

The night before the attempt there was a fog such as only occurs in this country, and then rarely. Such a fog that if you walked along a pavement, you could see neither the wall on one side nor the road on the other, and every lamp-post and every corner came upon you as a complete surprise. I consulted with Mirakoff what we should do if the same were to be the case next night. 'Adjourn the attempt for a month,' he said, and shrugged his huge shoulders. But we were more fortunate. December 26th opened with bright sunshine, and there was a frost, which made the blood race along the veins like quicksilver. Ah, my son, you know not the mingled tremor and ecstasy with which one awaits the hour to strike an immense blow for glory, for his Gracious Majesty our Emperor, and our beloved country!

I remember entering a café—eating-house—one afternoon shortly before the chosen day. It was one of those English establishments where beef and mutton are the chief articles of food supplied. A man sitting next to me addressed me with—

'A good many foreigners in Dover, now?'

'Are there?' I observed, carelessly. I eyed the man all over. He was simply an *ouvrier* of a shrewd kind. There was no danger to be feared from him. But there *was* danger if what he had noticed should become generally recognized. I longed for the period of action to come.

We had placed the preparations for the ball in good hands, so that we were not much troubled by that. In the course of the morning, as

A German view of 1882: 'The Tunnel has hardly been completed, when the British and the French are looking to see who will be the first of them to invade the other'

previously arranged, I received three telegrams. One was from Paris, another from Calais, a third from Cherbourg. Of course they were in cypher, and informed me that all was ready. I also received, late in the afternoon, the assurance from young *sous*-Lieutenant Beaujean, who had been round to the captains of our Dover contingent (the 2,000 mentioned before), that every man knew what to do, and was eager to take his part in our enterprise. The time for our ball to commence was nine o'clock at night. The time for the attempt on the three fortresses was an hour later. The great clock striking ten was to be our signal for action. This would necessitate my temporary absence from the ballroom; but this, I calculated, would not be noticed till too late.

For myself, I had selected the post of greatest danger, the attack on the fortifications on the 'Heights', and on the splendid Hay Hill or Harbour Fort. To Mirakoff I detailed the task of leading the assault on the Castle.

At ten minutes to ten we both set out, unobserved, unattended. At the shore end of High Street we shook hands and separated, I taking the right, by Snargate Street, to the base of the 'Heights', and he wending his way along the Esplanade to East Cliff Terrace, for the Castle was to be surprised by the entrance to it from the Cliff.

As I walked hurriedly along Snargate Street, the shops were all closed, as is usual at Christmas-time, and only a few foot-passengers were observed here and there. Carriages rolled along now and then: parties setting off to our ball. They would wonder where their hosts were gone to, when they arrived at the dancing-hall; but I had not time to think of that then. As I advanced, five men joined me without saying a word, and accompanied me onwards. Just where the Post Office stands, there were five other men laughing and talking, to all appearance—you would have thought—sailors the worse for liquor. When they observed us, they greeted us with ribald laughter, and followed behind us, as if out of drunken curiosity. Only a few yards further on was the side street leading directly to the entrance to the military shaft of which I have already told you. All seemed still as a desert when we entered it. Hardly had we arrived at the end, however, than, as if by magic, ten more figures quietly filed out of the dark shadows of walls and angles and ranged themselves at my side. A revolver and a short sword were their arms, concealed by their cloaks. The others were only armed with a revolver. And there, fronting us, was the blank wall with the door in it leading into the shaft!

I motioned the others aside, and stepping forward, rapped heavily with the short sword I carried. A pause, and the door was half opened by a sentry. One man against twenty. But it was necessary to avoid making a noise, so I appeared boldly before the fellow, in my full ball-dress just as I had emerged from the dancing-hall. He recognized me at once, as I had calculated he would do, opened the door wide, and saluted me respectfully.

'Monsieur le Commandant Fitzroy', I said enquiringly. 'He has not come to the ball. Is he here?'

'The Colonel—not gone,' said the man stupidly, and evidently wondering at the whole affair.

'I wish this note taken to him—at once,' I said. 'At once' was my signal. The sentinel was looking down at the note I had handed him. Quick as thought, two of my troop had sprung on him, thrown him to the ground, and gagged him. One of them gave him a touch on the head to keep him quiet. We all entered quietly, and shut the door behind us.

Then up the steps I sprang, and soon reached the elevated platform at the top, where was another door, as I have described, which communicated directly with the interior. Here I followed exactly the same plan. There was, I knew, only a single sentinel placed here also. But, so bad fortune decreed, on this particular night three other soldiers were gossiping at the gate in his company.

The moment the portal opened, I was confronted with the sentinel in the foreground, grasping his musket, and lolling against the wall behind him were the three others! But I was not taken unprepared for the emergency. Suddenly I decided to change my tactics. I called excitedly to these men, who knew me well by sight: 'Your Colonel! I have brought your Colonel! He is outside—he is here! Help him! He is ill!' They were staggered for a moment. The next, and humanity had triumphed over discipline. They dashed through the gate to succour their Commandant, and were overcome before they had time to utter a shout.

Then my twenty heroes poured in. Not a moment was to be lost. There were six hundred English soldiers in the fortress, we knew. Leaving a couple of men behind to guard the gate, I and the others rushed on, avoiding the barracks, avoiding the armoury, to a small court close to the officers' quarters, on the south side of the fortification. Here, as I knew, was a postern connecting directly with a part of the deep moat which ran round the works. We only met one man as we raced forward—a sleepy artilleryman, coming out of a door in his shirt-sleeves and forage cap. My sword was through him before he had time to give the alarm. As yet there was no opposition, and no cry to show we were discovered. We reached the postern safely, and opened it with ease. I drew back the bolts, and then, my son, I fervently thanked Heaven that had guarded us safely hitherto. For outside that postern, lying along the grassy hillside right up to the lip of the moat, were five hundred of our men, armed to the teeth. As I opened the small gate, and gave the agreed signal, suddenly the grass became alive with men, who slid, climbed, tumbled to the bottom of the deep trench, and then rushed forward.

Ah! I knew we were safe then. As I stood there, cheering them on, and saw them dash boldly into the fortress, with eyes gleaming and teeth set, I gloried in the skill which had, under Providence, directed us so far.

As for the garrison, it had not the faintest notion that anything extraordinary was occurring. They were idling about their quarters, as soldiers do—some in the yard, some leaning out of the windows, others amusing themselves in the bagatelle room. The surprise was absolute. On a sudden they found hundreds of armed men in their midst, around them, everywhere. I shouted that whoever resisted would be shot down. I assure you, we were obliged to allow no nonsense. Two or three, enraged, began using their fists; but it was the last time they ever used them. A guard, who was pacing, a little way off, up and down in front of the armoury, fired off his rifle as a danger-signal. The next instant he had dropped, with innumerable revolver bullets in his body. It was no time to stand on ceremony. And so the garrison was cowed, demoralized, without officers or word of command, and surrendered at discretion. The celebrated fortification of the 'Heights' had passed into our hands.

But there remained the other Fort—that on Hay Hill, or Shakespeare's Cliff, overlooking the Harbour—the greatest difficulty of all!

Directly our prisoners were secured, I hastened to the underground passage. Our men had made short work of the one sentinel guarding it at this end. But, as I told you, at the other end, where the subway leads into the Hay Hill Fort, there was not only a strong door, with *two* sentries guarding it, but the impossibility of opening it by stratagem.

By this time I was reinforced by a large contingent that had been waiting in the fields skirting the Folkestone road. With five hundred men, I considered that I could take the Hay Hill Fort, and hold it when taken. I allowed only one torch to be carried along the passage. Half-way, I ordered that to be extinguished. Then, with one comrade, I advanced stealthily, till a light was visible under the bottom of the ponderous door which blocked the end. We held our breaths. Yes, two sentries—we heard them distinctly, in conversation with each other. We heard one man say:

'I tell you it was a rifle-shot I heard.'

And the other replied, grumpily:

'Nonsense! Boys with popguns, more like.'

Then an angry altercation ensued. Now was a fine opportunity. I had decided to blow this door up from our side. It would have been of no use to adopt the former ruse, and knock for admission. The presence of anybody in the deserted subway late at night would alone have excited suspicion.

It was a massive iron screen, rather than a door. But I had arranged all; and silently we placed against it a small oblong-shaped box containing the explosive. I laid the train, and motioned my comrade back. Then I lit it, and quickly retreated. But I could not help the fuse fizzing somewhat. Almost immediately afterwards there was a terrific explosion. I threw myself flat on my face, half suffocated and stunned. But—Heaven be praised!—the door was in fragments. In fragments?—it no longer existed! We rushed in over the breach. I had calculated that we should take the men before they had time to fly to their arms; but it turned out even better than that. At the noise of the explosion, the soldiers all came flocking like geese towards the place, wondering what had happened. Their capture was ridiculously easy. Soon they were marched off in batches. The great Harbour Fort, England's key, the *clavis et repagulum regni*, was ours!

As you may suppose, these Dover fortresses were not without the means of communicating with other garrisons, and with the outside world generally. There was a telegraphic office in the Harbour Fort. The wires burrowed under the town, came up in the Castle, burrowed again, and emerged somewhere in the country, where they connected with the general telegraphic system of the kingdom. It was over the entrance of a miserable-looking little shed that I saw the word 'Telegraphs' written; and it was at the door, on the threshold, that I suddenly beheld, face to face, our foe, the man whom we had suspected, and who had suspected us. Judge my surprise to see, standing quietly there, a cigar in his mouth, Lieutenant Cameron!

'Ah, ha! Monsieur le Traître!' he cried, gaily. 'You have arrived just in time to be informed of the failure of your little conspiracy.'

'Take one of these cigars,' I said; 'you will find them better than your own.'

'And that Russian scoundrel,' he shouted passionately—'tell him from me that he is foiled too. You may have taken Dover by your underground tricks. You have not captured the rest of England. Let me tell you that troops are already on their way from Shorncliffe, Canterbury, and Chatham. London itself is warned. It was *I* who sent the messages.' He was really proud of his achievement.

'You think your troops are now advancing to recapture Dover, then?' I asked. 'Allow me to inform you, Monsieur le Lieutenant, that you are wrong.'

'Why so?'

I took out a cigar, and lit it leisurely.

'For this reason, Lieutenant Cameron: *the communication is cut.*'

It was true. Mirakoff and I had arranged that beforehand. And by this time, we knew, both stations and all post-offices would be in the hands of the Russian Guards, who were to be in waiting on the coast road, and surprise the town directly they received our signal showing that the forts were in our possession.

'I know you are lying,' the Lieutenant remarked, quietly enough; and before I could divine what his intentions were, he had drawn a revolver from his pocket and discharged it at my head. Had his nerves been sound, I should not now be writing to you, my dear son. As it was, a moment later he was struck down by one of our men.

Just then I heard the boom of the great clock of the town. Half-past ten! Half an hour and ten minutes had sufficed to place these 'impregnable' Dover fortifications in our hands. For I made no doubt that Mirakoff too had succeeded, and that we possessed the Castle as well.

But it was time, by all the rules of propriety, for me to remember my guests; for, to tell the truth, I had been hitherto shamefully neglecting the duty of politeness.

I had not, when I re-entered the ballroom, been absent from it more than three-quarters of an hour in all. Apparently, however, I had contrived to irritate *one* at least among my guests. This was Colonel Fitzroy himself, the Commandant, who seemed quite red and oppressed with rage. He was standing on the large raised däis at one end of the spacious hall, and round him were several of the officers of the garrison, among them the Surgeon-Major, whom I have mentioned before as one of whom we had suspicions. He was whispering something to the Colonel. I looked round the room anxiously to see if Mirakoff was visible anywhere. No; the dancing and gaiety were going on just as before; but, as yet, no Mirakoff.

As I approached the brilliant group of English officers at the end of the room, Colonel Fitzroy came to meet me, and said, in a loud voice: 'This is a pretty way to behave to your guests, Monsieur le Vicomte. This is what you Frenchmen call French leave, I suppose. In England it is the rule for the host to be present at his own entertainment.'

The Colonel's choler did not affect me much now. However, I pleaded politely that 'a most important and pressing engagement' had kept me absent so long—which was true.

'The Major,' went on the Colonel, turning to the Surgeon of the East Kent Regiment, 'says he has heard the sound of an explosion in the Hay Hill Fort. He also says—'

'He says what is true,' interrupted the gruff Englishman, stepping close up to me, 'that you, Monsieur le Vicomte, or whatever you call yourself, were seen talking last evening to some *gentlemen* who are suspected to be *Russian spies*!'

Of course I laughed at him. It was my cue to gain time by any means in my power. Mirakoff's continued non-appearance created a real feeling of dismay in my mind.

'You are mistaken,' I remarked quietly to the enraged Surgeon; 'and may I ask you this question—Could you and your friends recognize a Russian if you were to see one?'

'Certainly,' and as he said so he pointed to the door.

Mirakoff was entering! His face was flushed; his clothes ruffled; his manner denoted intense excitement. He strode through the dancers, who gazed with astonishment, though the dancing and the music never ceased or slackened. 'The Castle is ours,' he hissed in my ear; 'more than that, all is ready. The hall is surrounded. You can hear the tramp—there!'

Before I had time to prevent him, he had stepped up to Colonel Fitzroy, and stamping his foot with passion, exclaimed—

'You are in a trap, my fine officer, you and your England together. We have you now safe. Dover is ours—ours! Resist,' he cried, as the officers who heard him put their hands to their swords, 'and you shall all be shot down like wolves, without mercy.'

As he said this, he brandished his great arms, and pointed wildly towards the entry. There, over the heads of the dancers could be seen, filing slowly in, the ranks of our devoted infantry, and the dark hue of the uniform of the detachment of the Preobajensky Guards. While outside, the tramp, tramp, and the clang of arms, now drowned even the joyous sound of the dance-music; the music and the dancing both ceased suddenly.

'What is this?' shouted the Colonel. The whole room was in consternation. Women screamed and fainted; men stood as if spellbound. The officers drew their swords. I would, my dear son, that you could conjure up in your imagination that wonderful yet terrible scene, as I can!

'What does this mean?' screamed rather than shouted the Governor of Dover, the wild, stupid British boar caught fairly in our toils.

'It means treachery, no doubt,' said the Surgeon-Major, coolly. 'But one traitor shall suffer for it.' And before anybody could interfere, he had snatched a sword from an officer, and passed it with a vindictive lunge through poor Mirakoff's body. He fell with a deep groan.

The *mêlée* which ensued baffles description, and I had to use my sword in self-defence. They do not yield willingly, these English. I never beheld a more determined or heroic stand than that made by these few officers, in that crowded ballroom, with no weapons but their parade swords to fight with. They disdained to accept quarter. But of what use was such bravery? They resisted heroically—in vain, for all were cut down or shot.

And the next morning, my son, over the once proud Tower and Town of Dover, over the magnificent Harbour Fort, and upon those grassy 'Heights', there waved the Tricolor of our beloved France, in unison with the Imperial Eagle of the Russian Czar. By that time fifty thousand men had been safely landed; all night long they had been ceaselessly coming. They were a hundred and thirty thousand in twenty-four hours more. Then we heard that the Shorncliffe Camp had been captured.

But I will not weary you, who know them so well, with all the subsequent steps of that short but decisive campaign, the taking of Chatham, the attempted defence and capture of London, of Birmingham, Bristol, and the other great towns of the kingdom, inasmuch as you have already, doubtless, studied these details with the aid of your experienced military tutors. But what I have related to you now can be known to nobody in Europe better than to myself; so accept, my dear son, my report, derived from actual experience, of how Dover was captured.

As for the Commandant, Colonel Fitzroy, he was so shockingly wounded that his life was despaired of for long; but he lived. The doctors who attended him told me that in his fever he was always imagining that an invader was landing at Dover, and that by means of his favourite balloons they were at once destroyed! But those famous 'autopropellers' of his were never used. When he became convalescent, he was one day standing at a window of the Lord Warden Hotel, looking at some French military stores being landed. Suddenly he became violently agitated! There—there—before his eyes, was a cargo of war balloons, all exactly like his beloved Wilkinsonian autopropellers, yet stamped with the mark of the Toulon arsenal, where they had been manufactured—for, of course, the secret was no secret to our Emperor! It was too much for the Colonel. They tell me he became ill again—was taken to an asylum—and died.

It seems, I confess, but yesterday that England was still a mighty empire; but yesterday poor Mirakoff and I were plotting her ruin in a private room of a fashionable Dover hotel. I cannot but pity the nation; but their humiliation, as it was occasioned by sheer recklessness, by avarice for the gains of trade, and by blind stupidity, appears to my judgement to have been fully deserved.

Forgive more from my pen, my dear child. Your mother joins me in the expression of devoted affection. Continue by your conduct and your application to your studies to afford us the same satisfaction that you have ever done.

Your loving Father,

* * * *

In a Conning Tower

How I Took *HMS Majestic* into Action

HUGH OAKLEY ARNOLD-FORSTER

Have you ever stood within a conning tower? No; then you have not set foot in a spot where the spirit of man has borne the fiercest and direst stress to which the fell ingenuity of the modern world has learnt to subject it. You have not seen the place where the individual wages a twofold contest with the power of the tempest and the violence of the enemy, where, controlling with a touch and guiding with his will the gigantic forces of Nature, he stands alone in the presence of death, and asserts amidst the awful crash of the mental and physical battle the splendid majesty of the spirit of man. For indeed there is nothing grander, more consoling to humanity, than the power of man to hold his own, unshaken and unshakeable, in the face of unknown and incalculable dangers, upborne by the high inspiration of personal courage, by devotion to duty, or by the power of faith.

'Such a gift is vouchsafed to man'; but it is often bought at a great price, and often, though life be spared to him who wins it, and though the human protagonist comes out a victor in the contest, he survives with the scars of the terrible conflict burnt in for ever upon his inmost soul.

I have known a man, a giant in mind and body, emerge from the ordeal with hair blanched in an hour by the dread and strain of the conflict. Another I could tell you of, he who writes these lines, to whom the struggle between fear and duty, between terror and pride, brought the keenest suffering and the hardest trial which a man can bear.

Yes, I use the words 'fear' and 'terror'. I who have fought not without honour and success for my sovereign and my country, who bear on my breast the cross for valour, and whose name is not unknown among my countrymen and my comrades.[1]

But let me come to the story I have to tell you. You have never set foot inside a conning tower. Let me do the honours of my old ship, and let me ask you to go with me on board *HMS Majestic*, as she lies at anchor at Spithead. There she floats, a heavy mass upon the water, ugly enough no doubt to an artist's eye, but with a certain combination of trimness and strength very grateful to a sailor, and especially to a sailor who knows every inch of her within and without, and whose duty it has been to make use of her terrible powers in war.[2]

It is but a little way from the gig alongside on to the deck, and the ship in a bit of a sea is all awash where we stand. But we can take many a green sea on board the *Majestic* without being any the worse, and it takes a good deal to upset the equanimity of 12,000 tons. Step through the door there. Stoop and raise your feet, for it is a strait gate. Now turn and look at the door you have passed. Talk of a banker's strong room, what banker in the world has a door like that: twelve inches of iron and steel, with a face that will turn all the 'villainous centre-bits' that ever were forged? But the door must needs be strong, for the treasure it has to keep behind it is the honour of the flag, and those who knock will come with a rat-tat equal to 50,000 tons on the square foot. Now climb again: here we have more space, and things look more like the old man-of-war of the story books. Six guns on a broadside and over a hundred men in the battery. Ah, when I think of that gun-deck as I saw it once! You mark the racer of this after gun; come forward now to No. 3 on the port side. All that is new work, a single shell ripped the battery side away for fifty feet from this point where you stand. Carriages, bulk-heads, girders, beams, crumpled and torn like a tangle of bunch grass by an autumn gale.

This is the spot to which I wish to lead you. This is the conning tower of *HMS Majestic*. A chamber scarce six foot across, encumbered as you see with a score of appliances which diminish the scanty space which it affords. Touch the wall in front of you: a formidable partition, is it not? Twelve inches of solid steel and iron, and carried down far into the framework of the ship. Note too above your head a solid roof of steel. This is the fighting position of the *Majestic*. 'The fighting position,' you will say, 'but how can an action be conducted from a spot from which no enemy is visible?' Stand here and bring your eye to the level of the armour-plating, and mark the narrow slit between the arched cupola above us, and the steel walls of the chamber; sweep your eye round, and the whole horizon will come within your view. Look down, and in front of you is the sharp bow of the ship, and the two long white muzzles of the guns protruding many feet from the forward turret. Now look inside at the fittings of the conning tower, and read the inscriptions on the brass tablets

'Swept and battered by the point-blank discharge of the terrible artillery, the *Majestic* still held her course'

which surround it. Over that group of speaking-tubes on your right you see the words, 'Bow torpedo tube' and 'Above-water torpedo tube'. On the left is the voice tube to the engine-room. That key completes the circuit which discharges the great guns.

Here in the centre is the steam steering-wheel, binnacle, and compass. 'All very trim and ship-shape,' you will say, 'and an immense convenience to the commanding officer to have all the arrangements of the ship brought under his hand.'

Convenient, yes! But let your imagination come to the aid of your observation. Here lies the great ironclad, 'a painted ship upon a painted ocean'; but see her as I have seen her; think, if you can, of what is meant by the accumulation of forces within this little space; and try to realize, as clearly as any man who has not passed through the ordeal can realize, the strain upon the human mind which is placed in absolute control of this mighty engine in the day of battle.

Every Englishman who is worth his salt knows something of the glorious naval annals of his country. The names of Rodney, Howe, and Nelson are happily and rightly household words among us; we honour and revere those splendid masters of their art. Courage, skill, and a magnificent patriotism were theirs. All that their country demanded of them they did. But compare for a moment the position of any one of those great officers in the action, and that which the fearful ingenuity of modern science has imposed on their successors. On the one hand, we had the Admiral standing on his quarterdeck, his star upon his breast, the central figure of his crew, animating them by his presence, and inspiring the group of officers who stand around him with the spirit which his great example in previous victories has set them. By his side stands the Master; it is his business to sail and navigate the ship. The first lieutenant, charged with the discipline of the crew and the fighting of the guns, will see that there is no slackness, no want of skill in working the long tiers of the broadside carronades; an easy task, for it does not require either his vigilance or the example of his subordinates to strengthen the fierce rivalry between each gun's crew. Already the order has been passed that it is the duty of each ship to lay itself alongside of the enemy and to remain there till she has struck. The Master will lay the ship alongside, and the grimy gunners will continue to discharge their pieces at point-blank range until the wooden wall of the opposing ship is battered into a shapeless mass of smoking timber, and until the joyful news comes from the deck that the enemy's ensign has sunk from the peak in token of submission.

That was in the olden time. What are the conditions of modern war?

Here in this spot is concentrated the whole power of the tremendous machine which we call an ironclad ship.

Such power was never till the world began concentrated under the direction of man, and all that power, the judgement to direct it, the will to apply it, the knowledge to utilize it, is placed in the hands of one man, and one only.

What is this power?

Talk of Jove with his thunderbolts, of Nasmyth with his hammer! The fables of mythology and the facts of latter-day science! Where has there ever been anything to compare to it? Here in the conning tower stands the captain of the ship, and beneath his feet lie hidden powers which the mind can scarcely grasp, but which one and all are made subservient to his will, and his will alone. Picture him as he stands at his post before the battle begins; all is quiet enough, there

The engagement between the ironclad *Monitor* and the Confederate *Merrimac* in the War between the States changed naval technology overnight

is scarcely a sound save the lapping of the water against the smooth white sides of the ironclad, and no outward sign of force save the ripple of the parted waters falling off on either side of the ram as it sheers through the water. But mark that white thread escaping from the steam-pipe astern, a fleecy vapour rising into the air and nothing more! But what does it mean? It means that far down below some thirty glowing furnaces are roaring under the blast of steam; that in the great cylindrical boilers the water is bubbling, surging, struggling, as the fierce burning gases pass through the flues; and that the prisoned steam, tearing and thrusting at the tough sides of the boilers, is already raising the valves and blowing off at a pressure of 100 pounds. It means that the captain in his conning tower has but to press the button by his side, and in a moment the four great engines will be driving the twin screws through the water with the force of 12,000 horse power, and that the great ship with the dead weight of 12,000 tons will be rushing onwards at a speed of over twenty miles an hour.

In her turret and in her broadside batteries there is a deep hush of expectation: but there too, waiting to respond to the 'flash of the will that can', lie forces of destruction which appal the imagination.

Far down below our feet in the chambers of the great guns lie the dark masses of the powder charges. A touch, a spark, and in a sheet of flame and with the crash of thunder the steel shot will rush from their muzzles, speeding on their way 2,000 feet in a second, and dealing their blow with the impact of 60,000 foot-tons—5,000 pounds weight of metal discharged by one touch of the captain's hand. Nor is this all; another touch and another signal will liberate the little clips which detain the four Whitehead torpedoes in their tubes. A puff of powder, a click as the machinery is started and the two screws are set off whirling, and with a straight silent plunge the long steel torpedoes will dive into the water, and at their appointed depth will speed on their way thirty miles an hour on their awful errand of destruction. Move that switch, and through the dark wall of the night a long straight beam will shoot forth with the radiance of 40,000 candles, turning the night into day.

A word spoken through that tube will let loose the hailstorm of steel and lead from the quick-firing and machine-guns on the upper deck and in the tops. A discharge of shot and shell, not to be counted by tens or scores but by hundreds and thousands, a storm before which no living thing can stand, and under which all but the strongest defences will wither and melt away like a snow bank under an April shower.

And, last and most terrible of all, there is one other force ready to the captain's hand: a force, the sum of all the others, and which, if rightly utilized, is as irresistible as the swelling of the ocean tide, or the hand of Death. By your side and under your hand are the spokes of the steam steering-wheel; far forward under the swirling wave, which rises round the ship's cut-water, lies the ram, the most terrible, the most fatal of all the engines of maritime warfare. It is the task of the hand which turns that little wheel to guide and to direct the fearful impact of the ram.

Think what the power confided to one man's hand must be; 12,000 tons of dead weight driven forward by the frantic energy of 12,000 horse-power, plunging and surging along through the yielding waves, at a speed of ten feet in every second, and with a momentum so huge that the mathematical expression which purports to represent it to the mind conveys no idea to an intelligence incapable of appreciating a conception so vast. To receive a blow from the ram is death, the irretrievable catastrophe of a ship's career. To deliver such a blow is certain victory. It is with the captain, and with the captain alone, as he stands here in the conning tower, that the responsibility of inflicting or encountering this awful fate lies.

Now you will understand what I mean when I say that never since the world began have such forces been placed in the hands of a single man, whose eye alone must see the opportunity, whose judgement alone must enable him to utilize it, and whose hand alone must give effect to all that his courage, his wisdom, and his duty prompt.

Perhaps you will ask what business have I, a naval officer, to allow such notions as these to run through my brain; what business have I to talk about anxiety or responsibility? The sailor's duty is plain; he has got to find the enemy, to fight him, and to beat him. If he is either fearful or anxious, he is a man out of place. But unfortunately, naval officers are after all made of much the same stuff as other people; and there are certain circumstances in which their minds, however carefully tutored and prepared, are as much open to the strain of terror and anxiety as those of their comrades upon shore. Habit, personal courage, and a sense of duty may enable them to overcome these enemies, but they feel their assaults. Do not believe a man when he tells you that he does not know what fear is on going into an action; above all, do not believe it of the captain of a modern ironclad when about to engage with an enemy of equal strength. True, he has nothing to do but to carry out the duties which years of practice have taught him how to perform; but the heart never beat in a human frame whose pulsation was not quickened by the presence of danger. Sit at home and study the phenomena of electricity, codify the laws of the elements, and analyse the progress of the lightning with a Leyden jar and an electrometer, and you will doubtless learn to contemplate the prospect of a thunderstorm with a purely scientific interest. But stand alone in the night on the mountain side, amid the roar and flash of a tropical storm, and you must be either more or less than human if your imagination and your spirit are not moved and awed by the fierce play of Nature. And so it is with those who in the time of battle have to command a ship of war.

By a piece of good fortune which had not fallen to the lot of my colleagues, I had been two years in command of my ship when the late war came upon us. I knew her, as I have said, from stem to stern, from her armoured 'top' to her iron keel, and by day and by night, in my waking hours and in my dreams, I had been going through every conceivable form of engagement which my experience or my imagination could suggest as likely to fall to the lot of the *Majestic*. But sleeping or waking, by the light of experience or by the light of fancy, I ever saw one supreme moment when I should stand in this

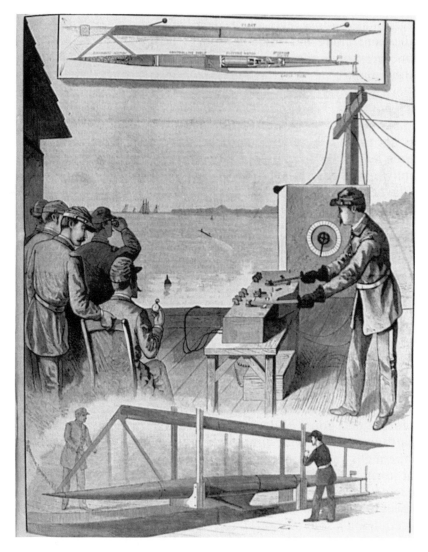

The illustrated magazines never failed to give their readers the latest news about new naval weapons

conning tower, and should be called upon to take into my hand for good or for ill, for success or failure, the mighty power of the ship, and to make myself responsible for the honour of the flag, the safety of the ship, and the lives of the crew.

And always one great fact remained present to my mind, that it was I, and I alone, who must do this thing; that on *my* judgement, on *my* skill, on *my* courage, must depend the issue of the day. I cannot describe to you how deeply this feeling of responsibility weighed upon my spirit, and how earnestly I prayed that when the time of trial came I might be found worthy of the post I held.

Well! At last the time did come. Everybody knows how strangely things were done at the outset of the war, and everybody remembers the merciful escapes from destruction, due not to forethought but to chance, which enabled the country to survive the blunders and the wanton carelessness of the Administration, and to live through the first shock of the war. Luckily, we all know too how, after chance had given us this happy and undeserved respite, the successes of our seamen, backed by the energy of our constructors, enabled us to regain and to assert that mastery of the sea which we had so nearly lost.

It was in the earliest days of this happier period, when the need for organization and system had begun to dawn upon the official mind, but before much had been done to give effect to the newly-awakened conviction, that the *Majestic* was ordered to join the Mediterranean fleet.

We steamed out of Portsmouth Harbour alone. It was a mad thing, and everybody knew it.

It was an axiom, which every one of the gentlemen at Whitehall had long ago committed himself to on paper, that no heavy ironclad should go to sea in time of war without an attendant squadron of cruisers, despatch vessels, and torpedo-boats. But beggars must not be choosers; there was urgent need for my ship in the Mediterranean, and all our cruisers, despatch vessels and torpedo-boats had too much to do in performing the immediate duties, which the stress of the situation and the want of any reasonable organization had forced upon them, to allow of their attending the *Majestic* on her southward journey.

It is not easy to describe my feelings when our sailing orders arrived; the mingled sensations which passed through my brain would be hard to analyse. At last the moment had come when the supreme ambition of my life was to be realized, and I was to command one of Her Majesty's ships in actual war. At the same time, the total want of any experience to guide me in the enterprise which it was now my duty to undertake, and the feeling of uncertainty as to the correctness of the theories which my studies in peace-time had led me to form, weighed upon my spirit to a painful degree. I must admit, however, that as we passed the Warner Light, and I telegraphed 'full speed ahead', my feeling was one of extraordinary exhilaration.[3] It is not easy to describe the mental atmosphere which seemed to pervade the ship; but one characteristic struck me as being of good omen; and that was the feeling of cheerfulness and good fellowship which seemed to animate all ranks of the ship's company.

One odd incident I remember as peculiar to myself. I had fully determined before I left port that I would dismantle my cabin of all the pretty knick-knacks and ornaments of which I was so proud, and which made it so charming and comfortable a retreat. When, however, the actual moment came for carrying my intention into effect, I felt an indescribable reluctance to give the necessary orders, and in the end I went to sea with scarcely a visible alteration having been effected in the arrangements of my cabin. The contrast between the pretty and homelike surroundings in which I studied once more my plan of action, and the terrible realities of the situation with which I might at any moment find myself face to face, dwells with a singular distinctness in my memory.

Our object being to reach Gibraltar unmolested and in good fighting trim, we naturally gave the shore a wide offing.

We had passed the Lizard Light some two hours when we came in contact with the first evidences that the ocean had become the scene of a bloody and fatal conflict.[4] It was at this point that we fell in with *HMS Shannon* slowly making her way homewards, and bearing plain marks of the strife in which she had been engaged. We exchanged signals with her, but she reported that she had not seen an enemy's ship for forty-eight hours. It was not till long afterwards that we learnt the particulars of the engagement from which she had just emerged. How, overtaken by a protected cruiser, she had lost no less than eighty men in the vain attempt to work her broadside guns; how, preserved from destruction by her armoured belt, she had maintained herself until, by a lucky discharge of the new nine-inch BL gun, which the Admiralty, in a fit of unwonted prescience, had placed in the bows, she had succeeded in exploding a heavy shell in a vital part of the enemy's ship; how safe, from pursuit, but with her crew decimated and her armour in splinters, she had made her way back to Plymouth, a testimony to the gallantry of her crew and to the error of her designers.

It was two o'clock on the following day that the look-out sighted a strange vessel hull down on the port bow. It was not long before the diminished distance between the two vessels revealed to us the three funnels and the raking masts of one of the enemy's fast cruis-

The spectacular victories of the Japanese fleet in the war with Russia raised questions about the future of capital ships

ers. A good glass enabled us to detect two torpedo-boats steaming along under her quarter. I knew at once what our friend was about, and I longed for a swift companion whom I might despatch in pursuit; but such good fortune was not to be. After making a careful inspection of us, the stranger went about, and steaming at full speed was soon beyond the horizon. To follow her was impossible, nor would it have been consistent with my instructions had I possessed the three extra knots which would have put me on an equality with her; but I was pretty sure, and the event proved that I was right, that she had not paid us her visit of inspection for nothing.

During the whole of the following night we were steering west-south-west, and our object in keeping so far from the land had been fulfilled, for we had sighted nothing but a homeward-bound British steamer from Valparaiso, which had made a clear run at an average rate of sixteen knots, and had not been molested by any enemy.

It was just after seven bells in the morning watch that the look-out man on the top signalled a vessel hull down on the port bow. It was a fairly bright morning, and the distance, as far as we could calculate, between ourselves and the vessel in question was about twelve miles.

Whoever the stranger might prove to be, there was little necessity for any extra precaution on board the *Majestic*. Throughout the night the water-tight doors had been closed; all movable bulkheads and unnecessary fittings had long ago been removed and stowed. Every man knew his station, and there was not the slightest occasion to hurry the men over their breakfast; the only difficulty was to keep them from their fighting stations, or from any point from which a view of the stranger could be obtained. In a very few minutes it became apparent that, whether friend or foe, the newcomer was heading directly for us. Our orders were not to seek an engagement; in this case it was evident that we should scarcely have an opportunity of refusing one, provided that we held our course, and that it was an enemy's ship that was in sight.

We were not long in doubt upon this head. In less than ten minutes not only the form but the colours of the stranger became clearly apparent, and the colours were those which it was our duty at any cost to lower.* The ship itself was as familiar to me as the flag which she bore. In these days, when photography and an elaborate professional literature have recorded the form and peculiarity of every important ship-of-war afloat, it would have been strange had I not recognized the formidable lines of the antagonist with which we were so soon to be in conflict. But my acquaintance with my adversary was a more intimate one than any which the study of books could have conferred. It was not three months since I had been on board of her. Nor was this all; not only did I know the ship, but I knew who was in command of her. Many a time had I met Captain C—— when he represented his country as naval attaché in London. A more gallant officer, a more accomplished gentleman, never wore the uniform of the honourable service to which he belonged.

I confess that, when I first realized who was my opponent, a sensation of a very peculiar kind passed through my brain. On the one hand, feeling as I did perfect confidence in my ship and in my crew, and rejoicing, as every man in my position would have done, at this opportunity of performing the highest duty of my profession, I was gratified that my opponent was a man whose defeat must add a special lustre to the efforts of my crew if they should be successful. On the other hand, I felt, as I stood on the bridge as the two ships neared each other, that the conflict must inevitably be not merely between material appliances on either side, but between the brain

---

* We learnt subsequently that the ironclad had been attended by the cruiser and torpedo-boats which we had seen on the previous day. Her auxillaries had remained in port to coal, with orders to follow at speed in a few hours. Happily, on leaving port they had been picked up by HM ships *Blenheim* and *Cossack*, which, after a running fight of an hour-and-a-half, had sunk the torpedo-boats and captured the cruiser.

and the heart of two men whose fortunes and whose reputations were equally at stake; and I knew that the great ship that was bearing down upon us was guided by a master mind, which would be quick to seize an opportunity, ready to strike, and merciless to gain victory at any cost. It was to be a battle, no doubt, but it was also to be a duel, and a duel to the death.

In less than half an hour from first sighting the enemy, the distance between us was reduced to a little over two miles. The crew were at their quarters, the guns were loaded, the torpedoes were charged and ready for action, and the boilers were blowing off at their highest pressure; for it had always been my fixed determination to fight an engagement at full speed. Up to this time I was standing close to the chart house on the upper bridge; perhaps not the wisest place to have selected, but I was determined to avail myself as long as possible of the full power to sweep the horizon which my entry into my appointed station in the conning tower would so inevitably curtail. It was hard at such a moment to believe that the peaceful aspect before us must be changed before we were many minutes older into a hideous tempest of fire and blood. Many of us on both sides had served our respective countries for many years, but there was not one of us to whom the circumstances of the approaching battle were not absolutely new and beyond experience. The ship was making 105 revolutions and was running at a very high speed, over seventeen knots; but the only sound was the crash of the engines, as familiar to us as the very pulsation of our own hearts and scarcely more noticed. By my side stood two of my officers, my gunnery and navigating officers, my signalman, and one of his staff. The time for conversation had gone by; we had said all that had to be said, but one more remark remained to be made.

'Mr Maitland,' I said to the staff-commander, 'I shall not require your services; this will be a matter of tactics, and not of navigation; we may be in need of officers before the day is out. I must ask you to leave the bridge; I know you will regret it, but the interests of the service demand it.'

The words were scarcely out of my mouth, and the officer had hardly left the ladder, when a tongue of flame shot forth from the forward barbette of the enemy, and a thick eddying bank of white smoke rolled and tumbled over her bows, driven forward by the blast of the great gun. There was a pause, short enough indeed in our ordinary reckoning of time, but fully long enough for anxious and excited nerves to appreciate ere the hostile message reached its destination. Suddenly, some twenty yards ahead of the *Majestic*, there rose into the air a vast column of water, and the eye, naturally following the direction of the shot, marked the great jets which sprang up far into the distance as the projectile ricocheted over the water.

The action had begun, and sooner than I had expected. The range was a long one—too long to my thinking—but evidently the enemy was not of the same opinion. The time had come when duty demanded that I should take my appointed station. I descended to the conning tower, followed by my subordinates. As I passed down the ladder, I saw the men duly posted at their stations in the tops and on the superstructure, in charge of the quick-firing guns. In the battery the larger quick-firing guns were loaded and ready. Nothing was wanted in that part of the preparations which my eye could reach, and I had the happy certainty that there was no detail in all the dark recesses of the ship which required vigilance and skill for its superintendence which had not been cared for by my officers.

A strange thrill came over me as I entered the conning tower. No one can analyse the sensations of such a moment; but one feeling I recall with pleasure and gratitude, whether it were due to the happy inheritance of that English temperament and those English traditions which will reveal themselves in the time of danger, even to those who have been least conscious of enjoying the advantages they confer; whether it were the overmastering interest of the situation itself, and the professional instinct which compelled me to regard the whole proceeding as a problem of absorbing interest, I cannot say. But of this I am certain: that from that moment the feeling of doubt and anxiety, which I must admit had been for many hours past one of the sensations of which my mind was most deeply conscious, passed away, and was replaced by a feeling of mental exaltation, and of keen and almost oppressive appreciation of the conditions of the fight.

However, I had little time at the moment to consider my sensations. I at once requested Lieutenant Mannering to communicate my orders with regard to laying the two heavy guns in the forward turret, and a general instruction was passed to the guns in the battery to reserve their fire until special orders were received from me. By this time the ships were within 2,000 yards of each other, the enemy about two points on our port bow. Again I saw the bright flash spring from her sides, and in a moment it was followed by a shock which shook the *Majestic* from stem to stern. This time there was no error in the aim, and the steel shot had struck the ship on the thick plating abaft the turret. Subsequent examination showed a scar six inches deep; but the blow had been a slanting one, and the projectile flew off at an angle, and passed into the sea astern of us.

The authors of *Trafalgar Refought*, 1905, intended 'to produce a vivid picture of likely happenings at sea had Nelson lived in this present year of grace'

The time had come to give as good as we got. We were not near enough as yet to allow of the guns being successfully laid by my direction, and I passed the word down to bring both the turret guns to bear upon the enemy, and to fire as soon as she came on the sights. With a roar and with a crash which shook the tower in which I stood, the monster guns spoke their first word in war. Neither in the conning tower nor on the upper deck could the result of the shot be seen, but the signalman in the top gave us the welcome news that one shot at any rate had gone home. The guns' crews immediately commenced reloading, and looking through the slit of the tower I watched with intense anxiety the course of the enemy. There was a discharge from her decks, and in an instant there burst forth in front of my face, in all appearance on the very bow of the *Majestic*, a sheet of flame, followed by a crack like the rending of the thundercloud. At the same moment, with a din such as I had never heard in such close proximity, the broken fragments of the bursting shell beat down upon deck, on turret, on conning tower. The destruction was instantaneous, and within a certain area it was complete.

Stanchions, bollards, bulwarks—the deck itself—were ripped and torn like so much paper; but the solid face of the turret held its own with ease, and the muzzles of the guns, to my immense satisfaction, remained untouched.

A second shot was more disastrous, striking the battery on the port side about halfway down its length; it passed through the iron skin as though a gossamer and, bursting against the after-bulkhead, spread ruin and death through the crowded space. Never had a single shot worked more havoc, never did men recover themselves under such a stress with such coolness and bravery, as did the survivors in the battery of the *Majestic*. I had deep reason to congratulate myself upon the order which I had previously given, that the guns' crews on the starboard side should go below until their guns could actually be brought to bear. But for this order, the carnage would have been terribly increased. Meanwhile my gunners were not idle, and the great guns had again tried the thickness of the enemy's sides, this time firing chilled shell, which proved by their detonation that they had found an obstacle.[5]

It was now the crisis of the battle, for I saw the enemy rapidly changing course, and porting her helm make a circuit which would soon bring her broad on our port beam. Two courses were open to me: one was to hold on, to accept the encounter and run past at close quarters, exchanging fire on the beam; but a moment's consideration convinced me that to do so would be to favour the manoeuvre which my adversary had commenced, and which I had anticipated from the outset. Once abaft my beam, his after-barbette guns would be as serviceable for attack as his forward guns had already proved themselves to be. I was, unluckily, not in the same plight; my single stern gun was not of a calibre to engage singly against such odds. At any cost I must keep my turret bearing on the foe. The alternative course therefore alone remained open to me.

I knew the turning circle of my ship to a yard, and in an instant I determined what to do. I would hold on.

The two ships were now in a blaze from stem to stern, the tops, the superstructure and the batteries in sheets of flame; my own fire, alas! diminished by the fatal shell which had played such havoc in my main battery.

Suddenly I saw that the time had come. The enemy was already heading in towards us, and in another moment his starboard guns would have opened upon us. Suddenly I gave the order 'Starboard, hard-a-starboard'. The order was executed as soon as given, and the splendid ship, answering to the helm, came round with a swift, steady rush that made my heart leap for joy. We were within three hundred yards, and with our starboard bow presented to the enemy we rapidly approached to an even closer and more perilous range. The fire from the tops and superstructure had now slackened, for we had realized with sorrowful certainty the truth which modern warfare has revealed to us, that no exposed crew can live under the close fire of machine-guns. The loss on either side had been terrific for so short an engagement, and mere physical inability to load and work the guns had for a time caused the fire to slacken. It was not my intention that the ship should complete the half circle, and suddenly porting the helm, I bore down diagonally on the starboard quarter of the enemy.

It was at this moment that both my antagonist and myself resorted to another of the great weapons of destruction that had been confided to us, but which had not as yet been called into play. I had given a general instruction to the officers in charge of the torpedo-tubes to exercise their discretion in discharging their weapons as soon as I informed them that a suitable stage in the operations had been reached. I now gave the required signal, and it was at this moment, as I was subsequently informed, that the starboard White-head was discharged. Almost at the same instant, one of the few observers left in the top, a midshipman who had found his way up there since the machine-gun fire had slackened, noted that a similar step had been taken by the enemy. I need hardly say that I was unable myself to observe either of the incidents which I have just related; the position of the conning tower, the thickness of the smoke, and, above all, my intense preoccupation prevented my appreciating the danger to which at that moment my ship was exposed. By a fortunate chance, however, an action of mine beyond all doubt averted the peril which I did not myself foresee. The discharge of the torpedoes on either side was evidently almost coincident with my sudden alteration of course.

The *Majestic*, which a few moments before had been almost broad on the enemy's beam, had yielded to the pressure of the rudder and was already heading obliquely towards the other ship. Our own torpedo, running with an accuracy and speed which left nothing to be desired, passed close under the stern of our adversary. The chance which diverted our attack proved also our protection.

The midshipman marked the moment of the discharge of the enemy's torpedo, and his eye followed the line of bubbles as it advanced with furious speed in the direction of the *Majestic*. Against the Whitehead torpedo once fairly launched against an unprotected ship there is no defence; the track of the terrible projectile is plainly visible to the eye, but no power can avert its course or parry the fatal blow. Seething and hissing, the torpedo came nearer; if the ship steadies on this course she must inevitably be struck; the hand which controls her is in the conning tower, and he who directs it is all unconscious of what depends upon the next movement of the little wheel in front of him. But the ship is not yet round, the slight pressure on the spokes is maintained, the steam steering-engine passes it on with its full power to the rudder, and the ship steadily swings up to starboard. It is touch and go: the hundredth part of a point less and the striker will come full against the bow of the iron-clad, and the great problem of the value of the Whitehead torpedo in war will have been illustrated by a practical example which perhaps few of the ship's company will live to study. But no! Hidden for a second under the curling swell above the ram, the hissing bubbles reappear, hastening away on our port bow, and this time, at any rate, the *Majestic* is saved.

But to return to my own immediate part in the engagement. The ship, whose course had been in the shape of an S, was now completing her second half-circle, and the guns trained over the beam were still bearing upon the enemy as she steamed away from us. The starboard battery was remanned, and on both sides the firing was renewed with great vigour, though with a diminished accuracy which told that the loss of the leading men in the guns' crew and the fierce stress of the fight had produced their natural consequences. Suddenly, amidst the din of the firing, and easily distinguishable above the thunder of the guns, came the report of a fierce rapid explosion, followed by an instantaneous cessation of the enemy's fire. It was impossible to see what had taken place, but the fact remained beyond doubt, and I instantly determined to avail myself of it. It had been my intention to have kept my course at right angles to the enemy for a time, so that I might steam out of torpedo range, and again take up an end-on position.[6] But this idea was instantly abandoned. Once more the helm was put hard-a-port, and once more the *Majestic* circled round on the further side of her adversary. In a moment firing was renewed, and the enemy, to my surprise, came gradually round to port, as though about to cross my bows. It is a source of unfailing thankfulness to me to remember that at this crisis of the battle my mind was cool and collected, and my judgement perfectly clear. I turned to the lieutenant, and bade him transmit my orders through the ship. The orders were simple: 'Lay both guns ahead, full speed and prepare to ram.'

I stood with the steering-wheel in my hand watching every movement of the enemy; for a freshening breeze now carried the smoke swiftly away. It was evident that something of serious importance had taken place; her speed was diminished, for the interval between the ships decreased much more rapidly than the lateral distance.

I was convinced that for a time at any rate my adversary had lost control over his ship. We were now separated by a distance of less than 300 yards, and still the same apparent indecision marked the movement of the enemy, who was moving slowly with almost a full broadside presented to us, and somewhat on our starboard bow. Suddenly she appeared to gather full way, and her head began to come in slightly towards us. But it was too late; the time had come. I moved my hand, and the officer by my side flashed my will to the great turret guns. On both sides there was a roar and a crash which, had I not witnessed what befell a moment later, would have been the most terrific experience of my life. So much I can recollect, but the next few moments remain a blank on my memory. I was stunned, but the loss of consciousness was only for a few instants. I recovered to find myself leaning against what had an instant before been the wall of the conning tower, but which now was but a fragment of the wreck with which everything around me seemed overwhelmed.

The view, which had hitherto been obscured by the low roof of the tower, was now open, for not only had the roof gone, but a huge piece of the solid wall of the tower itself had been caught by the impact of the great steel shot, and now lay in bent fragments and huge slabs on the iron deck below. Of the three who, a moment before, had stood together in the tower, I was the only survivor. My signalman, crushed and mangled by the débris of the armour, lay in front of me. By my side my lieutenant had sunk down dead, his breast pierced by a single fragment of the flying metal. I raised my hand to my eyes to brush away the mist which I felt gathering upon them, and I found that my face was streaming with blood; but, while reason was left to me, it could only be concentrated on one thought and one object: that which lay before me.

Swept and shattered by the point-blank discharge of the terrible artillery to which she had been exposed, the *Majestic* still held her course, and her course was that on which I had launched her. On either side the last bolt was sped, the gun had had its final word; a greater power was now to give its decision, and from that decision there was no appeal.

Those who attach any value to the humdrum division of time and

'Then, with a deep, grinding, terrible crash, the ram did its work'

distance by the ordinary standards of arithmetic and the clock-face, will doubtless be able to calculate for their own satisfaction that the period occupied in traversing 250 yards at a speed of twenty miles an hour is to be reckoned in seconds only, and that the briefness of the allotted time gives no scope for the operations of the mind. Those who have ever stood in such a position as I stood in at that moment will laugh at these dogmatic calculations, and will know as I know that each second, and each portion of a second, is pregnant with its keen and separate consciousness.

The time, so heavily laden with the weight of the unknown result which it was about to produce, crept heavily along. But the end came at last. To the last moment, from the high deck and superstructure of the enemy, the fire from the machine-guns was maintained with a certain degree of energy. Our opponent lay between us and the southern sun, and I can at this moment remember the instant when the low bow of the *Majestic* entered the shadow she cast upon the water. Then, with a deep, grinding, terrible crash, the ram did its work. We had struck the enemy about fifty feet from her bow, and the slight change in her direction made the blow a slanting one.[7]

The *Majestic* shivered from stem to stern, and I could actually see the ironwork on the bow ripping and splintering as it forced its way into the opposing side. But it was not there that the fatal wound had been given. Far underneath the water-line, the protruding ram had struck a blow from which no human power could save the victim. For a moment all was still, save for the sound of the stretching and rending of the iron; then suddenly, with a steady but certain heave, the great ship seemed to bow down towards us. I watched her for a moment, long enough to see the surface of the deck as it showed up with the heel of the ship, and then I knew no more. The strain was over, my work was done, and it was not till a month later that I opened my eyes in Haslar hospital and came back once more to the land of the living.

Little remains for me to tell, but you will ask how the two ships fared in the encounter. Of the condition of my adversary I can tell you but little, for no subsequent examination revealed the work of our guns. Within a quarter of an hour after the ram of the *Majestic* struck her, the last vestige of the splendid ship had sunk beneath the waves, her hull absolutely broken in two by the force of the collision. We had time to save some hundred and twenty of her crew, and from them we learnt something of the effects of our cannonade. A projectile from our forward turret had struck one of a pair of barbette guns at four feet from the muzzle. The chase of the gun which was thus struck had been broken clean away, and the gun alongside of it had been so far dislodged from its slide that the loading gear had become unserviceable. The rapid discharges of the heavy quick-firing guns had been most destructive, and it was to a hundred-pound shot from one of these that the catastrophe, to which in all probability we owed our victory, was due. Falling full upon the side of the ship in the neighbourhood of the broadside torpedo discharge, the shot had carried a piece of the plate bodily inwards; and had come in contact with the striker of the Whitehead torpedo, just as it was about to leave the impulse tube. An explosion had instantly followed, the report of which we had heard, but of whose effects we had no conception at the time. Seventy pounds of gun-cotton exploding between decks had created havoc which might well appal the bravest. Nor was this all. The blast of the explosion had driven a heavy piece of metal against the connections of the steam steering-gear, and for a moment all control over the movements of the ship had been lost. Before the fatal moment the ship was again in hand; but it was too late, and the sequel has already been told.

One other fact we were able to discover: the last discharge from our turret guns, at 300 yards, had gone home. One shot, piercing the armoured belt like paper, had cut a passage through the ship almost from stem to stern. The other, striking the conning tower, had in an instant destroyed the gallant captain of the ship, together with all those who stood round him.

On our side, with the exception of the final catastrophe, the results had been no less terrible. The central battery, torn as I have already pointed out by a heavy projectile, had been riddled through and through by smaller shell of every description. No less than ninety of our brave fellows had fallen in this part of the ship in a courageous attempt to keep up the fire of the broadside guns. In the tops and on the superstructure, our losses were only limited by the number of men whom I had allowed to expose themselves in those dangerous positions. On the superstructure not one man in ten escaped without a casualty of some sort; but the thick walls of the turret had proved an adequate protection. With the exception of No. 1 of the starboard gun, who had been struck dead by a machine-gun bullet in the very act of aligning the sights, not a single man of either gun's crew had been touched.

But the outside of the turret showed the terrible nature of the attack to which it had been exposed. On the port side was a grazing dent ten inches in length, and scoring the round surface of the turret for a yard or more. A shell exploding on the glacis plate had broken away the iron in more than one place. While more remarkable than all the other injuries was the spot where a salvo of five simultaneous or successive blows from the six-inch guns had struck the steel-faced plating within the space of a square yard. It was at this point that the armour had suffered most, and the accumulated force of the attack had shivered the metal, which, starred and cracked in every direction, had fallen down in heavy fragments eight inches thick upon the deck.

The last discharge of the heavy guns, which had well-nigh proved fatal to me, had struck the *Majestic* in two places. The first shot, passing through the thin plating at the bow like paper, had imbedded itself deep in the forward bulkhead. The second shot, striking the crown of the conning tower, had carried away the iron roof and a large portion of the wall of the structure. Not a single shot was fired during the whole of the action from our after-gun. The blow of the ram which had annihilated our enemy had not seriously damaged the *Majestic*. The strain had shaken and dislocated the plating around the bow, but the consequent leakage was well kept in check by the collision bulkhead, and was mastered by the steam-pumps. But our loss in men, in protection, and in ammunition was too grave to allow of any alternative but a return into port, and the officer who succeeded me in command wisely decided upon adopting this course.

We returned to Portsmouth on the fifth day after leaving it. A single action, lasting less than thirty minutes, had decided the fate of two of the most powerful ships in the opposing navies.

As for myself, as I have told you, it was not till many days afterwards that I regained consciousness and learnt the facts which I have now recounted to you. During the weary period of my delirium, I acted over and over again every scene in the drama in which I had been recently engaged. Nor, when the light of reason returned, did the preoccupation pass from my mind, but from that time to this, and from now till the end of my life, the great crisis of my existence has ever been, and must ever be, the terrible time that I spent in the day of battle in the conning tower of *HMS Majestic*.

The Stricken Nation

HUGH GRATTAN DONNELLY

> The multitude lives only among the shadow of things in the PRESENT: the learned, busied with the PAST, can only trace whence, and how, all comes; but he who is one of the people, and one of the learned, the true Philosopher, views the natural tendency and terminations which are preparing for the FUTURE.
>
> Isaac Disraeli

The pages of universal history may be scanned in vain for a record of disasters, swifter in their coming, more destructive in their scope, or more far-reaching in their consequences, than those which befell the United States of America in the last decade. Standing on the threshold of the twentieth century, and looking backward over the years that have passed since the United States first began to realize the tremendous possibilities of the impending crisis, we are amazed at the folly and blindness which precipitated the struggle, while bewildered and appalled by its effect on the destinies of mankind.

In 1891 we behold a nation! A Republic of sixty-two millions! A heterogeneous mass of humanity welded by the benign influence of Liberty into a homogeneous nationality: contented, prosperous, powerful; an intelligent, refined, progressive people; peace and plenty within their borders from the Atlantic to the Pacific, and from the shores of the Great Lakes to the Gulf.

In 1892, we see the shattered fragments of the once great Republic. We read with tear-dimmed eyes of its tens of thousand of heroes fallen in defence of its flag, of its thousands of millions of treasure wasted in tardy defence, or paid in tribute to the invader. We see its great cities in ruins, its commerce destroyed, its Treasury bankrupt, and its people plunged in the direst depths of privation and despair; and finally, as we write, we can discern evidences of the beginning of that vast conspiracy which shall alter the destinies of the people of the Western World for ages to come.

The Dream of Security

The United States in 1890 was at peace with the world. So far as could be seen, there was nothing in our international relations that could afford the slightest cause for uneasiness. We had, it is true, some trifling questions regarding the Canadian fisheries, which, although suffered to remain unsettled for years, gave nobody the slightest concern. Our neighbors in the south were friendly and there were no diplomatic questions, calculated to cause irritation, in sight in any part of the globe. The country was prosperous. The Republican Party was in power for good or evil. The domestic questions which divided the people were mainly concerning revenue; and, when finally settled, the friendly differences to which their discussion had given rise were forgotten. The National Treasury was full to overflowing; the vast material resources of the country were being developed with unprecedented rapidity; capital found ample investment, and labor was well paid and contented; while our commerce, which during the war had been almost destroyed, showed signs of a permanent revival after long years of depression. Altogether, the American people could well afford to look backward and view their past with pride and complacency, and look to their future with pleasurable confidence.

Harrison's administration up to this time had been fairly respectable.[1] True, the Cabinet was, with one exception, of very mediocre material, but, as the President himself was a person of very ordinary ability, he could hardly have been expected to surround himself with men of greater intellectual capacity than himself. The political problems presented to the administration were not difficult of solution. The great questions growing out of the war—the status of the Negro, reconstruction, and the financial question—had been disposed of. The far-seeing and sagacious Secretary of State, James G. Blaine, had carried through his pet project of a Pan-American Congress and had made some progress in creating a sentiment favorable to commercial union and political friendship among the nations of the Western World.[2]

These efforts were watched with jealous interest by the nations of Europe. It meant the beginning of a struggle for commercial supremacy, in which the United States, with its geographical and political advantages, might reap vast rewards. It meant a decrease in British, German, and French influence in the South American nations; and it meant, above all, an increasing power and weight for the United States as a factor in determining the political future of

The cover-page illustration of *The Stricken Nation* prepared readers for the worst possible future

Central and South America. In no part of Europe did this effort to extend the influence of the United States meet with more attention than in England; but, with the exception of some bitter comment in *The Times* and other leading Tory organs, there was little outward show of resistance or resentment.[3] This was fully in accord with the spirit of British diplomacy. It was in fullest consonance with the policy pursued by that nation for years—a policy which, in its relations with the United States, had always secured for Her Britannic Majesty's Government the happiest results. It was the perfection of Machiavellianism.

In 1861, the traditional envy and hatred of England towards the United States could no longer be concealed. It was felt that the time had come when British orators, British journalists, and British statesmen could speak freely their sentiments, and that there was no longer occasion to disguise their real feelings by such wretched cant as 'Our common language, our common blood and our common religion.' All the professed friendship for the American nation proved to be the merest sham. English ships were let loose to prey upon our commerce; her money bought arms and munitions of war for the Confederacy; her sailors manned the rebel privateers, and each reverse to the Union arms was hailed with joyful acclaim from Land's End to John O'Groats, as if it were an English victory. The war ended and the Union was preserved. Gradually, but speedily, the tune was changed. We were once again the 'Greater England beyond the seas.' 'Shakespeare and Milton were our common heritage'; 'The bonds that bound the two great English-speaking peoples were bonds of blood and affection'; and so on *ad nauseam*. Froude and Dean Stanley and their tribe came over and preached fraternity and went back laden with American gold and bespattered with American gush. American toadies aped English fashions, and Anglomania raged from the Atlantic to the Pacific. And Her Majesty's Government's coddle kept American statesmen quiet and made each administration a handy and subservient adjunct of the British foreign office.

Successive administrations were befooled and duped by this shallow trick. Under Arthur's administration,[4] Frelinghuysen, who was Secretary of State, was a weak and plastic tool of the British Minister; and in every instance in which he played at diplomacy, where the interests of the American and British nations were concerned, the victory remained with the English. Such was the success of the British policy with a Republican administration; it was even greater with the Democratic administration which followed. President Cleveland appointed as his Secretary of State Mr Thomas F. Bayard, of Delaware. Mr Bayard had scarcely taken office when he began to give evidence of sycophantic adherence to English views and aims. His willingness to sacrifice the interests of his own country in order that he might gain the cheap reputation of being a successful treaty-maker was beyond all precedent; but the crowning infamy was in the bringing home of the American Minister at the Court of St James—a respectable old fossil named Phelps who had been dragged from deserved obscurity up among the Vermont mountains—to lobby through the American Senate a treaty, in which Mr Bayard had surrendered every point to the British Government, and against the ratification of which the American nation rose with splendid unanimity and righteous indignation. That treaty was rejected by the Senate.

British diplomacy encountered in James G. Blaine a statesman of vastly different mental calibre to that of his immediate predecessor in the office of Secretary of State. His chiefest claim to the respect and admiration of the American people was his intense patriotism. He was neither to be duped by Lord Salisbury's sophistry nor blinded by specious arguments of the British Minister at Washington. He had, it is true, the ambition to be considered a successful treaty-maker, and to leave the impress of his individuality on the history of the times in which he was in power; but he was not the man to sacrifice the interests or the honor of his country to gain that end. And so, when the interminable fisheries question was again taken up by Harrison's administration, British diplomacy received a check; and for the first time in many years it was found that the American people had as their spokesman a man keenly alive to the strength of his position and assertive and aggressive enough to maintain it. Negotiations, however, were begun for the settlement of the question and were proceeding without apparent difficulty when an event occurred which changed the complexion of affairs and brought the American people face to face with their relentless and traditional foe.

Portents of the Storm

Restless activity, and wanton aggression—especially when dealing with weaker powers—have been the controlling factors in British diplomacy for centuries. History presents an unbroken record of arrogant and unjust attacks on the integrity of every nation in the world where a pretext could be found for asserting English domination. This policy had been consistent and continuous, and it had succeeded so well in every part of the world as to be thoroughly justified, in the eyes of the British people, by the accomplished results. It had given the Crown valuable possessions in every quarter of the globe, and there were in Europe, Asia, Africa, and Australia portions of the Empire as loyal to the throne as Great Britain itself. Encouraged by the pusillanimous and sycophantic policy pursued by successive administrations in the United States, British diplomacy found in the American continent a new and promising field for the exercise of its powers. British influence was paramount in Mexico. Concessions for railway and steamship lines were freely granted in that country—and its rich commerce, after the American lines had been crowded out by British subsidized steamships, was wholly in the hands of Englishmen. The same remarks apply to the South American nations—particularly to Paraguay and Honduras, where the more aggressive policy was pursued, and where the political movements were largely controlled by British influence.

On the north, Canada was becoming more and more a standing menace to the Republic. Fortified by the assurance of British support when the emergency requiring it should arise, its press and public men assumed a tone of irritating defiance to and contempt for the United States. England had drawn liberally on the Imperial Exchequer for the material development of the Dominion and had resorted to every artifice to strengthen the bonds of political union and to increase and strengthen the loyalty of the people to the British Crown. A new order of Canadian nobility had been created by Her Britannic Majesty; a royal princeling had traversed the country to meet with enthusiastic demonstrations of attachment to himself and family; and from one end of the country to the other the super-loyal manifestations of unswerving fidelity to the British Crown left no doubt of the genuineness of the feeling which prevailed.

But it was not alone to the sentimental that the British Government gave its attention. It was the practical, after all, that was to be the prime factor in the results which shrewd and farseeing British statesmen were enabled to anticipate. Liberal subsidies were granted for the development of new steamship lines, and large appropriations were made for public works—notably for building strategic railways and for the improvement of water-ways, the navigation of which would be important in the event of war. The great fortifications of Halifax and Quebec were strengthened and a mighty fortress erected at Victoria,[5] Vancouver Island, to dominate the Northern Pacific. Ship after ship arrived from England with heavy guns from the royal arsenals at Chatham and Woolwich to fortify the British citadel on the Pacific slope, and in 1891 Canada, in its power to resist attack on the seaboard, was almost as impregnable as England itself.

There was something else being done, as it afterwards transpired. Thirty-six light-draft but powerfully armed gunboats, carrying guns of heavy calibre, were secretly constructed in the British dock-yards. They were of a new design and were referred to as 'portables'. Built in sections, they could be shipped to any part of the world and put together in a few weeks. On June 5, 1891, the first six of these boats had arrived by the Allan Line steamship, and they were placed at different points on the Canadian shores of the lakes. This was done in strictest secrecy. The sections were numbered and ready, but were not to be put together. *They were to be kept till wanted.*

Canada had for years subjected American fishing vessels to an unwarranted and humiliating espionage by her armed cruisers. This was not alone in Canadian waters but sometimes extended as far as the Grand Banks. American vessels, flying the American flag, manned by American seamen, and owned by American citizens, had been seized and taken into Canadian ports for some real or fancied violation of Canadian fisheries regulations. Some of these vessels had been sold; in some cases fines were imposed; in all cases the seizures were made with a haughty and contemptuous indifference to American feelings that showed that Canadian officials felt perfectly secure in the perpetration of high-handed outrages. There were, of course, feeble protests made by Frelinghuysen and Bayard when the outrages were reported: but a carefully worded letter from the British authorities proved a sufficient salve to injured American pride, and one outrage had been forgotten before another was perpetrated. During the debate on the Fisheries Treaty in the American Senate the Canadian officials redoubled their vigilance, and when that treaty was finally rejected they resumed their policy of harassing and annoying the American fishermen with a vindictive persistency more than before.[6] Cleveland's administration, with Mr Bayard as the figure-head of its foreign affairs, submitted. It opposed a policy of meekness and weakness to British brag and bluster. Matters were in the same unsettled condition when Harrison's administration came into power, and when Blaine was made Secretary of State. For some time after, the more flagrant outrages stopped. It was felt in London and Ottawa that Blaine was not the man to be insulted with impunity, and that an outrage on the American flag would be equivalent to a declaration of war. This was not what was desired at that time. *They were not quite ready.*

Having thus hurriedly and imperfectly glanced at the condition of affairs as existing at the opening of a decade, the most momentous in all American history, let us, briefly and concisely as may be, relate the events which, following in rapid and bewildering succession, led to the declaration of war. It is manifestly impossible, in the limits of a brief review of this character, to dwell at length on minor details which, however interesting and important in enabling posterity to judge of the cause and effect of the mighty conflict in its wider political aspect, are beyond the scope of the present work.

Until Canada began to insist upon what may be termed the 'headland line'—that is to say, to assume jurisdiction on the high seas, no matter how far the disputed point might be, provided it was within a line running direct between headlands on her coast, there was but little disposition on the part of the American people to object to her vexatious rules and regulations. It was freely conceded that Canada had absolute jurisdiction within a line *conforming to her coast outline* and three miles therefrom. But when in her pride and arrogance the Dominion insisted upon extending this line, it was felt it was high time to protest. This was done with some degree of vigor by Mr Blaine, but neither the British Government nor the Canadian authorities would concede the point at issue. Then, too, the Behring seal fisheries began to be fruitful of dispute, and Canadian sealers steadily encroached on American waters in defiance of the American Government. They went so far as to arm and threaten fight if their illegal traffic should be interfered with. These were two of the questions open for settlement between her Britannic Majesty's Government and the United States when the incidents occurred which put an end to all negotiations and left the questions at issue to be decided on by the stern arbitrament of war. It is only necessary for the purpose of this work to tell the story in the fewest possible words.

Reaching the fishing banks early in June, 1892, the American schooner *Monroe*, Captain Abner Grant commanding, had met with more than usual good fortune, and with a full cargo had squared away for Portland, Maine, to which port she belonged, and from which she had sailed two weeks before. The return voyage had hardly begun when the *Monroe* encountered a succession of violent gales, during which she narrowly escaped foundering, and in which she was so badly damaged that it was impossible to reach Portland. After making a harbor of refuge on the Canadian coast, and receiving such repairs as could be made, the *Monroe* resumed her voyage. She had scarcely cleared the harbor, and was unquestionably within the three-mile limit, when she was discovered by the Canadian fisheries cruiser *Middleton*. The *Middleton*, coming from the south'ard, laid her course so as to intercept the Yankee schooner, but the latter, with a brisk breeze, was almost a match in sailing qualities for the steamer. The latter's signal to heave-to was either not observed on board the *Monroe*, or, if observed, was ignored, and the schooner continued on her way.

At this time an accident to the *Middleton's* machinery caused some delay, which gave the American vessel a start of several miles, and she was fast putting a long stretch of blue water between herself and her pursuer. But the delay on the part of the *Middleton* was of short duration. Repairs were quickly made, and, with every pound of steam she could carry, the Canadian cruiser started in pursuit of the Yankee fisherman. A stern chase is proverbially a long chase, but steam at last proved too much for sail, and the *Middleton* gained on her prey. She was now within gunshot, and both vessels fully fifteen miles from the shore, and clearly out of and far beyond the headland line. Boom! A solid shot ricocheted ahead of the American schooner. Captain Jackson's answer was to run up the Stars and Stripes to the main, and keep crowding-on canvas. But British blood was up. The long gun on the *Middleton* was carefully trained and sighted, and, at the word, fired. Crash! The twelve-pound solid shot had hit the mark, and the foremast of the American vessel went by the board, carrying everything with it, and the hapless and helpless schooner lay tossing on the waves at the mercy of the enemy. Two men had been killed.

The *Middleton* steamed up alongside her crippled prize, and five minutes thereafter her chief officer and five men were on the deck of the American vessel. 'Haul down your flag, you damned Yankee,' was the command. Captain Grant drew his revolver. Another moment he was overpowered and in irons, the American flag was hauled down, the British colors run up, and the *Middleton*, as its crew gave cheer after cheer, was master of the situation. A hawser was made fast, and the cruiser, going about, headed for the Canadian coast, towing an American vessel, which had been attacked and fired upon on the high seas.

Eastward, while the chase by the *Middleton* of the helpless schooner was going on, there had appeared on the horizon the twin spars of a vessel, which, in the excitement, neither pursued nor pursuer had noticed. But on board that vessel there were watchful eyes, and at the sound of the firing her bow was turned to the spot, and with every pound of steam she could carry the stranger headed for the scene of the outrage. Hardly had the *Middleton* got under weigh with her prize—scarcely had the Union Jack taken the place of the American flag which had been outraged—than the reverberation of a sixty-pounder startled the crews of both the Canadian cruiser and her prey. And there, coming up within a mile, in all her stately beauty, was the American gunboat *Bennington*, a living witness of the outrage perpetrated against the flag. Five minutes later on the *Bennington* was alongside, and the Canadian and her prize under her guns. 'Surrender!' was the demand of the American. The commander of the *Middleton*, for answer, pointed to the British flag flying. There was a brief parley, but it was to the point. The American vessel had been witness to the outrage to the flag on the high seas. Five minutes later the British flag was hauled down. The captain of the *Middleton*, with some show of bluster, demanded a reason for the 'outrage'. 'Piracy on the high seas,' was the reply.

Within thirty-six hours thereafter the *Bennington* steamed into Portland, Maine, with the *Middleton*, and American prize-crew on board, under her guns; and the rescued Yankee schooner *Monroe* in tow. The event was an epoch. *It was the beginning of war!*

The Declaration of War

An event fraught with such tremendous consequences as were clearly in sight naturally created the most profound sensation in both continents. The American people were for the moment stunned. It was felt that the signal had been given for a conflict, the end of which no man could foresee. The press, without distinction of party affiliation, recognized the extreme gravity of the situation; and, contrary to all precedent, counselled extreme moderation among the people, and an abstinence from any action calculated to increase excitement or augment the difficulties in the way of an honorable and speedy settlement. The leading journals of both the political parties hastened to assure the administration of the confidence and support of all the people; and a United Nation, sinking all difference on domestic questions, awaited with a suppressed intensity that defies description the outcome of an incident which had startled the civilized world.

In England the sensation was beyond that created by any event since the beginning of—the Crimean War. But there was none of that calmness and suppression of feeling which characterized the American people. The papers, headed by the London *Times* and the *Standard*, were unanimous in their opinion on the duties of the government. That opinion may be summed up in a few words. It was that no explanation would suffice. An outrage had been perpetrated on the British flag, and the dignity of the British empire was at stake. The government was urged to demand 'Unconditional surrender; an unqualified apology; ample money reparation; or to declare war.' The original cause—the attack by an armed Canadian cruiser on a helpless American vessel— was wholly ignored. It was the capture of the *Middleton* by the *Bennington* only that was considered. All else but the capture of a vessel flying their flag was forgotten. The British Minister at Washington had been prompt to act. Twelve hours after the arrival of the *Bennington* and *Middleton* in Portland, his ultimatum was in the hands of Secretary Blaine, and its contents were in possession of the Cabinet in what proved to be the most important meeting held since the beginning of the Civil War.

Shortly after the adjournment of the Cabinet, the terms of the ultimatum submitted became known throughout the length and breadth of the Union. There was no misunderstanding the purport of the communication addressed by the British Minister to the American Government. His demands were that the *Middleton* should be immediately released and escorted by the *Bennington* to the entrance of the harbor of Portland; that the British flag be restored and saluted by the *Bennington*; that the officer in command of the American gun-boat should be dismissed from the service for 'an unprovoked and unprecedented insult to the British flag'; that an ample and unqualified apology be tendered to the British Government; and that a money indemnity be paid to the Dominion of Canada, to be divided among the officers and crew of their cruiser as some reparation for the indignity to which they had been subjected. 'In the event of any or all of these conditions being refused,' the British Minister added, 'I am instructed by Her Majesty's Government to demand my passports.'

With the publication of this document, from New York to San Francisco there arose such a swell of patriotic indignation—such an outburst of American feeling—as had not been witnessed since the firing on the flag that floated over Fort Sumter. North and south, east and west, there was but one opinion: that any American statesman who should submit to such terms was deserving of everlasting infamy and universal execration. A great wave of national excitement surged across the continent with irresistible force, and with one voice the American people demanded that no steps be taken that would result in an ignominious and disgraceful surrender.

The negotiations which followed were brief. The administration

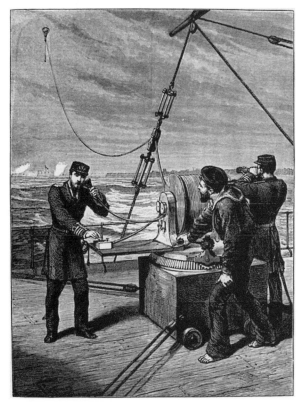

Front-page news for the readers of *The Graphic*: 'The Warfare of the Future—An Aerial Battery'

refused point-blank to accede to the demand of the British Government, while professing entire readiness to submit the questions at issue to arbitration, or to agree to the appointment of a joint high commission, to determine the responsibilities of the parties to the conflict. Twenty-four hours thereafter the British Minister sailed, under direct instruction from the home government, from New York on the Cunard line steamship. It was felt that, by this action, the last hope of a peaceful settlement had passed away; but now that the terrible imminence of war was so apparent, the heart of the nation stood still for a moment, hoping that some fortunate occurrence would avert the dread calamity. Meantime, the cables were actively employed in pour parlies between Washington and London; and the American Government had reason to hope that its manifest desire to avert a conflict would not be altogether fruitless on the other side.

But to all its conciliatory telegrams—to all its suggestions for such delay as might give the tremendous excitement pervading both countries time to subside, and allow reason to exercise its sober sway—there was but one answer: 'Her Majesty's Government,' concluded Lord Salisbury, in answer to the American Minister in London, 'cannot recede from the position it has taken; and the only terms that can be accepted are those contained in the memorandum submitted by Her Majesty's Minister in Washington to the Hon. the Secretary of State.' In other words, an abject apology and a humiliating surrender was the only course left for the American people; either that—or War!

Retreat was impossible. The American Government in its reply renewed its desire for a peaceful settlement; recounted the incidents which led to the capture of the *Middleton*; and, appealing to the judgment of the world for the justice of the position it had assumed, left the responsibility for the result upon the English Government and the English people. And now the American people, conscious of the tremendous perils which confronted them, sprang with splendid unanimity and spontaneous enthusiasm, tempered by a realization of their position, to the support of the Government. Thousands of volunteers were enrolled in each State; the American flag was in sight everywhere to encourage the halting and inspire the brave; and throughout the nation there was heard the busy note of preparation for the coming struggle. Since it was to be war, war let it be.

In no part of the country was the enthusiasm so great as in the West. Every village had its volunteers under arms, and the people were apparently eager for the beginning of the struggle. The Cincinnati *Enquirer* voiced the public sentiment in these words: 'North and south, east and west, there is but one opinion. We have tried every means to avert war; now, let it come! The American people, proudly conscious of the righteousness of their cause, and appealing to history for the vindication of their motives—this great nation, conscious of its strength and power, will not shrink from any sacrifice that may be demanded.' Cincinnati was several hundred miles from the seaboard; and it was not yet clearly apparent how Cincinnati and the interior could suffer much by the war, no matter how fiercely it raged on the coast line. Cincinnati and other cities subsequently discovered several things they had not known, or had forgotten at this time. The feeling that prevailed at this time may be judged from more than the contemporary utterances of the press. In all public assemblages every device to fire the American heart was resorted to. The speeches were of the most inspiring character, and no popular entertainment was without its topical song bearing on the issue. One of these enjoyed phenomenal popularity. It was the merest doggerel, but it caught the popular fancy. Here is a sample verse:

> The British boast they'll scourge our coast
> From Northern Maine to Texas.
> And give us hell with shot and shell,
> And otherwise will vex us.
> The boasting knaves! They're scurvy slaves
> From Land's End to Northumbria!
> Our Yankee steel again they'll feel—
> We'll give 'em Hail Columbia!

It was such songs as this, and speeches as were punctuated with cheers at every reference to the American flag, American rights, and American honor; and such editorials as expressed the popular feeling in 'Millions for defence—not one cent for tribute', that kept the enthusiasm of the people up to the highest pitch. The loyalty of the nation and its readiness to make sacrifices when called upon were to be speedily tested. On the morning of the 22nd day of June the American people realized that the die was cast. *England had declared war!*

The Terrible Awakening

There now came to the American nation a terrible awakening from that dream of security in which it had indulged for years and years. It found itself vulnerable where it should have been invincible; weak when it should have been strong; powerless, when its strength should have been irresistible. Its coastline of 4,000 miles was undefended at any point by a single fortification capable of successfully resisting attack by modern warships carrying guns of the heaviest calibre. Its arsenals were useless for the manufacture of modern ordnance; its guns were of an obsolete pattern, and of no use; its navy, small as it was, was scattered; its vessels for harbor defence existed only on paper in plans filed at the Navy Department. Most of the powerful ironclads that might have served in the hour of need, vessels of the type of the monitors *Puritan, Montinvant* and others, were rotten hulks in League Island, Brooklyn, Pensacola, and Norfolk navy yards.

Oh, the shame of it! Oh, the folly of it! Now began at every city and on every harbor the work which should have been begun and finished years before. Every gun foundry was ordered to work night and day to turn out the heaviest artillery possible; and at the Midvale Steel Works in Philadelphia, at Bethlehem, at Watervliet, and other points, orders were given for eight-hour shifts—three to the day. Thousands of men were at work on the fortifications of every city, and the entire engineer corps of the United States Army was found insufficient to supply the demand, while civil life afforded but few officers of practical training and experience.

There were a million men who could be put under arms; but there was no enemy for them to attack—no adversary that they could meet in a field of battle to repulse. Then the cry was raised for an invasion of Canada; but there were no modern rifles with which to arm the troops, and even in the matter of field artillery we were far behind any second-rate power in Europe. Troops were hurriedly sent from the interior to all the seaboard cities; but for what? Goliath was helpless and stationary with his club, while David advanced in leisurely security to smite the giant in the forehead with the missiles from his sling! In the mean time, every British vessel in American ports was under orders by cable to sail for home; and in great fleets they sailed away, some in ballast, some with half cargo, some crowded to the uttermost capacity with passengers anxious to get beyond the reach of the dangers impending. And, like a covey of frightened partridges, the American coasting vessels ran for the nearest ports out of the way, as they fondly hoped, of the destroyers which were hourly looked for from every headland in the offing. In New York, Boston, Philadelphia, Baltimore—in fact, in every city on the Atlantic seaboard or on the Gulf, in the cities on the Lakes and along the Pacific Coast, the first feeling of apprehension and alarm had speedily developed into universal panic and dismay. In New York and Boston a reign of terror prevailed. The rich and well-to-do were fleeing by thousands to the interior, business was suspended, and order was rapidly giving place to anarchy. To sum up in a word, it was panic from Portland to the Rio Grande!

England was ready! England had been making ready for this for years. Her statesmen were far-seeing. They knew that some day the struggle was to come; and their policy for generations had been to be fully in readiness when it did come. On the Continent she had nothing to fear. Her differences with the Great Powers had been settled, and the *entente cordiale* which existed between the British and German Governments was a guarantee that no overt act on the part of Russia or France—both supposed to be favorably disposed to the United States—would be tolerated to her injury without prompt interference by Germany. Her navy was in magnificent condition and in the highest state of efficiency, and ready at a moment's notice for aggressive action. Her defences at home were as perfect as could be; not that there was any fear of attack by the United States—such an idea was ridiculous!—but that England knew that the nation that was not prepared to resist attack is the nation that invites it. But it was not alone at home that England had been preparing, and was now fully prepared to act on the occasion that had now arrived. For years she had been steadily drawing a cordon around the American nation—north, south, east, and west—and it was now complete. It was when Americans examined the map that they realized how helplessly and hopelessly they were in the power of their hereditary enemy. When we look at the map and see how admirably the British policy of preparation had been carried on, we are at a loss whether to wonder more at the statesmanship which, through generations, had carried forward the plan to perfection, or at the criminal blindness and supineness of the American people who had allowed it to proceed without question.

North were Halifax and Quebec; Bermuda on the east; Kingston on the south-east; and Vancouver on the north and west! These fortifications, bristling with armaments that made them impregnable; these harbors, protected and defended by the heaviest guns, assuring ports of refuge for the merchantmen and ports of rendezvous, with enormous supplies of coal, provisions, and ammunition for the equipment of cruisers; these British outposts, within forty-eight hours' steam of the richest American cities, were now, it was afterwards discovered, thoroughly in readiness for all demands that could be made upon them.

So much for the ports on the seaboard. Now, for the condition of affairs on the Lakes. Almost immediately with the arrival of the news of the capture of the *Middleton* came orders by cable to construct the gunboats which had been built in sections in England and forwarded to Canada long before. There had been six originally. There were now twenty-one; and a week after the order was given every available man that could be put to work was busy night and day putting the gunboats together under the direction of skilled naval constructors sent out from England. It had been forgotten by American statesmen, but not by English, that the treaty of 1817 between the United States and England limited each nation to a small naval force upon the Lakes. Americans had forgotten that the springing up of the scores of cities and towns—Chicago, Detroit, Cleveland, Erie, and a host of others—should have demanded an abrogation of this treaty long before. They forgot that our vast boundary on the north was now at the mercy of British gunboats, and that, even if that nation had not had a navy for lake service then ready, their sea-going vessels, drawing fourteen feet, could pass the rapids of the St Lawrence and the Falls of Niagara by canals, and obtain entrance from the high seas to the Lakes. Which, in fact, is exactly what they did. All this had been pointed out to Americans before, but it made no impression. The dangers were only delusions existing in the brains of alarmists, and of those who had no sympathy with the sentiments of everlasting amity expressed and existing and always to exist between the two great branches of the Anglo-Saxon race, with the common heritage of Shakespeare, and so on and so forth. Such was the condition of affairs at the outbreak of the war.

Preparations for National Defence

By the earliest light of dawn on the morning of July 1, 1892, the advance guard of the British fleet was sighted off Fire Island, and the news that the enemy was now within striking distance of New York was instantly telegraphed throughout the entire country. As ship after ship appeared on the horizon, it was soon ascertained that this advance guard was the British North Atlantic squadron, comprising the *Bellerophon*, the *Canada, Comus, Partridge*, and *Buzzard*, under the command of Rear-Admiral Watson. These vessels, in obedience to orders, separated as they neared the coast, in such a manner as to effectually blockade the entrance to the harbor from Sandy Hook to Fire Island. They made no sign of antagonism; merely steamed slowly up and down, watching, waiting.

Then, throughout the Union, anxious hearts asked the question, 'How is New York defended?' 'What have we done to resist attack by a hostile fleet?' And as the truth became known, the people were dismayed and astounded. New York's defences—but why speak of them? There were none! New York, the great metropolis of the Western Continent, was, so far as its fortifications were concerned, absolutely at the mercy of the enemy. In the harbor on Governor's Island fortifications *commenced in 1831 were found unfinished in 1892!* Cause assigned: no appropriations. Fort Wood of course was incomplete—cause assigned: no appropriations. Fort Hamilton, commanding the Narrows; Fort Lafayette, Fort Wadsworth, Fort Tompkins, the Glacis gun battery, north of Fort

Tompkins; Battery Hudson, on Statten Island; the North Cliff battery, were all useless. Their works were out of repair, and, had they been long ready to receive their guns, there were none to supply. On the Sound approach, Fort Schuyler and Willett's Point Fort were antiquated in design and incomplete. *The defences of every American port on the Atlantic, on the Pacific, on the Lakes, and on the Gulf were found in the same condition; and not one American city, subject to attack from the sea, was found to possess a single defensive work of modern construction, or to be supplied with modern guns of such calibre as to afford a fighting chance against an enemy equipped for action according to the requirements of the time!* What wonder that the American people hung their heads with shame! What wonder that, in their heart of hearts, they called down maledictions on the men responsible for this crime against a nation!

Yet the country had not altogether lost hope. In every shipyard, on every fortification, in every gun foundry, and in every arsenal, thousands and tens of thousands of men were at work day and night in the preparations for defence. On the morning of July 2, the British squadron was still in sight. Not a gun had been fired, and it was hoped that the communications known to be passing between the American and British Governments might yet avert the danger. The silence of the British men-of-war was construed to mean that they had orders to await the outcome of the negotiations which were fondly believed to be progressing favorably. But this hope was soon dispelled. During the day sail after sail appeared in the offing, and before nightfall not less than twenty-one British men-of-war had concentrated within sight of Fire Island. And now all hope fled. It was seen that the delay in action on the part of the British fleet was simply to give time to bring together an invincible force, against which resistance would be useless, and which could crush, if need be, the combined American navy. This fleet was the most powerful that had been concentrated for offensive operations in history. It comprised, besides the vessels composing the North Atlantic squadron already referred to, *HMS Blake*, 9,000 tons, carrying two 9.2 inch guns; the *Repulse*, the *Resolution*, the *Devastation*, the *Trafalgar*, the *Inflexible*, the *Iron Duke*, and the *Royal Sovereign*, all armored or protected cruisers of the highest modern tonnage and armament; besides a number of torpedo cruisers, and light-draft, fast-sailing gunboats. And this mighty squadron, as night fell, was, in obedience to the signal rockets which could be plainly seen from the higher buildings in New York, making ready for the work of the morrow.

Hardly had the intelligence of this mighty squadron's appearance off New York harbor been flashed across the country than universal dismay was created by the telegrams from a dozen other points announcing the appearance or the approach of British men-of-war. The British Pacific squadron, as fast as intelligence reached vessels comprising it, began to concentrate off San Francisco; and the hurrying fleet of fugitive American coasters reported that the Delaware and Chesapeake Bays, commanding the approaches to Philadelphia and to Baltimore and Washington, were already in possession of the enemy. From Kingston, Jamaica, a British force had already sailed to threaten the Gulf ports, and on the Lakes the first four of the light-draft gunboats had been completed, and were already reinforced by two or three light-draft cruisers, which had found their way from Halifax to places assigned them. Portland, Boston, Charleston, Savannah, and other cities reported ominous signs of impending danger, and a general exodus of people who could get away to the interior. There was a blockade of the American coast now in existence which effectually put a stop to all commerce except that on the inside lines.

England, it was now plainly seen, was preparing to strike a blow, the effects of which would be felt for centuries to come. She had been preparing for just such a crisis for years, and was now fully prepared. With nothing to fear in Europe, she could concentrate all her forces for an attack which she well knew the United States was powerless to resist. For years her spies and agents had been at work in every department of the American government. She knew the weakest of our weak defences better than even our own engineers. She had on file plans of every port, charts of every harbor, tables of the valuation of every seaport town, particulars of our torpedo arrangements; and she had her own soldiers specially detailed for the duty, in the guise of enlisted men in every branch of our service. There were British spies on our ships, British spies in our arsenals; and British influences had for years been powerful enough to defeat every attempt that was made to get appropriations for defence. This was accomplished by American representatives whose election to Congress to perform this very duty had been secured by a lavish outlay of British gold.

Now that the English fleet was in position; now that a score of British cannon, some of them sixty-seven-ton guns, capable of throwing a 1,250-pound shell a distance of ten miles, were trained on New York; now that it was merely a matter of hours when half the cities of the Atlantic coast would be under the guns of a hostile British fleet—what hope remained? There were those who proclaimed that England would never dare to bombard a helpless city—to commit such an outrage on civilization—to draw upon herself the universal execration of mankind. These people forgot that such considerations never weighed with England when a blow was to be struck against her enemy. They forgot that her long and bloody record was against it. They forgot that they had to deal with a nation that justified the employment of Indian savages against American women and children during the Revolutionary war; that exulted in the blowing of Sepoys from the mouths of cannon; that bombarded, in spite of the protests of the world, Alexandria in Egypt. They forgot that this was the merciless foe with which they had to deal. And they forgot that the hereditary and traditional hatred of the British nation against their chiefest rival for commercial supremacy would justify any action that would crush the American Republic and avenge the defeat inflicted by that nation on the British arms in the Wars of the Revolution and the War of 1812.

On the morning of July 3, the Mayors of New York and Brooklyn, the dignitaries of the religious denominations, prominent members of the banking and commercial and shipping interests, and a number of foreign consuls, in all a body of over one hundred representative citizens, had steamed down the bay in response to a peremptory summons from the British Admiral. They were taken on board a gunboat, and no time was lost in acquainting them with the gravity of their position. 'New York,' said the British officer, 'is at our mercy. It will be spared on these conditions: an absolute and immediate surrender; the payment of FIVE HUNDRED MILLIONS OF DOLLARS within twenty-four hours; and an uncontested occupation of such points in the harbor by vessels of this fleet as may be designated.' The committee stood transfixed. They appealed for delay, for an opportunity to confer with the national authorities, for mercy on the helpless city. The Admiral was inexorable. 'The tribute must be paid within the time named. If it is not,' added the Admiral, 'you will instantly remove all noncombatants, as I will open fire in twenty-four hours.' The terms became known in New York immediately on the return of the committee, and a panic began that was simply indescribable. The people by hundreds of thousands were flying in all directions, and all semblance of order was soon at end. The British Admiral was as good as his word. When he had spoken, *New York was already doomed to destruction.*

The Destruction of New York

Reddened by the glare of flames from hundreds of its buildings; its streets drenched with the blood of thousands of its people slain; a mob of 10,000 of the scum of its population, delirious with drink and despair, pillaging the palaces of its millionaires and committing the most fiendish outrages upon the weak and helpless; its splendid architectural monuments, churches, hotels, schools crumbling to ruin beneath the terrible missiles which were falling with unerring aim and with titanic force; the crash of solid shot, spreading ruin on every side; the shriek of shells speeding in their flight, and leaving where they fell a track of death and destruction; the hoarse shouts of command from the Spartan band of heroes who braved death in its most terrible shape in a vain effort to save the city; the cries and moans of the wounded; the yells and screams of the frenzied fugitives, who ran hither and thither vainly trying to find shelter from the deadly hail of iron or to escape the falling walls; the roar of the awful conflagration which now raged on both sides of Broadway, from Chambers Street to Madison Square, and which was spreading east and west with terrific rapidity—such was the terrible tableau of a terrestrial hell presented by New York City on the night of July 4, 1892.

Yielding no jot of his terrible purpose, the British Admiral had given orders for the bombardment of the city almost simultaneously with the departure of the citizens who had come to beg for mercy. There was, it is true, a few hours' delay; but the delay was caused in waiting signals from another British fleet which had been reported making its way towards New York by the Sound. This fleet consisted of the *Temeraire*, the *Black Prince*, and the *Thunderer*, all representative of the most powerful ships in the British navy, and a number of swift-sailing but powerfully armed gunboats—in all, eight vessels. These found no trouble in making the passage by the Sound until they reached the fort at Willet's Point. Here they were fired on, but two shots from the *Black Prince* reduced that antiquated structure to a battered ruin, and compelled its speedy evacuation. The garrison withdrew to Flushing, and an hour after the long buildings used as quarters on the fort were in flames. At four o'clock on the afternoon of the 3d of July, the British fleet had taken position in Flushing Bay; and as night fell its signals to the fleet off Sandy Hook announced that all was in readiness for the work of destruction to begin.

Giving the answering signal, the British Admiral gave orders for a simultaneous attack, and the dread havoc began. The booming of

THE FALL OF WASHINGTON

Washington suffers the same fate as New York

the great guns of such terrible monsters as the *Black Prince* and the *Temeraire* was followed by a combined roar of cannon from the entire fleet; and then there rained upon the hapless, helpless, defenceless city such destruction as had not been seen on earth since Almighty God visited his terrible wrath upon the fire-swept Cities of the Plain. There was no waste of shot or shell. From the first, the distance had been as accurately judged as if the gunners were at practice on a stationary hulk in Portsmouth Harbor. It had been confidently believed that the guns of the fleet would be of insufficient power to reach New York City, and that Brooklyn would be the first to suffer. But this proved to be a mistake. At the beginning of the bombardment, Brooklyn escaped comparatively uninjured, the elevation of the guns enabling New York to be reached at every point from Canal Street down to the Battery. St Paul's Church, the Astor House, and the City Hall were among the first buildings to be struck, and then the great newspaper offices on Park Row. Then shell after shell began to fall in the densely populated poorer districts lying towards the East River, and an hour after the bombardment began a shot crashed into the New York end of the Brooklyn Bridge. Two hours later a fifty-four-inch shell exploded about three hundred feet from the Brooklyn side of the bridge, and an hour later that vast structure had parted and was in ruins.

And now fire began to add its dreadful horrors to the scene. Flames burst forth in a dozen different places, the greatest fire at this time being in the centre of the dry-goods district; while further up town there were a dozen buildings burning in as many blocks. It was now seen that nothing could save the city from total destruction. The flames speedily got beyond all control, and were spreading in all directions. In the mean time, tens of thousands of the poorer inhabitants had taken refuge in the upper part of the city, believing that they were out of danger. But their sense of security was soon rudely disturbed. Shots from the fleet in Flushing Bay began falling up as far as Fortieth Street, and St Patrick's splendid cathedral was among the first of the uptown structures to receive the shock. One of its great towers had fallen, crashing through the roof, and killing hundreds of people who were praying in the vast temple.

It was at this time that all semblance of order in the upper part of Manhattan Island began to be lost. Hitherto the police and the National Guard combined had managed to keep the riotous and desperate elements in control; but as block after block was abandoned, and the frenzied and maddened people became savage and desperate with liquor, there began to be concerted attacks on the banks and jewelry stores and the residences of the rich. For a time, by desperate courage and by a free use of arms, the police and soldiers seemed likely to succeed in their efforts to prevent a general sacking of the city; but as the shells from the ships in Flushing Bay began to explode, causing the most frightful casualties, they were forced to give way at several points. This was the beginning of the end. The mob—or, rather, the mobs, for half-a-dozen of them were at work along Madison and Fifth Avenues, and as far down town as they could venture to meet the fire, now sweeping upward with tremendous fury—were apparently the only people left in the city; and then began scenes which cast into the shade the most horrible excesses of the French Revolution. Men were shot down like dogs trying to defend their dear ones; women and children were attacked on the open streets; and, drunken with fury and the feeling of absolute license, the wretches aided the enemy in wantonly applying the torch in the finest residences in New York; and soon, for miles along the great uptown thoroughfares, the palatial residences were a raging, seething mass of flames.

Reaching points beyond Harlem River, and encamped by hundreds of thousands along the Jersey flats and from the heights of the Palisades, and from every point to which they had fled for safety, the desolate people, on the next morning, beheld under the great clouds of smoke which hung over Manhattan Island the ruins of New York. Fires were still burning fiercely in a score of places; but the scarred and blackened ruins of its buildings, the shipping in its harbor burnt to the water's edge, the awful silence of desolation which prevailed, told all that there remained to tell of the fate of the commercial metropolis of the Western World.

The Doomed Cities of the Coast

Any attempt to follow in detail the occurrences of dreadful import which happened in rapid succession after the fall of New York would be useless. It would require the genius of a Gibbon or a Macaulay to describe the long chapter of disasters which befell the American Republic, and a library of ponderous tomes to record the list of the wounds inflicted by a victorious and remorseless enemy. Perhaps a republication of some of the dispatches from different points, as they appeared in the New York papers—which papers, by the way, were then published in Plainfield, NJ—will give some idea of the extent of the calamities which befell the nation:

Chicago, July 11—Panic prevails here. A fleet of Canadian and British gunboats is reported within one hour's sail of the city. Thousands of people are flying to the interior, and abandoning their property . . . *Later*—The British fleet has appeared, and is now taking position off the city. A demand has been made for the payment of three hundred millions of dollars, under penalty of immediate bombardment . . . *Later*—Chicago authorities have pledged the city for the amount of the tribute demanded, and the British fleet, with guns shotted and ready for action, awaits payment.

Boston, July 6—The British fleet opened fire on the city at six o'clock this morning. Fort Warren opened fire on the man-of-war *Hercules*, but did no damage; and the guns on Fort Winthrop were useless. Fort Independence made no attempt at resistance. The city at this writing—9 a.m.—is on fire, and in danger of total destruction. God help us!

Philadelphia, July 6—It has been learned that the British fleet, now increased to sixteen vessels by recent arrivals from Bermuda, is advancing up the Delaware. Our city is absolutely helpless, there being no defences. A meeting has been called by the Mayor, and authority has been given to pay whatever tribute may be demanded . . . *Later*—League Island is in the hands of the enemy, and the city at its mercy. Three hundred millions is the price to be paid the invaders.

Portland, Maine, July 7—This city has capitulated, and British forces have taken possession of Forts Gorges, Preble, and Scammel, and are busily engaged in mounting guns of heavy calibre. Not one of these forts had a piece of ordnance to repel attack, and the capitulation of the city was inevitable.

Washington, July 10—All the government archives are being removed from this city, and troops have been concentrated here to guard government property. It is proposed to temporarily remove the seat of government to Springfield, Ill. The occupation of the city by the British fleet, which has now captured Norfolk, and to which Fortress Monroe, after a gallant struggle, surrendered last night, is inevitable.

Baltimore, July 10—The city surrendered to the British at nine o'clock this morning.

New Orleans, July 11—Advices from South Pass say that British cruisers have command of all approaches, and that no vessel can enter or depart without certain capture.

San Francisco, July 13—The British Pacific fleet has its guns trained on this city. We have no means of defence, and surrender and the payment of any tribute demanded is inevitable.

Cleveland, Ohio, July 9—This city has been bombarded and is in flames.

To continue the list is useless. Every city of any importance on the seaboard and on the Lakes was promptly invested by the enemy, and any refusal to pay the enormous tribute demanded was speedily followed by bombardment.

So much for the coast. What of the interior? With the first approach of the enemy, a universal stampede of the panic-stricken people began. Naturally, the well-to-do were the first to fly, and those who remained were among the most desperate and vicious of the population. As the danger became more imminent, all restraint of the dangerous classes was at an end, and the most frightful excesses were committed. It is estimated that the united sum of the tribute paid by the beleaguered cities in the first ten days of July amounted to 1,600 millions of dollars. The loss of life was enormous. In New York City alone it is estimated that over 12,000 people were killed and wounded by shot and shell, or crushed by the falling buildings before they could escape, or consumed in the awful conflagration which raged for three days succeeding the bombardment. The few ships that constituted the American navy were speedily destroyed or captured. They had no ports of refuge, and fell an easy prey to the swarm of British cruisers that were off the coast.

The cities in the interior of the country and the thousands of towns and villages far removed from danger of attack or invasion by sea or land felt from the beginning a sense of security to which the seaboard places were strangers. The concentration of large bodies of troops in the vicinity of some of these places, and the influx of thousands of fugitives, created a temporary prosperity. But it was only temporary. With the closing of our ports and the destruction of our shipping, the immense harvest of the year found no market abroad, and the advances of the banks to move the crop, now deprived of a market, created a financial panic. One by one the banks began to fail; an era of financial stress ensued; the great stores and manufactories began to suspend, and the enormous drain on the country to pay tribute soon produced its inevitable result. Money became scarce; work there was none; and soon there came a time when hunger began to be felt among the laboring masses of all the great cities. The results may be imagined. Bread riots began in many places, and a time of dire distress and privation followed. The rich were poor, and the poor were penniless.

At last, when every city of any importance on the Atlantic, on the Lakes, or on the Pacific slope had been captured, or bombarded, or spared in consideration of the payment of tribute of unparalleled amounts, British vengeance began to show signs of satiety; and a temporary cessation of hostilities was agreed upon to give time for the assembling of Congress to take action on the terms upon which the British Government was willing to declare peace. All our forts, originally planned for the defence of our cities, were now in possession of the enemy, and the Union Jack had replaced the Stars and Stripes on every fortification on the seaboard. Thousands of troops had now arrived from England, and garrisons were established, while the works were mounted with British guns *turned against the cities* that had capitulated, or that had been destroyed during the bombardment. It is true that within the entire country, a score of miles from the coast, the authority of the United States prevailed, but it was merely nominal. The nation was rapidly drifting into a state of anarchy. Many members of Congress had fled, fearing the vengeance of the people they had betrayed by their failure to provide for a defence of the coast; and when, on August 5, Congress convened at Springfield, Illinois—the temporary capital—scarcely more than half the members of the Senate and House answered to their names.

No pen can describe the scene which followed when the House was called to order. Strong men cried like children as they contemplated the ruin of their country; and some, losing control, called aloud upon God to avert further calamity. The session was brief. It had been called to consider the terms dictated by the victorious enemy. And when these terms became known, there was called by the President a day of fasting and prayer for all the people, that Divine intercession be asked to save the Union of the Fathers from everlasting ruin.

During the brief session of Congress—it only lasted twenty-one days—the Nation was plunged into the deepest despair. The sombre hues of mourning were to be seen on every side; the public buildings were draped in black; all places of amusement were closed, and in the churches of all denominations religious services were being held almost without intermission. The voice of the people was hushed to a whisper, an universal sadness and despondency prevailed among all classes of society. It was felt that hope had fled, and that nothing remained for the once proud and mighty American people but a future of degradation and despair.

The Treaty of Peace

On the morning of the third day after the assembling of Congress, the President laid before the Senate the communication from the British Government covering 'the terms upon which Her Britannic Majesty's Government would consent to a cessation of hostilities'. It was now for the first time that the American people realized their utter helplessness in the power of their hereditary, relentless, vindictive, and bitter enemy. Every important seaboard city had either been reduced to ruins or was under the guns of the enemy's fleet; hundreds of millions had already been paid in tribute to avert destruction of those that had escaped bombardment; the vast armies that had sprung up like magic for the invasion of Canada were held helpless and impotent by the ultimatum of the British authorities that the invasion of Canada at any point by an American force would compel the opening fire on every city that had hitherto escaped destruction and that was within range of the guns of the investing squadrons. From Philadelphia, Chicago, Baltimore, San Francisco, New Orleans, and many smaller cities came agonized appeals from the people to avert their destruction. And in the face of all these supplications there was but one thing to do—countermand the order for the invasion of Canada and await the conditions of peace which were daily expected from London.

Some historians have taken the ground that the American forces should have pushed forward despite the British warning of such terrible retaliation. It has been urged that the threats of deliberate bombardment of helpless cities which had already paid tribute to avert their destruction would never have been carried into effect. But the people on the seaboard knew too well that the same terrible foe that had already reduced New York and Boston to ruins would stop at no step, however wanton and merciless, that would further crush their helpless adversary.

Nor were they mistaken. From the moment the first gun was fired, the British authorities, anticipating the result for which they had been secretly preparing for years, had already determined to make peace on such terms as would for ever crush their only rival for the commercial and political supremacy on the Western continent. Briefly stated—and divested of the many minor details with which each proposition was elaborated—the terms of peace dictated by the British Government were as follows:

1. The payment of a war indemnity by the United States of

America, of 10,000 millions of dollars within a period of twenty years from the signing of a treaty of peace.

2. The uncontested occupation by British forces of such forts in the Atlantic, Gulf, Pacific, and Lakes as Her Majesty's Government shall designate.

3. The abrogation of the Treaty of 1817, in so far as it applied to the presence of British men-of-war on the Lakes; Her Majesty's Government to have full rights to maintain such a fleet as in its judgment shall be necessary for the protection of British interests; but no American vessels of war to be constructed except for revenue purposes.

4. California, Oregon, Florida, and parts of Louisiana to be hereafter designated to be added to the British Crown.

5. An entire disarmament of all American forces except certain numbers of State militia as may hereafter be agreed upon.

6. The war indemnity to be a first claim upon all American revenues, and three British Commissioners to have charge of such revenues until said indemnity be paid.

Now that the purpose of England became manifest, a purpose that unmistakably meant the destruction of the American Republic, a tremendous outburst of popular feeling followed. In all the interior cities, at every point removed from danger from the guns of the enemy's fleet, great meetings were held to protest against such shameful surrender of American rights. Tens of thousands more of volunteers sprang to arms in every State, and the universal sentiment proclaimed was that, rather than submit to such humiliating and degrading terms, resistance should be carried on until the last man fell and the last dollar was expended in defence of the flag and the liberties of American free-men.

England, during the temporary truce granted by the British commander, had not been idle. Every possible emergency that might arise during the war had been foreseen; every contingency had been provided for. For years before, every steamship in her merchant marine had been constructed on certain plans approved of by the Admiralty; and at the first signal of war all the great transatlantic steamships sailing under her flag were ordered to her naval dockyards. Some were speedily equipped as transports; others, mounted with batteries of moderate calibre, were soon transformed into cruisers, and ordered to different points to relieve the regular men-of-war in foreign stations, which, in turn, were despatched to certain designated American ports, and the whole fleet of ocean tramps were speedily commissioned as store and supply ships and sent as tenders to the great fleets anchored in American waters. The result was that, while the American Congress was awaiting the terms proposing peace, England had time to assemble the mightiest armada of history and invest every port on the Atlantic seaboard. And now, in addition to the greater cities which were helpless under the guns of her ironclads, scores of smaller cities—Galveston, Savannah, Charleston, Norfolk, New London, and many others— were in the power of the enemy when the signal should be given for a renewal of hostilities.

England had no further need to temporize. It was no longer a proposal to discuss the terms of peace. Within forty-eight hours after the terms above-named had been submitted, the ultimatum was received. No further delay could or would be granted; the immediate and unconditional acceptance of each and every condition was demanded or every city within range of British cannon would be reduced to ruins. *This meant, now that England had had all the time she needed to get her fleet into position, every place of any importance on the Atlantic or Pacific seaboard, the Gulf, or the Lakes.*

Little now remains to be told. The Stricken Nation, in the depths of its awful despair, appealed to the mercy of its victorious enemy. 'Her Majesty's Government,' the answer stated, 'after profound consideration of the petition, sees no reason to abandon its position, or to modify any of the terms upon the acceptance of which a treaty of peace can be concluded.' The appeal for delay in order that several of the States whose Senators had resigned should have time to elect new members to represent them in such a momentous crisis was peremptorily denied, and finally, on August 25, 1892, when Congress fled to escape the vengeance of an army of Americans from the interior, who demanded 'No Surrender', it was with the under-standing— although the fact was not then known—that a treaty had been signed.

Let us drop the curtain. The worst has been told. The treaty signed was never ratified, but in the changed aspect of the North American continent today is seen the results which followed the defeat of the United States and the consequent destruction and disruption of the American Republic. There remains the story of foreign intervention. There is yet to be told of the new nations built upon the ruins of the once mighty Union of States. The story will be told in the sequel to 'The Stricken Nation', and will be entitled 'The New America' by Stochastic.

Yet one more point remains; it is the purpose of this work. *It is to arraign before the American people their representatives in Congress, who in their blindness and folly were responsible for the defenceless condition of the great cities on this coast; who for years saw their fortifications crumbling into ruins for want of appropriations for their repair; who by their criminal neglect of their duties and their lack of patriotic statesmanship invited the dreadful calamity which befel the nation; and who, in the judgment of posterity, must be held accountable for the destruction of the Republic.*

The Raid of *Le Vengeur*

GEORGE GRIFFITH

The Dream of Captain Flaubert

It was the third morning after the naval manoeuvres at Cherbourg, and since their conclusion Captain Leon Flaubert, of the Marine Experimental Department of the French Navy, had not had three consecutive hours' sleep.

He was an enthusiast on the subject of submarine navigation. He firmly believed that the nation which could put to sea the first really effective fleet of submarine vessels would hold the fleets of rival nations at its mercy, and acquire the whole ocean and its coasts as an exclusive territory. To anyone but an enthusiast it would have seemed a wild dream, and yet only a few difficulties had still to be overcome, a few more discoveries made, and the realization of the dream would be merely a matter of money and skilled labour.

Now the Cherbourg evolutions had proved three things. The submarines could sink and remain below the surface of the water. They could be steered vertically and laterally, but, once ten feet or so below the water, they were as blind as bats in bright sunshine.

Moreover, when their electric head-lights were turned on, a luminous haze, through which it was impossible to see more than a few metres, spread out in front of them, and this was reflected on the surface of the water in the form of a semi-phosphorescent patch which infallibly betrayed the whereabouts of the submarine to scouting destroyers and prowling gun-boats. The sinking of a couple of pounds of dynamite with a time-fuse into this patch would have consequences unspeakable for the crew of the submarine, since no human power could save them from a horrible death.

It was the fear of this discovery that had caused the rigid exclusion of all non-official spectators from the area of the experiments. Other trials conducted in daylight had further proved that the dim, hazy twilight of the lower waters was even worse than darkness. In short, the only chance of successful attack lay in coming to the surface, taking observations, probably under fire, and then sinking and discharging a torpedo at a venture. This, again, was an operation which could only be conducted with any chance of success in a smooth sea. In even moderately rough weather, it would be absolutely impossible.

It was these difficulties which, joined to a thousand exasperatingly stubborn technical details, had kept Captain Flaubert awake for three nights. For him everything depended upon the solution of them. He was admittedly the best submarine engineer in France. The submarines had been proved to be practically non-effective. France looked to him to make them effective.

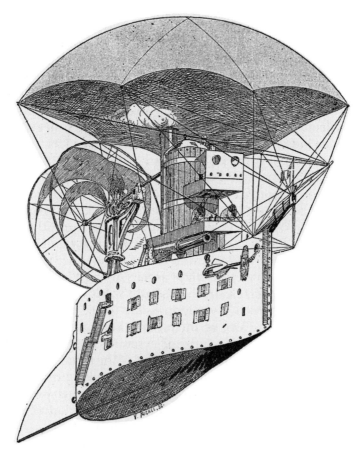

The fantasies of science fiction at times took no account of technological possibilities

The troubles in the far East and, nearer home, in Morocco had brought the Dual Alliance and the British Empire to the verge of war.[1] At any moment something might happen which would shake a few sparks into the European powder magazine. Then the naval might of Britain would be let loose instantly. In a few hours her overwhelming fleets would be striking their swift and terrible blows at the nearest enemy—France— and yet, if he could only give the submarines eyes which could see through the water, France could send out an invisible squadron which would cripple the British fleets before they left port, destroy her mightiest battleships and her swiftest cruisers before they could fire a single shot, and so in a few days clear the Narrow Seas and make way for the invasion of England by the irresistible military might of France. Then the long spell would be broken, and the proudly boasted Isle Inviolate would be inviolate no longer.

It was a splendid dream—but, until the submarines could be made to see as well as steer, it was as far away as aerial navigation itself.

Day was just breaking on the third morning when a luminous ray of inspiration pierced the mists which hang over the borderland of sleep and waking, of mingled dream and reality, amidst which Flaubert's soul was just then wandering.

He sat bolt upright in his little camp bed, clasped his hands across his close-cropped head, and, hardly knowing whether he was asleep or awake, heard himself say:

'*Nom de Dieu*, it is that! What foolishness not to have thought of that before. If we cannot see we must feel. Electric threads, balanced so as to be the same weight as water—ten, twenty, fifty, a hundred metres long, all round the boat, ahead and astern, to port and to starboard! Steel ships are magnetic, that is why they must swing to adjust their compasses.

'The end of each thread shall be a tiny electro-magnet. In-board they will connect with indicators, delicately swung magnetic needles, four of them, ahead, astern, and on each side; and, as *Le Vengeur*—yes, I will call her that, for we have no more forgotten Trafalgar than we have Fashoda—as she approaches the ships of the enemy, deep hidden under the waters, these threads, like the tentacles of the octopus, shall spread out towards her prey!

'As she gets nearer and nearer they will swing round and converge upon the ship that is nearest and biggest. As we dive under her they will point upwards. When they are perpendicular, the overhead torpedo will be released. Its magnets will fasten it to the bottom of the doomed ship. *Le Vengeur* will sink deeper, obeying always the warning of the sounding indicator, and seek either a new victim or a safe place to rise in. In ten, fifteen, twenty minutes, as I please, the torpedo will explode, the battleship or the cruiser will break in two and go down, not knowing whose hand has struck her.[2]

'Ah, Albion, my enemy, you are already conquered! You are only mistress of the seas until *Le Vengeur* begins her work. When that is done there will be no more English navy. The soldiers of France will avenge Waterloo on the soil of England, and Leon Flaubert will be the greatest name in the world. *Dieu Merci*, it is done! I have thought the thought which conquers a world—and now let me sleep.'

His clasped hands fell away from his head; his eyelids drooped over his aching, staring eyes; his body swayed a little from side to side, and then fell backwards. As his head rested on the pillow a long deep sigh left his half-parted lips, and in a few moments a contented snore was reverberating through the little, plainly-furnished bedroom.

A Dinner at Albert Gate

Curiously enough, while Captain Leon Flaubert had been worrying himself to the verge of distraction over the problem of seeing under water, and had apparently solved it by substituting electric nerves of feeling for the sight-rays which had proved a failure, Mr Wilfred Wallace Tyrrell had brought to a successful conclusion a long series of experiments bearing upon the self-same subject.

Mr Tyrrell was the son of Sir Wilfred Tyrrell, one of the Junior Lords of the Admiralty. He was a year under thirty. He had taken a respectable degree at Cambridge, then he had gone to Heidelberg and taken a better one, after which he had come home, entered at London, and made his bow to the world as the youngest D.Sc. that Burlington Gardens had ever turned out.

His Continental training had emancipated him from all the limitations under which his father, otherwise a man of very considerable intelligence, suffered. Like Captain Flaubert, he was a firm believer in the possibility of submarine navigation; but, like his unknown French rival, he, too, had been confronted with that fatal problem of submarine blindness, and he had attacked it from a point of view so different to that of Captain Flaubert that the difference of method practically amounted to the difference between the genius of the two nations to which they belonged. Captain Flaubert had evaded the question and substituted electric feeling for sight. Wilfred Tyrrell had gone for sight and nothing less, and now he had every reason to believe that he had succeeded.

The night before Captain Flaubert had fallen asleep in his quarters at Cherbourg, there was a little dinner-party at Sir Wilfred Tyrrell's house in Albert Gate. The most important of the guests from

Wilfred's point of view was Lady Ethel Rivers, the only daughter of the Earl of Kirlew. She was a most temptingly pretty brunette with hopelessly dazzling financial prospects. He had been admiring her from a despairing distance for the last five years, in fact ever since she had crossed the line between girlhood and young womanhood.

Although it was quite within the bounds of possibility that she knew of his devotion, he had never yet ventured upon even the remotest approach to direct courtship. In every sense she seemed too far beyond him. Some day she would be a countess in her own right. Some day, too, she would inherit about half a million in London ground-rents, with much more to follow as the leases fell in, wherefore, as Wilfred Tyrrell reasoned, she would in due course marry a duke, or at least a European prince.

Lady Ethel's opinions on the subject could only be gathered from the fact that she had already declined one Duke, two Viscounts, and a German Serene Highness, during her first season, and that she never seemed tired of listening when Wilfred Tyrrell was talking— which of itself was significant if his modesty had only permitted him to see it.

But while he was sitting beside her at dinner on this momentous night, he felt that the distance between them had suddenly decreased. So far his career had been brilliant but unprofitable. Many other men had done as much as he had and ended in mediocrity. But now he had done something; he had made a discovery with which the whole world might be ringing in a few weeks' time. He had solved the problem of submarine navigation, and, as a preliminary method of defence, he had discovered a means of instantly detecting the presence of a submarine destroyer.

He was one of those secretive persons who possess that gift of silence, when critical matters are pending, which has served many generations of diplomats on occasions when the fates of empires were hanging in the balance.

Thus, having learnt to keep his love a secret for so many years, he knew how to mask that still greater secret, by the telling of which he could have astonished several of the distinguished guests round his father's dinner table into a paralysis of official incredulity. But he, being the son of an official, knew that such a premature disclosure might result, not only in blank scepticism, for which he did not care, but in semi-official revelations to the Press, for which he did care a great deal. So when the farewells were being said, he whispered to his mother:

'I want you and father and Lady Ethel and Lord Kirlew to come up to the laboratory after everyone has gone. I've got something to show you. You can manage that, can't you, mother?'

Lady Tyrrell nodded and managed it.

Wilfred Tyrrell's laboratory was away up at the top of the house in a long low attic, which had evidently been chosen for its seclusion.

As they were going up the stairs Wilfred, sure of his triumph, took a liberty which, under other circumstances, would have been almost unthinkable to him. He and Lady Ethel happened to be the last on the stairs, and he was a step or two behind her. He quickened his pace a little, and then laying his hand lightly on her arm he whispered:

'Lady Ethel—'

'Oh, nonsense!' she whispered in reply, with a little tremble of her arm under his hand. 'Lady Ethel, indeed! As if we hadn't known each other long enough. Well never mind what you want to say. What are you going to show us?'

'Something that no human eyes except mine have ever seen before; something which I have even ventured to hope will make me worthy to ask you a question which a good many better men than I have asked—'

'I know what you mean,' she replied in a whisper even lower than his own, and turning a pair of laughing eyes up to his. 'You silly, couldn't you see before? I didn't want those Dukes and Serene Highnesses. Do something—so far I know you have only studied and dreamt—and, much and all as I like you—Well, now?'

'Now,' he answered, pulling her arm a little nearer to him, 'I have done something. I quite see what you mean, and I believe it is something worthy even of winning your good opinion. Here we are; in a few minutes you will see for yourself.'

The Water-Ray

The laboratory was littered with the usual disorderly-order of similar apartments. In the middle of it, on a big, bare, acid-stained deal table, there stood a glass tank full of water, something like an aquarium tank, but the glass walls were made of the best white plate. The water with which it was filled had a faint greenish hue and looked like sea-water. At one end of it there was a curious looking apparatus. A couple of boxes, like electric storage batteries, stood on either side of a combination of glass tubes mounted on a wooden stand so that they all converged into the opening of a much larger tube of pale blue glass. Fitted to the other end of this was a thick double concave lens also of pale blue glass. This was placed so that its axis pointed down towards the surface of the water in the tank at an angle of about thirty degrees.

'Well, Wallace,' said Sir Wilfred as his son locked the door behind them, 'what's this? Another of your wonderful inventions? Something else you want me to put before my lords of the Admiralty?'

'That's just it, father, and this time I really think that even the people at Whitehall will see that there's something in it. At any rate, I'm perfectly satisfied that if I had a French or Russian Admiral in this room, and he saw what you're going to see, I could get a million sterling down for what there is on that table.'

'But, of course you wouldn't think of doing that,' said Lady Ethel, who was standing at the end of the table opposite the arrangement of glass tubes.

'That, I think, goes without saying, Ethel,' said Lord Kirlew. 'I am sure Mr Tyrrell would be quite incapable of selling anything of service to his country to her possible enemies. At any rate, Tyrrell,' he went on, turning to Sir Wilfred, 'if I see anything in it, and your people won't take it up, I will. So now let us see what it is.'

Tyrrell had meanwhile turned up a couple of gas-jets, one on either side of the room, and they saw that slender, twisted wires ran from the batteries to each of the tubes through the after-end, which was sealed with glass. He came back to the table, and with a quick glance at Lady Ethel, he coughed slightly, after the fashion of a lecturer beginning to address an audience. Then he looked round at the inquiring faces, and said with a mock professional air:

'This, my lord, ladies, and gentlemen, is an apparatus which I have every reason to believe removes the last and only difficulty in the way of the complete solution of the problem of submarine navigation.'

'Dear me,' said Lord Kirlew, adjusting his *pince-nez* and leaning over the arrangement of tubes, 'I think I see now what you mean. You have found, if you will allow me to anticipate you, some sort of Röntgen ray or other, which will enable you to see through water. Is that so?'

'That is just what it is,' said Tyrrell. 'Of course, you know that the great difficulty, in fact, the so far insuperable obstacle in the way of submarine navigation has been the fact that a submerged vessel is blind. She cannot see where she is going beyond a distance of a few yards at most.

'Now this apparatus will make it possible, not only for her to see where she is going up to a distance which is limited only by the power of her batteries, but it also makes it possible for those on a vessel on the surface of the water to sweep the bottom of the sea just as a search-light sweeps the surface, and therefore to find out anything underneath, from a sunken mine to a submarine destroyer. I am going to show you, too, that it can be used either in daylight or in the dark. I'll try first with the gas up.'

He turned a couple of switches on the boxes as he said this. The batteries began to hum gently. The tubes began to glow with a strange intense light which had two very curious properties. It was just as distinctly visible in the gaslight as if the room had been dark, and it was absolutely confined to the tubes. Not a glimmer of it extended beyond their outer surfaces.

Then the big blue tube began to glow, turning pale green the while. The next instant a blaze of greenish light shot in a direct ray from the lens down into the water. A moment later the astonished eyes of the spectators saw the water in the tank pierced by a spreading ray of intense and absolutely white light. Some stones and sand and gravel that had been spread along the bottom of the tank stood out with magical distinctness wherever the ray touched them. The rest, lit up only by the gas, were dim and indistinct in comparison with them.

'You see that what I call the water-ray is quite distinct from gaslight,' said Tyrrell in a tone which showed that the matter was now to him a commonplace. 'It is just as distinct from daylight. Now we will try it in the dark. Lord Kirlew, would you mind turning out that light near you? Father, turn out the one on your side, will you?'

The lights were turned out in silence. People of good intelligence are as a rule silent in the presence of a new revelation. Every eye looked through the darkness at the tank. The tubes glowed with their strange light, but they stood out against the darkness of the room just like so many pencils of light, and that was all. The room was just as dark as though they had not been there. The intense ray from the lens was now only visible as a fan of light. Tank and water had vanished in the darkness. Nothing could be seen but the ray and the stones and sand which it fell on.

'You see,' said Tyrrell, 'that the ray does not diffuse itself. It is absolutely direct, and that is one of its most valuable qualities. The electric lights which they use on the French submarines throw a glow on the top of the water at night, and so it is pretty easy to locate them. The surface of the water there, you see, is perfectly dark. In fact the water has vanished altogether. Another advantage is that this ray is absolutely invisible in air. Look!'

An artist's impression of 1885 shows a submarine vessel attaching explosives to a warship

As he said this he tilted the arrangement of tubes backwards so that the ray left the water, and that moment the room was in utter darkness. He turned it down towards the tank and again the brilliant fan of light became visible in the water.

'Now,' he continued, 'that's all. You can light the gas again, if you don't mind.'

'Well, Wallace,' said Lord Kirlew when they had got back to the library, 'I think we can congratulate you upon having solved one of the greatest problems of the age, and if the Admiralty don't take your invention up, as I don't suppose they will, eh, Tyrrell?—you know them better than I do—I'll tell you what I'll do; I'll buy or build you a thirty-five knot destroyer which shall be fitted up to your orders, and until we get into a naval war with someone, you can take a scientific cruise and use your water-ray to find out uncharted reefs and that sort of thing, and perhaps you might come across an old sunken treasure-ship. I believe there are still some millions at the bottom of Vigo Bay.'

Before Lady Ethel left, Tyrrell found time and opportunity to ask her a very serious question, and her answer to it was:

'You clever goose! You might have asked that long ago. Yes, I'll marry you the day after you've blown up the first French submarine ship.'

In The Solent

For once at least the British Admiralty had shown an open mind. Sir Wilfred Tyrrell's official position, and Lord Kirlew's immense influence, may have had something to do with the stimulating of the official intellect, but, at any rate, within a month after the demonstration in the laboratory, a committee of experts had examined and wonderingly approved of the water-ray apparatus, and HM destroyer *Scorcher* had been placed at Tyrrell's disposal for a series of practical experiments.

Everything was, of course, kept absolutely secret, and the crew of the *Scorcher* were individually sworn to silence as to anything which they might see or hear during the experimental cruise. Moreover, they were all picked men of proved devotion and integrity. Every one of them would have laid down his life at a moment's notice for the honour of the Navy, and so there was little fear of the momentous secret leaking out.

Meanwhile, international events had been following each other with ominous rapidity, and those who were behind the scenes on both sides of the Channel knew that war was now merely a matter of weeks, perhaps only of days.

The *Scorcher* was lying in the South Dock at Chatham, guarded by dock police who allowed no one to go within fifty yards of her without a permit direct from headquarters. She was fitted with four water-ray instalments, one ahead, one astern, and one amidships to port and starboard, and, in addition to her usual armament of torpedo-tubes and twelve three-pounder quick-firers, she carried four torpedoes of the Brennan type which could be dropped into the water without making the slightest splash and steered along the path of the water-ray, towards any object which the ray had discovered.

The day before she made her trial trip, Captain Flaubert had an important interview with the Minister of Marine. He had perfected his system of magnetic feelers, and *Le Vengeur* was lying in Cherbourg ready to go forth on her mission of destruction. Twenty other similar craft were being fitted with all speed at Cherbourg, Brest, and Toulon. *Le Vengeur* had answered every test demanded of her, and at the French Marine the days of the British Navy were already regarded as numbered.

'In a week you may do it, mon Capitaine,' said the Minister, rising from his seat and holding out both his hands. 'It must be war by then, or at least a few days later. Prove that you can do as you say, and France will know how to thank and reward you. Victory today will be to those who strike first, and it shall be yours to deliver the first blow at the common enemy.'

At midnight a week after this conversation a terrible occurrence took place in the Solent. Her Majesty's first-class cruiser *Phyllis* was lying at anchor about two miles off Cowes Harbour, and the *Scorcher* was lying with steam up some quarter of a mile inside her. She was, in fact, ready to begin her first experimental voyage at 1 a.m. She had her full equipment on board just as though she were going to fight a fleet of submarines, for it had been decided to test not only the working of the water-ray, but also the possibility of steering the diving torpedoes by directing them on to a sunken wreck which was lying in twenty fathoms off Portland Bill. The Fates, however, had decided that they were to be tried on much more interesting game than the barnacle-covered hull of a tramp steamer.[3]

At fifteen minutes past twelve precisely, when Tyrrell and Lieutenant-Commander Farquar were taking a very limited promenade on the narrow, rubber-covered decks of the *Scorcher*, they felt the boat heave jerkily under their feet. The water was perfectly calm at the time.

'Good Heavens, what's that?' exclaimed Tyrrell, as they both stopped and stared out over the water. As it happened they were both facing towards the *Phyllis*, and they were just in time to see her rise on the top of a mountain of foaming water, break in two, and disappear.

'A mine or a submarine!' said Commander Farquar between his teeth; 'anyhow—war. Get your apparatus ready, Mr Tyrrell. That's one of the French submarines we've been hearing so much about. If you can find him, we mustn't let him out of here.'

Inside twenty seconds, the *Scorcher* had slipped her cable, her searchlight had flashed a quick succession of signals to Portsmouth and Southampton, her boilers were palpitating under a full head of steam, and her wonderful little engines were ready at a minute's notice to develop their 10,000 horse power and send her flying over the water at thirty-five knots.

Meanwhile, too, four fan-shaped rays of intense white light pierced the dark waters of the Solent as a lightning flash pierces the blackness of night, and four torpedoes were swinging from the davits a foot above the water.

There was a tinkle in the engine-room, and she swung round towards the eddying area of water in which the *Phyllis* went down. Other craft, mostly torpedo-boats and steam pinnaces from warships, were also hurrying towards the fatal spot. The head-ray from the *Scorcher* shot down to the bottom of the Solent, wavered hither and thither for a few moments, and then remained fixed. Those who looked down it saw a sight which no human words could describe.

The splendid warship which a couple of minutes before had been riding at anchor, perfectly equipped, ready to go anywhere and do anything, was lying on the weed-covered sand and rock, broken up into two huge fragments of twisted scrap-iron. Even some of her guns had been hurled out of their positions and flung yards away from her. Other light wreckage was strewn in all directions, and the mangled remains of what had so lately been British officers and sailors were floating about in the mid-depths of the still eddying waters.

'We can't do any good here, Mr Tyrrell,' said Commander Farquar. 'That's the work of a submarine, and we've got to find him. He must have come in by Spithead. He'd never have dared the other way, and he'll probably go out as he came in. Keep your rays going and let's see if we can find him.'

There was another tinkle in the engine-room. The *Scorcher* swung round to the eastward and began working in a zigzag course at quarter speed towards Spithead.

Captain Flaubert, however, had decided to do the unexpected, and thirty minutes after the destruction of the *Phyllis*, *Le Vengeur* was feeling her way back into the Channel past the Needles. She was steering, of course, by chart and compass, about twenty feet below the water. Her maximum speed was eight knots, but Captain Flaubert, in view of possible collisions with rocks or inequalities on the sea-floor, was content to creep along at two.

He had done his work. He had proved the possibility of stealing unseen and unsuspected into the most jealously guarded strip of water in the world, destroying a warship at anchor, and then, as he thought, going away unseen. After doing all that, it would be a pity to meet with any accident. War would not be formally declared for three days at least, and he wanted to get back to Cherbourg and tell the Minister of Marine all about it.

The *Scorcher* zigzagged her way in and out between the forts, her four rays lighting up the water for a couple of hundred yards in every direction, for nearly an hour, but nothing was discovered.

'I believe he's tried the other way after all,' said Commander Farquar after they had taken a wide, comprehensive sweep between Foreland and Southsea. 'There's one thing quite certain, if he has got out this way into the Channel, we might just as well look for a needle in a haystack. I think we'd better go back and look for him the other way.'

The man at the wheel put the helm hard over, the bell tinkled full speed ahead in the engine-room. The throbbing screws flung columns of foam out from under the stern, and the little black craft swept round in a splendid curve, and went flying down the Solent towards Hurst Point at the speed of an express train. Off Ryde she slowed down to quarter speed, and the four rays began searching the sea bottom again in every direction.

Le Vengeur was just creeping out towards the Needles, feeling her way cautiously with the sounding indicator thirty feet below the surface, when Captain Flaubert, who was standing with his Navigating Lieutenant in the glass-domed conning-tower, lit by one little electric bulb, experienced the most extraordinary sensation of his life. A shaft of light shot down through the water. It was as clean cut as a knife and bright as burnished silver. It wavered about hither and thither for a few moments, darting through the water like a lightning flash through thunderclouds, and then suddenly it dropped on to the conning-tower of *Le Vengeur* and illuminated it with an almost intolerable radiance. The Captain looked at his Lieutenant's face. It was almost snow white in the unearthly light. Instinctively he knew that his own was the same.

'*Tonnerre de Dieu!*' he whispered, with lips that trembled in spite of all his self-control. 'What is this, Lieutenant? Is it possible that these accursed English have learnt to see under water? Or, worse still, suppose they have a submarine which can see?'

'In that case,' replied the Lieutenant, also in a whisper, 'though *Le Vengeur* has done her work, I fear she will not finish her trial trip. Look,' he went on, pointing out towards the port side, 'what is that?'

A dimly-shining, silvery body about five feet long, pointed at both ends, and driven by a rapidly whirling screw had plunged down the broad pathway of light and stopped about ten feet from *Le Vengeur*. Like a living thing, it slowly headed this way and that, ever drawing nearer and nearer, inch by inch, and then began the most ghastly experience for the Captain and his Lieutenant that two human beings had ever endured.

They were both brave men, well worthy of the traditions of their country and their profession; but they were imprisoned in a fabric of steel thirty feet below the surface of the midnight sea, and this horrible thing was coming nearer and nearer. To rise to the surface meant not only capture but ignominious death to every man on board, for war was not declared yet, and the captain and crew of *Le Vengeur* were pirates and outlaws beyond the pale of civilization. To remain where they were meant a death of unspeakable terror, a fate from which there was no possible escape.

A secret weapon of 1849: the Austrians send balloons with incendiary devices against Venice

'It is a torpedo,' said the Lieutenant, muttering the words with white trembling lips, 'a Brennan, too, for you see they can steer it. It has only to touch us and—'

A shrug of the shoulders more expressive than words said the rest.

'Yes,' replied Captain Flaubert, 'that is so, but how did we not know of it? These English must have learnt some wisdom lately. We will rise a little and see if we can get away from it.'

He touched a couple of buttons on a signal board as he said this. *Le Vengeur* rose fifteen feet, her engines quickened, and she headed for the open sea at her best speed. She passed out of the field of the ray for a moment or two. Then three converging rays found her and flooded her with light. Another silvery shape descended, this time to the starboard side. Her engines were put to their utmost capacity. The other shape on the port side rose into view, and ran alongside the conning-tower at exactly equal speed.

Then *Le Vengeur* sank another thirty feet, doubled on her course, and headed back towards Spithead. The ray followed her, found her again, and presently there were the two ghostly attendants, one on each side, as before. She turned in zigzags and curves, wheeled round in circles, and made straight runs hither and thither, but it was no use. The four rays encircled her wherever she went, and the two torpedoes were ever alongside.

Presently another feature of this extraordinary chase began to develop itself. The torpedoes, with a horrible likeness to living things, began to shepherd *Le Vengeur* into a certain course. If she turned to starboard then the silvery shape on that side made a rush at her. If she did the same to port the other one ran up to within a yard or so of her and stopped as though it would say: 'Another yard, and I'll blow you into scrap-iron.'

The Lieutenant was a brave man, but he fainted after ten minutes of this. Captain Flaubert was a stronger spirit, and he stood to his work with one hand on the steering wheel and the fingers of the other on the signal-board. He knew that he was caught, and that he could expect nothing but hanging as a common criminal. He had failed the moment after success, and failure meant death. The Minister of Marine had given him very clearly to understand that France would not be responsible for the failure of *Le Vengeur*.

The line of his fate lay clear before him. The lives of his Lieutenant and five picked men who had dared everything for him might be saved. He had already grasped the meaning of the evolutions of the two torpedoes. He was being, as it were, steered into a harbour, probably into Portsmouth, where in time he would be compelled to rise to the surface and surrender. The alternative was being blown into eternity in little pieces, and like the brave man that he was, he decided to accept the former alternative, and save his comrades by taking the blame on himself.

He touched two more of the buttons on the signal-board. The

engines of *Le Vengeur* stopped, and presently Tyrrell and Commander Farquar saw from the deck of the *Scorcher* a long, shining, whale-backed object rise above the surface of the water.

At the forward end of it there was a little conning-tower covered by a dome of glass. The moment that it came in sight the *Scorcher* stopped, and then moved gently towards *Le Vengeur*. As she did so the glass dome slid back, and the head and shoulders of a man in the French naval uniform came into sight. His face looked like the face of a corpse as the rays of the searchlight flashed upon it. His hair, which an hour ago had been black, was iron-grey now, and his black eyes stared straight at the searchlight as though they were looking into eternity.

Then across the water there came the sound of a shrill, high-pitched voice which said in perfectly correct English:

'Gentleman, I have succeeded and I have failed. I destroyed your cruiser yonder, I would have destroyed the whole British Navy if I could have done so, because I hate you and everything English. *Le Vengeur* surrenders to superior force for the sake of those on board her, but remember that I alone have planned and done this thing. The others have only done what I paid them to do, and France knows nothing of it. You will spare them, for they are innocent. For me it is finished.'

As the *Scorcher's* men looked down the rays of the searchlight, they saw something glitter in his hand close to his head—a yellow flash shone in the midst of the white, there was a short flat bang, and the body of Captain Leon Flaubert dropped out of sight beside the still unconscious Lieutenant.

Le Vengeur was taken into Portsmouth. Her crew were tried for piracy and murder, and sentenced to death. The facts of the chase and capture of *Le Vengeur* were laid before the French Government, which saw the advisability of paying an indemnity of ten million dollars as soon as *Le Vengeur*, fitted with Wilfred Tyrrell's water-ray apparatus, made her trial trip down Channel and blew up half-a-dozen sunken wrecks with perfect ease and safety to herself.

A few weeks later, in recognition of his immense services, the Admiralty placed the third-class cruiser *Venus* at the disposal of Mr Wilfred and Lady Ethel Tyrrell for their honeymoon trip down the Mediterranean.

The declaration of war of which the Minister had spoken to Captain Flaubert remained a diplomatic secret, and the unfortunate incident which had resulted in the blowing up of a British cruiser in time of peace was publicly admitted by the French Government to be an act of unauthorized piracy, the perpetrators of which had already paid the penalty of their crime. The reason for this was not very far to seek. As soon as Wilfred Tyrrell came back from his wedding trip, *Le Vengeur* was dry-docked and taken literally to pieces and examined in every detail. Thus, everything that the French engineers knew about submarine navigation was revealed.

A committee of the best engineers in the United Kingdom made a thorough inspection with a view to possible improvements, and the result was the building of a British submarine flotilla of thirty enlarged *Vengeurs*. And, as a couple of these would be quite sufficient for the effective blockade of a port, the long-planned invasion of England was once more consigned to the limbo of things which may only be dreamt of.

The Green Curve

MAJOR-GENERAL SIR ERNEST SWINTON

Je créai six commissaires pour faire la description des bouches inutiles, et après bailler ce rôle à un chevalier de Saint-Jean de Malte, accompagné de 25 ou 30 soldats, pour les mettre dehors . . .

Ce sont les lois de la guerre; il faut être cruel bien souvent pour venir à bout de son ennemi; Dieu doit être bien miséricordieux en notre droit, qui faisons tant de maux.

Montluc, Siege of Sienna

I

'Yes, you certainly make a point there—but I'm afraid it cannot be done. I quite see, of course, that under certain circumstances it might be advisable, purely from a military point of view; but there are also other considerations—weighty considerations, I may say— and it cannot be done; at least, not at present.' As he said these words the Minister put on his well-known smile—that smile which had disarmed so many.

'But if not possible at present, do you not think we ought to be prepared to take this step shortly—at a moment's notice?' replied the other.

'Yes; in so far as measures can be taken that will not cause excitement. You see—I'll be frank with you'—here the set smile again showed the teeth of the speaker under his carefully waxed black moustache—'we cannot do it on account of the result that such action may have on the Public—we cannot afford to do it. The Public is ignorant of any such necessity, and would not understand. They are, of course, still quite confident, I hope not unreasonably, and look upon the rosy side of affairs—'

'Yes; remember the Parisians and their cry of "*À Berlin!*" Remember—' interrupted the other.

But the mandarin suavely held up his hand and continued sonorously: 'And look upon the rosy side of things, as I say. Such an extreme—not to say drastic—step would certainly inflict great hardships on non-combatants, and would excite apprehension. It would be bound to have an adverse effect on the Government. Believe me, we have considered the matter from all sides. Of course, I quite understand and, I hope, appreciate the line you are taking up: all the military advisers have—perhaps quite naturally— urged similar forcible methods; but are not your fears somewhat groundless?'

At that moment there was a discreet tap at the door. A secretary entered and looked with a deferential air of inquiry at the Minister, who, seeing that he brought some papers, broke off his argument. The other bowed, and with a grunt of dissent strode to the window. As he stood reading with his back to the light his face was in shadow, but his attitude and manner of reading betokened a character the antithesis of that of the Minister, who was now immersed in the papers just brought in.

The business, which chiefly consisted in signing the papers handed to him, with now and then a word of explanation, did not take long. After a final 'Yes, sir, quite,' the secretary noiselessly vanished, and the Minister sat back, gently tapping his fingers together over his ample waistcoat. While endeavouring to recall the exact portion of his peroration reached before the interruption, he gazed benignly round the well-appointed room, which was large and had a long table in the centre. The number of despatch-boxes and the lavish display of official stationery upon the table showed it to be a government office.

As the Minister sat on, tapping his finger-tips together, his cuffs made a rattling which at last attracted the attention of his more highly-strung companion, who looked up with a frown. Seeing that the secretary had gone, he returned to the charge.

'I think you should read this. You have not seen it: it has only just reached me. It's his last letter to me, in which he again specifically discusses this very point. As you will see, he demonstrates once more that, if things go at all against us, the place is bound to be besieged, and that either the useless civil population should be sent away now at once, or a very much larger food-supply stored there than has heretofore been arranged for or contemplated. He favours the former course, as making matters simpler and easier for the defence. But see for yourself what he says,—the portion of his letter on this subject begins here. As you know, he is no alarmist, and his opinion, supporting as it does so many others, must surely carry great weight.'

The Minister took the papers but did not read. 'I don't think it will do much good, General, my wading through all this'—he flipped through the pages. 'I know it all: I have seen former reports, and I don't suppose there's anything new. It represents the ultra-military point of view, which has been already considered. We have decided, if possible, quietly to increase the stock of food so as to provide for the whole population. Of course, if opportunity offers, we might— er—persuade a few old people to go; but we must wait till the Public realizes the necessity for the move before doing anything on a large scale. Possibly people will then go readily and not have to be forced. Compulsion is always *so* undesirable in these matters. Then, perhaps, we might leave the matter to the discretion of the future military governor of the place; we should not like to commit him to any course beforehand, or to tie his hands!'

'But, quite apart from the great disadvantage of saddling that poor man with such a difficult question at a time when he will have so much else to do, I do not think you understand that it will increase the hardship ten-thousand-fold if the wretched people have to be turned out once the town is invested. It will then practically mean the starvation of them all, and will be an atrocity. Now, it is possible and involves comparatively little hardship. Why not tell the Public the truth and act? Lead them, don't follow. Of course, they will acquiesce, once they know the position.'

'Oh, come, come,' smiled the Minister, 'isn't that a little strong? War is a brutal matter, but surely you don't imply that, even were the place besieged, the enemy would not allow the harmless civil population—non-combatants—a safe-conduct through their lines? You make our enemies out to be savages of the worst type. We live in different times from the siege of Jerusalem, you know! As to your last suggestion—why, it is not within the sphere of practical politics. Impossible, absolutely.'

'I don't think you realize what War is. Starvation is one of the weapons of a besieger—as history has proved, one of the most powerful. If the opposing general conducting the siege were to assist the defenders by allowing them to send out their women and children after the siege has commenced, he would be a traitor to his country and should be shot! From what I know of our enemy's notions of war and of the character of the man who will probably undertake any siege, I do not think this likely. Have you read his last work, *Vae Victis; or The Ethics of War?*'

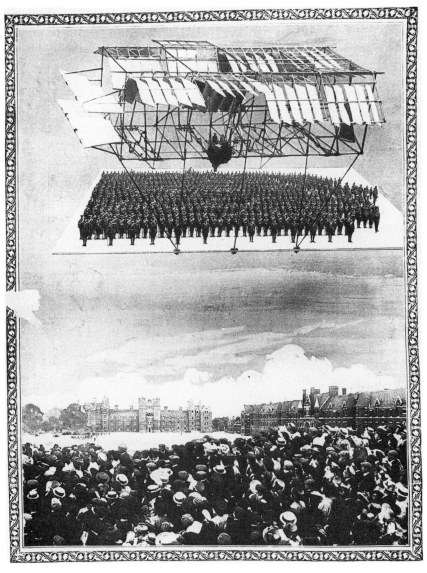

The first air-landing troops in history? The aptly named *Falsiloquus Pennatus* takes off on
1 April 1909

'No, I have not. I have no—'

'You should. I will send you a copy. It has just been translated. It
treats of starvation as a weapon, and deals with the problems of *les
bouches inutiles*.

'Thank you very much, but of course many men write things

which they could not carry out in practice. I am afraid I should not be convinced by his theorizing. Besides, if he is the ogre that you imagine, the commandant of the fortress will make his arrangements accordingly!'

'Yes—when it will be too late!' The speaker lost his patience. 'So it is really the "Public" that you rely on to judge when such a thing is necessary? The mob are the paid leaders and expert advisers of the nation? I can't help telling you that the Government are shirking their duty, but are not evading their responsibility, by trying to shelve the questions for some luckless general to settle when it is too late. I trust you may not have the blood of many harmless non-combatants, or of the whole garrison, on your hands, or be responsible for eventual defeat.' He spoke bitterly.

'Tut-tut, my *dear* General,' the Minister shrugged his shoulders in a deprecating way, 'it's absurd—quite impossible to talk like this. I am so much obliged—I'm sure we all are—for the trouble you have taken, but I do not think any useful purpose can be served by our continuing this discussion or attempting to reopen the matter. Your views have my fullest sympathy, I assure you; I will bear in mind what you have said. It shall not be lost sight of. Meanwhile let us hope for the best!' He smiled again, and his third chin nestled into his wide collar with an air of finality.

The hint was plain. With a curt farewell the other went out, sore at heart.

The Minister turned his chair round to his table, and absently repeated the shibboleth—'We must hope for the best.' But the catchword did not seem to convey comfort, for the smile had left his lips. It was some time before the busy scratching of his pen showed that he had once again got back into his stride, and was making his point in a masterly minute.

II

It was some weeks later: the storm had burst, and the war had gone badly. Winter had fastened upon the coast fortress; blizzard alternated with calm black frost; but far more paralysing than the grip of winter was the gradual constriction of the enemy's line of investment, for by land and sea the town was cut off from the world.

Upon a certain wild afternoon the office of the Military Governor and Fortress Commander looked gloomy and deserted—silent but for the roaring of the fitful gusts in the chimney, and the distant booming of artillery which could be heard at intervals. Suddenly these dull, muffled sounds changed to a shrill discord of wind whistling through the windows, as the door was thrown open and two men entered. Before it could be closed a shower of papers fluttered from the table, and the powdery snow, which had been driven through the broken panes, scurried across the floor in wisps, turning to a dirty grey as it picked up the dust.

'That's the place,' said the sergeant, as he pointed out a vacant space on the walls amidst the maps and proclamations with which they were covered, 'made for it.'

The private, whose mouth seemed full, only nodded and drew a hammer from his belt. Uncoiling a large roll they had brought with them, which was apparently a patchwork of smaller pieces pasted together so as to form one sheet, they set to work. The sergeant whistled while he held it straight against the wall; the other, daintily drawing tin-tacks one by one from his mouth, nailed it up. After the last nail had been driven, and after a final stepping-back to judge of the general effect, the remaining tacks were carefully ejected into a scrap of paper. No one could have accused these two of not being whole-hearted in their work, for they took as much trouble over the exact position and alignment of this ugly diagram as a youth over his first white tie.

'Doesn't look so bad after all; but I'll just thicken up the green a bit, as I have it on me,' said the senior, taking a chalk-pencil from behind his ear. 'Yes, that does it. The Colonel said it was to be plain and prominently placed. It is plain, it is prominent, and—it is neat. We've made a job of it.' He sucked his pencil and cocked his head on one side critically.

The well-worn platitude that the main points—the great issues of affairs—are often lost sight of by those immersed in working out the details was well illustrated at this moment. These two men were intelligent, and fully understood the meaning of the particoloured chart they had helped to prepare, and yet they were far more concerned with its exact position and appearance than they were with its meaning. Nevertheless, the message it conveyed was not altogether without importance to them personally.

The private solemnly screwed up the paper containing the tacks, put it in his pocket, and stuck the hammer in his belt. He looked all round the room. 'S'pose the Governor will be moving office again to-morrow. It's about time, as he's been here four days now!'

'Yes; it beats me how quick they find out where it is, after all the spies we've nobbled, and the flag kept flying at the wrong place too.

Of course they know who keeps the show going and who is the whole defence—in a manner of speaking. Why, it would be worth anything to them to drop a shell on The Butcher. Not but what he hasn't had some narrow squeaks already. If it wasn't for this ever-lasting shifting it would be worthwhile tidying up this place a bit—something crool, I call it.' He glanced round and snorted, his draughtsman's eye offended at the state of the room. After picking up and weighting the scattered papers, they stumped heavily from the room, chased out by the jeering cat-calls of the wind. They stumped, inasmuch as they made a great noise on the hard parquet floor; but it was more the shuffle of weak-kneed men who could not control their too heavy feet than the tramp of vigorous limbs. Perhaps it was due to the dull light of the leaden-hued sky, rendered gloomier by the dusty window, but both men certainly looked very ill. Their faces were haggard and grey, and their uniforms sagged about their bodies.

The room itself, which had so excited the disgust of the sergeant, presented a combination of opulence and squalor that was bizarre to a degree. Large and high, its furnishing was mostly rough and its condition altogether neglected. The parquet floor was dull, except in a track to the door. The ceiling was hand-painted; even in the dim light of this winter's afternoon could be seen the inevitable cupids wallowing among garlands of roses and ribbons upon a background of clouds. The remnants of Rose-du-Barri-coloured satin, which fluttered from the edges of the panels, showed what had been the wall covering—torn down to allow of the maps being nailed on the flat. Between the panels rococo metal sconces projected, and from the centre of the ceiling hung a florid electrolier in the same style. Most of the incandescent lamps were missing, and the blackened condition of those left told a tale of long use, while the candlesticks dotted about showed that no electric current was now available—searchlights devour so much!

Again the grey scurry on the floor: an elderly man came in. As he stamped round the room, taking off his gloves and shaking the snow from him, his eye was arrested by the new diagram. Unhook-ing his fur coat, he walked up and began studying it carefully. In spite of the self-congratulations of its draughtsman, it was at first sight a confusing chart, and as the Governor frowned at it, the dour expression of his square face became accentuated almost to grotesqueness.

The heading, printed in bold type across the top of the paper, was—

'Food Chart'.

The sheet was ruled in horizontal and vertical lines, which formed a checkered pattern. The ends of the horizontal lines were figured as a scale of 'Food', those of the vertical as a scale of 'Time'. From the left-hand top corner started four thick lines of different colours, which ran downwards towards the right in sloping curves. These curves intersected the bottom of the 'zero' line of the food-scale at four different points, each marked with a circle.

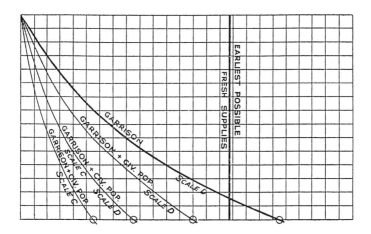

Beginning with the steepest, each curve was labelled as follows:

Red curve	Garrison	}	Scale C
	Civ. Pop.		
Blue curve	Garrison		Scale C
	Civ. Pop.		Scale D
Purple curve	Garrison	}	Scale D
	Civ. Pop.		
Green curve	Garrison		Scale D

Below was this explanatory note:

Scale C = Minimum scale of rations for fighting or working
Scale D = Minimum scale of rations for bare existence
Civ. Pop. = Civil Population (excluding those useful in defence, who are shown as 'Garrison')

The Governor gazed steadily at the diagram for some minutes, tracing with his finger the different curves of the food-supply down to the point where the last ration would be eaten. He pulled a paper out of his pocket and, after a few pencilled calculations, commenced counting along the days in the time-scale, when his Chief-of-Staff, a slightly younger man, entered and saluted.

'Ah, there you are! I see you have been able to get this done at last. I am glad, because I got some news today which I think will make the point all the clearer—so clear that even the Council must grasp it at once. I now know the date before which we cannot possibly get any food ships through the blockade. Of course, they may not come till long after—if at all—but they cannot come before then. Just look at this, and chalk up and mark the diagram at the date.'

He turned to take off his fur coat and hang it over a chair. The other took the paper, worked out a rapid sum, and marked a certain date in the horizontal time-scale of the diagram. He looked round for a coloured chalk, but seeing none seized a quill pen from the table and, dipping the plume into the red ink, drew a line up through the date—the wet feather leaving a brilliant smear of scarlet. 'Label it,' said the Governor, looking round.

With pain, for he was no draughtsman, the other printed against this line, 'Earliest Possible Fresh Supplies'.

The Governor joined him. They both looked at the diagram, then at each other.

'Well, sir, that settles it definitely,' said the staff-officer, and he whistled softly.

It did, indeed. The value of the chart was now increased tenfold, for it gave the absolute as well as the relative results of following the different curves. According to the Red Curve, the food would run out many weeks before the earliest possibility of relief; according to the Blue, the end would be closer to, but still before, the fateful day; while, following the Purple, it would be only a few days short. The Green was the only curve that intersected the 'zero' line to the right of the scarlet smear. As the earliest date for this was not fixed, but problematical, it was obvious that the green curve was the only one that could be followed with safety, and, even then, not more than a few days' margin would be obtained. It was but too clear that only by refusing to feed the useless members of the population, or, in other words, by turning them out to freeze and starve, could the beleaguered town have a fair chance of holding out.

'I'd like a certain friend of ours to be here now and see this,' continued the last speaker. It was unnecessary for him to utter any name or to specify him of the triple chin in order to be understood.

'Yes,' quietly said the other, 'I should like him to read his own death sentence in those curves!' There was no hint of jesting in this reply: the tone and expression of the speaker were grimness itself.

'Look here! I want some more explanation, as I prefer, if possible, to carry the Council with me, and they will want a lot. You see there has been no collusion, and the chart has not been faked to back up my views. The men who made it did not know of this last message; but the result has borne out in a marvellous way what I have said all along.'

'Very good, sir; I will fetch the Director of Supplies, who got the actual calculations made out.'

In a few moments he returned with that officer.

'Will you please explain how these figures have been arrived at,' said the Governor.

'The actual amounts of supplies, scales of rations, etc., I obtained from my returns, sir. The figures for the population I got from the Provost-Marshal. For the statistics, calculations, and forecasts I worked in conjunction with a committee of leading business men and some of the actuaries of the insurance companies. I got these gentlemen collected specially from the earthwork and other gangs. The principal actuary of the Peace and Plenty Assurance Company presided over the calculations. A lot of it was quite beyond me.'

'I see. Now, what exactly do you include under "Civil Population"? What we discussed the other day?'

'Yes.'

'In fact—the useless mouths?'

'Precisely. Would you like to see the figures, sir? Here they are.'

The elder man put out his hand, but hesitated, and did not take the proffered bundle. Instead, he muttered half to himself—

'No, no; it is better I shouldn't. It must be decided on principle— on the diagram. I don't want to know the numbers—it might affect my decision. God knows it is hard enough to do my duty without knowing all the results in detail. No,' he finished out aloud, 'I won't look at them! About the diagram, I don't see why the coloured lines should be curved. It seems that the decline for a uniform consumption should be a slanting line. Do you gradually decrease the ration scale?'

'No, sir, though the result is much the same. The curvature is caused by the decreasing daily consumption, owing to the increased proportion of deaths and—'

'Of course, yes; I had forgotten that for the moment. Did the civil experts collaborate cordially?'

'Very, especially the mathematicians. It was their own work they

Aerial bombardment from airships was taken for granted in tales of future warfare by the last decade of the nineteenth century

were coming back to—what they were bred up to do—and they enjoyed it after their long spell of navvy labour. They called it a "pretty problem". One poor fellow went quite off his head in his professional zeal, and lost all sense of proportion. He simply revelled in the curves! He said that the thing was capable of a "neat solution", for if we applied a suitably arranged sliding ration-scale to the casualty curve we should never eat our last ration!'

'What on earth did he mean?'

'I don't know, sir; but I took down what he said, as a matter of interest. He said—he said—here it is—that if we did this, the zero line of food would tend to become "asymptotic" to the curves and—'

'*What?*'

'Asymptotic to the curves, and that if a fire at the depot should cause a sudden drop in the food-supply, we could almost turn this drop into a "cusp" by making a sortie next day to bring up the casualties! He was also much grieved because, as we cannot put back the clock, we can never get a "node" in the—'

'That's enough; that's enough. What did you do with him?'

'Sent him back to pick-and-shovel work at once; thought him quite mad; but the other actuaries now state that, mathematically, he was correct, though it was of no practical value! The commercial men did not see the force of losing combatants simply to produce a "cusp", and said it was not business.'

'Well, well, many more will go like that before we've done, I expect. Anything more I should know about the working out before the Council meets?'

'Yes, I forgot to mention that certain events are expressly excluded from this prognostication—earthquakes, large assaults, or fire in supply depots; also, we have estimated every edible in the food total.'

'Thanks. It's all only too clear,' said the Governor. Then, turning to his chief of staff, he added: 'Please have draft orders got out in detail for carrying on according to the green curve, from the day after to-morrow. I have decided finally, and shall force it through the Council of Defence now, by the aid of that diagram. Let me see the orders after the Council meeting. We meet in an hour, and until then I want to be undisturbed. Tell the ADC I do not wish to see any one upon any subject not vital.'

'Very good, sir.'

The wind whistled, and the Governor was alone.

III

He pushed one of the gilt chairs covered with stained brocade up to the stove and sat heavily down. The winter's day had drawn to its close, and in the fitful light of the candles, towards which his face was turned, the deep-set eyes, square chin, and bristly moustache gave an impression of the man's nature. His face was almost brutal in its severity, though it was not on account of his appearance that he had been dubbed 'The Butcher'. From the dark and frayed strip of silk on his breast, it was evident that he was much decorated; could the colours of the ribbons have been distinguished, it would also have been clear that he had seen much service.

Dogged to obstinacy, he was not cursed with too much imagination, and he pursued to the bitter end what he thought to be the path of duty, regardless of side-issues. Formed of tougher material than the majority of his fellow-countrymen, he played the bloody game of war with a stern logic, untouched by the opportunism and hysterical humanitarianism that was helping to sap the vitality of his country. He was, therefore, popularly but quite erroneously, supposed to be careless of human life. Being matter-of-fact, he realized that success in war is as important today as ever it was, for defeat means economical if not physical death to the conquered. He could appreciate the meaning of that expression *saigner à blanc*; moreover, he knew how eminently ripe for such an operation was his own nation—grown rich and soft through years of peace and money-making. Expecting no misplaced mercy from his enemy, he never accorded it himself. To this trait, and to the fact that, with a true sense of proportion, he had not hesitated upon one occasion to sacrifice a large number of his own men in order to gain more than a compensating advantage elsewhere, he owed his nickname. Given at first in execration by the hasty and ignorant, it had grown to be a name, if not of affection, at least of confidence. To the soldiers under him, it was almost a term of endearment.

Painfully taking off his stiffened gaiters and boots, he placed his aching feet upon the guard-rail of the stove and took a tobacco-pouch from his pocket. As he withdrew the pouch, a dog's-eared photograph fell out. For a minute he gazed sadly at it before picking it up. It was the portrait of a lady and a child, and as The Butcher gazed, his nickname seemed a libel.

Sombre indeed were his thoughts, for never perhaps since the Middle Ages, when life was cheap, had unhappy soldier to face such a problem. It had haunted him ever since he had been driven into this coast town with his field army and had taken command of the fortress. Finding the whole population in the place without adequate food, he had foreseen what must happen. Now it had come to the point. The diagram had made matters so mathematically

Technological warfare carried to the limit of the imagination in Wells's *War of the Worlds,*
1898

clear that the facts had to be faced. His own mind had long since
been made up; but now the Council of Defence must see the
inevitable course. It needed no highly coloured imagination to

realize what the green curve meant to those evicted in such weather, and The Butcher was certainly under no delusions. It meant death from exposure and starvation to hundreds of his own race—men, women, and little ones. This was different from losing soldiers in action, or even shooting down the populace in a food riot. Not responsible for it, he as much as possible kept his thoughts from the man who had placed him in this position. His course of action determined on, he tried not to dwell on the horrors of the inevitable; but, when alone, his mind reverted to the subject. He sat on, wearied, wrestling with his dreadful thoughts, his rough features lit up in the semi-gloom by the glow from his pipe. Do what he would, he could not blot out from his sight the starving crowd, wandering blindly in the snow between the hostile armies; and the group on the photograph kept intruding itself on the scene! As to the chance of the besiegers receiving the refugees or giving them passage, it never entered his head. He knew War, and he knew his enemy.

Suddenly, a more dreadful possibility, suggested to him by some one more imaginative, recurred to him with insistence. Even when at length his eyes closed, his pipe went out, and his head drooped forward, it continued to occupy his dreams.

* * *

He was in one of the advanced works of the girdle of forts—where he had spent the previous night—standing alone in the snow. Close in front was a searchlight, whose beam slowly swept to and fro across the landscape. Not far off, to one side and well clear of the beam, was its observer. Though no snow was falling, the bitter wind now and then whirled up little clouds of it from the ground, which, as they eddied through the ray of light, flashed out like dazzling swarms of fire-flies dancing past. He was close enough to hear the 'phit-phit' which ended the wild career of those flakes which chanced to encounter the metal projector, heated by the electric arc spluttering within.

Between the gusts the air cleared, and he caught a glimpse over the undulating country towards the enemy's lines, a long distance off. From this stretch of country all vegetation had been cleared, but its billowy nature still provided shelter unsearched by the light, where masses might collect unseen. Close in front he saw the inner wire-entanglement standing out black and cruel against the snow, and farther out the repetition of this pitiless web of barbed wire—a continuous grey band.

The enemy seemed to him to be inactive. A strange quiet reigned over their lines, and between the howling gusts the silence was only broken by the hiss of the carbons, the distant bark of an oil-engine, and the noise of sleeping men as they snored and muttered. Just behind the parapet lay the line of figures wrapped in blankets and skins. They were, except the look-outs, indeed asleep in spite of the continual rustling and coughing. Now and again there were snatches of incoherent babble, and even of laughter, but no notice was taken by their companions or by the few officers and non-commissioned officers pacing up and down close to him. After each gust, gigantic shadows danced over the country as the collected snow was rubbed off the lenses by a gloved hand; occasionally the light was altogether cut off for a period. He stood watching. Everything seemed going well.

A bell rang under the light emplacement, and the recumbent telephone operator swore deeply as he got up with his blankets clinging to him, and placed the cold instrument to his tingling ear. It was a message from some one at the next fort, who imagined that he saw something. The ray from their light could be seen fixed steadily towards the North-West. An officer came to the instrument, and a brief conversation ensued over the wire. A gong sounded, and with a clicking noise the needle of a dial close to the telephone jerked to a certain bearing. The search-light above quietly swung to the desired direction, while the officer joined the observer.

The Butcher followed. There, right away among the ghostly sand-dunes, now that the converging rays of light were focused on the spot, something could be distinguished in the concentrated rays. Something moving—a dark body—a mass against the snow. He could only come to one conclusion: it was the enemy advancing to an assault—madness on their part unless they succeeded in effecting a surprise. The officer looked long, then, placing a whistle between his lips, blew. This signal was taken up and repeated on all sides till the air was full of shrill sound. The observers continued to watch. The whole place became alive, though there was no shouting, no real noise; but despite the efforts to preserve silence, the click of opening magazine cut-offs and the metallic rattle of cartridge-clips were unmistakable.

The Butcher tried to estimate the direction and rate of advance, and after a short pause, evidently for the same purpose, the observing officer whistled again twice. The light was turned off, and the ray from the other fort also disappeared. For a few minutes the quiet bustle continued as guns were unhooded and trained, and piles of ammunition uncovered. The hot-water bags, which had been nestling against the water-jackets of the machine-guns, were thrown aside. Two or three baby search-lights were now got ready, each in its own little emplacement. They could throw a dispersed beam for a comparatively short range over a wide area—just what was required for the coming slaughter. The long-range concentrated beam had served to pick up the quarry far away; but when it came to the 'kill', the whole front would be flooded with the glare from those baby lights, the special role of which it was to dazzle the sheep and light up the shambles. The electric circuits to the mines among the entanglements were again tested, the connections made to the firing-keys by which these volcanoes would be made to erupt.

Here and there a man took off his glove and sucked his trigger-finger to get the numbness out, for the cold metal seared as if already hot. The great light deceptively shone forth again once or twice, and glared everywhere but in the right direction, for there was no need to impress overmuch on the enemy, now marching to his doom across the snow, that they had been seen.

Silently in the dark and the stabbing cold, The Butcher waited; he was pleased—not that he gloated over the coming slaughter, but his soldier's instinct could not but be soothed by the impending success and by the way things had been done. His ideas had been carried out to the letter, and not a soul had asked either advice or orders. All had known their duty, all had done it. There had been no hesitation, no useless gun-fire at uncertain ranges: once discovered, the enemy had been as far as possible lured on to certain destruction. When their silent masses should reach the flat beyond the outer obstacle, the defences dark and noiseless in front of them, their hopes would rise high; but when, checked by the entanglement and struggling in the maze of barbed wire, a flood of light from those earthworks suddenly blinded and threw them into a blaze of glare—! To pursue the matter further was too much even for *him*—and what good? These things had to be.

Whilst allowing his thoughts to run ahead, he had stood calm, but elsewhere the tension had now become extreme. Only one finger trembling over-hard against a trigger and the whole plan would be given away—the victims warned. It was a moment when a man—well-meaning but of untrained nerve—might spoil the greatest *coup*.

It was strange, indeed, but no such hail of shrapnel was falling on these works as might have been expected with an assault so close. Nor was there the usual amount of firing from the enemy's lines: what there was seemed to be directed elsewhere. The hum of rifle-bullets even was absent. The enemy must indeed be mad! To assault from such a distance, and to neglect to assist this assault in forcing by their gun-fire the defenders to keep under cover! Of course, it was to help towards a surprise; but he wondered.

There was now a general rustling among the men. Though seeing nothing, all had an undefinable feeling that the moment was close, very close. He himself was infected by the contagion—his pulse quickened. Suddenly his heart almost stopped as the true reason for the absence of the enemy's fire struck him dizzy. Those silently advancing masses were not the enemy. Great God! He knew now! They were the Useless Mouths that had been thrust out. The picture of the wanderers in the snow again came before him. He could see them, and among them he could distinguish—!

He tried to shout—to warn the waiting garrison not to open fire— that it was not the enemy; but horror had frozen his voice, which rattled in his throat. He tore open his collar, shouted again, but not a soul heard or even looked up. He tried to run forward to touch them—to shake them; he could not move—his feet were frozen so hard to the ground that the effort was agony. While he struggled he heard the snick of the breech-blocks. Grip tightened on rifle and machine-gun handles were clutched.

As he made one more frantic effort to shout, a rocket shot up in the distance, leaving behind it a parabolic green trail in the sky. There was one loud report and a flash—!

* * *

He awoke.

That he had knocked over a candle in his struggles or that his feet were scorching, he did not notice, for he was in a cold sweat, dazed and trembling.

The dread dream still held him. As he gazed vaguely round, in the gloom he saw the diagram, and the hateful green curve—that curve which marked out so clearly where duty lay—caught his eye and brought him back to the facts. Getting up, he looked at his watch, then stamped up and down in his stockinged feet oblivious of snow, dust, or nails. A great struggle was going on within him—a struggle between conscience and sentiment. Every time he faced the chart and saw that curve, the cause of duty received an impulse. Every time he turned away the dream again possessed him, and a feeling of humanity prevailed. He tried to reason. He tried to persuade himself that his fears were groundless, that no such horror could occur, for all would be warned when the wretched souls were turned out. But he knew too well that on a dark night anything may happen; so he anew tried to persuade himself that to be shot, even by their own kith and kin, was after all a more speedy, a more merciful end, than to be frozen. His efforts were all in vain.

He walked to the door, opened it, stopped in hesitation, and then came back to his chair, leaving the door ajar. Once again the shrilling of the wind and the fluttering of the papers on the wall filled the air. There was a tearing sound and, alas for the sergeant's handiwork! One corner of the diagram tore off its nail and hung flapping to and fro. The green curve was hidden. One influence on the side of duty was gone.

He looked up. Though not superstitious, he muttered—'So be it!'

His mind once again made up, his expression relaxed. He rang. The Chief-of-Staff entered, a paper in his hand, much surprised to find the Governor sitting with boots and gaiters off in that icy draught.

'I have changed my mind. Have you made out the orders I told you?'

'Yes, sir; here they are.'

The Governor took the paper, and, to the astonishment of his junior, tore it in small pieces.

'I now want you to make out draft orders according to the purple curve over there, and let me see them.'

'But, sir, you remember what that means?' said the staff-officer. 'Surely—'

'Yes. I remember. I have made up my mind not to turn them out, and to take the chance. I know what you wish to say—that the food won't last. I have thought of that—I'll risk it. We must take risks sometimes. Now I'm due to meet the Council; but my task will be easier than I thought.'

He started up and would have left the room bootless as he was, had not the Chief-of-Staff pointed out his condition.

'By the way, please have that diagram taken down: I shall not want it any longer. If you need to refer to it for orders, destroy it afterwards.'

His bewildered subordinate stood speechless. He noticed, as his chief left the room, that the tough man appeared at last to be ageing. He walked almost feebly.

IV

The Dives Restaurant was well filled.

The bald-headed man, with the gold glasses and the pendulous lower lip, finished his peach with gusto, and beckoned to one of the polyglot waiters hovering about the special party in this hotel— one of the fashionable rendezvous of the capital. It was a man's dinner, but the private room in which the diners were seated opened out into the large restaurant, filled, in spite of bad times, by a crowd of men and women seated at small tables. The crowd was what is termed 'Smart', inasmuch as all were clean, richly dressed, and of outwardly unimpeachable solvency; many, too, were distinguished, or, at least, sufficiently well known for their presence to be noted next day in the society column of the papers.

The large room presented a brilliant and gay scene, and the style of the whole hotel expressed that note of luxury demanded by the Sybarites of every capital from the resorts which aim at being the vogue. To the lucky mortals able to pay for its hospitality, the winds were indeed tempered, and all the senses were lulled by the atmosphere of protection and refined luxury. The carefully regulated temperature, though now perhaps a trifle oppressive after the long meal, gave no hint of the winter outside, for no draught could penetrate the revolving doors and double windows. The eye, while pleased by the subtle colour scheme of the decorations and the bright dresses, was undazzled by any direct rays of crude light, for the electric lamps were placed behind a cornice, and the rooms were illumined only by diffused radiance, and by the soft glow of the table lamps in their pink silk shades. The steps of the busy waiters made no sound on the thick carpet; even the sensuous music of the string orchestra was modulated by the discreet distance at which the performers were situated. The babble in the restaurant rose in waves of sound which, however, were never so loud as to hinder the conversation in the private rooms.

A casual glance this winter night at the gay scene in the Dives or in any similar pleasure resorts of the capital would scarcely have given the impression that war had been raging for some months, or that it had been on the whole unsuccessful. 'The Front' was far away, and though many people were mourning, and more were inclined to be pessimistic, the life of the capital continued on the surface much as it had done during peace: people were born, were married, died; business was carried on as far as the general depression permitted. The froth of the population especially still insisted on having its excitements. But the real state of the public mind could have been gauged as much from the way that any trifling success was received as from the savage and ignorant criticism hurled at the army and its generals for every set-back.

The first appearance of the Martian warriors in Wells's *War of the Worlds*

The full-lipped man, having carefully selected another peach, proceeded to peel it with that strict attention to business which had made him what he was. Conversation had flagged during this dinner, notwithstanding the flushed look on some of the faces. The one topic in the minds of all had been tacitly shunned, with the result that was to be expected from such continuous effort at repression. All round the same effect was noticeable. There was an additional reason for any lack of sparkle at this special party, for the intended guest of the evening—the Minister with the triple chin— had, at the last moment, been prevented by pressure of weighty affairs from attending. His absence was not entirely unexpected, and surmises as to its cause had been avoided until the moment of mental and physical relaxation which arrives with coffee and cigars.

'Of course, it must be more bad news,' said one gloomily, as he swung his chair round.

'We have got nothing else for some time. If it had been good the Government would have made the most of it, and would have published it this morning. I suppose it is unavoidable, but I wish we had more details. For instance, I don't like the lack of news about The Butcher at all. The reports are much too vaguely rosy: when it comes to analysing the basis for the official optimism, we find precious little. I don't like it a bit. If only our guest had come, we might have got some pronouncement from him: there's a man for you!'

There was a chorus of assent and then a pause. The bald gentle- man, who had just finished his second peach, deliberately dipped his plump fingers into the scented water of his finger-bowl, removed the gilded band of his cigar, cut it with the same care that he had bestowed on peach-peeling, and lovingly licked the end. When it was alight, he looked at the glowing point to make certain it was burning evenly, wiped his glasses, then spoke in a voice of husky satisfaction which proclaimed he had at last dined, and was for the time beyond the reach of fate.

'Yes—he is a man; but careful, prudent, far-seeing, and square, and therefore we should have got nothing from him unless there were definite good news. But anyway, I have great faith in The Butcher: he makes War with a capital W, and does not play at it. He won't surrender.'

'Why, do you know anything?' was the question snapped out from two or three directions: the speaker was the sort of magnate that gets news early.

'No, I know no more than you do—no more than is public; but I use my brains and make deductions.'

'It's an absolute shame that they do not give us more informa- tion,' interrupted another angrily. 'Here we are, paying for this infernal war, and treated like children, getting nothing but the veriest flapdoodle served out to us. I think censorship is all right in reason; but there are limits. Do they think we can't stand bad news?'

'No,' went on the man opposite, 'but officialdom likes keeping the public in ignorance, for then it obtains a sense of superiority. Of course, the ostensible reason of this secrecy is that the enemy should not be helped by information, which is all right as far as it goes; but my idea is that they keep things secret long after the necessity has passed. It's quite sound keeping intentions dark, but the enemy know of past events as soon as we do. No, no,' he continued mysteriously, 'there's more in it than that. They're hiding something—want to screen somebody—or they're rigging a bit. Take this siege; why, we know nothing of what has really happened. Every one seems content to have confidence in The Butcher! They say he's the right man in the right place, and use other catch phrases, but facts are what we want. The individual is not everything.'

'There you are wrong,' interposed the man with the glasses; 'that's just what does count. It's the individual—the personality—that counts. I take an altogether personal view of the matter, and if any one else but The Butcher were in command, I should have sold. As it is, I am a Bull. Can I say more? He is the best man we have. As I've often said, our army is too luxurious—wants too much—our soldiers are too soft; but not The Butcher. We need hardy men, and I think he is about the only one. Give me hardy soldiers, I say.' With that he shivered slightly, and an attentive waiter at once went up and closed one of the doors.

'He is certainly the strongest man we have,' added another. 'If they had followed his advice all along we should have done much better, but he has been hampered as usual by the statesmen—I mean politicians. Of course I don't *know*, but I believe many of his recommendations haven't been accepted. Anyhow, it's no good moping over possibilities. There may be no bad news. Why anticipate?'

'Quite, why anticipate?' echoed his neighbour—a fair specimen of the gilded youth of the nation, who had hitherto been chiefly noticeable for his bored look. This tired young man wore his hair long: it was dark, glossy hair, brushed straight from his sloping forehead. The receding chin and two prominent teeth seen in profile suggested a rodent; the oily hair well plastered down further suggested a rodent which had eaten its way through a keg of butter. 'Why anticipate? I say,' he repeated, well pleased with his contribution. 'Eh, what?' and replaced an exaggerated cigarette-holder between his lips.

After this there was a pause, perhaps quite naturally, in the conversation, and the whole party listened to the wild music of the reputed Tziganes, who were again playing. It was a lament, the sad refrain being taken up in the bass. As the last low wailing notes of the violoncello died away through the rooms, the hush became general. The vibrations of the strings had awakened too many memories for conversation—faces had grown sad.

The long silence following the music was harshly broken by a distant baying noise from the street, which grew louder as it was repeated at rapid intervals. The current of reverie was interrupted, and there was a universal movement to give orders to the waiters, for this sound—the cry of newsvendors selling special war editions—had become familiar to all. It was impossible to distinguish what was being shouted in hoarse tones, and the papers were awaited with impatience; all pretence at indifference was cast aside.

Returning with the others, one waiter rushed into the private room with three or four papers, which were torn from his grasp. The man with the glasses, being near the door, got the first copy. He read the scare heading—all there was—out loud, in a horror-struck wheeze:

'UNSUCCESSFUL SORTIE. GOVERNOR WOUNDED. STARVED FORTRESS SURRENDERS!!'

Quite softly he wheezed again to himself—'Fortress surrenders!' Then, dropping his cigar, he sank into his chair and added, 'And I have been buying! *Buying!*'

The rooms were now filled with exclamations, shouts, and even oaths; many were cursing The Butcher, few were taking his part. The band struck up the opening bars of the latest exotic dance, but was shouted into silence, and the dejected revellers began to disperse.

The man with the glasses sat on, fingering his glass of *crème de menthe*. Again he panted, 'If it had been any other I should not have backed him. Ah!—damn him, damn him! Traitor! I wonder where he failed?'

Tremulously raising his glass, he drained the warming cordial. As it flowed, a film of the sticky liqueur clung to the curve of the glass, and, catching the light, gleamed momentarily emerald.

That night The Butcher lay dying in the enemy's hands—his last moments embittered by the idea that he had betrayed his country.

That night also—in the capital—a certain politician lay sleepless. Perhaps he, too, may have thought—?

The Trenches

CAPTAIN C. E. VICKERS

This remains the tactical problem of all ages, how to get men enough together within efficient killing distance of their enemy.

War and the World's Life, p. 97

I

'I WISH that organ would dry up! It puts me off so that I can't read this thing.'

'Yes,' responded Major Swann; 'the first time it came and played "Sing me to Sleep" outside here, it seemed rather a jest. But the organ-grinder's sense of humour must be getting less keen: he doesn't know when we've had enough. I've sent a messenger outside to move him on.'

The organ droned on outside for a minute or so, and then stopped rather suddenly in the middle of a pathetic note, as if some of the tune had been bitten off.

As you may perhaps have guessed, it was at the War Office: the speakers were Captain Marshall and Major Swann, who sat at large desks on opposite sides of a large room cheerfully hung round with a fair array of drawings and maps, conspicuous among which was one showing British possessions and colonies in red. The former officer seemed to have a lot of correspondence to deal with, for big bundles of papers were piled on one side of the table, and he would from time to time pick one up, untie the red tape which confined it like a belt, look through a letter, write something, and then throw the bundle into a big basket which stood on the floor by him. Major Swann seemed to have to do with plans and drawings rather, for there were many rolls of them on his desk and some spread out on an adjacent table: besides, there were cases of shallow drawers labelled with names of fortresses and barracks. The man of plans was engaged at the moment in measuring and comparing some particulars, using dividers and rule, occasionally referring to a sheet of notes,—evidently, from his knitted brows, a troublesome thing to understand or settle.

Rather a keen-eyed man, this Swann. Not much hair left on his head; but what there was, fair and curly. Gold-rimmed glasses, behind which a quizzical expression occasionally gleamed. You could see when he stood up that he was broad-shouldered and energetic-looking. Not an office man, you would think; as a matter of fact, he had spent a good deal of his time on the Indian frontier, and again on designing and constructing roads and bridges—work in which there is more nerve and resource called for than is always admitted.

It had pleased the Powers that Be, however, to think it a good idea to bring in a man with field experience to deal with questions concerning the design of military buildings and so on. Not, indeed, that the military chiefs are wont to undervalue experience—it is the political people who can't see the value, because in their own line it isn't wise to be too practical—but it isn't always easy to find the round peg to fit the hole. Major Swann was nothing loth. He rather liked living in London, though he would sometimes say that if he only tried to come too punctually he would acquire a daily-bread-face—like other toilers. 'Regular habits are one road to perdition in the Service,' he would say.

Marshall sighed—'Some of these old stories are awfully complicated. This began by being a question about drainpipes; and here has some one managed to switch it off on to a disquisition about carrier-pigeons, and I can't quite make out where the pipe ends and the pigeon begins! I wish to goodness they'd stick to one subject!'

'Some of the big bosses think too much about their fads, and too little about the main question,' rejoined Swann. 'By the bye, *à propos* of that, I've got a man coming to see me about a patent drain-excavator this morning. He's American, I fancy; and I guess he'll just about make the Great American Eagle flap around this benighted office. Don't go away when he comes. I'll probably need your moral support; and, besides, you can remind me of an engagement if he gasses too much.'

'Another of your interviewers! I suppose I shan't get any work done,' remarked Marshall, 'do you want me to take notes?'

At this moment the door opened, and another man came in rather hurriedly, holding a yellow slip of paper in his hand. He approached the senior officer. 'Say, John Henry, when are you going to let us have the designs of Queen's Battery? The old man is asking after them, and anyway I've got a return to make out showing how things are getting on.'

'Well, Harris,' responded Major Swann (affectionately known as John Henry), after making some inquiries down a speaking-tube, 'they're tracing them in the drawing room. You'll have them in a day or two. I suppose there isn't any frantic hurry?'

'Only that they're going to have another pow-wow, and alter the scheme, I suppose. I must say Defence Policy changes a bit too quick for me. No sooner have we got a programme safely finished—and sometimes no more than started—than a new Board of Admiralty comes in or something, and it's all got to be done again. I must say, the Admiralty usually move mighty slow, but when they do change their minds, it's like an earthquake or a cataclysm. Now, according to my scheme—'

'You don't seem to have much to do, Harris,' broke in Marshall, heaving a big bundle of papers into his basket, and carefully lighting a pipe. 'Thought you had a fight on with the finance people!'

'Cruel fellow you are, Marshall, to remind me of so painful a subject. I had a hint that it would be better to declare peace if I didn't want to get disliked. What I say is, how can one keep up one's

The Land Ironclads go into action in Wells's tale of armoured warfare

profesh while polishing the seat of one's pants on an office chair, unless one does a little fighting now and then, if it's only on paper? But the hatchet is buried, the tomahawk rusts forgotten! By the bye, are any of you fellows going to the manoeuvres?'

'Look here, my lad,' interjected Major Swann, 'I'm rather busy just now. Do you mind holding your Strategy Board in the next room? There's an American josser coming to see me about a machine of his, and I haven't had time to read up the papers he sent me about it yet.'

Harris went out again, somewhat hurt, perhaps, for he had rather a good conceit of himself; and silence fell on the room for a while.

Presently a messenger came in with a piece of paper. 'The gentleman seems in a hurry to see you, sir.'

'All right. Take these papers away.'

The newcomer was a keen-faced, rather restless-looking citizen of the United States. He advanced and shook the Major warmly by the hand. The latter motioned him to a chair.

'Glad to see you, sir. They didn't know much about things upstairs, though they were mighty polite; but I managed to make them understand at last that I wanted to see the man who deals with these things, and hadn't merely come to talk. You will be interested in this here machine, Major. It's just about the latest and cutest idea in trenching machines—trench along through any darned thing: just set it to the width and depth, and it'll go along any distance you please, and you can follow up with the pipes as fast as your men can lay them.'

'Oh, I understand quite well that the machine is intended for cutting out drain or irrigation trenches; but I want to know a little about its pace and weight, and how it is drawn, and what it will cut through, and all that.'

'See here, sir; that machine will just move right along by its own power through pretty well any sort of soil, same as if it was butter. It'll heave out the stuff into a dump-cart if you like, or else it'll leave it alongside the trench, handy for you to put it in again when you're ready. Now, I reckon if your department were to try one of them, they'd soon quit usin' any sort of hand work for trenchin'. Cuts better and quicker, and you don't need any gang boss behind to jolly up the men diggin'. As to the stuff—we can supply pretty well any sort of cutting tools, and don't mind takin' chunks out of any sort of rock, short of what needs blasting anyway.'

'Ought to be pretty handy, Mr Emery, if it will do all that,' said Swann; 'but you know what a Government Department is—fair to moderately slow taking up new ideas. First of all, they'll want me to report all about it, and refer back two or three times for more particulars; then somebody will suggest referring to a committee, then the committee has to be appointed and to meet, then the committee will talk and may make experiments, and get out volumes of statistics— and, finally, they'll find out there isn't any money to buy one till next year.'

'Well, sir, I'm not afraid of your red tape. I did imagine you would understand the masheen, of course—'

'I don't see,' said Major Swann, a little nettled, 'why you wanted to come and see me, if that's all. Of course, we're always pleased to explain anything you want to know, but we have all particulars of your machine in the papers you sent, haven't we? Of course, I can't tell you what may be decided.'

'Well, see here, Major. Your durned old War Office moves mighty slow, and it sort of seemed to me that calling round might hustle things a bit. Your War Department needs something to aid its digestion now and then. Now in my country, when a businessman sees a good thing he's right on to it like a perching cassowary. I did reckon from your face that you see some good points about it: isn't it so?'

'Well, you mustn't ask me to give myself away, Mr—er—Sandpaper. It seems to me sound enough, but in an office like this there are a good many people all to have their whack about an invention. I suppose you wanted us to take it up as an invention? And then we usually get the local officers to experiment with it and report, and it all takes time.'

'Reminds me a bit,' ejaculated the visitor, 'of the young fellow who said on the Morning After that he only needed a Glass of Water and a few Kind Words. I thought you might be able to give me some idea what chance there was of getting orders.'

'Oh, I know it's disappointing; but governments move very, very slow—else perhaps it would not be so well worthwhile getting government contracts. However, I did want to ask you one or two things. Our mechanical people thought one or two of the dodges rather ingenious. Just a moment: I'll unroll the drawing. Now would you explain to me what that spiral spring does?'

'That little whing-whang with the butterfly-nut? Oh! that's . . .'

They were lost in a maze of technicalities, and perhaps we won't trouble to follow them.

'Do you know,' remarked the elder officer, 'that man will come and sit on the doorstep every day till something happens. I think it's a good thing . . . By Jove! I think it's a great thing. I see an idea. Marshall, I believe there are possibilities, but (gloomily) I suppose that means sending it to the Inventions Committee.'

'To the Grave of Inventions, eh?' said Marshall. 'Do they ever say anything except *No further action recommended*, or *Too expensive*, or something really solid and British like that? Keep calm, and let your illusions cool off. I don't know what it all was, as I've been trying to straighten out a Pay case while you've been confabulating with that hairy-headed man. Tell me about it as we go across to lunch. By the bye, did you go to see the new Gaiety piece?'

II

It was drawing towards evening, and the noise seemed inclined to subside. At the farmhouse amidst the trees, where the General had made his headquarters, certainly the roar of battle had never come near enough to be really disturbing: the heavy concussion of the big guns, the screech of shell, the rattle of musketry all day, had been merged into a sort of dull rumble, like a heavy thunderstorm reverberating, rising, and falling, but not that crashing, rending, ear-splitting tornado of sound which reigned on the battle-field itself. Generals have too much to think of to expose themselves in the day of battle to so many upsetting influences. It is sufficient to come out and view the development when all the combinations have been made.

Centre of a great nervous system as it was, there were a good many people going to and fro round that house of the many telephone wires. Officers would ride up and dismount every now and then, and there were a group of orderlies outside to look after horses and take messages.

Inside, in the sitting-room, where chairs and a conglomeration of impedimenta had been shoved unceremoniously to one side, a youngish man in khaki uniform was standing at the long table under the window. A big drawing was set out before him, consisting, apparently, of a number of separate pieces fixed down by drawing-pins. Coloured pencils, rulers, and some saucers of ink lay on a side table, with his belts and gear. It was a large-scale map. He held a telephone to his ear, and was at the same time consulting a sheaf of papers and making notes. Presently he put down the telephone and, taking up a small box, began to sort out and stick in little flags here and there on the map—red and blue, the former marked with various names.

If one had been looking over his shoulder, one would see by degrees a sort of pattern emerging from the arrangement of pin-flags, and that the red contour lines on the map marked out a sort of series of ridges and hills on this side and that, between which there was open ground. There were some blue lines, too, indicating streams, and an occasional splash of green or blob of black.

He sighed a little and muttered to himself, 'They don't seem to have got much forrarder. I wish we knew more about that section on their right centre; but I don't suppose we shall ever get a proper sketch for it now'; and then, apparently inconsequently, 'Poor chap!'

The fact was that the sketches of the enemy's position which the topographical officers had been sent out to get were not all perfect. One of them had got killed before he had finished, and the party sent out in search of him had brought back a very imperfect sketch only.

The door from the inner room opened, and an elder man looked in. He was tall and thin, a dark burnt face with prominent nose and deep-set sharp eyes more or less concealed by heavy gold-rimmed glasses. He looked very weary, but moved briskly, and spoke with a certain crisp decisiveness which would at once draw attention.

'Are you about ready, Williams? The General wants to look at the map. He's been busy with the Ordnance and Supply people, and there isn't too much time to settle the orders.'

'Yes, sir; I've got all the information plotted, but of course reports keep coming in. I'm not very sure about the cavalry.'

The elder man went in again, closing the door softly.

Williams resumed the telephone.

'Oh, by the way,' said Colonel Anson, looking in again, 'just try and catch the Chief Engineer and get him to come here.'

'Very good, sir; I can get him on the telephone.'

Bald-headed and spectacled, Colonel Anson did not at all give the impression of a brilliant strategist, and yet he was the Chief of Staff of this great army, the man who calculated out the moves necessary to fulfil his general's plan of campaign. Indeed, the more brilliant and dashing the general, the more cool and calculating does his principal general staff officer need to be. A little mistake may ruin everything. Anson had been known from time immemorial as The Professor—a professor, mind you, who was a terror to the superficial soldier, he had such a way of penetrating by some searching remark into the depths of the shallow one's ignorance.

There are so many things to be thought of in running a campaign. If it is easy to order troops about, things like finding where they go to, keeping track of what happens, and giving them what they want, those need an eye; and behind the spectacles there was indeed a sharp eye.

The General—it was, of course, Axe—was a man of a very different temperament, quick and bluff, but nervous. He excelled in an intuitive grasp of the situation and in judgement of men. Wont as he was to set them hard tasks, his power of putting in a few words what he wanted done, and his unfailing appreciation of good work, made him a born leader. To look at, he was rather short and tubby, spruce and tough, a hard rider to hounds in peace, and one who held on like a burr in war.

The General's temper was somewhat ruffled when he came in. Indeed, it was not surprising, for, as Williams had been heard to remark, affairs had not got much forrarder during the day, and the reports of the Ordnance and Supply officers had shown that affairs were not going absolutely like a machine. One can imagine the difficulties in getting up all the stores that may be wanted, but a trifling oversight may upset big plans.

'I can't make out why they were such idiots. Any fool could guess we'd need more picks and shovels!' he was remarking as he came in. 'Let's see that big map. Give me a pair of dividers, and tell me the scale.'

The two men bent over the map for a few minutes, then Anson said, 'I think it makes clear what I was saying. Unless we can manage to establish ourselves closer to some bit of their line, I don't see how we are to break it.'

'Yes, but you know yourself that time is everything. We simply can't afford to stay here facing them until their fleet has time to get up the coast. Of course, it's only a possibility; but if they did get there, we'd be absolutely diddled. I haven't an army to detach.'

'Well,' responded the other, 'supposing we played the holding game, spread out the troops quietly along the front, and sent off Vigner's Division with some extra mounted infantry to try and get round. Get out the general map, Williams. With luck it might have a good moral effect. I've got a man in my department who knows every inch of the country—used to have some sort of carrier business hereabouts. It would be a chance.'

'It would be a chance,' echoed the General; 'but from what Vigner told me—you didn't talk to him, did you?—his men aren't worth much at the moment. They had it pretty hot, and I'm afraid their losses have been rather heavy. Have you the casualty returns?'

'No; the casualty returns are not in yet. Shall I telephone?'

'No; I'm not sure that we can't manage something.' He studied the map again. 'That's the key of the position!' and he put his finger on a place where a rise in the ground was indicated.

'Ah, here's Spofforth!'

And in fact, it was Colonel Spofforth who came in at this moment. The Chief Engineer looked fatigued and rather overdone. He had spent a tiring day. Away from the battle, his business had been mainly with the organization of his supplies and his machinery. The handmaid arm, it is true, does not often fight battles, but it sometimes contributes a good deal towards winning them. Without water an army cannot exist for long: it is the engineer's province to provide water. If the transport cannot get up supplies fast enough, it is the engineer who organizes the railway service. When the enemy's fire waxes too deadly, it is he who plans the trenches, and with mine and gabion makes slow but sure approaches.

'Spofforth, it seems as if this were going to be a sort of siege affair—your department, I think. I want your views as to what you're prepared to do. Don't say it's a matter of space and time!'

'Thank you, General, but perhaps you will excuse my saying I'm not quite *au fait* with the situation. I've had to spend nearly all my day at the Park seeing to demands of stores and a lot of pure business, which doesn't show yet; but we've got some useful things just come. Perhaps, if Colonel Anson would show me on the map?'

The three heads bent over the map, Anson explaining, quoting figures of the men available (he had a wonderful memory for figures), pointing out what reports he had of the enemy, giving a sketch of the day's fighting.

The Chief Engineer nodded at intervals. 'I suppose,' he said at last, 'if we could put some approaches through during the night towards that place I have my finger on, it would make a good base for tomorrow's attack?'

'If the enemy don't move their guns,' said Anson.

'They're bound to stick to that salient,' said the General; 'it commands their line.'

'Well, sir, I think the trenching machines that have just been got ready—they're in my Park—might do the trick. If I might use your telephone it would save time. Start from the point just north-east of Harrod's Store—there's a strong post there, I think you said?'

III

(From our Correspondent)

For the moment things seem to be at a deadlock: the armies have been at grips, but have had to draw off without any advantage gained on either side. It almost seems as if the conflict were like to resolve itself into pseudo-siege operations. And yet, how suddenly may the kaleidoscope of war be shaken and the picture be changed. The pattern of the struggle is indeed intricate. Battles are waged not merely between men, but between opposing generals. Uncle Toby manoeuvred his forces on the bowling-green; even so do generals shift them—on the map—and the orders go out by telegraph, and the men march, they fight, they struggle, the guns roar: wounds, carnage, it is all but part of the working out of a calculation; men, guns, battalions, companies, horse, foot, and artillery, all are merely the bits which go towards making up the pattern. The machine has begun to dominate war, but the directing power is in the general's brain, and it is between generals that the game is played.

The machine! . . . But it seems such a simple, almost obvious, notion to evolve a machine that shall dig trenches, that shall be able to move unconcernedly across open ground where no man can show himself scatheless, secure under its turtleback of steel, inconspicuous, minding all the hail of lead as little as rain, patient. They have nicknamed it The Snail, but it can burrow forward like a mole![1]

Last evening we correspondents were, for the first time, allowed a little freedom to go forward and see the dispositions. Up to now, as you know, we have but been allowed to get as far as headquarters and the depots, and have had to reconstruct the situation as best we might from the meagre information vouchsafed us by the Intelligence Department. It was a strange feeling to walk through the quiet night, conscious how it was charged with the electricity of combat, soon to burst again into din and struggle; to pass alone the line of eminences which mark our position, making detours now and then to avoid the obstacles—complex wire arrangements; looking across the flat featureless plain which separates us from the entrenchments of our opponent—a level varied but by dim shadows.

In front of us in the trenches men sleeping, their arms at hand: how many of them sleeping to awaken for the last time, who can prophesy. Advanced again, sentries and patrols, the screen which interposes and guards against efforts to pry into our dispositions.

'Little clumps of men, outflanked and unable to get away'. A scene in Wells's 'The Land Ironclads', *Strand Magazine*, 1903

Behind us in the woods others, supports and reserves—a little wondering, perhaps what role they will have to play on the morrow; some of them waking, thinking of home and of you mayhap; some wakeful and restless, some—but who shall say how each is affected by the thought of fighting! Behind the hill, the guns, their muzzles poking up grimly towards the sky. The artillery are alert, for it is they above all who must be ready against any sudden move across the plain. Farther back again, the railway; trains faintly rumbling hither and thither, distributing ammunition, stores, provisions—the railway never seems to be idle.

All this evening, indeed, the troops have been moving again in spite of their wearisome day. It has been a puzzling business, this game of living chess. Vigner's division is now somewhere away on the right, Klepside's is near us, Arkwright's away over there. There seem to be regiments everywhere, men everywhere, ready to move on.

Luckily, I met a friend up at the front, Captain Cuthbert, with whom I had made acquaintance in the train coming here, when he was carrying dispatches. An officer in charge of dispatches is allowed some extra room in the train to himself, and he was kind enough to make space for a tired correspondent. It is remembered to his credit with a grateful remembrance.

'Cuthbert,' said I, 'what do you think about the situash? what's your regiment going to do?'

'Oh, the same old game, I suppose: going out and getting potted at. What you scribes call "the hail of lead", and all that sort of thing: first digging like a mole, and then sitting in a beastly trench, and never getting a chance to draw a bead on the other people. This time they say we're going to make a real dart at 'em, though. They've given us each a picture of the trenches.' And he produced a neat little map, showing, in zigzag lines, a sort of scheme of approach trenches.

'Going to dig all that?' says I. 'You'll have a bit of a day's work. Your men have all got picks and shovels, I suppose?'

'Oh, my men are very nice and snug down there in the blindages. Quite a good egg, the arrangement; come and look. My dug-out's just down beyond there—"Picnic Villa", they call it. No, sir, we aren't to do any digging. The machine takes on all that.'

And above the moon is shining, pale; scurrying clouds dim her disc. But no; who cares for the moon, with those searchlights ceaselessly gleaming, staring here and there, prying out to discern anything moving over the plain that separates us from the enemy, that coveted mile or so that must be crossed before the day is lost or won! Were it not for those flaring lights, it would seem as if both sides were resting, renewing their strength against the moment when the first gun shall usher in the renewal of the storm.

Resting! No; there is a new sound. Somewhere down below something has begun to be busy. Something is at work amid the mists of the plain. It is as if a little reaping-machine had set out to cut some ghostly corn. No, not quite a reaping-machine—more like some mammoth death-watch. It must be some strange animal: something endowed with life, for is not that another calling to its mate?

Cuthbert's little dug-out, which he shares with the other officers of his company, is snugger than one might suppose: these old hands know how to take care of themselves, and if the grub is not very rich, the company is very cheery. It is agreeable to be among these young fellows, whose thoughts for the morrow are mainly of the chances of having a dash at the enemy, and who display such a keen interest in reminiscences of other wars.

Sounds from without penetrate now and then, but they tell me I can't see anything: the mist has thickened, and now the dark has come on; that it would not be safe to go dodging round—men keeping guard at night are rather apt to have short ways with suspicious coves, you know. We are getting sleepy, and so, finally, we all turn in. They remind me, who must stay awake a little longer to write, that we shall all have to be stirring early enough anyway.

And so the night passes.

With the grey dawn someone pokes in a head and warns us to awake. An old hand does not take long turning out, and I know that it behoves me to be about business, if I would be in time for the overture. The guns may be tuning up soon. With a hasty God-speed, I leave my friends and am climbing the rise to near where I saw the battery last night.

From up here, as the mist lifts, the country spreads out like a great panorama: first, the higher ground, whence they tell me the enemy has been firing, looms forth. Wherever the action is going, the direction and observation must be done from somewhere over there—one can imagine some sort of Intelligence reaching forth antennae, groping more or less blindly, for so it must be in the fight, to tell what is toward and carry back news to the brain behind. It is too far to make out anything by mere vision.

The silvery mists linger over the plain for a while; gradually the veils fade away. It reminds one somewhat of observing Mars, for through the mists one begins to discern something like canals—from up here, that is: they show very little from the enemy's side. They are the trenches. And as one sees more clearly, one recognizes how regularly patterned they are—one recalls the little plan with its zigzag lines. It is The Snail's work!

But all this has not been done without casualty. There are two or three battered heaps still smoking. Those bursts of fire which we heard last night have not been without some result: some of the machines have been wrecked, and some of the gallant drivers have been sacrificed—but a wonderful network of trenching has been accomplished.

On our side, too, things are moving. From here I can see lines of men assembling and melting away, moving off slowly but surely into the plain, vanishing, it would seem, into the ground. They are occupying the trenches.

At last! One can imagine a button being pressed somewhere. There is a burst of battle away on the right. The day has begun. . . .

IV

(From our Correspondent)

The volume of artillery fire has been growing—it seems feeble to describe it as a crescendo effect; howitzer and mortar belch forth projectiles from their murky throats; with roar of explosion and scream of shell overhead, the air is full of noise, of things hurtling, of rattle and bang. It is the bass of a thunderous concerto, in which the voice part is to be taken by the rifle.

Day has been creeping up, and now we see more clearly across the plain. Like some cloud-burst, the intensity of shell-fire has concentrated on the rising ground just opposite us, and plume after plume of smoke rises into the air as the shells burst over where the enemy's trenches are, though we cannot distinguish them. Preliminary bombardment they say is a thing of the past, but this is not preliminary bombardment: just as when, at the siege of San Sebastian, the stormers lay down to let the hail of shell pass over them, so the function of the artillery fire is now to keep down the shooting of the defenders while our men creep forward and draw nearer the doomed lines. As we watch we can make out a swarm of dark figures, like ants from an ant-hill, crawling forward, each carrying a burden.

Some of them fall, some are dragged back to the trench, some remain crouching behind the little mound of sandbags: now and then something bursts, and the scene is shrouded in a cloud of smoke—it is a hand-grenade. Bit by bit, however, the little mound grows, something is gained.

The pitiless whirl and smash of shell and the incessant thunder of the guns keep on; one's head whirls, and it seems as if one's eardrums must burst. The intensity of the fighting is concentrating on the ground in front of us. And all the time a sort of trickle of men is coming back from the trenches: slowly moving, this stream, the waste, the expended, stretchers bearing back wounded to the dressing-stations.

It is a bludgeon business when you come to close quarters. I have

Repair work going on inside the gas-chambers of the giant zeppelins in H. G. Wells's *The War in the Air*, 1908

seen men in the trenches fighting with picks and crowbars, with any convenient weapon, in the heat of hand-to-hand combat: a shovel in the hands of a strong man makes a very fair substitute for a cleaver. Fighting in the trenches is veritably a bloody affair.

Look yonder. As if something has burst forth, a swarm of black things scatters out from their cover. We are hand to hand now. Here and there, gleams: they are bayonets. The line dashes forward, wavers; it is almost swallowed up in yellowish dust: rifle and bayonet are doing their deadly work; men dash up to the trenches, impelled by the fury which urges them to try and get at the foemen concealed by the sod cover: but the riflemen are steady, each is ensconced in his niche, each has a good view over the ground from his concealment: few reach the trench, many gasp, stagger, and fall as the rifle speaks to them; the line thins, straggles. My God! The attack has failed!

A long and exasperating struggle, this, in front of the salient hill, and yet we can see that the Chief means to make a desperate effort to take it. Again and again, men are hurled at it with sandbag and rifle. Little clusters form themselves behind the painfully accumulated cover here and there; but they are isolated, at a standstill: it seems as if plan had been lost.

Only a while ago I told you what wonderful trenching the machine had done last night. How is it no attempt has been made today? No one quite knows. Perhaps it is that all the machines have been knocked out, or else their cutting gear is blunted, or else the petrol supply has run out. And yet, even while we are asking, a fresh development has taken place. A machine is at work again. I can see through my glasses a turtle-backed affair pushing out from the advanced trench, something half concealed in a cloud of dust, the same sort of cloud which a motor makes on a dusty day. The guns thunder out, but the rushes of ants have ceased for a while.

The machine has not been idle. It has been eating forward, a devious path enough, slantingly so as to avoid the plunging fire. It is drawing nearer. But will it get near enough to assault from? Will not the enemy ply their hand-grenades with as deadly effect as before?

They are bringing up some other clumsy-looking affair into the advanced trench; men have, of course, been occupying the line and keeping up the fire, but what is this to do?

It is a mortar, a childish-looking thing of wood, hooped like a barrel, mounted in a sort of heavy perambulator. They have jammed it in the trench. Truly its range is small, no more than a few yards, but it is to throw something more than a shell: a pinch or so of powder will suffice to lift a sort of portmanteau of dynamite, a dangerous load truly, and it is no wonder that the men are withdrawn round the bend of the trench and the artillery fire concentrated to batter the enemy's head cover while the device is preparing. Once it goes off prematurely, as a crater in our trench testifies; but we are not without a second resort.

Preparation seems slow—oh, how slow to the man behind the field-glasses. At last all is ready. One hears nothing, one has been all but deaf these hours past anyway; but a cloud, scattering like the fingers of an outspread hand, announces that the charge has attained its target. Clods, boulders, tatters of men, and scraps of timber soar into the air, pelting the ground with their wreck. It has cleared that trench, for but a hole in the ground remains.

The stormers are ready. For the last time they dash forward; this time they lodge themselves securely, they empty their magazines along the neighbouring trenches. They have obtained a hold. Vigner has been watching for this moment, and has been pouring his last reserves down the arteries which feed his front. The machine is working furiously, and picks and shovels, entrenching tools and bayonets make the soil fly. An approach is secured. The enemy's reserves are too late to drive them out. The hill is taken!

It is needless to describe in detail how our troops push along the hill, once this commanding point is gained. It is easy to rake the remainder of the position, till at last the moment for the general advance comes.

We are in possession, and the enemy has drawn off. Now our weary men must hasten to harry the rear-guard as it strives to cover the retreat. But many guns have been left behind, and alas! many, many gallant men.

But there is no time to count up fully the gains and losses of the day. My part is to hurry to the telegraph office and to tell you, as fully as they will let me, that we have pushed the enemy back, we have gained a stage on the road, we have been able at last to cry 'Check!' War is a complex and a terrible game. And the end is not yet.

The Secret of the Army Aeroplane

A. A. MILNE

[Mr WILLIAM LE QUEUX wishes to deny indignantly that the following tale was written by him. On the contrary, he identifies himself completely with the proprietor of the *Daily Mail* in deprecating the publishing of scare stories. As the proprietor of the *Daily Mail* truly says, such stories 'place England and Englishmen in a ridiculous and humiliating light before the German people'. At the same time, Mr LE QUEUX is bound to confess that the story printed below bears an astonishing resemblance to his latest imaginative work, *Spies of the Kaiser*—a book only just published, but written in the days of his hot and unregenerate youth, many weeks ago.]

'Yes,' said my friend, Ray Raymond, as a grim smile crossed his typically English face, looking round the chambers which we shared together, though he never had occasion to practise, though I unfortunately had, 'it is a very curious affair indeed.'

'Tell us the whole facts, Ray,' urged Vera Vallance, the pretty fair-haired daughter of Admiral Sir Charles Vallance, to whom he was engaged.

'Well, dear, they are briefly as follows,' he replied with an affectionate glance at her. 'It is well known that the Germans are anxious to get hold of our new aeroplane, and that the secret of it is at present locked in the inventor's breast. Last Tuesday a man with his moustache brushed up the wrong way alighted at Basingstoke Station and inquired for the refreshment-room. This leads me to believe that a dastardly attempt is about to be made to wrest the supremacy of the air from our grasp.'

'And even in the face of this, the Government denies the activity of German spies in England!' I exclaimed bitterly.

'Jacox,' said my old friend, 'as a patriot it is none the less my duty to expose these miscreants. To-morrow we go to Basingstoke.'

Next Thursday, then, saw us ensconced in our private sitting-room at the Bull Hotel, Basingstoke. On our way from the station I had noticed how ill-prepared the town was to resist invasion, and I had pointed this out bitterly to my dear old friend, Ray Raymond.

PROCLAMATION.

CITIZENS OF LONDON.

THE NEWS OF THE BOMBARDMENT of the City of Newcastle and the landing of the German Army at Hull, Weybourne, Yarmouth, and other places along the East Coast is unfortunately confirmed.

THE ENEMY'S INTENTION is to march upon the City of London, which must be resolutely defended.

THE BRITISH NATION and the Citizens of London, in face of these great events, must be energetic in order to vanquish the invader.

The ADVANCE must be CHALLENGED FOOT BY FOOT. The people must fight for King and Country.

Great Britain is not yet dead, for indeed, the more serious her danger, the stronger will be her unanimous patriotism.

GOD SAVE THE KING.

HARRISON, *Lord Mayor.*

MANSION HOUSE,
LONDON, *September 3rd,* 1910.

'THE ENEMY'S INTENTION is to march upon the City of London, which must be resolutely defended.' An illustration in William Le Queux's notorious *Invasion of 1910*

'Yes,' he remarked grimly; 'and it is simply infested with spies. Jack, my surmises are proving correct. There will be dangerous work afoot tonight. Have you brought your electric torch with you?'

'Since that Rosyth affair, I never travel without it,' I replied, as I stood with my back to the cheap mantel-shelf so common in English hotels.

The night was dark, therefore we proceeded with caution as we left the inn. The actions of Ray Raymond were curious. As we passed each telegraph pole he stopped and said grimly, 'Ah, I thought so', and drew his revolver. When we had covered fifteen miles, we looked at our watches by the aid of our electric torches and discovered that it was time to go back to the hotel unless we wished our presence, or rather absence, to be made known to the German spies; therefore we returned hastily.

Next morning Ray was recalled to town by an urgent telegram; therefore I was left alone at Basingstoke to foil the dastardly spies. I stayed there for thirteen weeks, and then went with my old friend to Grimsby, he having received news that a German hairdresser, named Macdonald, was resident in that town.

'My dear Jack,' said my friend Ray Raymond, his face assuming that sphinx-like expression by which I knew that he had formed some theory for the destruction of his country's dastardly enemies, 'tonight we shall come to grips with the Teuton!'

'And yet,' I cried, 'the Government refuses to admit the activity of German spies in England!'

'Ha!' said my friend grimly.

He opened a small black bag and produced a dark lantern, a coil of strong silk rope, and a small but serviceable jemmy. All that burglarious outfit belonged to my friend!

At this moment the pretty fair girl to whom he was engaged, Vera Vallance, arrived, but returned to London by the next train.

At ten o'clock we proceeded cautiously to the house of Macdonald the hair-dresser, whom Ray had discovered to be a German spy!

'Have you your electric torch with you?' inquired my dear old college friend.

'I have,' I answered grimly.

'Good! Then let us enter!'

'You mean to break in?' I cried, amazed at the audacity of my friend.

'Bah!' he said. 'Spies are always cowards!'

Therefore we knocked at the door. It was opened by two men, the elder of whom gave vent to a quick German imprecation. The younger had a short beard.

'You are a German spy?' inquired Ray Raymond.

'No,' replied the bearded German in very good English, adding with marvellous coolness, 'to what, pray, do we owe this unwarrantable intrusion?'

'To the fact that you are a spy who has been taking secret tracings of our Army aeroplane!' retorted by friend.

But the spy only laughed in open defiance.

'Well, there's no law against it,' he replied.

'No,' retorted Ray grimly, 'thanks to the stupidity of a crass Government, there *is* no law against it.'

'My God!' I said hoarsely.

'But my old friend Jacox and I,' continued Ray Raymond, fixing the miserable spy with his eye, 'have decided to take the law into our own hands. I have my revolver and my friend has his electric torch. Give me the tracings.'

„Hm! – Der Ball will überlegt fein! – Direkt werde ich ihn nicht machen können!"

Ironic German view of Edward VII, seen as an international political player snookered in his foreign policy manoeuvres

'Gott—no!' cried the German spies in German. 'Never, you English cur!'

But Ray had already extracted a letter from the elder man's pocket, and was making for the door. I followed him. When we got back to our hotel he drew the letter from his pocket and eagerly examined it. I give here an exact copy of it, and I may state that when we sent it to His Majesty's Minister for War, he returned it without a word!

Berkeley Chambers,
Cannon Street, E.C.

DEAR SIR,—In reply to yours of the 29th ult. we beg to say that we can do you a good line in shaving brushes at the following wholesale prices:

Badger . . . 70s. a gross
Pure badger . . . 75s. a gross
Real badger . . . 80s. a gross

Awaiting your esteemed order which we shall have pleasure in promptly executing,

We are, Sir,
Yours obediently
WILKINSON and ALLBUTT
Mr James Macdonald

That letter, innocent enough upon the face of it, contained dastardly instructions from the Chief of Police to a German spy! Read by the alphabetical code supplied to every German secret agent in England, it ran as follows:

Phrase 1: 'Discover without delay secret of aeroplane's successful descents.'
Phrase 2: 'Forward particulars of best plan for blowing up
  1. Portsmouth Dockyard;
  2. Woolwich Arsenal;
  3. Albert Memorial.'
Phrase 3: 'Be careful of Jack Jacox. He carries a revolver and an electric torch.'

'Ah!' said my friend grimly, 'we were only just in time. Had we delayed longer, England might have knelt at the proud foot of a conqueror!'

'Ha!' I replied briefly.

Next morning we returned to the chambers which we shared together in London, and were joined by Vera Vallance, the pretty fair daughter of Admiral Sir Charles Vallance, to whom my old friend was engaged. And, as he stroked her hair affectionately, I realized thankfully that he and I had indeed been the instruments of Providence in foiling the plots of the German spies!

HOW WILL IT ALL END?
WHEN WILL GERMANY STRIKE?

[*It will end now, before our readers strike*—EDITOR]

The Unparalleled Invasion

Excerpt from Walt Nervin's 'Certain Essays in History'

JACK LONDON

It was in the year 1976 that the trouble between the world and China reached its culmination. It was because of this that the celebration of the Bi-centennial of American liberty was deferred. Many other plans of the nations of the earth were, for the same reason, twisted and tangled and postponed. The world awoke rather abruptly to its danger; but for over seventy years, unperceived, affairs had been shaping toward this very end.

The year 1904 logically marks the beginning of the development that, seventy years later, was to bring consternation to the whole world. The Japanese–Russian War took place in 1904, and the historians of the time gravely noted down that that event marked the entrance of Japan into the comity of nations. What it really did mark was the awakening of China. This awakening, long expected, had finally been despaired of. The Western nations had tried to arouse China, and they had failed. Out of their native optimism and race egotism, they had therefore concluded that the task was impossible—that China would never awaken.[1]

What they failed to take into account was this: *that between them and China was no common psychological speech.* Their thought processes were radically dissimilar. The Western mind penetrated the Chinese mind but a short distance when it found itself in a fathomless maze. The Chinese mind penetrated the Western mind an equally short distance when it fetched up against a blank, incomprehensible wall.

It was all a matter of language. There was no way to communicate Western ideas to the Chinese mind. China remained asleep. The material achievement and progress of the West was a closed book to her. Back and deep down on the tie-ribs of consciousness, in the mind of the English-speaking race, was a capacity to thrill to short Saxon words; back and deep down on the tie-ribs of consciousness of the Chinese mind was a capacity to thrill to its own hieroglyphics.

The Chinese mind could not thrill to short Saxon words, nor could the English-speaking mind thrill to hieroglyphics. The fabrics of their minds were woven from totally different stuffs. They were mental aliens. And so it was that Western material achievement and progress made no dent on the rounded sleep of China.[2]

Came Japan and her victory over Russia in 1904. Now, the Japanese race was the freak and paradox among Eastern peoples. In some strange way, Japan was receptive to all that the West had to offer. Japan swiftly assimilated Western ideas, and digested them and so capably applied them that she suddenly burst forth, full-panoplied, a world-power. There is no explaining this peculiar openness of Japan to the alien culture of the West. As well might be explained any biological sport in the animal kingdom.

Having decisively thrashed the great Russian Empire, Japan promptly set about dreaming a colossal dream of empire for herself. Korea she had made into a granary and a colony; treaty privileges and vulpine diplomacy gave her the monopoly of Manchuria. But Japan was not satisfied. She turned her eyes upon China. There lay a vast territory, and in that territory were the hugest deposits of iron and coal in the world—the backbone of industrial civilization. Given natural resources, the other great factor in industry is labor. In that territory was a population of 400 million souls—one-quarter of the total population of the earth. Furthermore, the Chinese were excellent workers, while their fatalistic philosophy (or religion) and their stolid nervous organization constituted them splendid soldiers—if they were properly managed. Needless to say, Japan was prepared to furnish that management.

But, best of all, from the standpoint of Japan, the Chinese was a kindred race. The baffling enigma of the Chinese character to the West was no baffling enigma to the Japanese. The Japanese understood the Chinese character as we could never school ourselves nor hope to understand. The Japanese thought with the same thought-symbols as did the Chinese, and they thought in the same peculiar grooves. Into the Chinese mind the Japanese went on, where we were balked by the obstacle of incomprehension. They took the turning that we could not perceive, twisted around the obstacle, and were out of sight in the ramifications of the Chinese mind, where we could not follow.

They were brothers. Long ago, one had borrowed the other's written language, and untold generations before that they had diverged from the common Mongol stock. There had been changes, differentiations brought about by diverse conditions and infusions of other blood; but, down at the bottom of their beings, twisted into the fibers of them, was a heritage in common, a sameness in kind, that time had not obliterated.

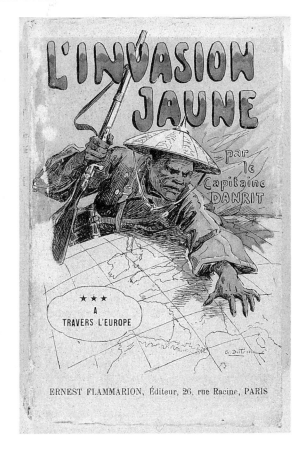

The 'Yellow Peril' was the theme of Commandant Danrit's tale of 1905

And so Japan took upon herself the management of China. In the years immediately following the war with Russia, her agents swarmed over the Chinese Empire. A thousand miles beyond the last mission station toiled her engineers and spies—clad as coolies, or under the guise of itinerant merchants or proselyting Buddhist priests—noting down the horse-power of every waterfall, the likely sites for factories, the heights of mountains and passes, the strategic advantages and weaknesses, the wealth of the farming valleys, the number of bullocks in a district or the number of laborers that could be collected by forced levies. Never was there such a census, and it could have been taken by no other people than the dogged, patient, patriotic Japanese.

But in a short time, secrecy was thrown to the winds. Japan's offi-cers reorganized the Chinese army. Her drill-sergeants made over the medieval warriors into twentieth-century soldiers, accustomed to all the modern machinery of war and with a higher average of marksmanship than the soldiers of any Western nation. The engin-eers of Japan deepened and widened the intricate system of canals, built factories and foundries, netted the Empire with telegraphs and telephones, and inaugurated the era of railroad-building. It was these same protagonists of machine civilization who discovered the great oil-deposits of Chunsan, the iron-mountains of Whang-Sing, the copper-ranges of Chinchi; and they sank the gas-wells of Wow-Wee, that most marvelous reservoir of natural gas in all the world.

Japanese emissaries were in China's councils of empire. Japanese statesmen whispered in the ears of Chinese statesmen. The political reconstruction of the Empire was due to them. They ousted the scholar class, which was violently reactionary, and put into office progressive officials. And in every town and city of the Empire, newspapers were started. Of course, Japanese editors dictated the policy of these papers, which policy they got direct from Tokyo. It was the newspapers that educated and made progressive the great mass of the population.

China was awake at last. Where the West had failed, Japan had succeeded. She had transmuted Western culture and achievement into terms that were intelligible to the Chinese understanding. Japan herself, when she awakened so suddenly, had astounded the world. But at the time she was only 40 million strong. China's awak-ening, what with her 400 millions and the scientific advance of the world, was frightfully astounding. She was the Colossus of the nations, and soon her voice was heard in no uncertain tones in the affairs and councils of the nations. Japan egged her on, and the proud Western peoples listened with respectful ears.

China's swift and remarkable rise was due to the superlative quality of her labor perhaps more than to anything else. The Chinese was the perfect type of industry. For sheer ability to work, no worker in the world could compare with him. Work was the breath of his nostrils. Liberty, to him, epitomized itself in access to the means of toil. To till the soil and labor interminably was all he asked of life and the powers that be. And the awakening of China had given its vast population not merely free and unlimited access to the means of toil, but access to the highest and most scientific machine-means of toil.

China rejuvenescent! It was but a step to China rampant. She discovered a new pride in herself, and a will of her own. She began to chafe under the guidance of Japan. But she did not chafe long. In the beginning, on Japan's advice, she had expelled from the Empire all Western missionaries, engineers, drill-sergeants, merchants, and teachers. She now began to expel the similar representatives of Japan. The latter's advisory statesmen were showered with honors and decorations, and sent home. The West had awakened Japan, and, as Japan had requited the West, so Japan was now requited by China. Japan was thanked for her kindly aid, and flung out, bag and baggage, by her gigantic protégé.

The Western nations chuckled. Japan's rainbow dream had gone glimmering. She grew angry. China laughed at her. The blood and the swords of the samurai would cut, and Japan rashly went to war. This occurred in 1922, and in seven bloody months Manchuria, Korea, and Formosa were taken away from her, and she was hurled back, bankrupt, to stifle in her tiny crowded islands. Exit Japan from the world-drama. Thereafter she devoted herself to art, and it became her task to please the world greatly with her creations of wonder and beauty.

Contrary to expectation, China did not prove warlike. She had no Napoleonic dream, and was content to devote herself to the arts of peace. After a period of disquiet, the idea was accepted that China was to be feared not in war, but in commerce. It will be seen that the real danger was not apprehended. China went on consummating her machine civilization. Instead of a large standing army, she developed an immensely larger and splendidly efficient militia. Her navy was so small that it was the laughing-stock of the world; nor did she attempt to strengthen it. The treaty ports of the world were never entered by her visiting battleships.

The real danger lay in the fecundity of her loins, and it was in 1970 that the first cry of alarm was raised. For some time all the territories adjacent to China had been grumbling at Chinese immigration; but now it suddenly came home to the world that China's population was 500 millions. Since her awakening, she had increased by 100 million. Burchaldter called attention to the fact that there were in existence more Chinese than white-skinned people. He added together the population of the United States, Canada, New Zealand, Australia, South Africa, England, France, Germany, Italy, Austria, European Russia, and all Scandinavia. The result was 495 millions. And the population of China overtopped this tremendous total by 5 millions. Burchaldter's figures went around the world, and the world shivered.

For many centuries China's population had been constant. Her territory had been saturated with population; that is to say, her territory, with its primitive method of production, had supported the maximum limit of population. But when she awoke and inaugurated the machine civilization, her productive power enormously increased. At once the birth-rate began to rise and the death-rate to fall. Before, when population pressed against the means of subsistence, the excess population had been swept away by famine. But now, thanks to the machine civilization, China's means of subsistence had been enormously extended, and there were no famines; her population followed on the heels of the increase in the means of subsistence.

During this time of transition and development of power, China had entertained no dreams of conquest. The Chinese was not an imperial race. It was industrious, thrifty, and peace-loving. War was looked upon as an unpleasant but necessary task that must be performed at times. And so, while the Western races had squabbled and fought and world-adventured against one another, China had calmly gone on working at her machines and growing. Now she was spilling over the boundaries of her Empire—that was all, just spilling over into the adjacent territories, with all the certitude and terrifyingly slow momentum of a glacier.

Following upon the alarm raised by Burchaldter's figures, in 1970 France took a long-threatened stand. French Indo-China had been overrun, filled up, by Chinese immigrants. France called a halt. The Chinese wave flowed on. France assembled a force of 100,000 on the boundary between her unfortunate colony and China, and China sent down an army of militia soldiers a million strong. Behind came the wives and sons and daughters and relatives, with their personal household luggage, in a second army. The French force was brushed aside like a fly. The Chinese militia soldiers, along with their families—over five millions all told—coolly took possession of French Indo-China, and settled down to stay for a few thousand years.

Outraged France was up in arms. She hurled fleet after fleet against the coast of China, and nearly bankrupted herself by the effort. China had no navy. She withdrew into her shell like a turtle. For a year the French fleets blackened the coast and bombarded exposed towns and villages. China did not mind. She did not depend upon the rest of the world for anything. She calmly kept out of range of the French guns, and went on working. France wept and wailed, wrung her impotent hands, and appealed to the dumbfounded nations. Then she landed a punitive expedition to march to Peking. It was 250,000 strong and it was the flower of France. It landed without opposition, and marched into the interior. And that was the last ever seen of it. The line of communication was snapped on the second day. Not a survivor came back to tell what had happened. It had been swallowed up in China's cavernous maw, that was all.

In the five years that followed, China's expansion, in all land directions, went on apace. Siam was made a part of the Empire, and, in spite of all that England could do, Burma and the Malay Peninsula were overrun; while, all along the long south boundary of Siberia, Russia was severely pressed by China's advancing hordes. The process was simple. First came the Chinese immigration (or, rather, it was already there, having come there slowly and insidiously during the preceding years). Next came the clash at arms and the brushing away of all opposition by a monster army of militia soldiers, followed by their families and household baggage. And finally came their settling down as colonists in the conquered territory. Never was there so strange and effective a method of world-conquest.

It was at this time that Burchaldter revised his figures. He had been mistaken. China's population must be 700 millions, 800 millions—nobody knew how many millions; but, at any rate, it would soon be 1,000 millions. Burchaldter announced that there were two Chinese for every white-skinned human in the world, and the world trembled. China's increase must have begun in 1904. It was remembered that since that date there had not been a single famine. At 5 millions a year increase, her total increase in the intervening seventy years must be 350 millions. But who was to know? It might be more. Who was to know anything of this strange new menace of the twentieth century—China, old China, rejuvenescent, fruitful, and militant!

The Convention of 1975 was called at Philadelphia. All the Western nations, and some few of the Eastern, were represented. Nothing was accomplished. There was talk of all countries putting bounties on children to increase the birth-rate; but it was laughed to scorn by the arithmeticians,who pointed out that China was too far in the lead in that direction. No feasible way of coping with China was suggested. China was appealed to and threatened by the United Powers, and that was all the Convention at Philadelphia came to. And the Convention and the Powers were laughed at by China. Li Tang Fwung, the power behind the Dragon Throne, deigned to reply.

'The Great Wall of China
After the Unparalleled
Invasion of 1976'

'What does China care for the comity of nations?' said Li Tang Fwung. 'We are the most ancient, honorable, and royal of races. We have our own destiny to accomplish. It is unpleasant that our destiny does not gibe with the destiny of the rest of the world, but what would you? You have talked windily about the royal races and the heritage of the earth, and we can only reply that that remains to be seen. You cannot invade us. Never mind about your navies. Don't shout. We know our navy is small. You see, we use it for police purposes. We do not care for the sea. Our strength is in our population, which will soon be 1,000 millions. Thanks to you, we are equipped with all modern war machinery. Send your navies. We will not notice them. Send your punitive expeditions—but first remember France. To land half a million soldiers on our shores would strain the resources of any of you. And our thousand millions would swallow them down in a mouthful. Send a million, send 5 million, and we will swallow them down just as readily. Pouf! A mere nothing, a meager morsel. Destroy as you have threatened, you United States, the 10 million coolies we have forced upon your shores—why, the amount scarcely equals half of our excess birth-rate for a year.'

So spoke Li Tang Fwung. The world was nonplussed, helpless, terrified. He had spoken truly. There was no combating China's amazing birth-rate. If her population was 1,000 millions and was increasing 20 millions a year, in twenty-five years it would be 1,500 millions—equal to the total population of the world in 1904. And nothing could be done. There was no way to dam up the monstrous overspilling flood of life. War was futile. China laughed at a blockade of her coasts. She welcomed invasion. In her capacious maw was room for all the hosts of earth that could be hurled at her.

But there was one scholar that China failed to reckon with—Jacobus Laningdale. Not that he was a scholar, except in the widest sense. Primarily, Jacobus Laningdale was a scientist, and, up to that time, a very obscure scientist—a professor employed in the laboratories of the Health Office of New York City. Jacobus Laningdale's head was very like any other head, but in that head he evolved an idea. Also, in that head was the wisdom to keep that idea secret. He did not write an article for the magazines. Instead, he asked for a vacation.

On September 19, 1975, he arrived in Washington. It was evening, but he proceeded straight to the White House, for he had already arranged for an audience with the President. He was closeted with President Moyer for three hours. What passed between them was not learned by the rest of the world until long after.

Next day the President called in his Cabinet. Jacobus Laningdale was present. The proceedings were kept secret. But that very afternoon Rufus Cowdery, Secretary of State, left Washington, and early the following morning sailed for England. The secret that he carried began to spread, but it spread only among the heads of governments. Possibly half a dozen men in a nation were intrusted with the idea that had formed in Jacobus Laningdale's head. Following the spread of the secret sprang up great activity in all the dockyards, arsenals, and navy-yards. The people of France and Austria became suspicious, but so sincere were their government's calls for confidence that they acquiesced in the unknown project that was afoot.

This was the time of the Great Truce. All countries solemnly pledged themselves not to go to war with any other country. The first definite action was the gradual mobilization of the armies of Russia, Germany, Austria, Italy, Greece, and Turkey. Then began the eastward movement. All railroads into Asia were glutted with troop trains. China was the objective: that was all that was known. A little later began the great sea movement. Expeditions of warships were launched from all countries. Fleet followed fleet, and all proceeded to the coast of China. The nations cleaned out their navy-yards. They sent their revenue cutters and despatch boats and lighthouse-tenders, and they sent their most antiquated cruisers and battleships. Not content with this, they impressed the merchant marine. The statistics show that 58,640 merchant steamers, equipped with searchlights and rapid-fire guns, were despatched by the various nations to China.

And China smiled, and waited. On her land side, along her boundaries, were millions of the warriors of Europe. She mobilized her militia to the number of five times as many millions, and waited for the invasion. On her sea-coasts she did the same. But China was puzzled. After all this enormous preparation, there was no invasion. She did not understand. Along the great Siberian frontier all was quiet. Along her coasts, the towns and villages were not even shelled. Never in the history of the world had there been so mighty a gathering of war-fleets. The fleets of all the world were there, and day and night millions of tons of battleships plowed the brine of her coasts. And nothing happened. Nothing was attempted. Did they think to make her emerge from her shell? China smiled. Did they think to tire her out, or starve her out? Again China smiled.

But on May 1, 1976, had the reader been in the imperial city of Peking, with its population of 11 millions, he would have witnessed a curious sight. He would have seen the streets filled with the chattering yellow populace, every queued head tilted back, every slant eye turned skyward. And high up in the blue he would have beheld a tiny dot of black, which he would have identified as an aeroplane. From this aeroplane, as it curved its flight back and forth over the city, fell missiles—strange, harmless-looking missiles, tubes of fragile glass that shattered into thousands of fragments on the streets and housetops. But there was nothing deadly about these tubes of glass. Nothing happened. There were no explosions. It is true that several Chinese were killed by the tubes dropping on their heads from so enormous a height; but what were three Chinese against an excess birth-rate of 20 millions?

One tube struck perpendicularly in a fishpond in a garden, and was not broken. It was dragged ashore by the master of the house. He did not dare to open it, but, accompanied by his friends and surrounded by an ever-increasing crowd, he carried the mysterious tube to the magistrate of the district. The latter was a brave man. With all eyes upon him, he shattered the tube with a blow from his brass-bowled pipe. Nothing happened. Of those who were very near, one or two thought they saw some mosquitoes fly out. That was all. The crowd set up a great laugh, and dispersed.

As Peking was bombarded by glass tubes, so was all China. The tiny aeroplanes, despatched from the warships, contained only two men each, and over all cities, towns, and villages they wheeled and curved, one man directing the ship, the other throwing the glass tubes.

Had the reader been in Peking again six weeks later, he would have looked in vain for the 11 million inhabitants. Some few of them he would have found, a few hundred thousand, perhaps, their carcasses festering in the houses and in the deserted streets, and piled high on the abandoned death-wagons. But for the rest, he would have had to seek along the highways and byways of the Empire. And not all would he have found fleeing from plague-stricken Peking, for behind them, by hundreds of thousands of unburied corpses by the wayside, he could have marked their flight.

As it was with Peking, so it was with all the cities, towns, and villages of the Empire. The plague smote them all. Nor was it one plague, nor two plagues: it was a score of plagues. Every virulent form of infectious death stalked through the land. Too late the Chinese Government apprehended the meaning of the colossal preparations, the marshalling of the world hosts, the flights of the tiny aeroplanes, and the rain of the tubes of glass. The proclamations of the Government were in vain. They could not stop the 11 million plague-stricken wretches fleeing from the one city of Peking to spread disease through all the land. Physicians and health officers died at their posts; and death, the all-conqueror, rode over the decrees of the Emperor and Li Tang Fwung. It rode over them as well, for Li Tang Fwung died in the second week, and the Emperor, hidden away in the Summer Palace, died in the fourth week.

Had there been but one plague, China might have coped with it. But from a score of plagues, no creature was immune. The man who escaped smallpox went down before scarlet fever; the man who was immune to yellow fever was carried away by cholera; and if he were immune to that too, the Black Death, which was the bubonic plague, swept him away. For it was these bacteria, and germs, and

'A Gramophone lecture on China's death at the Duluth Institute of Microcosmology in the year 1977'

microbes, and bacilli, cultured in the laboratories of the West, that had come down upon China in the rain of glass.

All organization vanished. The Government crumbled away. Decrees and proclamations were useless when the men who made them and signed them one moment were dead the next. Nor could the maddened millions, spurred on to flight by death, pause to heed anything. They fled from the cities to infect the country, and, wherever they fled, they carried the plague with them. The hot summer was on—Jacobus Laningdale had selected the time shrewdly—and the plague festered everywhere.

Much is conjectured of what occurred, and much has been learned from the stories of the few survivors. The wretched creatures streamed across the Empire in many-millioned flight. The vast armies that China had collected on her frontiers melted away. The farms were ravaged for food, and no more crops were planted, while the crops already in were left unattended and never came to harvest. The most remarkable thing, perhaps, was the flights. Many millions engaged in them, charging to the bounds of the Empire, to be met and turned back by the gigantic armies of the West. The slaughter of the mad hosts on the boundaries was stupendous. Time and again, the guarding line was drawn back twenty or thirty miles to escape the contagion of the multitudinous dead.

Once the plague broke through and seized the German and Austrian soldiers who were guarding the borders of Turkestan. Preparations had been made for such a happening, and, though 60,000 soldiers of Europe were carried off, the international corps of physicians isolated the contagion and dammed it back.

Such was the unparalleled invasion of China. For that billion of people there was no hope. Pent in their vast and festering charnel-house, all organization and cohesion lost, they could do naught but die. They could not escape. As they were flung back from their land frontiers, so they were flung back from the sea. Seventy-five thousand vessels patrolled the coasts. By day their smoking funnels dimmed the sea-rim, and by night their flashing searchlights plowed the dark and harrowed it for the tiniest escaping junk. The attempts of the immense fleets of junks were pitiful. Not one ever got by the guarding sea-hounds. Modern war machinery held back the disorganized mass of China, while the plague did the work.

But old war was made a thing of laughter. Naught remained to him but patrol duty. China had laughed at war, and war she was getting; but it was ultra-modern war, twentieth-century war, the war of the scientist and the laboratory, the war of Jacobus Laningdale. Hundred-ton guns were toys compared with the micro-organic projectiles hurled from the laboratories, the messengers of death, the destroying angels that stalked through the empire of a billion souls.

During all the summer and fall of 1976, China was an inferno. There was no eluding the microscopic projectiles that sought out the remotest hiding-places. The hundreds of millions of dead remained unburied, and the germs multiplied; and, toward the last, millions died daily of starvation. Besides, starvation weakened the victims and destroyed their natural defenses against the plague. Cannibalism, murder and madness reigned. And so China perished.

Not until the following February, in the coldest weather, were the first expeditions made. These expeditions were small, composed of scientists and bodies of troops; but they entered China from every side. In spite of the most elaborate precautions against infection, numbers of soldiers and a few of the physicians were stricken. But the exploration went bravely on. They found China devastated, a howling wilderness through which wandered bands of wild dogs and desperate bandits who had survived. All survivors were put to death, wherever found.

And then began the great task, the sanitation of China. Five years and hundreds of millions of treasure were consumed, and then the world moved in—not in zones, as was the idea of Baron Albrecht, but heterogeneously, according to the democratic American program. It was a vast and happy intermingling of nationalities that settled down in China in 1982 and the years that followed—a tremendous and successful experiment in cross-fertilization. We know today the splendid mechanical, intellectual, and artistic output that followed.

It was in 1987, the Great Truce having been dissolved, that the ancient quarrel between France and Germany over Alsace and Lorraine recrudesced. The war-cloud grew dark and threatening in April, and on April 17 the Convention of Copenhagen was called. The representatives of the nations of the world being present, all nations solemnly pledged themselves never to use against one another the laboratory methods of warfare they had employed in the invasion of China.

A Vision of the Future

GUSTAF JANSON

The start had originally been intended for midday. But as the commander-in-chief had expressed the wish to be present, the whole affair had been postponed for a few hours. The airman stood by his machine, waiting; a few sappers sat together in a group chatting. There was nothing for them to do after they had put the bombs in position. In front of the shed, the doors of which were thrown back, stood about twenty officers who had come together to witness their comrade's bold reconnaissance.[1]

The airman yawned slightly behind his hand, but the General's wish delayed the flight. He frowned and went over to watch one or two companies who were at drill a short distance away.

A man on horseback was approaching from the city.

The officers became mildly excited. Was something going to happen at last? Yes, the General must have finished his lunch.

The airman stretched himself and filled his lungs. Everything seemed to promise a successful flight. The sky was certainly overcast, but there was no reason to expect anything but calm weather. He could hardly have chosen a more suitable day.

'At last,' he murmured. A group of horsemen were coming from the city.

The soldiers stopped their drill. It would have been unfair to deprive them of the sight of the flying. The officers drew nearer.

'All ready, captain?' asked a lieutenant good-naturedly.

'All ready,' nodded the airman. He cast a final glance over the machine. No, nothing was missing. He signed to the sappers, who jumped up and took the places already assigned to them.

The General rode up with his escort and halted a little to one side of the hangar. He greeted the airman condescendingly, and saluted the group of officers with his gloved hand, and his clever eyes rested on the machine. He had always taken a lively interest in this new aid to military operations, and he never missed an opportunity of seeing a flight. He sprang lightly from his saddle and went up to the flying-machine. The long row of orders and medals on his breast glittered in the pale light, the gold flashed on his cap, his sword struck rhythmically against the patent leather of his left boot.

'Aha . . . aha . . . very good,' he said and smiled, showing two even rows of white teeth under his carefully waxed and brushed-up moustache. He nodded cheerfully to the airman. 'Now . . . shall we, captain?'

'Whenever you please, General.'

'Good. And the bombs, eh?' The General indicated the seven shells, placed where the airman could easily reach them.

'Yes.'

'Good. And you think you can be back again within half an hour?'

'If nothing unforeseen occurs . . .'

An artist's anticipation of
air warfare in 1910

'Good. Here on the drill ground?'

'If everything happens according to my calculations . . . yes.'

'I will await your return. May Our Lady and all the Saints protect you, captain!'

The General stepped back a pace. At a sign the sappers began to push the machine forward. The airman took his seat and started the motor experimentally. It was working perfectly.

The great flying-machine wobbled about. The ground was not its element. With mighty, outspread wings, which demanded air and space under them, the machine moved heavily forward for a few yards. The airman, from his seat, smiled at the officers.

His comrades saluted their daring friend with their hands to their caps.

The airman bowed slightly to the General, and then devoted his whole attention to the machine. The motor began to whirr. The flying-machine made a leap forward.

The sun broke through a rift in the clouds. The aeroplane had left the ground and was rising swiftly in a slanting direction. The wings shone, the metal of the frame glittered. The machine rose higher and higher, glided into the sunshine and again into the shadow; against the light background it looked like some great prehistoric insect.

Eager and interested, officers and men looked with upturned faces and blinking eyes after the vanishing aeroplane.

'Good,' exclaimed the General, 'very good!' His eyes shone, his orders and medals glittered. 'Sublime, gentlemen, simply sublime!' The flying-machine became smaller and glided into the infinite. The old General lowered his head and sank into deep thought. That which he had just seen was not only wonderful, it was rich with promise. What vistas opened before him . . . a glance into a future, so dazzling, that . . . that . . . 'Very good,' he said aloud, 'very good!'

A staff-officer was standing beside him and had said something of which he had not heard a word. An orderly came running up.

The General signed to the staff-officer to withdraw.

'The problem is solved,' he thought. 'We only need to take advantage of every improvement in the technique. What a pity I am too old to fly . . .'

The orderly saluted and went away, after having delivered his message, of which the General had not heard a syllable.

'What was that?' The old gentleman turned to the Major standing beside him. 'What was that newspaper with the article about the military aviation of today?'

'I have got it with me.'

'Very good. I will sit down here a little, whilst we are waiting. See that I am not disturbed.' He took the journal from the Major's hand and threw a searching glance towards the south. With what extraordinary rapidity these flying-machines were developing. New inventions followed one after another, and at this moment the most epoch-making ones were those for military purposes. 'Very good!' The General sat down on the cloak which his orderly had spread for him and began to turn over the pages of the newspaper handed to him by the major.

The airman had reached a height of from 600 to 800 yards. Gazing steadily ahead, he hastened on. The wind created by his speed was cool in his face. But he did not notice it. A hard smile played round his firmly closed lips. He was thinking of his two-fold task. The first thing to do was to find out the disposition of the enemy's troops and after that to harry and damage them as much as possible. He fancied he could still hear the voices of his brother officers, and his determination increased. He clenched his teeth and his expression grew hard. He was determined to carry out his mission. He was striving not only for the respect of his comrades and the praise of his superior officers; he was flying through the air so as to testify to the unquestionable superiority of the white races. The proofs were there, in the shape of seven powerful bombs. When he flung those down from the sky the proof would be overwhelming, then all contradiction would be silenced.

Behind him the propellers droned harshly and unceasingly. The rigid sand waves beneath him looked strangely confused. Here and there a village glimmered white in the midst of a group of palms.[2] He had not yet passed the advanced lines of his own countrymen. Oh, down there the soldiers were running together from all directions. What was the matter? They had perceived him, they were shouting 'Hurrah!' Triumphant and stimulating, the cry rose from below. He raised one hand from the steering-wheel and waved. He would have liked to descend a little, to have flown so near that they could have heard his answer. But he had no time, his goal was too far off. Quicker and quicker the machine flew through the ether. Look, there was the desert . . . the bare ground beneath him, the bare space above him, and he, the solitary man, floating between the two! A feeling of mighty power came over him.

'We men,' he thought, 'we masters of air and earth . . .' The airman's mission was a great and splendid one. When thousands of others like him traversed space at dizzy heights and with absolute safety, and descended exactly where they wanted to, then indissoluble bonds would be forged between the nations. The aeronauts were the true pioneers of progress, heralds who announced the new . . . no, the old, gospel: 'no more boundaries, no more walls between peoples'.

A sound, like a sharp crack, reached his ear. He looked down and smiled contemptuously. A dozen Arabs on horseback were racing madly in the same direction as himself. An expression of cruelty distorted the airman's youthful features. Those fellows down there . . . aha! . . . they were actually amusing themselves by shooting at him. His hand left the steering-wheel and moved towards the bracket on which a bomb was fastened. He owed them a visiting-card, those bare-legged, shouting rascals down there. It would have amused him to watch the effects of the explosion, but . . . well . . .

Again sand, nothing but sand. What was it he had been thinking about? Oh yes, the speech at the banquet given to the airmen who were setting out for the war. How did it go? Yes. 'The last important step has been taken, now there need be no obstacles, no delays. The elements have become the servants of mankind. Certainly, it happened now and then that they acted treacherously, but that they could be made to obey there was no doubt whatever. All that now remained was a mechanical problem, over the solution of which thousands of brains had been occupied for a considerable time. Mankind, always seeking a new problem to master, is hastening triumphantly to its completion. Will is the creative power which constructs out of nothingness. It was thanks to their extraordinary will-power that mankind was becoming more and more godlike. Today we hail as an accomplished fact that which, a few years ago, was nothing but a dream.' An excellent and highly characteristic speech.

Look . . . there were the Turkish lines. Trenches were being dug and . . . Why were all those thousands of soldiers formed in a square? Nobody down there seemed to have noticed the flying-machine as yet; it was a favourable moment for making observations. Why were all the soldiers standing with their rifles at their sides? And . . . What? Arab mollahs . . . they were burying those killed in the last fight. He could not have hoped for a better opportunity.

Two bombs were hastily detached and dropped.

'Ah . . . !'

A faint detonation sounded from below, and then another! Then followed wailings, and angry shouts . . . confusion.

'Hope you'll enjoy it!' murmured the airman, and smiled. The pioneers of civilization were showing what they were worth. Just look, they were shooting at him. So two bombs were not enough. Very well, let them have another!

The flying-machine rocked as though buffeted by the wind. The aviator saw the flaw at once; intuition told him the cause of it. With a quick movement everything was put right again. He smiled confidently. The instant it occurred, the nervous sensitiveness, so indispensable to an airman, had told him that something had happened. A second later the aeroplane had resumed its even flight.

What had occupied his thoughts just now? The dream which had become reality . . . That speech was really first-rate—did it not contain everything that was to be said on the subject? The vision of the future . . . the magnificent possibilities . . . How easy it had been for the speaker to silence the incredulous! Everything that man had ever produced had been set down as Utopian when it first appeared. Old men and wiseacres had always shaken their heads; dreary, unimaginative people had always shrugged their shoulders. And now everything that they had denied, everything that they had suspected, was respected and made use of continuously; all that had seemed to them useless was now indispensable. The impossible had proved simple and easy to accomplish.

The flying-machine glided on. No, there was nothing down here to be seen. He was behind the Turkish lines now. So far so good; he turned. But just a little way towards the east first of all.

'The restrictions of time and space have been removed,' he thought, and was once more overwhelmed in the torrent of words which had roused him to such enthusiasm when he had listened to them, and which would always remain in his memory: 'The human intellect had made subject to it earth, fire, water, and air. All these were being employed in the service of mankind.'

'What's that down there?' Oh, the red crescent on a white ground! So they had actually had the cheek to set up a field hospital so near the front! Did the enemy imagine that there was no means of punishing them for this audacity? Why, they had actually stretched a great white sheet right over the roof of the hospital! Perhaps another aviator had already flown over here. No; he could not remember having heard of such a thing . . . there! so much for the superiority of the civilization . . . one . . . two bombs . . . fools! The intoxication of flying and the sense of power aroused the desire for further triumphs. He saw the men down below running about in confusion; in the distance he could hear the shrieking and the noise. The aviator smiled. He was proud of his success.

Look! They were honouring him with gun-shots and curses. Fools! Did they not realize their inferiority? Had they not deserved their fate?

The propellers droned unceasingly; the machine throbbed softly. Down below there was nothing to be seen but sand. The furthest outposts of the enemy lay far behind the airman, and . . . no; a patrol party was creeping through a hollow between two hills. So they actually dared to penetrate so near to his countrymen's lines! That cried out for retribution. The prospect of hitting this handful of men with a bomb was very slight, but . . . the last bomb was taken from its bracket and fell through the air. What's the matter now . . . what? The soldiers down below had caught sight of him, they were putting their hats on their bayonets and waving . . . shouting hurrah . . . oh, they were his countrymen!

The flying-machine hurried onwards with greater speed than heretofore. The airman felt that his cheeks were burning and his heart beating. A strange mixture of terror and curiosity forced him to turn round and look down at the patrol party, which was plodding on its way slowly through the sand. There had been no detonation. The bomb had sunk into the loose sand and lay there half buried . . . until another occasion or for always—who could say?

There, there were the Italian lines. Shouts of hurrah, wavings, rejoicings . . . The airman thought of what he had thrown down just before. If the bomb had exploded and the men had been injured!

On the farther side of the group of palms, the camp from which he had started came in sight. The flying-machine began to descend . . . a little to the left . . . a little more.

The landing was accomplished without difficulty. Like a creature gifted with intelligence, the machine obeyed the will at the steering-wheel, a slight vibration still shaking every part of it.

The sappers ran up. The officers, whose numbers had doubled during his absence, drew nearer. The General stood up, folded his newspaper and handed it to the major who had hurried to the spot. From afar off, the Commander-in-Chief had sighted the returning flying-machine and had followed it with his eyes. A horse was frightened and shied, but soon became calm again.

'Welcome to the ground, Captain!' The General shook the airman by the hand. He was proud and delighted at this feat performed by an officer in his corps. 'Very good! What have you to report?'

In sentences of military abruptness the airman gave an account of his reconnoitring. The enemy's lines were almost parallel to their own, about like this . . . The airman drew a sketch in the sand. A few strong detachments . . . Arabs, cavalry therefore . . . had pushed forward towards the centre, smaller patrol parties were scattered over the district. He had dropped his bombs, but owing to the speed of his flight he had only been able to watch their effect at one spot. That had been near a field hospital . . . the enemy had stretched a white sheet with the red crescent on it over the roof . . . but he had not been taken in by this precaution.

'Very good,' nodded the General.

The flattered airman smiled. Shortly before that he had passed a large number of troops in square formation, they were evidently holding a military funeral. Judging from what he had seen the enemy had suffered tremendous losses in the last fight, and probably an officer of superior rank had been killed. Otherwise, why were they losing time by gathering together the troops in this way?

'Type of gun which Germany has prepared for checkmating the aeroplane-of-war and battle-airships'

'Make a note of that!' The General signed to the major at his side. He had already produced his notebook and was writing in it. 'Very good! Telegraph!'

The airman bowed slightly. In his opinion it would be well to reconnoitre again as soon as possible. The enemy might change his plans. There was nothing further to report.

'Thank you, Captain!' The General shook him warmly by the hand once more and stood for a few minutes sunk in thought. 'Gentlemen,' he began suddenly, turning to the officers, 'it is incredible how the technique of war has changed. Telephones, telegraphs, wireless communications, war makes use of all these. It presses every new invention into its service. Really most impressive. I have just been reading the latest aviation news from Europe. Our ally Germany and our blood-relation France possess at this moment the largest fleets of aeroplanes in the world. The distance between Metz and Paris can be covered in a few hours. The 300 aeroplanes which Germany possesses at this moment, all constructed and bought in France, could throw down 10,000 kilos of dynamite on to the metropolis of the world in less than half an hour. This is a positively gigantic thought! In the middle of the night, these 300 flying-machines cross the border, and before daybreak Paris is a heap of ruins! Magnificent, gentlemen, magnificent . . . ! Unexpectedly, without any previous warning, the rain of dynamite bursts over the town. One explosion follows close on the other. Hospitals, theatres, schools, museums, public buildings, private houses, all are demolished. The roofs break in, the floors sink through to the cellars, crumbling ruins block up the streets. The sewers break and send their foul contents over everything . . . everything. The water pipes burst and there are floods. The gas pipes burst, gas streams out and explodes and causes an outbreak of fire. The electric light goes out. You hear the sound of people running together, cries for help, shrieking and wailing, the splashing of water, the roaring of fire. And above it all can be heard the detonations occurring with mathematical precision. Walls fall in, whole buildings disappear in the gaping ground. Men, women, and children rush about mad with terror among the ruins. They drown in filth, they are burnt, blown to pieces in explosions, annihilated, exterminated. Blood streams over the ruins and filth; gradually the shrieks for help die down. When the last flying-machine has done its work and turned northwards again, the bombardment is finished. In Paris a stillness reigns, such as has never reigned there before.

'We can imagine, on the other hand, that the French have carried out this same operation against Berlin, or possibly London. Who knows what political combination the future may have in store? But be that as it may, it only remains to us gratefully to dedicate ourselves to the new and glorious task now set before us. Gentlemen, I bare my head before the marvellous and unceasing progress of mankind.' The General removed his cap, and his voice vibrated with gratitude to the merciful Providence which would perhaps grant that he would live to see this vision come true; and he continued: 'In the face of this triumphant progress which I have just described, I am not overstepping the mark when I say that we are approaching perfection.'

''Planes!'

FREDERICK BRITTEN AUSTIN

The reveillé sounded, and there was stir and movement in the mist-hung meadows where the brigade had passed the night.[1] The groups of huddled, recumbent figures clustered round the sodden embers of the bivouac fires awoke, and the men sat up, yawned, rubbed their eyes as they came to themselves out of that heavy, drugged sleep which follows after a forced march, and rose to their feet. Acutely conscious of the hunger unsatisfied overnight, they discussed, pessimistically, the chances of the supply train having arrived. Sergeants hurrying through the fog were stopped, questioned, and cursed as though they were responsible for the failure of the commissariat which their brief reply indicated.

Grumbling, tightening their belts, and stamping chilled and stiffened limbs, the men wandered, guided by the fall of the land, down to the stream, and filled their water-bottles. A babel of voices rose through the blanket of mist. Bad-tempered men, their faces white and drawn with fatigue, jostled against each other at the little stream, and swore at those who fouled it with muddy boots. Altercations arose, the pointless, endless bickerings of tired and hungry men. Suddenly a voice cried—'By G—d! They're at it! I heard a gun!'

'No—rot!'—'Yes, there was! He's right!' A chorus of such affirmations and denials arose.

'Shut up, you fools!' cried the first speaker. 'Listen!'

A hush came over the group of men as they stood with heads cocked on one side and faculties at strain. A dull boom, not very loud, but seeming none the less to shake the air, was heard distinctly. It was repeated almost before the sound had rumbled into silence.

The chorus of voices broke out afresh.

'He's right! They're at it!—How far away?—Eight miles!—Ten!—Five!'

The first speaker, who, as the discoverer of the phenomenon, seemed to consider himself as sole patentee of all knowledge to be derived from it, spoke authoritatively.

'Not more than seven and a half,' he said. 'Come on, boys; we'd better be getting back. They'll be wanting us presently.'

The news that a part of the army was fighting already a few miles away spread itself instantaneously over the meadows. Knots of men discussed the situation excitedly. Many—not officers only—spread maps upon the soaked grass, and, kneeling round them, pointed with finger or pipe-stem to the positions believed to be in hostile occupation—positions hotly contested on the moment by their comrades—and traced the line of march they considered probable. The sun, pale and watery, broke through the mist, and looked down upon the busy meadows.

A motor-car throbbed, hooting, along the narrow lane, and stopped at a gate leading into the fields. The Brigadier disengaged himself from a group of his staff and strode towards it. For a few minutes he stood in talk with a gray-moustached soldier in the car. A map was unfolded and spread out. The Brigadier bent over it, following the gray-moustached officer's finger. Then, with a nod, he stepped back and saluted. The car, after a warning hoot, shot forward along the lane.

The Brigadier went back towards his staff, watched, with excited interest, by every man near enough to perceive him through the mist.

A minute afterwards the bugle sang out the 'Fall in'. It was repeated, in quick and overlapping succession, like the various chimes of a country town, by bugle after bugle all over the meadows.

The chaotic mass of men collected, jostled, straightened itself into long lines, and stood still. There was a hurrying to and fro of officers. The captains stood, statuesque in the mist, in front of their companies.

Pursuant to the commands barked out successively, the lines thickened and turned into columns of fours, and, battalion after battalion, the brigade regiments marched across the fields and wheeled into the lane.

The regular beat of thousands of boots upon the earth as the brigade lengthened along the lane swelled into a heavy, endless sound that deadened the senses. Sharp-eared among the men contended as to whether the distant guns were still firing or no, but certainty was impossible in the tramp of the marching regiments.

Presently there was no doubt about the gun-fire. A succession of heavy reports, too distinct for thunder, smote the ears of the men. They looked, with an outburst of excited talk, eagerly at the sky before them. No sign of strife stained the pale blue of the heaven, but the sound continued—was never to cease, indeed, all that day.

Minute by minute, it swelled into a heavier, louder roar, that surged in the ears like a wave at each more marked concussion. Mounted officers rode along the column, hastening its pace.

The tired men, now getting into the swing of motion, had quickened it involuntarily at the sound; but greater efforts were required. 'Step it out now!'—'Forward!'—'No straggling!—'Forward!' rose at irregular intervals above the incessant tramp of the marching column. The men, shifting their rifles now to the shoulder, now to the trail, now slinging them across their backs in an effort to get some relief for the muscles tired out on the previous day, set their teeth and stepped sturdily forward. With the excitement of the battle fever, induced by that distant artillery fire, beginning to surge in their blood, they were conscious of their unsatisfied hunger only as a vague ache.

Up hill and down the column wound, twisting like a long, light-brown snake now to the right, now to the left between the narrow hedges; passing farmhouses; crossing streams; rousing little villages, where a few inhabitants had remained, into wakefulness; waking only echoes in others that were deserted, their windows boarded up; pressing always towards that persistent, swelling thunder of artillery, hastening to join the army that for the past week had been steadily forcing the enemy back.

There was an outburst of wild cries from the rear. The officers looked back. A staff-officer cantered along the column, shouting commands. The men were hurriedly pressed against the hedge. A battery of guns tore along the lane at a gallop, thundering past them as an express hurtles past a side-tracked train. Springing from stone or rut, the guns rushed through, the shouting drivers lashing their horses like jockeys in a race, the swaying gunners clinging tightly to their limber-seats and yelling jeers and witticisms at the huddled infantry. They were happily out of earshot of the responses.

'Getting close now,' was the opinion of the brigade. 'They wouldn't go far at that pace.' The unceasing thunder of the invisible artillery, now deafeningly intense, gave probability to the surmise.

The last wagon of the battery passed, and the infantry opened out into the lane again and resumed its march. The fancied nearness to the fray acted like a tonic on the men. Some one struck up a popular song, other voices joined in; and in a few moments, to a stirring chorus from thousands of throats, the column had quickened step. The thunderous menace of the battle in front of them filled the air, seeming to shake the blue sky, but the chorus held on, rhythmic to the tramp.

'Hallo! Look! There's an aeroplane!' The speaker was not alone to perceive it. Every man in the brigade had looked up to see the machine shoot over the wooded hills in front of them. The singing ceased.

'It's ours!—No, it isn't!—Yes! I know the pattern!—No!'

'It's the enemy's,' observed a tall man in the ranks mildly. 'Ours have bigger planes.'

The conviction that the machine was hostile spread. Men speculated anxiously as to whether it was a bomb-dropper or merely a scout.

'It can do what it likes with us, that's certain. D—d things!' said the mild man.

There was a general sigh of relief when the machine, after a circle overhead, whirred back harmlessly out of sight.

'They know we're coming, anyway,' said the mild man's right-hand file gloomily. Then, with a rising tone of excitement, he added, 'Look! they're firing at it!'

They saw the aeroplane lift into sight again over the trees, rising

'M. Blériot's flight across the Channel has resulted in a revival of those invasion scares that were so prevalent recently...'

rapidly. Puff-balls of smoke appeared in the air around, below it. Suddenly the machine stopped, pitched, dropped earthward in a dreadful headlong rush.

'Got him!' cried some one exultantly. 'He flew too low that time.'

'Halt!' The yellow-brown serpent contracted its length a little and stopped.

'What's up?' queried the men. 'Surely we're in time after all.'

The brigade had halted in a hollow of the wooded, enclosed country. On every side the view was bounded by tree-clad hills. Somewhere just over them, just out of sight, the stern match was being played. Along a line of ten miles or more, among those hills and woods, Life, wrought to fever-pitch, was exposing itself to Death. The thunder of a multitude of guns merged, mounting, into one terrible open roar that shook the earth and deafened the listening ears. Yet, save for the episode of the aeroplane, no sign of the strife had yet been visible.

After a few minutes of impatient waiting, the brigade moved on again, climbed the next hill, and descended the next valley—again, 'Halt!'

The head of the column had stopped just at the foot of the descent, tailing out its long body above it, behind it, over the last hill. Close now, evidently, to the clamorous strife, and afforded a view ahead, the men looked eagerly for visible signs of battle. In a water-meadow to the left of the road a cluster of white tents, splashed largely with red crosses, stood in the shade of a few trees. It was a field hospital. In front was one of the hills to which the last few miles had accustomed them—a steep acclivity, tree-covered, gashed with the ascending road, shutting out the view. As they looked, they saw an endless procession of ambulance carts trotting over the brow of that hill and descending, while a counter-procession of similar carts climbed back toilsomely up the slope. That was all. No other men were visible; and in that ear-destroying, open, expanding, continuous roar, those carts seemed to travel in an uncanny silence. Rapidly, ceaselessly, they came over the brow of the hill, bearing wrecked and broken men from that sea of sound which to the imagination lay just beyond it, out of sight. In the field hospital the surgeons worked like automata set to full speed. A tent-flap rising for a moment in a puff of wind revealed a sight that made the men in the leading files of the column look the other way hurriedly.

The brigade fretted, grumbled, cursed at its inaction. Across the low-lying meadows to the right a regiment of cavalry moved slowly—idly, it seemed. Nobody seemed to be doing anything. In the fever induced by the vast roar that seemed ever to be mounting to a pitch from which it must decline but yet never diminished, the men were guilty of blasphemy against the commander-in-chief.

'What's he playing at, anyway? Why doesn't he send us in?'

The cavalry regiment continued its quiet stroll across the meadow. The procession of ambulances streamed steadily down the hill. The roar of the invisible battle abated not at all. But still the brigade moved not.

Suddenly a mounted officer appeared galloping down the hill. He waved his hand wildly. Scarcely hearing the sharp monosyllabic orders, the brigade surged forward. Despite the restraining voices of the officers, it broke for a minute or two into the 'double', so eager were the men to rush into the fight. At last! And in the excitement of the crisis, men went oddly pale who had no consciousness of fear.

'Steady, men, steady! You'll want your breath presently!' cried the officers; and the brigade, against the sharp rise of the hill, fell into a slower step, swifter none the less than its pace during the march. The ambulances, stopped, were pressed against the hedges on either hand, and the column, heedless of the menace they symbolized, moved rapidly up between them, drawn at last into the battle-vortex.

At the top the road bent sharply to the right, and kept to the ridge. A knot of mounted officers awaited the brigade at the bend. The Brigadier cantered quickly up to them, and exchanged eager talk. As the leading files reached the summit, six heavy reports, in quick but regular succession, broke from a battery extended along the road to the right. Beyond it, for ten miles in that direction, scores of other batteries and hundreds of thousands of rifles were thundering, crashing, crackling against each other in a vast concerto of noise that, when the brain, now accustomed and half-oblivious to it, reperceived it, seemed to check the pulse. The brigade had arrived on the extreme left flank of the army at the moment when its forward movement was checked, forced back.

Quickly the battalions were distributed to positions along the ridge. Companies became semi-independent units. One broke into a farmhouse standing at the bend of the road, and hurriedly put it into a state of defence. Another lined the garden wall. A third occupied the orchard. One, supplied—who knew whence?—with picks and shovels, dug in all haste a shelter-trench across a potato field. The work was almost frantically performed, yet still the officers cried for speed. The battery on the right was firing rapidly, but the toiling men had no leisure to raise their eyes towards its target. They had a confused sense of yet more troops arriving, behind and on either side of them, and an intuitive knowledge of imminent danger. They dug on, blindly almost, delving for shelter against the coming storm. As yet, no shots fell near them.

At last, the trench finished, the water-cans filled, the cartridge-boxes placed at intervals, the line manned, they could look about them. The shelter-trench ran a little below the crest of a gradual slope down to a broad green valley. At the farther side of the valley dense woods descended. Below them was a farmhouse, to which a spur of the ridge led a rough track.

The officers gave the range to the edge of the woods. 'Nine hundred yards!' Men adjusted their sights in anticipation.

From those woods a horde of light-brown infantry was issuing. Battalion, company formations lost, a brigade in rout, the infantry emerged endlessly in swarms from the trees. They ran—in fear, it seemed to the men in the shelter-trench up above, of an imaginary foe. Officers rushed about the mass with brandished swords, like herdsmen rounding up cattle, and collected them into some order in the broad valley meadows. At the same moment, a company went at the double down the cart-track from the ridge to the outlying farmhouse. A few moments later the men watching above saw a little cloud of mortar-dust rise round the buildings. The company was knocking out loopholes.

The stream of infantry from the woods stopped. The last men, who had kept a loose formation, turned at every minute, and, dropping on the knee or prone, fired at the shelter they had just quitted. Then they ran on, to turn and fire again a few yards further on. A quiet, leisurely officer directed them. No enemy was visible or specially audible, but every now and then one of this rear-guard threw up his arms or fell in a heap. The routed brigade, now in some measure reformed, was marching up to the ridge. Presently the rear-guard followed it, leaving the valley empty, save for the stretched-out bodies here and there.

There was a pause. To the excited, watching men in the shelter-trench it was like the end of an act at a play. Then suddenly the batteries behind them—more than one now—roared, gun after gun in quick succession. The men in the trenches had not noticed the temporary cessation of their fire. As they spoke again, little curls of smoke began to rise slowly here and there above the tree tops, dark holes suddenly appeared in the blanket of foliage, a faint flash showed occasionally in the shadows. The waiting soldiers settled themselves in their trench, their fingers on the triggers, itching to fire. Still no enemy showed himself. The woods might have been deserted—a practice-target merely for the persistent guns.

'Look!' High above the woods, an aeroplane rushed at full speed towards them. Smoke-puffs burst out of the air below around it. Untouched, the machine came on, at an elevation too great for the angry guns. A murmur of impotent wrath ran along the trenches, a crackle of rifle-fire broke out. Superbly unscathed, the aeroplane rose above the ridge, turned, followed it; then, rising yet higher, fled back to its lair behind the woods. The harmless smoke-puffs followed it until it dropped out of sight.

Immediately almost the attention of the men on the ridge was attracted to the outlying farmhouse. It looked like a box of crackers going off by itself. A quick series of little explosions dotted the fields around it; sharp little puffs of smoke broke out on the roof, against the walls, round the fences, in the courtyard. The sound of these explosions was distinctly audible above the ear-crushing roar that all this time had never ceased. The explosions about the farmhouse multiplied. It looked like a little volcano in active eruption. The chimney-stack disappeared suddenly, the roof fell in great holes, the walls crumbled—it was as though invisible hands were tearing it down. Smoke and flame arose. The explosions, everywhere at once now, continued. There was no sign of the men that garrisoned it.

'Wonder where those guns are?' queried some one in the trench above. 'They'll be having a go at us in a minute.'

He had scarcely spoken when there was a long-drawn sharp wail, rising to a screech, in the air above. Immediately a succession of splitting crashes followed, somewhere behind them. Out of that noise the wail came again. A row of little white smoke clouds sprang out of the blue air in front of them with a deafening run of reports, followed on the instant by the high-pitched drone of shrapnel bullets. The drone had not died away before another series broke over the trench. Henceforth there was no cessation. It was a tornado that swept over the position. The stricken infantry cowered in their shelters, not daring to raise their heads.

The storm was at its height when the whistles of the officers shrilled out. Below them, in the valley, the enemy was debouching in a cloud of skirmishers from the wood. Heedless of the rain of shells, the infantry made ready for him, those panic-stricken in the trenches kicked meanwhile into activity. Down below, from the blazing ruins of the farmhouse, came a fusillade, faint in the roar that seemed to centre now upon the ridge. The men in the trenches took aim, and fired in a crackling roll. The crowd of dark-uniformed soldiers below were coming on in a rush, disdaining to seek cover, when they met the sheet of bullets. Numbers of them seemed to trip over an unseen obstacle. Others dropped as though felled by a blow on the head. Some sprang and twisted as if stung ere they sank down. Above, the men in the trenches, yelling, laughing, cursing, praying, singing in the battle fever, loosed bullets on them in a heavy shower. The batteries on the ridge beat them down with shrapnel till the crowded meadow looked like a rye-field in a hail squall.

Panic seized the dark soldiery. Men rushed hither and thither aimlessly, to leap into the air for a final fall headlong, or to be flung down with a dozen comrades under the smoke-puff which marked a bursting shell. Some threw themselves behind a scrap of cover and fired rapidly, vainly, at the terrible heights whence the flood of death poured on them. Others rushed almost alone towards them, until they collapsed suddenly, dramatically. The most hesitated, turned, looked from side to side, and then ran back, a chaotic rabble, to the shelter of the woods.

The attack had failed, but the hail of shells still beat upon the ridge, decimating the men in the trenches as they showed themselves to fire. Nevertheless, with the meadows below again clear, there was a lull for the defenders. They lay down again upon a litter of empty brass cartridge-cases, and submitted as patiently as they could to the shrapnel that crashed and droned above their heads. The weariness of the long marches had passed away, but hunger was an acute pain, and thirst a torture to parched throats and dry, swollen lips. The bottles and water-cans in the trenches were soon emptied. Groups, wild-eyed and grim, cast lots; and here and there men, hung all about with water-bottles, sprang out of the trench and raced, bending low, across the shell-swept field. Some fell or disappeared in a flash of flame. The most reached the farm buildings, and clustered about the well.

Down below in the valley, a dozen men—all that remained of the company—were running back from the ruins of the other farm-house.

The batteries behind—still further reinforced, it seemed—ceased not with their fire. The ground shook with their reports. Again smoke was curling up above the tree-tops of the woods.

Suddenly the whistles shrilled out anew.

Dark figures were emerging cautiously, in little groups, from the

'Mene Tekel Zeppelin' was the German way of saying that air power would be the end of British naval supremacy

wood. Taught by experience, they now availed themselves of every scrap of cover. More followed them, and yet more—an endless number. Again the crackling roll ran along the trenches. Again the shrapnel burst in quick puffs over their heads. They seemed to mind it as little as the grim defenders on the ridge heeded the shrapnel which still assailed them. Yard by yard, in little rushes, they pressed steadily forward, firing every time they dropped into cover. The ruined farmhouse was silent now, tenanted only by dead or helpless men. A crowd of dark soldiers made a rush for it, established themselves there. Again the sporadic explosions dotted the broken walls.

Forward, steadily forward, pressed the dark throng. The valley was filled with figures running towards the ridge, throwing themselves down, springing up again, spurting onward. Rifle bullets sang an ever louder song over the heads of the defenders in the trenches. The shrapnel burst viciously over the ridge. The quick reports of the guns merged into one incessant deafening roar. The roll of rifle-volleys went on endlessly.

Still the dark mass pressed onward, losing heavily, but creeping gradually nearer to the ridge which was its goal. The leading figures were already firing from the slope on the hither side of the ruined farmhouse.

The defenders nerved themselves for a supreme effort. The roll of the rifles swelled into ever louder volume. Fresh battalions came up and flung themselves down in the open along the ridge, firing swiftly. The batteries swept the slope with shells. The forward movement of the dark mass stopped. Confusion spread among it. It was the crisis of the attack.

Suddenly there was a cry along the ridge.

'Look! Oh, my Gawd! Look!'

Six aeroplanes, one behind the flanks of the other, like a flight of birds, were rushing towards them. High above the shells they came, and, as they approached, the shrapnel ceased to beat upon the ridge. The respite was for a moment only. Every man upon the ridge knew it, and in panic desperation they turned their rifles up to the machines and fired, emptying their magazines recklessly. In vain the officers strove to stop them, pointing to the men below now surging up scatheless to the attack. They fired wildly into the air against the onward-rushing menace, forgetting all else save the urgent necessity of crippling them ere they floated overhead.

The leading machine reached the ridge, slackened, and turned along it. A stream of small objects fell from her as she drove slowly onward. A succession of heavy explosions, a series of vivid eruptions, burst out along the crowded ridge. The ammunition wagons of a battery went into the air in a sheet of flame.

Her consort reached the ridge, turned, and did likewise. The rear machines imitated them as they came up. One followed the line of the shelter-trench across the potato-field. It seemed to the men in it that the earth exploded under their feet. Everything seemed swaying, rocking, in flame and paralysing sound. With a shriek they fled wildly—anywhere, amid an inferno of explosions. Behind them broke out a roar of cheers, a roll of murderous rifle-fire. The dark uniforms swarmed into the position, shooting down the fugitives, pursuing them with levelled bayonets at their backs.

A battery, caught in the midst of a struggle with maddened, plunging horses, was overrun. Another tore wildly through the crowd, knocking over all in its way. A mass of frenzied infantry, all order gone, all discipline lost, raced, fought, jostled, stumbled, in a mad rush for safety. In a torrent they poured, foot and guns, into the narrow road behind the ridge, trampling underfoot those who fell, shooting down those who tried to stay them, staring with wild eyes, yet blind with terror. Behind them rolled the rifle volleys of their foes.

Overhead the aeroplanes, their work done, sailed slowly back.

Danger!

Being the Log of Captain John Sirius

SIR ARTHUR CONAN DOYLE

It is an amazing thing that the English, who have the reputation of being a practical nation, never saw the danger to which they were exposed.[1] For many years they had been spending nearly a hundred millions a year upon their army and their fleet. Squadrons of dreadnoughts costing 2 millions each had been launched. They had spent enormous sums upon cruisers, and both their torpedo and their submarine squadrons were exceptionally strong. They were also by no means weak in their aerial power, especially in the matter of seaplanes. Besides all this, their army was very efficient, in spite of its limited numbers, and it was the most expensive in Europe. Yet, when the day of trial came, all this imposing force was of no use whatever, and might as well have not existed. Their ruin could not have been more complete or more rapid if they had not possessed an ironclad or a regiment. And all this was accomplished by me, Captain John Sirius, belonging to the navy of one of the smallest powers in Europe, and having under my command a flotilla of eight vessels, the collective cost of which was £1,800,000. No one has a better right to tell the story than I.

I will not trouble you about the dispute concerning the Colonial frontier, embittered, as it was, by the subsequent death of the two missionaries. A naval officer has nothing to do with politics. I only came upon the scene after the ultimatum had been actually received. Admiral Horli had been summoned to the Presence, and he asked that I should be allowed to accompany him, because he happened to know that I had some clear ideas as to the weak points of England, and also some schemes as to how to take advantage of them. There were only four of us present at this meeting—the King, the Foreign Secretary, Admiral Horli, and myself. The time allowed by the ultimatum expired in forty-eight hours.

I am not breaking any confidence when I say that both the King and the Minister were in favour of a surrender. They saw no possibility of standing up against the colossal power of Great Britain. The

Minister had drawn up an acceptance of the British terms, and the
King sat with it before him on the table. I saw the tears of anger and
humiliation run down his cheeks as he looked at it.

'I fear that there is no possible alternative, Sire,' said the Minister.
'Our envoy in London has just sent this report, which shows that the
public and the press are more united than he has ever known them.
The feeling is intense, especially since the rash act of Malort in des-
ecrating the flag. We must give way.'

The King looked sadly at Admiral Horli.

'What is your effective fleet, Admiral?' he asked.

'Two battleships, four cruisers, twenty torpedo-boats, and eight
submarines,' said the Admiral.

The King shook his head.

'It would be madness to resist,' said he.

'And yet, Sire,' said the Admiral, 'before you come to a decision I
should wish you to hear Captain Sirius, who has a very definite plan
of campaign against the English.'

'Absurd!' said the King, impatiently. 'What is the use? Do you
imagine that you could defeat their vast armada?'

'Sire,' I answered, 'I will stake my life that if you will follow my
advice you will, within a month or six weeks at the utmost, bring
proud England to her knees.'

There was an assurance in my voice which arrested the attention
of the King.

'You seem self-confident, Captain Sirius.'

'I have no doubt at all, Sire.'

'What then would you advise?'

'I would advise, Sire, that the whole fleet be gathered under the
forts of Blankenberg and be protected from attack by booms and
piles. There they can stay till the war is over. The eight submarines,
however, you will leave in my charge to use as I think fit.'

'Ah, you would attack the English battleships with submarines?'

'Sire, I would never go near an English battleship.'

'And why not?'

'Because they might injure me, Sire.'

'What, a sailor and afraid?'

'My life belongs to the country, Sire. It is nothing. But these eight
ships—everything depends upon them. I could not risk them.
Nothing would induce me to fight.'

'Then what will you do?'

'I will tell you, Sire.' And I did so. For half an hour I spoke. I was
clear and strong and definite, for many an hour on a lonely watch I

had spent in thinking out every detail. I held them enthralled. The King never took his eyes from my face. The Minister sat as if turned to stone.

'Are you sure of all this?'

'Perfectly, Sire.'

The King rose from the table.

'Send no answer to the ultimatum,' said he.

'Announce in both houses that we stand firm in the face of menace. Admiral Horli, you will in all respects carry out that which Captain Sirius may demand in furtherance of his plan. Captain Sirius, the field is clear. Go forth and do as you have said. A grateful King will know how to reward you.'

I need not trouble you by telling you the measures which were taken at Blankenberg, since, as you are aware, the fortress and the entire fleet were destroyed by the British within a week of the declaration of war. I will confine myself to my own plans, which had so glorious and final a result.

The fame of my eight submarines, *Alpha, Beta, Gamma, Theta, Delta, Epsilon, Iota* and *Kappa*, has spread through the world to such an extent that people have begun to think that there was something peculiar in their form and capabilities. This is not so. Four of them, the *Delta, Epsilon, Iota,* and *Kappa,* were, it is true, of the very latest model, but had their equals (though not their superiors) in the navies of all the great Powers. As to *Alpha, Beta, Gamma,* and *Theta,* they were by no means modern vessels, and found their prototypes in the old F class of British boats, having a submerged displacement of 800 tons, with heavy oil engines of 1,600 horse-power, giving them a speed of eighteen knots on the surface and of twelve knots submerged. Their length was 186 and their breadth 24 feet. They had a radius of action of 4,000 miles and a submerged endurance of nine hours. These were considered the latest word in 1915, but the four new boats exceeded them in all respects. Without troubling you with precise figures, I may say that they represented roughly a twenty-five per cent advance upon the older boats, and were fitted with several auxiliary engines which were wanting in the others.[2] At my suggestion, instead of carrying eight of the very large Bakdorf torpedoes, which are 19 feet long, weigh half a ton, and are charged with 200 pounds of wet gun-cotton, we had tubes designed for eighteen of less than half the size. It was my design to make myself independent of my base.

And yet, it was clear that I must have a base, so I made arrangements at once with that object. Blankenberg was the last place I would have chosen. Why should I have a *port* of any kind? Ports would be watched or occupied. Any place would do for me. I finally chose a small villa standing alone nearly five miles from any village and thirty miles from any port. To this I ordered them to convey, secretly by night, oil, spare parts, extra torpedoes, storage batteries, reserve periscopes, and everything that I could need for refitting. The little whitewashed villa of a retired confectioner—that was the base from which I operated against England.

The boats lay at Blankenberg, and thither I went. They were working frantically at the defences, and they had only to look seawards to be spurred to fresh exertions. The British fleet was assembling. The ultimatum had not yet expired, but it was evident that a blow would be struck the instant that it did. Four of their aeroplanes, circling at an immense height, were surveying our defences. From the top of the lighthouse I counted thirty battleships and cruisers in the offing, with a number of the trawlers with which in the British service they break through the mine-fields. The approaches were actually sown with 200 mines, half contact and half observation, but the result showed that they were insufficient to hold off the enemy, since three days later both town and fleet were speedily destroyed.

However, I am not here to tell you the incidents of the war, but to explain my own part in it, which had such a decisive effect upon the result. My first action was to send my four second-class boats away instantly to the point which I had chosen for my base. There they were to wait submerged, lying with negative buoyancy upon the sands in twenty feet of water, and rising only at night. My strict orders were that they were to attempt nothing upon the enemy, however tempting the opportunity. All they had to do was to remain intact and unseen, until they received further orders. Having made this clear to Commander Panza, who had charge of this reserve flotilla, I shook him by the hand and bade him farewell, leaving with him a sheet of notepaper upon which I had explained the tactics to be used and given him certain general principles which he could apply as circumstances demanded.

My whole attention was now given to my own flotilla, which I divided into two divisions, keeping *Iota* and *Kappa* under my own command, while Captain Miriam had *Delta* and *Epsilon*. He was to operate separately in the British Channel, while my station was the Straits of Dover. I made the whole plan of campaign clear to him. Then I saw that each ship was provided with all it could carry. Each had forty tons of heavy oil for surface propulsion and charging the dynamo which supplied the electric engines under water. Each had also eighteen torpedoes as explained and 500 rounds for the collapsible quick-firing twelve-pounder which we carried on deck, and which, of course, disappeared into a water-tight tank when we were submerged. We carried spare periscopes and a wireless mast, which could be elevated above the conning tower when necessary. There were provisions for sixteen days for the ten men who manned each craft. Such was the equipment of the four boats which were destined to bring to naught all the navies and armies of Britain. At sundown that day—it was April 10th—we set forth upon our historic voyage.

Miriam had got away in the afternoon, since he had so much farther to go to reach his station. Stephan, of the *Kappa*, started with me; but, of course, we realized that we must work independently, and that from that moment when we shut the sliding hatches of our conning towers on the still waters of Blankenberg Harbour, it was unlikely that we should ever see each other again, though consorts in the same waters. I waved to Stephan from the side of my conning tower, and he to me. Then I called through the tube to my engineer (our water-tanks were already filled and all kingstons and vents closed) to put her full speed ahead.

Just as we came abreast of the end of the pier and saw the white-capped waves rolling in upon us, I put the horizontal rudder hard down and she slid under water. Through my glass portholes I saw its light green change to a dark blue, while the manometer in front of me indicated twenty feet. I let her go to forty, because I should then be under the warships of the English, though I took the chance of fouling the moorings of our own floating contact mines. Then I brought her on an even keel, and it was music to my ear to hear the gentle, even ticking of my electric engines and to know that I was speeding at twelve miles an hour on my great task.

At that moment, as I stood controlling my levers in my tower, I could have seen, had my cupola been of glass, the vast shadows of the British blockaders hovering above me. I held my course due westward for ninety minutes, and then, by shutting off the electric engine without blowing out the water-tanks, I brought her to the surface. There was a rolling sea and the wind was freshening, so I did not think it safe to keep my hatch open long, for so small is the margin of buoyancy that one must run no risks. But from the crests of the rollers I had a look backwards at Blankenberg, and saw the black funnels and upper works of the enemy's fleet with the light-house and the castle behind them, all flushed with the pink glow of the setting sun. Even as I looked, there was the boom of a great gun, and then another. I glanced at my watch. It was six o'clock. The time of the ultimatum had expired. We were at war.

There was no craft near us, and our surface speed is nearly twice that of our submerged, so I blew out the tanks and our whale-back came over the surface. All night we were steering south-west, making an average of eighteen knots. At about five in the morning, as I stood alone upon my tiny bridge, I saw, low down in the west, the scattered lights of the Norfolk coast. 'Ah, Johnny, Johnny Bull,' I said, as I looked at them, 'you are going to have your lesson, and I am to be your master. It is I who have been chosen to teach you that one cannot live under artificial conditions and yet act as if they were natural ones. More foresight, Johnny, and less party politics—that is my lesson to you.' And then I had a wave of pity, too, when I thought of those vast droves of helpless people, Yorkshire miners, Lancashire spinners, Birmingham metal-workers, the dockers and workers of London, over whose little homes I would bring the shadow of starvation. I seemed to see all those wasted eager hands held out for food, and I, John Sirius, dashing it aside. Ah, well! war is war, and if one is foolish one must pay the price.

Just before daybreak I saw the lights of a considerable town, which must have been Yarmouth, bearing about ten miles west–south–west on our starboard bow. I took her farther out, for it is a sandy, dangerous coast, with many shoals. At five-thirty we were abreast of the Lowestoft lightship. A coastguard was sending up flash signals which faded into a pale twinkle as the white dawn crept over the water. There was a good deal of shipping about, mostly fishing-boats and small coasting craft, with one large steamer hull-down to the west, and a torpedo destroyer between us and the land. It could not harm us, and yet I thought it as well that there should be no word of our presence, so I filled my tanks again and went down to ten feet. I was pleased to find that we got under in 150 seconds. The life of one's boat may depend on this when a swift craft comes suddenly upon you.

We were now within a few hours of our cruising ground, so I determined to snatch a rest, leaving Vornal in charge. When he woke me at ten o'clock we were running on the surface, and had reached the Essex coast off the Maplin Sands. With that charming frankness which is one of their characteristics, our friends of England had informed us by their press that they had put a cordon of torpedo-boats across the Straits of Dover to prevent the passage of submarines, which is about as sensible as to lay a wooden plank across a stream to keep the eels from passing. I knew that Stephan, whose station lay at the western end of the Solent, would have no difficulty in reaching it. My own cruising ground was to be at the mouth of the Thames, and here I was at the very spot with my tiny *Iota*, my eighteen torpedoes, my quick firing-gun, and, above all, a brain that knew what should be done and how to do it.

When I resumed my place in the conning tower I saw in the periscope (for we had dived) that a lightship was within a few hundred yards of us upon the port bow. Two men were sitting on her bulwarks, but neither of them cast an eye upon the little rod that clove the water so close to them. It was an ideal day for submarine action, with enough ripple upon the surface to make us difficult to detect, and yet smooth enough to give me a clear view. Each of my three periscopes had an angle of sixty degrees, so that between them I commanded a complete semi-circle of the horizon. Two British cruisers were steaming north from the Thames within half a mile of me. I could easily have cut them off and attacked them had I allowed myself to be diverted from my great plan. Farther south a destroyer was passing westwards to Sheerness. A dozen small steamers were moving about. None of these were worthy of my notice. Great countries are not provisioned by small steamers. I kept the engines running at the lowest pace which would hold our position under water, and, moving slowly across the estuary, I waited for what must assuredly come.

I had not long to wait. Shortly after one o'clock, I perceived in the periscope a cloud of smoke to the south. Half an hour later a large steamer raised her hull, making for the mouth of the Thames. I ordered Vornal to stand by the starboard torpedo-tube, having the other also loaded in case of a miss. Then I advanced slowly, for though the steamer was going very swiftly we could easily cut her off. Presently I laid the *Iota* in a position near which she must pass, and would very gladly have lain to, but could not for fear of rising to the surface. I therefore steered out in the direction from which she was coming. She was a very large ship, 15,000 tons at the least, painted black above and red below, with two cream-coloured funnels. She lay so low in the water that it was clear she had a full cargo. At her bows were a cluster of men, some of them looking, I dare say, for the first time at the mother country. How little could they have guessed the welcome that was awaiting them!

On she came with the great plumes of smoke floating from her funnels, and two white waves foaming from her cut-water. She was within a quarter of a mile. My moment had arrived. I signalled full

'I stopped the engines, brought her to the surface, and opened the conning tower'

Conan Doyle's extraordinarily prophetic account of submarine warfare was matched by
the perception of the artist

speed ahead and steered straight for her course. My timing was
exact. At 100 yards I gave the signal, and heard the clank and swish
of the discharge. At the same instant, I put the helm hard down and
flew off at an angle. There was a terrific lurch, which came from the
distant explosion. For a moment we were almost upon our side.
Then, after staggering and trembling, the *Iota* came on an even keel.
I stopped the engines, brought her to the surface, and opened the
conning tower, while all my excited crew came crowding to the
hatch to know what had happened.

The ship lay within 200 yards of us, and it was easy to see that she
had her death-blow. She was already settling down by the stern.
There was a sound of shouting and people were running wildly
about her decks. Her name was visible, the *Adela*, of London, bound,
as we afterwards learned, from New Zealand with frozen mutton.
Strange as it may seem to you, the notion of a submarine had never
even now occurred to her people, and all were convinced that they
had struck a floating mine. The starboard quarter had been blown in
by the explosion, and the ship was sinking rapidly. Their discipline
was admirable. We saw boat after boat slip down crowded with

people as swiftly and quietly as if it were part of their daily drill. And suddenly, as one of the boats lay off waiting for the others, they caught a glimpse for the first time of my conning tower so close to them. I saw them shouting and pointing, while the men in the other boats got up to have a better look at us. For my part, I cared nothing, for I took it for granted that they already knew that a submarine had destroyed them. One of them clambered back into the sinking ship. I was sure that he was about to send a wireless message as to our presence. It mattered nothing, since, in any case, it must be known; otherwise I could easily have brought him down with a rifle. As it was, I waved my hand to them, and they waved back to me. War is too big a thing to leave room for personal ill-feeling, but it must be remorseless all the same.

I was still looking at the sinking *Adela* when Vornal, who was beside me, gave a sudden cry of warning and surprise, gripping me by the shoulder and turning my head. There behind us, coming up the fairway, was a huge black vessel with black funnels, flying the well-known house-flag of the P and O Company. She was not a mile distant, and I calculated in an instant that, even if she had seen us, she would not have time to turn and get away before we could reach her. We went straight for her, therefore, keeping awash just as we were. They saw the sinking vessel in front of them and that little dark speck moving over the surface, and they suddenly understood their danger. I saw a number of men rush to the bows, and there was a rattle of rifle-fire. Two bullets were flattened upon our four-inch armour. You might as well try to stop a charging bull with paper pellets as the *Iota* with rifle-fire. I had learned my lesson from the *Adela*, and this time I had the torpedo discharged at a safer distance—250 yards. We caught her amidships and the explosion was tremendous, but we were well outside its area. She sank almost instantaneously. I am sorry for her people, of whom I hear that more than 200, including 70 Lascars and 40 passengers, were drowned. Yes, I am sorry for them. But when I think of the huge floating granary that went to the bottom, I rejoice as a man does who has carried out that which he plans.

It was a bad afternoon that for the P and O Company. The second ship which we destroyed was, as we have since learned, the *Moldavia*, of 15,000 tons, one of their finest vessels; but about half-past three we blew up the *Cusco*, of 8,000, of the same line, also from Eastern ports, and laden with corn. Why she came on in face of the wireless messages which must have warned her of danger, I cannot imagine. The other two steamers which we blew up that day, the *Maid of Athens* (Robson Line) and the *Cormorant*, were neither of them provided with apparatus, and came blindly to their destruction. Both were small boats of from 5,000 to 7,000 tons. In the case of the second, I had to rise to the surface and fire six twelve-pound shells under her water-line before she would sink. In each case, the crew took to the boats, and so far as I know no casualties occurred.

After that no more steamers came along, nor did I expect them. Warnings must by this time have been flying in all directions. But we had no reason to be dissatisfied with our first day. Between the Maplin Sands and the Nore, we had sunk five ships of a total tonnage of about 50,000 tons. Already the London markets would begin to feel the pinch. And Lloyd's—poor old Lloyd's—what a demented state it would be in! I could imagine the London evening papers and the howling in Fleet Street. We saw the result of our actions, for it was quite laughable to see the torpedo-boats buzzing like angry wasps out of Sheerness in the evening. They were darting in every direction across the estuary, and the aeroplanes and hydroplanes were like flights of crows, black dots against the red western sky. They quartered the whole river-mouth, until they discovered us at last. Some sharp-sighted fellow with a telescope on board of a destroyer got a sight of our periscope, and came for us full speed. No doubt he would very gladly have rammed us, even if it had meant his own destruction, but that was not part of our programme at all. I sank her and ran her east–south-east with an occasional rise. Finally we brought her to not very far from the Kentish coast, and the search-lights of our pursuers were far on the western skyline. There we lay quietly all night, for a submarine at night is nothing more than a very third-rate surface torpedo-boat. Besides, we were all weary and needed rest. Do not forget, you captains of men, when you grease and trim your pumps and compressors and rotators, that the human machine needs some tending also.

I had put up the wireless mast above the conning tower, and had no difficulty in calling up Captain Stephan. He was lying, he said, off Ventnor and had been unable to reach his station on account of engine trouble, which he had now set right. Next morning he proposed to block the Southampton approach. He had destroyed one large Indian boat on his way down Channel. We exchanged good wishes. Like myself, he needed rest. I was up at four in the morning, however, and called all hands to overhaul the boat. She was some-what up by the head, owing to the forward torpedoes having been used, so we trimmed her by opening the forward compensating tank, admitting as much water as the torpedoes had weighed. We also overhauled the starboard air-compressor and one of the periscope motors which had been jarred by the shock of the first explosion. We had hardly got ourselves shipshape when the morning dawned.

I have no doubt that a good many ships which had taken refuge in the French ports at the first alarm had run across and got safely up the river in the night. Of course I could have attacked them, but I do not care to take risks—and there are always risks for a submarine at night. But one had miscalculated his time, and there she was, just abreast of Warden Point, when the daylight disclosed her to us. In an instant we were after her. It was a near thing, for she was a flier, and could do two miles to our one; but we just reached her as she went swashing by. She saw us at the last moment, for I attacked her awash, since otherwise we could not have had the pace to reach her. She swung away and the first torpedo missed, but the second took her full under the counter. Heavens, what a smash! The whole stern seemed to go aloft. I drew off and watched her sink. She went down in seven minutes, leaving her masts and funnels over the water and a cluster of her people holding on to them. She was the *Virginia*, of the Bibby Line—12,000 tons—and laden, like the others, with food-stuffs from the East. The whole surface of the sea was covered with the floating grain. 'John Bull will have to take up a hole or two of his belt if this goes on,' said Vornal, as we watched the scene.

And it was at that moment that the very worst danger occurred that could befall us. I tremble now when I think how our glorious voyage might have been nipped in the bud. I had freed the hatch of my tower, and was looking at the boats of the *Virginia* with Vornal near me, when there was a swish and a terrific splash in the water beside us, which covered us both with spray. We looked up, and you can imagine our feelings when we saw an aeroplane hovering a few hundred feet above us like a hawk. With its silencer, it was perfectly noiseless, and had its bomb not fallen into the sea we should never have known what had destroyed us. She was circling round in the hope of dropping a second one, but we shoved on all speed ahead, crammed down the rudders, and vanished into the side of a roller. I kept the deflection indicator falling until I had put fifty good feet of water between the aeroplane and ourselves, for I knew well how deeply they can see under the surface. However, we soon threw her off our track, and when we came to the surface near Margate there was no sign of her, unless she was one of several which we saw hovering over Herne Bay.

There was not a ship in the offing save a few small coasters and little thousand-ton steamers, which were beneath my notice. For several hours I lay submerged with a blank periscope. Then I had an inspiration. Orders had been marconied to every foodship to lie in French waters and dash across after dark. I was as sure of it as if they had been recorded in our own receiver. Well, if they were there, that was where I should be also. I blew out the tanks and rose, for there was no sign of any warship near. They had some good system of signalling from the shore, however, for I had not got to the North Foreland before three destroyers came foaming after me, all converging from different directions. They had about as good a chance of catching me as three spaniels would have of overtaking a porpoise. Out of pure bravado—I know it was very wrong—I waited until they were actually within gunshot. Then I sank and we saw each other no more.

It is, as I have said, a shallow sandy coast, and submarine navigation is very difficult. The worst mishap that can befall a boat is to bury its nose in the side of a sand-drift and be held there. Such an accident might have been the end of our boat, though with our Fleuss cylinders and electric lamps we should have found no difficulty in getting out at the air-lock and in walking ashore across the bed of the ocean. As it was, however, I was able, thanks to our excellent charts, to keep the channel and so to gain the open straits. There we rose about midday, but, observing a hydroplane at no great distance, we sank again for half an hour. When we came up for the second time, all was peaceful around us, and the English coast was lining the whole western horizon. We kept outside the Goodwins and straight down Channel until we saw a line of black dots in front of us, which I knew to be the Dover–Calais torpedo-boat cordon. When two miles distant we dived and came up again seven miles to the south-west, without one of them dreaming that we had been within thirty feet of their keels.

When we rose, a large steamer flying the German flag was within half a mile of us. It was the North German Lloyd *Altona*, from New York to Bremen. I raised our whole hull and dipped our flag to her. It was amusing to see the amazement of her people at what they must have regarded as our unparalleled impudence in those English-swept waters. They cheered us heartily, and the tricolour flag was dipped in greeting as they went roaring past us. Then I stood in to the French coast.

It was exactly as I had expected. There were three great British steamers lying at anchor in Boulogne outer harbour. They were the

Caesar, the *King of the East*, and the *Pathfinder*, none less than 10,000 tons. I suppose they thought they were safe in French waters, but what did I care about three-mile limits and international law! The view of my Government was that England was blockaded, food contraband, and vessels carrying it to be destroyed. The lawyers could argue about it afterwards. My business was to starve the enemy any way I could. Within an hour the three ships were under the waves and the *Iota* was streaming down the Picardy coast, looking for fresh victims. The Channel was covered with English torpedo-boats buzzing and whirling like a cloud of midges. How they thought they could hurt me I cannot imagine, unless by accident I were to come up underneath one of them. More dangerous were the aeroplanes which circled here and there.

The water being calm, I had several times to descend as deep as a hundred feet before I was sure that I was out of their sight. After I had blown up the three ships at Boulogne I saw two aeroplanes flying down Channel, and I knew that they would head off any vessels which were coming up. There was one very large white steamer lying off Havre, but she steamed west before I could reach her. I dare say Stephan or one of the others would get her before long. But those infernal aeroplanes spoiled our sport for that day. Not another steamer did I see, save the never-ending torpedo-boats. I consoled myself with the reflection, however, that no food was passing me on its way to London. That was what I was there for, after all. If I could do it without spending my torpedoes, all the better. Up to date I had fired ten of them and sunk nine steamers, so I had not wasted my weapons. That night I came back to the Kent coast and lay upon the bottom in shallow water near Dungeness.

We were all trimmed and ready at the first break of day, for I expected to catch some ships which had tried to make the Thames in the darkness and had miscalculated their time. Sure enough, there was a great steamer coming up Channel and flying the American flag. It was all the same to me what flag she flew so long as she was engaged in conveying contraband of war to the British Isles. There were no torpedo-boats about at the moment, so I ran out on the surface and fired a shot across her bows. She seemed inclined to go on so I put a second one just above her water-line on her port bow. She stopped then and a very angry man began to gesticulate from the bridge. I ran the *Iota* almost alongside.

'Are you the captain?' I asked.

'What the —' I won't attempt to reproduce his language.

'You have food-stuffs on board?' I said.

'It's an American ship, you blind beetle!' he cried. 'Can't you see the flag? It's the *Vermondia*, of Boston.'

'Sorry, Captain,' I answered. 'I have really no time for words. Those shots of mine will bring the torpedo-boats, and I dare say at this very moment your wireless is making trouble for me. Get your people into the boats.'

I had to show him I was not bluffing, so I drew off and began putting shells into him just on the water-line. When I had knocked six holes in it he was very busy on his boats. I fired twenty shots altogether, and no torpedo was needed, for she was lying over with a terrible list to port, and presently came right on to her side. There she lay for two or three minutes before she foundered. There were eight boats crammed with people lying round her when she went down. I believe everybody was saved, but I could not wait to enquire. From all quarters, the poor old panting, useless war-vessels were hurrying. I filled my tanks, ran her bows under, and came up fifteen miles to the south. Of course, I knew there would be a big row afterwards—as there was—but that did not help the starving crowds round the London bakers, who only saved their skins, poor devils, by explaining to the mob that they had nothing to bake.

By this time I was becoming rather anxious, as you can imagine, to know what was going on in the world and what England was thinking about it all. I ran alongside a fishing-boat, therefore, and ordered them to give up their papers. Unfortunately they had none, except a rag of an evening paper, which was full of nothing but betting news. In a second attempt I came alongside a small yachting party from Eastbourne, who were frightened to death at our sudden appearance out of the depths. From them we were lucky enough to get the London *Courier* of that very morning.

It was interesting reading—so interesting that I had to announce it all to the crew. Of course, you know the British style of headline, which gives you all the news at a glance. It seemed to me that the whole paper was headlines, it was in such a state of excitement. Hardly a word about me and my flotilla. We were on the second page. The first one began something like this:

CAPTURE OF BLANKENBERG!

———

DESTRUCTION OF ENEMY'S FLEET

———

BURNING OF TOWN

———

TRAWLERS DESTROY MINE FIELD
LOSS OF TWO BATTLESHIPS

Is It The End?

Of course, what I had foreseen had occurred. The town was actually occupied by the British. And they thought it was the end! We would see about that.

On the round-the-corner page, at the back of the glorious resonant leaders, there was a little column which read like this:

HOSTILE SUBMARINES

Several of the enemy's submarines are at sea, and have inflicted some appreciable damage upon our merchant ships. The danger-spots upon Monday and the greater part of Tuesday appear to have been the mouth of the Thames and the western entrance to the Solent. On Monday, between the Nore and Margate, there were sunk five large steamers, the *Adela, Moldavia, Cusco, Cormorant,* and *Maid of Athens,* particulars of which will be found below. Near Ventnor, on the same day, was sunk the *Verulam,* from Bombay. On Tuesday the *Virginia, Caesar, King of the East,* and *Pathfinder* were destroyed between the Foreland and Boulogne. The latter three were actually lying in French waters, and the most energetic representations have been made by the Government of the Republic. On the same day *The Queen of Sheba, Orontes, Diana,* and *Atalanta* were destroyed near the Needles. Wireless messages have stopped all ingoing cargo-ships from coming up Channel, but unfortunately there is evidence that at least two of the enemy's submarines are in the West. Four cattle-ships from Dublin to Liverpool were sunk yesterday evening, while three Bristol-bound steamers, the *Hilda, Mercury,* and *Maria Toser,* were blown up in the neighbourhood of Lundy Island. Commerce has, so far as possible, been diverted into safer channels, but in the meantime, however vexatious these incidents may be, and however grievous the loss both to the owners and to Lloyd's, we may console ourselves by the reflection that, since a submarine cannot keep the sea for more than ten days without refitting, and since the base has been captured, there must come a speedy term to these depredations.

So much for the *Courier*'s account of our proceedings. Another small paragraph was, however, more eloquent:

> The price of wheat, which stood at thirty-five shillings a week before the declaration of war, was quoted yesterday on the Baltic at fifty-two. Maize has gone from twenty-one to thirty-seven, barley from nineteen to thirty-five, sugar (foreign granulated) from eleven shillings and threepence to nineteen shillings and sixpence.

'Good, my lads!' said I, when I read it to the crew. 'I can assure you that those few lines will prove to mean more than the whole page about the Fall of Blankenberg. Now let us get down Channel and send those prices up a little higher.'

All traffic had stopped for London—not so bad for the little *Iota*—and we did not see a steamer that was worth a torpedo between Dungeness and the Isle of Wight. There I called Stephan up by wireless, and by seven o'clock we were actually lying side by side in a smooth rolling sea—Hengistbury Head bearing north–north-west and about five miles distant. The two crews clustered on the whale-backs and shouted their joy at seeing friendly faces once more.

Stephan had done extraordinarily well. I had, of course, read in the London paper of his four ships on Tuesday, but he had sunk no fewer than seven since, for many of those which should have come to the Thames had tried to make Southampton. Of the seven, one was of 20,000 tons, a grain-ship from America, a second was a grain-ship from the Black Sea, and two others were great liners from South Africa. I congratulated Stephan with all my heart upon his splendid achievement. Then, as we had been seen by a destroyer which was approaching at a great pace, we both dived, coming up again off the Needles, where we spent the night in company. We could not visit each other, since we had no boat, but we lay so nearly alongside that we were able, Stephan and I, to talk from hatch to hatch and so make our plans.

He had shot away more than half his torpedoes, and so had I, and yet we were very averse from returning to our base so long as our oil held out. I told him of my experience with the Boston steamer, and we mutually agreed to sink the ships by gun-fire in future so far as possible. I remember old Horli saying, 'What use is a gun aboard a submarine?' We were about to show. I read the English paper to Stephan by the light of my electric torch, and we both agreed that few ships would now come up the Channel. That sentence about diverting commerce to safer routes could only mean that the ships

The cramped operating space in the first true submarine, *USS Holland*, which entered service in 1900

would go round the North of Ireland and unload at Glasgow. Oh, for two more ships to stop that entrance! Heavens, what *would* England have done against a foe with thirty or forty submarines, since we only needed six instead of four to complete her destruction! After much talk we decided that the best plan would be that I should dispatch a cipher telegram next morning from a French port to tell them to send the four second-rate boats to cruise off the North of Ireland and West of Scotland. Then when I had done this I should move down Channel with Stephan and operate at the mouth, while the other two boats could work in the Irish Sea. Having made these plans, I set off across the Channel in the early morning, reaching the small village of Etretat, in Brittany. There I got off my telegram and then laid my course for Falmouth, passing under the keels of two British cruisers which were making eagerly for Etretat, having heard by wireless that we were there.

Half-way down Channel we had trouble with a short-circuit in our electric engines, and were compelled to run on the surface for several hours while we replaced one of the cam-shafts and renewed some washers. It was a ticklish time, for had a torpedo-boat come upon us we could not have dived. The perfect submarine of the future will surely have some alternative engines for such an emergency. However, by the skill of Engineer Morro, we got things going once more. All the time we lay there I saw a hydroplane floating between us and the British coast. I can understand how a mouse feels when it is in a tuft of grass and sees a hawk high up in the heavens. However, all went well; the mouse became a water-rat, it wagged its tail in derision at the poor blind old hawk, and it dived down into a nice safe green, quiet world where there was nothing to injure it.

It was on the Wednesday night that the *Iota* crossed to Etretat. It was Friday afternoon before we had reached our new cruising ground. Only one large steamer did I see upon our way. The terror we had caused had cleared the Channel. This big boat had a clever captain on board. His tactics were excellent and took him in safety to the Thames. He came zigzagging up Channel at twenty-five knots, shooting off from his course at all sorts of unexpected angles. With our slow pace we could not catch him, nor could we calculate his line so as to cut him off. Of course, he had never seen us, but he judged, and judged rightly, that wherever we were those were the tactics by which he had the best chance of getting past. He deserved his success.

But, of course, it is only in a wide channel that such things can be done. Had I met him in the mouth of the Thames, there would have been a different story to tell. As I approached Falmouth I destroyed a 3,000-ton boat from Cork, laden with butter and cheese. It was my only success for three days.

That night (Friday, April 16th) I called up Stephan, but received no reply. As I was within a few miles of our rendezvous, and as he would not be cruising after dark, I was puzzled to account for his silence. I could only imagine that his wireless was deranged. But, alas! I was soon to find the true reason from a copy of the *Western Morning News*, which I obtained from a Brixham trawler. The *Kappa*, with her gallant commander and crew, were at the bottom of the English Channel.

It appeared from this account that, after I had parted from him, he had met and sunk no fewer than five vessels. I gathered these to be his work, since all of them were by gun-fire, and all were on the south coast of Dorset or Devon. How he met his fate was stated in a short telegram which was headed 'Sinking of a Hostile Submarine'. It was marked 'Falmouth', and ran thus:

> The P and O mail steamer *Macedonia* came into this port last night with five shell holes between wind and water. She reports having been attacked by a hostile submarine ten miles

to the south-east of the Lizard. Instead of using her torpedoes, the submarine for some reason approached from the surface and fired five shots from a semi-automatic twelve-pounder gun. She was evidently under the impression that the *Macedonia* was unarmed. As a matter of fact, being warned of the presence of submarines in the Channel, the *Macedonia* had mounted her armament as an auxiliary cruiser. She opened fire with two quick-firers and blew away the conning tower of the submarine. It is probable that the shells went right through her, as she sank at once with her hatches open. The *Macedonia* was only kept afloat by her pumps.

Such was the end of the *Kappa*, and my gallant friend, Commander Stephan. His best epitaph was in a corner of the same paper, and was headed 'Mark Lane'. It ran:

'Wheat (average) 66, maize 48, barley 50.'

Well, if Stephan was gone there was the more need for me to show energy. My plans were quickly taken, but they were comprehensive. All that day (Saturday) I passed down the Cornish coast and round Land's End, getting two steamers on the way. I had learned from Stephan's fate that it was better to torpedo the large craft, but I was aware that the auxiliary cruisers of the British Government were all over 10,000 tons, so that for all ships under that size it was safe to use my gun. Both these craft, the *Yelland* and the *Playboy*—the latter an American ship—were perfectly harmless, so I came up within a hundred yards of them and speedily sank them, after allowing their people to get into boats.

Some other steamers lay farther out, but I was so eager to make my new arrangements that I did not go out of my course to molest them. Just before sunset, however, so magnificent a prey came within my radius of action that I could not possibly refuse her. No sailor could fail to recognize that glorious monarch of the sea, with her four cream funnels tipped with black, her huge black sides, her red bilges, and her high white top-hamper, roaring up Channel at twenty-three knots, and carrying her 45,000 tons as lightly as if she were a five-ton motor-boat. It was the queenly *Olympic*, of the White Star—once the largest and still the comeliest of liners. What a picture she made, with the blue Cornish sea creaming round her giant fore-foot, and the pink western sky with one evening star forming the background to her noble lines.

She was about five miles off when we dived to cut her off. My calculation was exact. As we came abreast, we loosed our torpedo and struck her fair. We swirled round with the concussion of the water. I saw her in my periscope list over on her side, and I knew that she had her death-blow. She settled down slowly, and there was plenty of time to save her people. The sea was dotted with her boats. When I got about three miles off I rose to the surface, and the whole crew clustered up to see the wonderful sight. She dived bows foremost, and there was a terrific explosion, which sent one of the funnels into the air. I suppose we should have cheered—somehow, none of us felt like cheering. We were all keen sailors, and it went to our hearts to see such a ship go down like a broken eggshell. I gave a gruff order, and all were at their posts again while we headed north-west. Once round the Land's End, I called up my two consorts, and we met next day at Hartland Point, the south end of Bideford Bay. For the moment the Channel was clear, but the English could not know it, and I reckoned that the loss of the *Olympic* would stop all ships for a day or two at least.

Having assembled the *Delta* and *Epsilon*, one on each side of me, I received the report from Miriam and Var, the respective commanders. Each had expended twelve torpedoes, and between them they had sunk twenty-two steamers. One man had been killed by the machinery on board of the *Delta*, and two had been burned by the ignition of some oil on the *Epsilon*. I took these injured men on board, and I gave each of the boats one of my crew. I also divided my spare oil, my provisions, and my torpedoes among them, though we had the greatest possible difficulty in those crank vessels in transferring them from one to the other. However, by ten o'clock it was done, and the two vessels were in condition to keep the sea for another ten days. For my part, with only two torpedoes left, I headed north up the Irish Sea. One of my torpedoes I expended that evening upon a cattle-ship making for Milford Haven. Late at night, being abreast of Holyhead, I called upon my four northern boats, but without reply. Their Marconi range is very limited. About three in the afternoon of the next day I had a feeble answer. It was a great relief to me to find that my telegraphic instructions had reached them and that they were on their station.

Before evening we all assembled in the lee of Sanda Island, in the Mull of Kintyre. I felt an admiral indeed when I saw my five whalebacks all in a row. Panza's report was excellent. They had come round by the Pentland Firth and reached their cruising ground on the fourth day. Already they had destroyed twenty vessels without any mishap. I ordered the *Beta* to divide her oil and torpedoes among the other three, so that they were in good condition to continue their cruise. Then the *Beta* and I headed for home, reaching our base upon Sunday, April 25th. Off Cape Wrath I picked up a paper from a small schooner.

'Wheat, 84; Maize, 60; Barley, 62.'

What were battles and bombardments compared to that!

The whole coast of Norland was closely blockaded by cordon within cordon, and every port, even the smallest, held by the British. But why should they suspect my modest confectioner's villa more than any other of the 10,000 houses that face the sea? I was glad when I picked up its homely white front in my periscope. That night I landed and found my stores intact. Before morning the *Beta* reported itself, for we had the windows lit as a guide.

It is not for me to recount the messages which I found waiting for me at my humble headquarters. They shall ever remain as the patents of nobility of my family. Among others was that never-to-be-forgotten salutation from my King. He desired me to present myself at Hauptville, but for once I took it upon myself to disobey his commands. It took me two days—or, rather, two nights, for we sank ourselves during the daylight hours—to get all our stores on board, but my presence was needful every minute of the time. On the third morning, at four o'clock, the *Beta* and my own little flag-ship were at sea once more, bound for our original station off the mouth of the Thames.

I had no time to read our papers whilst I was refitting, but I gathered the news after we had got under way. The British occupied all our ports, but otherwise we had not suffered at all, since we have excellent railway communications with Europe. Prices had altered little, and our industries continued as before. There was talk of a British invasion, but this I knew to be absolute nonsense, for the British must have learned by this time that it would be sheer murder to send transports full of soldiers to sea in the face of submarines. When they have a tunnel they can use their fine expeditionary force upon the Continent, but until then it might just as well not exist so far as Europe is concerned. My own country, therefore, was in good case and had nothing to fear. Great Britain, however, was already feeling my grip upon her throat. As in normal times four-fifths of her food is imported, prices were rising by leaps and bounds. The supplies in the country were beginning to show signs of depletion, while little was coming in to replace it.

The insurances at Lloyd's had risen to a figure which made the price of the food prohibitive to the mass of the people by the time it had reached the market. The loaf, which under ordinary circumstances stood at 5*d*, was already at 1*s* 4*d*. Beef was 3*s* 4*d* a pound, and mutton 2*s* 9*d*. Everything else was in proportion. The Government had acted with energy and offered a big bounty for corn to be planted at once. It could only be reaped five months hence, however, and long before then, as the papers pointed out, half the island would be dead from starvation. Strong appeals had been made to the patriotism of the people, and they were assured that the interference with trade was temporary, and that with a little patience all would be well. But already there was a marked rise in the death-rate, especially among children, who suffered from want of milk, the cattle being slaughtered for food. There was serious rioting in the Lanarkshire coalfields and in the Midlands, together with a Socialistic upheaval in the East of London, which had assumed the proportions of a civil war. Already there were responsible papers which declared that England was in an impossible position, and that an immediate peace was necessary to prevent one of the greatest tragedies in history. It was my task now to prove to them that they were right.

It was May 2nd when I found myself back at the Maplin Sands to the north of the estuary of the Thames. The *Beta* was sent on to the Solent to block it and take the place of the lamented *Kappa*. And now I was throttling Britain indeed—London, Southampton, the Bristol Channel, Liverpool, the North Channel, the Glasgow approaches, each was guarded by my boats. Great liners were, as we learned afterwards, pouring their supplies into Galway and the West of Ireland, where provisions were cheaper than has ever been known. Tens of thousands were embarking from Britain for Ireland in order to save themselves from starvation. But you cannot transplant a whole dense population. The main body of the people, by the middle of May, were actually starving. At that date wheat was at 100, maize and barley at 80. Even the most obstinate had begun to see that the situation could not possibly continue.

In the great towns, starving crowds clamoured for bread before the municipal offices, and public officials everywhere were attacked and often murdered by frantic mobs, composed largely of desperate women who had seen their infants perish before their eyes. In the country, roots, bark, and weeds of every sort were used as food. In London, the private mansions of Ministers were guarded by strong pickets of soldiers, while a battalion of Guards was camped permanently round the Houses of Parliament. The lives of the Prime Minister and of the Foreign Secretary were continually threatened and occasionally attempted. Yet the Government had entered upon the war with the full assent of every party in the State. The true culprits were those, be they politicians or journalists, who had not the foresight to understand that, unless Britain grew her own supplies, or unless by means of a tunnel she had some way of conveying them into the island, all her mighty expenditure upon her army and her fleet was a mere waste of money so long as her antagonists had a few submarines and men who could use them. England has often been stupid, but has got off scot-free. This time she was stupid and had to pay the price. You can't expect Luck to be your saviour always.

It would be a mere repetition of what I have already described if I were to recount all our proceedings during that first ten days after I resumed my station. During my absence, the ships had taken heart and had begun to come up again. In the first day I got four. After that I had to go farther afield, and again I picked up several in French waters. Once I had a narrow escape through one of my kingston valves getting some grit into it and refusing to act when I was below the surface. Our margin of buoyancy just carried us through. By the end of that week the Channel was clear again, and both *Beta* and my own boat were down West once more. There we had encouraging messages from our Bristol consort, who in turn had heard from *Delta* at Liverpool.

Our task was completely done. We could not prevent all food from passing into the British Islands, but at least we had raised what did get in to a price which put it far beyond the means of the penniless, workless multitudes. In vain, Government commandeered it all and doled it out as a general feeds the garrison of a fortress. The task was too great—the responsibility too horrible. Even the proud and stubborn English could not face it any longer.

I remember well how the news came to me. I was lying at the time off Selsey Bill when I saw a small war-vessel coming down Channel. It had never been my policy to attack any vessel coming *down*. My torpedoes and even my shells were too precious for that. I could not help being attracted, however, by the movements of this ship, which came slowly zigzagging in my direction.

'Looking for me,' thought I. 'What on earth does the foolish thing hope to do if she could find me?'

I was lying awash at the time and got ready to go below in case she should come for me. But at that moment—she was about half a mile away—she turned her quarter, and there to my amazement was the red flag with the blue circle, our own beloved flag, flying from her peak. For a moment I thought that this was some clever dodge of the enemy to tempt me within range. I snatched up my glasses and called on Vornal. Then we both recognized the vessel. It was the *Juno*, the only one left intact of our own cruisers. What could she be doing flying the flag in the enemy's waters? Then I understood it, and turning to Vornal, we threw ourselves into each other's arms. It could only mean an armistice—or peace!

And it was peace. We learned the glad news when we had risen alongside the *Juno*, and the ringing cheers which greeted us had at last died away. Our orders were to report ourselves at once at Blankenberg. Then she passed on down Channel to collect the others. We returned to port upon the surface, steaming through the whole British fleet as we passed up the North Sea. The crews clustered thick along the sides of the vessels to watch us. I can see now their sullen, angry faces. Many shook their fists and cursed us as we went by. It was not that we had damaged them—I will do them the justice to say that the English, as the old Boer War has proved, bear no resentment against a brave enemy—but that they thought us cowardly to attack merchant ships and avoid the warships. It is like the Arabs who think that a flank attack is a mean, unmanly device. War is not a big game, my English friends. It is a desperate business to gain the upper hand, and one must use one's brain in order to find the weak spot of one's enemy. It is not fair to blame me if I have found yours. It was my duty. Perhaps those officers and sailors who scowled at the little *Iota* that May morning have by this time done me justice when the first bitterness of undeserved defeat was passed.

Let others describe my entrance into Blankenberg; the mad enthusiasm of the crowds, and the magnificent public reception of each successive boat as it arrived. Surely the men deserved the grant made them by the State which has enabled each of them to be independent for life. As a feat of endurance, that long residence in such a state of mental tension in cramped quarters, breathing an unnatural atmosphere, will long remain as a record. The country may well be proud of such sailors.

The terms of peace were not made onerous, for we were in no condition to make Great Britain our permanent enemy. We knew well that we had won the war by circumstances which would never be allowed to occur again, and that in a few years the Island Power would be as strong as ever—stronger, perhaps—for the lesson that she had learned. It would be madness to provoke such an antagonist. A mutual salute of flags was arranged, the Colonial boundary was adjusted by arbitration, and we claimed no indemnity beyond an undertaking on the part of Britain that she would pay any damages which an International Court might award to France or to the United States for injury received through the operations of our submarines. So ended the war!

Of course, England will not be caught napping in such a fashion again! Her foolish blindness is partly explained by her delusion that her enemy would not torpedo merchant vessels. Common sense should have told her that her enemy will play the game that suits them best—that they will not enquire what they may do, but they will do it first and talk about it afterwards. The opinion of the whole world now is that if a blockade were proclaimed one may do what one can with those who try to break it, and that it was as reasonable to prevent food from reaching England in war-time as it is for a besieger to prevent the victualling of a beleaguered fortress.

I cannot end this account better than by quoting the first few paragraphs of a leader in *The Times*, which appeared shortly after the declaration of peace. It may be taken to epitomize the saner public opinion of England upon the meaning and lessons of the episode.

> In all this miserable business, [said the writer] which has cost us the loss of a considerable portion of our merchant fleet and more than 50,000 civilian lives, there is just one consolation to be found. It lies in the fact that our temporary conqueror is a power which is not strong enough to reap the fruits of her victory. Had we endured this humiliation at the hands of any of the first-class powers, it would certainly have entailed the loss of all our Crown Colonies and tropical possessions, besides the payment of a huge indemnity. We were absolutely at the feet of our conqueror and had no possible alternative but to submit to her terms, however onerous. Norland has had the good sense to understand that she must not abuse her temporary advantage, and has been generous in her dealings. In the grip of any other power, we should have ceased to exist as an Empire.
>
> Even now we are not out of the wood. Some one may maliciously pick a quarrel with us before we get our house in order, and use the easy weapon which has been demonstrated. It is to meet such a contingency that the Government

has rushed enormous stores of food at the public expense into the country. In a very few months the new harvest will have appeared. On the whole, we can face the immediate future without undue depression, though there remain some causes for anxiety. These will no doubt be energetically handled by this new and efficient Government, which has taken the place of those discredited politicians who led us into a war without having foreseen how helpless we were against an obvious form of attack.

Already the lines of our reconstruction are evident. The first and most important is that our Party men realize that there is something more vital than their academic disputes about Free Trade or Protection, and that all theory must give way to the fact that a country is in an artificial and dangerous condition if she does not produce within her own borders sufficient food to at least keep life in her population. Whether this should be brought about by a tax upon foreign foodstuffs, or by a bounty upon home products, or by a combination of the two, is now under discussion. But all Parties are combined upon the principle, and, though it will undoubtedly entail either a rise in prices or a deterioration in quality in the food of the working-classes, they will at least be insured against so terrible a visitation as that which is fresh in our memories. At any rate, we have got past the stage of argument. It *must* be so. The increased prosperity of the farming interest, and, as we will hope, the cessation of agricultural emigration, will be benefits to be counted against the obvious disadvantages.

The second lesson is the immediate construction of not one but two double-lined railways under the Channel. We stand in a white sheet over the matter, since the project has always been discouraged in these columns, but we are prepared to admit that, had such railway communication been combined with adequate arrangements for forwarding supplies from Marseilles, we should have avoided our recent surrender. We still insist that we cannot trust entirely to a tunnel, since our enemy might have allies in the Mediterranean; but in a single contest with any power of the North of Europe, it would certainly be of inestimable benefit. There may be dangers attendant upon the existence of a tunnel, but it must now be admitted that they are trivial compared to those which come from its absence. As to the building of large fleets of merchant submarines for the carriage of food, that is a new departure which will be an additional insurance against the danger which has left so dark a page in the history of our country.

Frankreichs Ende im Jahre 19??

ADOLF SOMMERFELD

Before the Storm

For a long time, rumours of war had appeared like dark clouds on the political horizon in Europe. Years ago, that is in the summer of 1911, there had been diplomatic thunder and lightning. Everyone was reckoning on an Anglo-German war, and they were all worried about the consequences of the conflict between Turkey and Italy. No one could forecast where the storm would break out.[1]

The Italo-Turkish War finally ended—to the advantage of Italy and with the concurrence of the European powers. Of course, the peace agreement had again given England and France the chance to use every kind of diplomatic trick in order to shear the Turkish sacrificial lamb and share the spoils between them; and if Russia, the spoilt darling of these two nations, had not forcefully intervened at the last moment, they would no doubt have already come to blows. Despite the outward show of good will, the mistrust continued. England alone had made a serious effort to maintain correct relations with Germany, at least in business matters. This had nothing to do with feelings of kinship. It was because, in all parts of the great British Empire, the very foundations were beginning to shake. Like the writing on the wall that Belshazzar had once seen, the coal strikes and their social consequences spelt out the fearful *Mene, Tekel, Upharsin* of war.

Meanwhile, Russia was slowly but surely loosening her ties with the Entente powers and, without showing her hand, was getting on with the development of her army and navy. As far back as Bismarck's time, the western ambitions of Russian diplomacy had been declining; for the mailed fists of Germany and of her ally Austro-Hungary had hindered every imperialist attempt to move westwards. This had led to the 'colonial policy' which had come to such an inglorious end in the disastrous war with Japan.

Moreover, the growing power of Japan was pushing Russia ever nearer the south-west and the south, and into those territories that greedy England claimed as her own. So, from the very first, a peaceful understanding between Russia and England was impossible, despite the apparent cordiality of the Entente. For a long time Russia had been flirting with the Triple Alliance. That was the only way she had of keeping England in check during peace-time; and, if war came, this understanding would allow her to occupy those territories, central to her colonial ambitions, that were already part of the British Empire or were to come under British protection at the first favourable opportunity. To this end, Russia had made a secret treaty with Germany which gave her a free hand in this area; for the Russian diplomats were smart enough to leave a loophole in their Entente agreement with England that allowed them to slip out of their obligations whenever it suited them. In fact, the Entente Treaty between Russia, France, and England was no more than a defensive arrangement. For Russia had only one obligation—to come to the aid of her two allies in the event of an attack on them by the Triple Alliance. The Russians knew full well that such an attack did not figure in the plans of the Triple Alliance, so that from every point of view the Entente was a risk-free arrangement. Not only did it allow them to live on the best of terms with the states of the Triple Alliance, but also it enabled the Russians to make secret treaties with other powers. If, for example, England and France should make a combined attack on the Triple Alliance, Russia could remain neutral; and in return for that neutrality the nations of the Triple Alliance would permit Russia to invade India and occupy Persia and Afghanistan.

England and France knew nothing of this secret treaty. They only suspected that, on the occasion of a meeting between the German Emperor and the Czar at Potsdam, there had been an important 'personal understanding', and ever afterwards they mistrusted their Russian friend. From that time forward, England and France made every effort to win over the Turks so that, whenever it was necessary, they could light a fuse in Paris or London that would touch off an explosion in Russia. This relationship of the two powers explained their attitude when the Italians and the Turks made peace. The Turks had long determined to keep to the defensive. Split by factional interests and continually endangered by internal unrest, they asked for nothing more than to see the sun rise daily over the crescent on the dome of San Sophia—even though that last symbol of a long forgotten world was also destined to pass away. But all the attentions of England and France could do nothing to spur the lethargic Turks to any kind of offensive action. Indeed, the general impression was that, if the Turks ever bestirred themselves, disaster would surely follow.

And then there were the false prophets who found out how mistaken they had been when they had seen a docile puppet in the former heir apparent, Franz Ferdinand—the present Emperor Franz—and had forecast a clerical government for Austria. As everyone knows, and all history bears witness to the fact, heirs to the throne always change their colours as soon as they are called to take on the duties of government. The Emperor Franz soon learnt how to distinguish between his religious convictions and political necessities. He pressed on energetically with the old Austro-Hungarian policy in the Balkans; and he not only enlarged his fleet, as he had contracted to do with the members of the Triple Alliance, but also kept his army well prepared for all eventualities.

The Albanian troubles and the decline in Ottoman prestige made the situation increasingly dangerous, and that led to a secret understanding between Austro-Hungary and Danilo, King of Montenegro.[2] This laid down that, if any serious European conflict were to endanger peace in the Balkans, Montenegro would occupy Albania and Epirus with the help of the Austro-Hungarians; and for their part they would send an army corps by way of Novi Bazar to Salonica. In like manner, the other Balkan states—Bulgaria, Serbia, Romania—were working secretly to carve up Turkey. Long ago they had formed an offensive–defensive alliance. This required that, if the situation deteriorated, Serbia and Bulgaria were to occupy the Turkish territory east of the River Vardar. The ambitions of Romania were to secure free navigation in the Black Sea and to conclude advantageous commercial treaties.

* * *

Italy had become a flourishing industrial and colonial power, thanks to a tax on foreigners which had greatly reduced the annual invasion of honeymoon couples and idle tourists. Those who had formerly made their living from the foreigners now had to devote themselves to industry. They invested their accumulated capital; they cultivated their waste-lands; and very soon flourishing centres with the most modern industrial plant appeared in the desolate Campagna. There were regular passenger and freight services between Ostia, the port of Rome, and Tripoli, the capital of the Italian colonial possessions; for, soon after the departure of the Italian forces, and after the Arabs had been convinced that the Italians were tolerant in religion and humane in conduct, they settled down and became the best of friends with the Italians. This process

One of the many serial accounts of the next great war that appeared between 1903 and
1914

of peaceful evolution led to the massive development of Italy as a
maritime power. The most important naval bases were fortified. The
numbers of Italian dreadnoughts, cruisers and torpedo-boats
increased year by year, so that the navies of Austria and Italy dominated the Mediterranean. Since emigration had decreased in Italy,
their land forces came close to doubling, and that is without counting the recently established colonial units in Libya.

* * *

Spain now became what Italy had once been—the land of the love-sick and of the nature-lovers. Every year foreign visitors poured many millions of pesetas into Spain, and that financial input was an immense benefit for the thrifty and simple inhabitants. The economy picked up in a few years, and before long Spain was well on the way to becoming a great power once again.

Although there was a general, somewhat artificial, peace throughout Europe, Spain had not known real tranquility for years because of France. Not that the French looked enviously at the growing prosperity of their southern neighbours: the root cause was the chronic difficulty of the situation in Morocco. There had been almost daily expectations of a war between France and Spain, but at all times England had known how to reduce the tension, although the skirmishing went on continuously. Today it is not easy to say who was responsible for this discord; but older people can still remember that, as far back as the Moroccan crisis with Germany, the French had looked enviously at the Spanish negotiations in North Africa. Ever since Germany had, as a friendly gesture, given France a free hand in Morocco, the French had become increasingly extravagant in their conduct of affairs.

Today it is quite apparent that France is suffering from incurable political hysteria. Their chauvinism in matters of national defence is proof of that. Although the steady drop in their birth-rate points to the decline of France as a military power, the Gallic cock has gone on crowing about the greatness of France. And yet, if we look more closely at this 'greatness', to our amazement we find it is a matter of auxiliary troops that the imagination has endowed with magical powers. In fact, these auxiliaries are no more than a collection of black, badly uniformed Nigger troops, aeroplanes, submarines, and all sorts of unimportant technical 'novelties'. France had long ago given up relying on herself, and was now looking for salvation in alliances and technical inventions . . . 'There can be no pact with a race of serpents.'

Already in 1869, the skills of Émile Ollivier and Napoleon III had failed them, when they sought to coax the southern German states into an alliance against Prussia; and in the end, when the great war appeared unavoidable, all France exulted in anticipation of a brilliant victory.[3] Her victory was going to astonish the world because France, and France alone, had those technical inventions that the French believed would inevitably give them the victory. In spite of the Mitrailleuse and the Chassepot rifle, however, there was not— Oh! Horror!—even the shadow of a victory for France. Those

technical marvels, so the story went later on, had been handed over
secretly and treacherously to the enemy. Only in that way could the
French sustain their belief in their technical superiority, for genius
and courage are unfortunately of no avail against treachery. So, the
French still go on boasting about their superiority, forgetful of their
earlier defeat and unmindful of the fundamental truth that nowadays technological know-how is not the monopoly of any one
nation. Inanities about military technology cannot defeat the enormous numbers of men who come face to face in modern warfare.
The war of today requires a vast mass of combat-ready fighting men,
then comes up-to-date equipment, and then tactics—tactics—
tactics.

Although an ever-decreasing population had given France good
reason to avoid provocation—for there was no sure way of gauging
the capacity of her black troops when face-to-face with a European
enemy and in a different climate—nevertheless, the French had
been trying for years to drive the Spaniards from North Africa. The
first disputes began with the military occupation of the French zone.
The Spaniards followed suit in their own territory; and most days
the French and Spanish troops came to blows. The officers of the
two countries forgot about all forms of international courtesy; and in
consequence there were many duels that claimed victims from both
sides. More than once, the news agencies would telegraph round the
world that France had declared war on Spain. In fact, there had been
occasions when the order for mobilization had been ready for signa-
ture in Paris; but, always at the last moment, British diplomats had
intervened at the express wish of their King and damped down the
bellicose ardour of the French. It was never possible, however, to
obtain a final reconciliation with Spain. On the contrary, the cold
showers that kept on coming from London only managed to raise
the temperature.

The development of Morocco was proceeding too slowly for the
French. They felt they had to bestir themselves, and in order to steal
a march on the Spaniards they began to build a railway. The Spanish
Cabinet at once sent a note to Berlin, since the terms of the Franco-
German Agreement on Morocco did not allow France to build a
railway in her own territory before the line from Tangier to Fez had
been opened. The German Ambassador in Paris drew attention to
these facts, and received the very courteous reply that construction
would be stopped. In fact, the French went on secretly with their
railway. This incident resulted in some six furious notes in one
month from Germany to France, and the last of them came close to

an ultimatum. In order to watch over events, the German Government sent the small cruiser *Schwalbe* to Moroccan waters. When the French saw the German flag in Agadir, they were at first a little surprised. Then they remembered that some years previously a similar little ship, all ready for serious business, had dropped anchor in the same place, only to return somewhat ingloriously to the Fatherland. But, since gratitude is totally foreign to the French character and any peaceful approach is considered pure weakness, they quickly passed from their initial consternation to total contempt. The German sailors, who occasionally went ashore from the *Schwalbe*, were called the most disgusting names. Fortunately they did not understand, although the faces of the French soldiers spoke of anything but friendship and respect.

Then, quite suddenly, something unbelievable and incomprehensible happened. On a dark and stormy night, not a star in the sky, the grave-like silence broken only by the waves crashing against the barren coast—there was the most dreadful explosion. A column of flame and smoke shot up into the air, and a jumble of wreckage and human remains cascaded into the heaving waves. The little cruiser *Schwalbe* had disappeared, crew and all, in one explosion. At first it was thought that it must have been an internal explosion. However, since the movement of French troops on the frontier of the Spanish territories had already aroused suspicion, the German Government considered that the event called for an inquiry, and to this end sent a commission of military and technical experts.

Meanwhile a Spanish soldier had found a large piece of torpedo casing on the shore, and handed it over to his superior officer. This important discovery was communicated to the German commission, once they had arrived, and they proceeded with their inquiries in that direction. That same day, two divers went down to the sea-bed where the hull of the *Schwalbe* was lying; and they established beyond all doubt that a torpedo fired at close range had hit the cruiser, for the point of impact was still clearly visible. Since it could only have been a French attack, a wireless signal in code sent the facts immediately to Berlin. Even without this, there could be little doubt about the hostile intentions of the French. Whilst the members of the commission were working on the beach they were often in danger of life and limb, as rifle bullets whistled round their ears.

* * *

What happened in Berlin, when the dreadful catastrophe was made known, defies all description. The *Berlin Lokalanzeiger* was the first to print the news of the French attack on the *Schwalbe* in a special edition. Half an hour later the Zimmerstrasse was packed with vast crowds, all eager for more news. There the first cries of '*Nieder mit Frankreich!*' were raised, and the people began to assume threatening attitudes. Since the local section of the district police were incapable of handing the situation, the Chief of Police dispatched a detachment from the mounted force. In the meantime the crowd, possessed with anger and anxiety, swayed backwards and forwards like a sea of heads until huge searchlights flashed out the final details of the shameful deed in enormous letters on the dark night sky. A single, frightful cry like that of an animal in pain rose up from the vast mass of people. Then they began to push and to press against one another. They were all running and shouting—an army of men and women of all sorts, and all in the greatest rage, stormed down the Charlottenstrasse in the direction of the Unter den Linden.

Fortunately, the Chief of Police had had timely warning of the danger, and, with all available men from headquarters and from the other sections, he rushed to the Pariser Platz in order to protect the French Embassy from a sudden attack by the mob. The wisdom of this move was soon apparent. Hardly had the police set up their road-block, when the crowd arrived, all maddened with feelings of rage and revenge. The sight of the police cordon made them even wilder. From this mass of humanity came a savage, unintelligible cry, and then came separate threats.

Suddenly a shot rang out—the signal for the attack. Everywhere savage fighting began; on this side the call of duty and on that side the national honour. The flat police sabres flashed in the air; the horses of the mounted constabulary reared up and fell on the crowd, which neither moved nor gave way. On the north side of the square the police cordon collapsed, and at once the window panes of the embassy showered on to the pavement, as axes hacked away at the entrance. The whole square was crammed with angry groups of people, and amongst them one could see mounted policemen fighting for their lives. Here and there a shining police sabre rose up above the mob as an officer sought to regain his section. The wounded lay all over the place, groaning and moaning, whilst the horses that had thrown their riders were bolting along to the nearby Tiergarten and even on to the Unter den Linden; and countless souvenirs of the riot—helmets, clothing, hats, walking-sticks, even wigs and pigtails—were left littering the pavements.

Every moment the situation became more dangerous. Through the smashed windows of the French Embassy, one could see fear on the pale faces of the servants as they rushed here and there; and visible in the background there was the figure of a woman in smart clothes who was wringing her hands in desperation. A section of the front door had already been shattered, when help finally arrived. From the south, galloping up along the Unter den Linden, came the Dragoon Guards. From the north came two battalions of the IIIrd Guards-Infantry Regiment, hastening along at the double with fixed bayonets. Before such a show of force, the mob had to give way, and in a few minutes the square had been cleared and the troops had taken over. The crowd spread themselves through the neighbouring streets. Throughout that night, however, there was no rest for Berlin.

That night the French Ambassador and his family did not remain in the embassy. They had received an invitation to stay with the British Ambassador, and so they were saved from having to see what the Germans are like when they are roused. These events took place in July 19?? The Reichstag was summoned to assemble as soon as possible, and most of the members who were on holiday or on their estates came immediately to Berlin, so that two days after the Battle of the Pariser Platz the House was in session. It was a stormy meeting. No one paid any attention to the Order of the Day from the Allied governments. From every part of the House, from all the parties, and from the visitors' gallery there came but one call: War! War!

Next day war was declared, and the French diplomats received their passports. Two days later Germany had finished mobilization. The general enthusiasm beggared description. As the Kaiser drove along the Linden in an open carriage with the aged Empress at his side, blue cornflowers rained down on them from all sides in token of past victories.[4]

The Road to War

Although all the major European powers had for decades been preparing energetically for a great war, the declaration of war on France came like a bolt from the blue. In Vienna and Rome the Parliaments were at once assembled, and after furious debates it was decided, almost unanimously in Vienna and with a two-thirds majority in Rome, to comply with the terms of the Triple Alliance and immediately break off diplomatic relations with France. Paris laboured in vain to represent the German declaration of war as an act of imperialistic brutality and the *Schwalbe* incident as a calculated pretext. It was, they said, for an international commission, not for a German court, to investigate any crime committed by the French.

In keeping with their instructions, the Ambassadors of Austro-Hungary and Italy left Paris without paying further attention to the French quibbles. Everywhere there was tension as the rest of Europe waited to see what the attitude of England and Russia would be. The German Government had prudently prepared for hostilities with England. They had signalled all their ships on the high seas or in foreign ports that they were to keep an eye on all freighters bound for England, especially those *en route* from South America or India. In the event of a declaration of war, which would be notified by wireless, they were to seize their cargoes and make for the nearest neutral ports.

Of course, England had less to fear from a naval war with Germany than she had from a blockade. If her supply lines from South America and India were cut, starvation would most probably lead to an internal crisis. Moreover, the British politicians had reason to think seriously about the danger of civil unrest in India, the concentration of American troops on the Canadian frontiers, and the movement for independence in Australia and South Africa. Nevertheless, it was a most difficult decision to make, and several weeks passed before London informed the European powers that Britain would remain neutral so long as British interests were not affected. This somewhat general statement was later properly tied up, in all details, and written into a special treaty with the Triple Alliance.

Silence reigned in Russia. For all that, however, there were signs that something extraordinary was going on in the Tsarist Empire. In the west, line-regiments from the interior replaced the garrisons that had been maintained by the Guard regiments, and these were transferred who knows where. The German and Austrian Governments followed these movements with close attention, and responded by keeping their own forces on the Russian borders up to strength. Then, when it came out that the Russian troops had been sent to Tashkent, people realized what was going on. In fact, the news soon came that the first Russian regiments had marched into India. Since the British declaration of neutrality prevented the Russians from going any further, their troops remained for the time being on the borders of India. Russia delayed no longer, and informed the Triple Alliance that she would remain neutral.

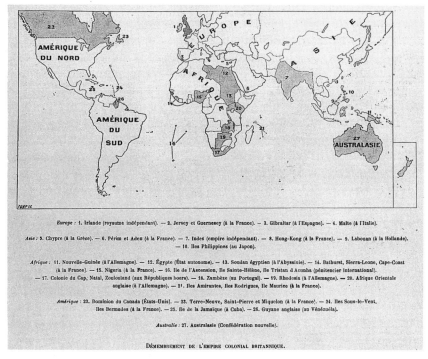

Europe : 1. Irlande (royaume indépendant). — 2. Jersey et Guernesey (à la France). — 3. Gibraltar (à l'Espagne). — 4. Malte (à l'Italie).

Asie : 5. Chypre (à la Grèce). — 6. Périm et Aden (à la France). — 7. Indes (empire indépendant). — 8. Hong-Kong (à la France). — 9. Labouan (à la Hollande). — 10. Iles Philippines (au Japon).

Afrique : 11. Nouvelle-Guinée (à l'Allemagne). — 12. Égypte (État autonome). — 13. Soudan égyptien (à l'Abyssinie). — 14. Bathurst, Sierra-Leone, Cape-Coast (à la France). — 15. Nigeria (à la France). — 16. Ile de l'Ascension, Ile Sainte-Hélène, Ile Tristan d'Acunha (pénitencier international). — 17. Colonie du Cap, Natal, Zoulouland (aux Républiques boers). — 18. Zambèze (au Portugal). — 19. Rhodesia (à l'Allemagne). — 20. Afrique Orientale anglaise (à l'Allemagne). — 21. Iles Amirantes, Iles Rodrigues, Ile Maurice (à la France).

Amérique : 22. Dominion du Canada (États-Unis). — 23. Terre-Neuve, Saint-Pierre et Miquelon (à la France). — 24. Iles Sous-le-Vent, Iles Bermudes (à la France). — 25. Ile de la Jamaïque (à Cuba). — 26. Guyane anglaise (au Vénézuéla).

Australie : 27. Australasie (Confédération nouvelle).

DÉMEMBREMENT DE L'EMPIRE COLONIAL BRITANNIQUE.

This French division of the British Empire was the last word in military projections

These acts by the two Entente states came as a crushing blow for the French and had a crippling effect on all their military preparations, since they had counted on British and Russian support. The most accomplished French diplomats rushed off to London and St Petersburg to save what could be saved from the Entente. Everywhere they found the doors closed against them; and from everyone they had the same answer: 'Our treaty is purely defensive. You have attacked Germany and, contrary to international law, you have blown up a friendly German vessel and its crew. You are on your own now, and you face the consequences of your rash action.' Thus, France was thrown back on herself, and so the French General Staff decided to start by keeping on the defensive until a favourable opportunity opened up the possibility of going over to the offensive. In the meantime, the French navy had orders to harass the enemy along the Italian coasts and in the German areas of the North Sea.

For defence reasons, the fortresses and the garrisons along the eastern and southern frontiers were reinforced and supplied with ample stores of food. The rest of the French forces were so disposed that they covered Paris with three large concentrations stretching from north to south. Each army corps was supported by dirigible airships and by several air squadrons, and the black army which had been stationed in the south for several years was distributed between the different army corps. Thanks to the neutrality of Britain and Russia, the Austrians and the Germans had a free hand. In like manner, the alliance with Austria meant that Italy had no frontiers to guard, whilst the Austrian fleet was asked to protect her Adriatic coastline. Consequently, Germany was able to put the greater part of her twenty-three army corps into the field, leaving the Austrian forces to assume a covering role, to act as a reserve, or to maintain the necessary frontier duties in the East and South. Spain had likewise mobilized, but had not declared war on France. It was enough for her to take up strong positions in the Pyrenees and to strengthen the garrisons in the ports.

* * *

Two days after the declaration of war, the French and German forces had already clashed on the frontier, but so many German troops had entered France that their superiority in numbers had an overwhelming effect on the French frontier towns and fortresses. The stretch of country from Thionville to Sedan was occupied almost without fighting. From Thionville to Verdun there were sharp outpost actions; but when the French took refuge in the fortress of Verdun, they were surprised by the Germans and the fortress was taken by storm. The German troops who had taken Nancy were now able to move north-west towards Verdun and south towards Neufchâteau. The rear-guard followed in the same direction and joined up with the Bavarian and Württemburger regiments before Belfort, whilst the troops from Baden and from Hesse linked up with the Austrian *Kaiserjäger* and took up positions near Dijon and Besançon.

A tremendous battle with heavy casualties was raging at Belfort; but in the end the defenders could not hold out any longer against the devastating fire of the German artillery, and they surrendered. With the fall of Belfort, 10,000 French, officers and other ranks, marched away to captivity. The small fortress of Besançon in like manner surrendered after the first gun-fire, and only Dijon put up any real opposition. However, after the small forts were wiped out and the main fortress came under heavy bombardment, the heroic defenders laid down their arms. It was here that a Zeppelin cruiser, two Parsifal airships, and thirty flying machines came into action for the first time, launching bombs at the fortress and causing immense destruction. It was reported that two of these bombs, filled with a special explosive, had set fire to a whole district of the town with the loss of some 500 men.

Some of the troops, set free by this surrender, now advanced on Lyons, the well-known centre of the silk industry. The population consisted of well-to-do manufacturers and workers. The latter had always been anti-militarist, and they considered that the war, which took the bread from their mouths, was a criminal attack on their economic interests. Even before the arrival of the Germans, there had been trouble that only military force could put down. And now, when they saw the enemy besieging the fortress, the rage of the workers against the military burst out again; and the factory owners, whether they liked it or not, from fear of violence from the embittered labour force, were obliged to join in the anti-militarist action of their workers. Two factions emerged in Lyon: the militarists, that is the garrison troops, and the anti-militarists, the most part of whom were the ordinary people. The French troops were, therefore, obliged to remain within the fortifications and behind the ramparts, for as soon as they appeared in the streets, they were abused and harassed by the populace. The first sortie of the garrison came to nothing. They fled back exhausted through the streets and squares, back to the safety of the fortifications, to the jubilation of the populace. Next day the whole town was covered with huge posters that showed a hare holding the *Tricoleur*, and beneath the scornful words: *C'est la Garde de Lyon!*

Shortly before dawn on the day following this sortie, the enemy artillery opened up again. The shells rained down on the town, flashing and crashing like some tremendous storm, rudely waking the inhabitants from their slumbers, and leaving them in the grip of a universal panic. Then three courageous men stole along to the Town Hall, and under incessant gun-fire hoisted the white flag on the tower. Seconds later, a couple of well-aimed shots from the garrison brought down the flag and the flag-pole. The general anxiety grew steadily and, to complete the misery of the townsfolk, that evening a *Schütte-Lanz* balloon, a *Siemens-Schuckert* airship, and a number of aeroplanes appeared over the city and dropped their bombs right on target. During the night, the populace got together and decided to compel the garrison to surrender. They acted at once on their decision: armed with fowling-pieces, old muskets, and the most extraordinary weapons, they moved in separate groups to the case-mates where they demanded with the most frightening threats an end to the fighting. The gallant soldiers were united in their refusal to sacrifice the honour of the nation, and so a small-scale civil war began. Whenever the German attack was most serious and the garrison was fully occupied with defending itself, a shower of stones would rain down on the ramparts. Many a soldier, fighting there in defence of his Fatherland, fell victim to the enemy within— shot from behind, or stabbed in the back, or struck down by a stone. In these circumstances it was easy going for the besiegers. Deserters had revealed the state of the town, so that there was no reason to take Lyon by storm. Accordingly, they left the city to 'Providence'— that is, to the struggle going on inside the town.

On the sixth day after the beginning of the siege, the German and Austrian troops were able to enter Lyon; and the garrison received full military honours in recognition of their bravery. In less than a fortnight, the entire eastern part of France had fallen to the enemy and all the largest fortresses had been taken. Some 18,000 French soldiers and more than 200 officers had been taken prisoner. The French casualty list was enormous, but the total German losses were 1,200 dead and 1,500 wounded.

By this time, the German army had taken up positions in eastern France along a zig-zag line with their main western bases at Sedan, Verdun, Neufchâteau, and Dijon, and their eastern bases at Thionville, Nancy, Belfort, and on in a straight line through Besançon to Lyon. In the eastern sector the Austrian army and some German units provided the reserve. This arrangement allowed the German forces to move out from any point in their western line on offensive missions and return to designated positions without any fear of attacks from the flank or the rear. This distribution of the strategic reserves was made possible by the skilful arrangement of the German state railways. As early as the first decade of the twentieth century, the French generals had proposed a similar railway system for their country, but they had no success.

Meanwhile in Italy three army corps, drawn from the garrisons of Piedmont, Lombardy, and Tuscany, had moved into France. They had serious clashes in the border towns, but everywhere the French were forced to yield to superior numbers. The passage of Mont Cenis and Monte Viso was carried through with such speed and secrecy that the first the French outposts knew of the enemy was when they were already well on their way to the high plateau fortress of Briançon. So rapidly did the Italians encircle the town that the support troops in the surrounding strong-points, who had the task of reinforcing the garrison of the fortress, could scarcely get to Briançon in time. During the first few days it was all quiet at Briançon, since the defenders would not risk a sortie and the Italian artillery did little damage; moreover, the Italians had no balloons and no aeroplanes. But on the fifth day of the siege luck came their way, when by a singular mischance the fortress fell into their hands. From daybreak they had been firing incendiary shells that set fire to the roofs of a few houses but did little serious damage, since most of the buildings were old structures built with massive stone blocks. Suddenly and simultaneously, two projectiles landed in the old powder magazine, a crumbling ruin which for reasons of economy had been left half repaired. There was a colossal explosion. For close on half an hour nothing could be seen, since a dense cloud of smoke covered the shattered town and city. Then the *Alpenjäger* stormed forward with fixed bayonets, but there was no fighting. The garrison met them half-way with the white flag and asked for the right to leave as free men—a request that was willingly granted.

With the help of the remaining inhabitants, the Italians restored order. They set up a large hospital where those French wounded in the explosion received first aid. Without any fortress to hold back their advance, the Italian army took up the following positions in the south-west frontier areas of France: from Chambéry south-west to Grenoble, then south-east past the ruins of Briançon to the fortress of Embrun, from there south to Digne, and on south-east as far as Grasse. All these places were occupied and fortified. The mass of the French Army of the South had retreated to the interior of the country.

Of far greater consequence than these achievements, however, was the colonial war the Italians had begun against the French in Tunis and Algiers. For a long time the greater part of the population in these places had been Italian, and this situation had not altered with the colonial developments in Tripolitania and Cyrenaica. So, it was easy enough for the Italians, with the support of their compatriots, to establish themselves there. The Libyan army of Italy, composed for the most part of Arabs and Somalis, went off happily to the war; but very soon it became clear that their eagerness for battle declined markedly when they had to face their fellow Muslims from Tunis and Algiers. In effect, it came to shadow-boxing between the Muslim troops, with the result that most of the French colonial troops fraternized with the enemy, and only a fraction of them followed their French officers. The latter were left powerless with a handful of troops in the middle of a hostile Italian population; and some gave themselves up while others took the first opportunity to return to France. In less than a month, the Italians were the masters of Tunis and Algiers; and, in keeping with the terms of the Triple Alliance, the Italians at once annexed the two provinces in the sure knowledge that, even if the war ended badly, Austria and Germany would see to the eventual cession of those territories that they had already promised the Italians as the price for their military support.

Meanwhile the German General Staff had directed the Italian Commander-in-Chief to cut off the retreat of the troops in Toulon, Marseilles, and the other coastal garrisons. To this end, the Italians were to take up a strong position between Digne and Carcassonne so that from there they could the better harass the ports and take them with a combined sea and land attack. The Italians, therefore, left only a small force at Grasse. They then made south-west from Digne in three columns and pressed on directly to take Avignon, Nîmes, Montpellier, and Carcassonne. There was heavy fighting before Avignon and Montpellier, where the Bersaglieri for the first time came face to face with the Senegalese infantry. The Africans were good marksmen, but they were not up to the tactical ability of European troops and their trenches gave them hardly any protection—not to mention the recklessness with which they flung themselves at such crack shots as the Bersaglieri. After several hours of fighting, with the Italians shooting as calmly as if they were on a firing range, almost half the Blacks had bitten the dust. Again, the Senegalese custom of bringing their wives and children with them when they went campaigning proved impractical in European conditions; for it was impossible for them to endure the interminable cries and lamentations of their women and children without feeling some demoralizing effect. Consequently all these family groups were a hindrance to an orderly retreat.

So, when the Bersaglieri carried the enemy entrenchments by storm and those black devils had rushed back to their camp in panic-stricken flight, total chaos followed. The women threw themselves in front of their men, and together with their children they became an impenetrable mob. In vain did the French officers shout out their orders, for all discipline goes when the Blacks see that danger threatens their women-folk. So, the Italians had the pleasure of taking prisoners not only the remainder of the Senegalese troops, but also their wives and children, their widows and orphans. Only the future can tell how the Italian Supreme Command will settle things with their women and children prisoners. According to the rules of war, those soldiers who lay down their arms become prisoners of war; but there is no mention of what should be done with women and children. If the Italians abandoned the women and children, they would risk an uprising of the Negroes as well as losing their reputation as humane soldiers. If, however, the Italian Government were to feed the black families, it would cost them much, especially if the war went on for long; and in keeping with international law they would not be able to claim any compensation from the enemy. Clearly, the Senegalese troops had given the international law experts a hard nut to crack.

The annihilation of their black regiments, all killed in action or taken prisoner, came as a great shock to the rest of the French troops. They had expected military marvels from them, partly because of their dexterity and their skill as marksmen, partly because of their terrifying appearance; for it was not by simple chance that the French had rigged them out in such frightening clothes. However, the French gentlemen had forgotten that we are no longer living in the epoch of the Cimbri and the Teutons who could terrify a Roman army. Nowadays, we have all become so accustomed to seeing black faces—in everyday life and on the stage—that a Negro porter or coachman attracts no more stares than average, and even small children have lost all fear of 'the Black Man'. Moreover, in modern warfare hand-to-hand fighting becomes possible only in the last phase, when the battle has already been won along the firing lines where not less than 1,500 metres separate one side from the other. At this distance appearance and smell have no function in combat, so that, when troops go into the attack, their nostrils filled with smoke powder and dust, they are not like to faint away at the sweat and stench of black soldiers.

When the Italians entered Avignon, they found that the enemy had already left the town so that they were able to make themselves at home there. Nîmes was taken without a blow, and so was Carcassonne. In Montpellier they let the Italians enter without any sign that there would be opposition; but, no sooner had their troops scattered through the streets and squares than suddenly all the windows opened and there came a hail of bullets from the hidden French soldiers. At first there was a frightful confusion, and many Italians were killed in this treacherous way. Then the Italians reformed and attacked the houses. Where internal barricades prevented their entry, they destroyed the houses from top to bottom, and then proceeded to impose a fitting punishment on the city. The town hall was razed to the ground, the mayor was taken prisoner, court-martialled, and shot; all inhabitants found with weapons met the same fate.

The killing went on into the night. From time to time single shots ran out, for a fraction of the French soldiers preferred a hero's grave to captivity. When the sun rose next day over Montpellier, it seemed as if an earthquake had destroyed the town. Everywhere there were smoking ruins, and in all the squares and streets there were great piles of unburied corpses. Even the dead had not been left in peace. The cemetery, which was once one of the sights of the town, now looked as if a hurricane had smashed it to pieces. Ancient oaks and weeping willows were shattered and shrivelled; hundred-year-old ivies had been ripped from the walls and lay in twisted heaps. The walls had collapsed; shells had torn open many graves; and in one place the coffin had been smashed, the skeleton reduced to powder, and only a white arm bone, a finger trembling as if in menace, appeared from the shattered grave.

War is war! All the east and south of France was held by the Allied armies. They had only to close the iron ring from Sedan to Carcassonne to seal the fate of France.

By Land and Sea

The Supreme Command of the French army was well aware of the growing danger. Throughout the country, the recent defeats had sparked off a storm of protests against the General Staff: their failures in strategy had disheartened the nation. Already there were rumours that the enemy was three miles from Paris, when in fact the Allied armies had not yet moved from their positions on the frontiers. In the midst of this general depression, the news of the destruction of the French Mediterranean fleet came like a thunderclap.

A few days after the outbreak of war three Italian mine-layers had, with the permission of Spain, closed the Straits of Gibraltar with a barrier of contact mines that stretched from Tarifa to Ceuta; and they had closed the Suez Canal by sinking a cargo ship near Aden. At that time the French squadron, which was then patrolling the coasts of North Africa and Palestine, had no option but to proceed at full speed to Toulon and there prepare for a naval engagement; and as a consequence of this retreat a number of gun-boats and torpedo-boats had fallen to the combined force of Austrian and Italian destroyers. In Toulon, all the French vessels made up an imposing battle fleet as they moved to their stations outside the harbour. Three cruisers and some torpedo-boats went off on reconnaissance, but for days they saw nothing, because most of the Italian

WE, WILHELM,

GIVE NOTICE to the Inhabitants of those provinces occupied by the German Imperial Army, that—

I MAKE WAR upon the soldiers, and not upon English citizens. Consequently, it is my wish to give the latter and their property entire security, and as long as they do not embark upon hostile enterprise against the German troops they have a right to my protection.

GENERALS COMMANDING the various corps in the various districts in England are ordered to place before the public the stringent measures which I have ordered to be adopted against towns, villages, and persons who act in contradiction to the usages of war. They are to regulate in the same manner all the operations necessary for the well-being of our troops, to fix the difference between the English and German rate of exchange, and to facilitate in every manner possible the individual transactions between our Army and the inhabitants of England.

WILHELM.

Given at POTSDAM, *September 4th*, 1910.

German Imperial Decree from William Le Queux, *The Invasion of 1910*

The above is a copy of the German Imperial Decree, printed in English, which was posted by unknown German agents in London, and which appeared everywhere throughout East Anglia and in that portion of the Midlands held by the enemy.

armoured vessels (dreadnoughts) were located in the ports of Genoa, Spezia, Livorno, and Porto Ferrajo, and all were in contact with one another by means of the Marconi system. Other warships, reinforced by Austrian dreadnoughts and torpedo-boats, were on patrol in the Tyrrhenian Sea and along the southern coast of Sicily as far as Tripoli. The rest of the Austrian fleet controlled the Ionian Sea and barred entrance to the Adriatic with a double line of warships between Otranto and Valona. Since Britain had declared the English Channel a neutral zone, France had to avoid the less than attractive possibility of a fleet engagement in the North Sea.

Late in the evening, three Italian cruisers and four destroyers had steamed slowly out of Genoa on a reconnaissance mission. This small squadron was sighted by the French scouting vessels near Nice but they failed to realize how close they were; and the French reconnaissance was equally poor, since they signalled the battle fleet at Toulon that a large Italian squadron had appeared. As the Italian cruisers steamed on through the night with masked lights, they observed dense patches of smoke on the horizon. These undoubtedly came from a large enemy force. The suspicion soon became certainty; and, after sending a detailed wireless report to the Italian flagship in Genoa, the Italian cruisers and their escort turned round and made for home waters at top speed, with the enemy on their heels.

Meanwhile the Admiral in Genoa had signalled the squadrons in Spezia and Porto Ferrajo that they were to sail at once and cut off the enemy near Cape Corso in Corsica. With his ships, he steamed westward along the coast towards San Remo so that he would be in a position to attack at the right moment. Two dreadnoughts and three destroyers were detached from the Livorno squadron, and according to plan they sailed towards the enemy in order to decoy the French into pursuing them. The leading vessel in the French fleet had hardly come in sight when the searchlights began to play upon the Italian ships; and even before they had time to change direction, enemy gun-fire had damaged the smoke-stacks of two ships and the bow of another.

This slight success emboldened the French. They extended their line of battle into a large half-circle, and in this formation they pursued the enemy vessels in the hope of encircling and destroying them. As the leading vessels in this formation approached Cape Corso, they came in range of the speeding dreadnoughts. Suddenly searchlights flashed from east and south; and at once the first shells from the Italian ships whistled through the air and burst on the decks of the French warships. These took up the attack, and in the brilliant glare of the searchlights a naval engagement began that has no parallels in history. The heavy guns had a fearful effect, for even the most heavily armoured vessels had no defence against them. All the while the warships manoeuvred, now turning, now zig-zagging, employing every tactical move to avoid the enemy shells or to score a direct hit on the opposition. Thus, a single shot from an Italian ship penetrated to the boiler room of a French dreadnought and sent it to the bottom after the gun turrets and the bridge had been blown sky high.

Since the French were able to manoeuvre freely to the north and were superior in numbers, they were able to inflict heavy losses on the Italians. Although both sides were equal in seamanship and in the accuracy of their gunfire, a third of the Italian ships were destroyed or put out of action by the French. The French suffered the same scale of damage, but their numerical superiority made it easier for them to support their losses. The battle had raged on for two hours, with honours even between the two sides, when the Italian flagship and the main fleet approached from the north for the decisive action. Before the French had time to appreciate their situation, the Italian battleships had come between the French fleet and all hope of retreating north or west. The sea-battle now took on the appearance of a tiger hunt. Although the French did all they could to escape the cordon of destruction, in less than an hour all their ships were out of action. Those not already sunk were taken in tow as war prizes and brought to Porto Ferrajo. There Napoleon Bonaparte had once come after fate had first dealt him a heavy blow, and from there he had gazed on his place of exile.

On the Italian side, the squadrons from Spezia and Livorno had suffered the greatest damage, whilst the ships in the flagship group and those that had been stationed in Porto Ferrajo had come off lightly and had no loss of life to report. A few days later these ships sailed off as a battle-fleet to seize the naval port and the town of Toulon. When the Italians arrived, the French mine-layers were at work seeking to close the entrance with contact mines and sending floating mines on their way. A few well-placed rounds sent the mine-layers to the bottom, but it was not possible to enter the harbour until it had been cleared of mines. Since the Italian guns, like all modern naval armaments, had a considerable range, the town could be shelled. Although the bombardment had no apparent success, there was such panic in the fortress that the commandant was unable to look to the defence of the civil population. For three weeks, the Italian fleet remained off Toulon doing nothing else but distressing the fortress and demolishing a few houses every day. Clearing the mines had no effect on the situation, since the small blockading squadron could not come within range of the enemy artillery without running the risk of being blown up by the large-calibre guns of the fortress. So, Toulon might have been able to hold out for a long time, if the intervention of the Italian army had not changed the situation.

On the instructions of their Supreme Command, the Italian troops in Nîmes, Avignon, and Digne separated their forces and set off with their heavy artillery to attack Toulon from the north. On the way there they moved through an almost empty countryside, since inhabitants had taken refuge in the town. Close on 10,000 people had made for Toulon with the alarming news that the enemy were coming. That only served to increase the general confusion, since the siege of the town had prompted fears of famine. The commander of the fortress resolved to train all able-bodied men up to 50 years of age in the use of arms as rapidly as possible. He had decided that, with the support of the fortress artillery, he would engage the enemy in battle before the gates of the city. The Italians, however, had got wind of this decision from their spies, and accordingly they modified their plans in so far as they divided their forces into two battle-groups. One group with the support of their heavy artillery was to attack the town; the other—riflemen, a section of the machine-gun battalion, and cavalry—would take on the small fortress defence force. The assault on the ramparts was to take place in the opposite direction, and it would start only when the other attack had gone in.

Whilst the engagement between Toulon and Hyères was going on, the other Italian troops to the north and south of the fortress had taken up their positions and had begun to fire on the town. At the same time the warships joined in the bombardment, with the result that the cannonade terrified the break-out group. They all turned and fled back in panic to the safety of the fortifications. The Italian cavalry pursued them all the way to the ramparts, killing several hundred French soldiers and taking 1,200 prisoners. But the brave fortress commander still did not lose hope. He defended the place with the courage of a lion, but despite all his efforts he could do nothing more to prevent the fall of Toulon. To the west, north, and south, most of the French guns had fallen silent; the ramparts had been in part demolished; and the enemy artillery had brought death and destruction ever closer. At this moment of their greatest danger, the fortress commander decided to save himself and his men from the shame of captivity. He handed over responsibilities to his second-in-command and, with those who wished to follow him, went off to one of the eastern case-mates where they kept their powder magazine. There he blew himself up with all of his men. When the Italians saw the smoke from their ships, they thought that a shell had caused the explosion. Soon afterwards, however, two flags were hoisted simultaneously (one white, the other black). One announced the surrender of the town, and the other signalled a dreadful catastrophe.

The Toulonnais resigned themselves to their fate; and, when the Italians occupied the town, they gave their Italian cousins a friendly reception. In two days' time, the main body of the Italian army moved back again to their old positions in the north, leaving a small garrison which was strong enough to deal with any unrest. With the fall of Toulon, the defence of Marseilles was no longer feasible, so the mayor decided to open negotiations in order to avoid needless fighting. The Italian GHQ was willing to treat with them: they allowed the free departure of the garrison; they put occupying troops in Marseilles; and the Toulon naval command dispatched two dreadnoughts and a number of torpedo-boats as guard-ships to Marseilles. In this way, the Italians gained the command of the Mediterranean with a single victorious sea battle.

* * *

In the meantime, the French Supreme Command had divided their forces into two groups—a Northern and a Southern Army. The Northern Army had still not engaged the enemy, whereas the Southern Army consisted of the remnants from the recent unfortunate battles, increased and strengthened by new troops from the north. This army had positioned itself in a half-circle about Paris so that the French troops in Reims, Châlons, Chaumont, Langres, and Châtillon faced the German line from Sedan, Thionville, Verdun, Nancy, Neufchâteau, Belfort, and Dijon. The French had their headquarters in Orléans. The Southern Army had dug in at Limoges, Moulin, and Creuzot, and had considerable forces ready in reserve positions at Nevers and Châteauroux. Had this Southern Army attacked Lyon, they might have broken through and the French would probably have retaken the fortresses of Lyon, Dijon, and Besançon; for the whole area between Chambéry and Lyon was unoccupied: the Austrian and German positions did not go beyond Lyon and the Italians were entrenched at Chambéry. This French attack did not take place, either because they were not well informed about the enemy positions, or because they had no desire to go over to the offensive.

Before the Germans changed their positions, they filled in the Lyon–Chambéry gap, since the Italians wheeled westwards from Grenoble and Chambéry and so established communications between Lyon and Grenoble. Again the Germans returned to the offensive. The troops on the eastern points of the zig-zag line, as well as those stationed in Thionville, Nancy, and Belfort, moved forward to the east and reinforced the troops who were at combat readiness in their positions at Sedan, Verdun, Neufchâteau, and Dijon. At this point the Germany army, together with the Austrian reserve troops, made up a united and exceptionally strong fighting force on which the fate of the French Northern Army depended. In order to take effective action against the Southern Army, the Germans made up an independent army corps from the large garrisons in Dijon and Lyon together with reinforcements from their Northern Army. These last were covered by Italian troops from Lyon.

The German attack began simultaneously along the entire front. First of all, they had to take the great fortress of Reims, if possible, by a feint followed by a surprise attack. The plan failed, however, because the French dirigibles had observed all the movements of the advancing German troops, so that when the Germans attacked Reims from all sides the enemy were waiting and repulsed them with heavy losses. Since the fortress garrison did not present a threat to future operations, it was decided to starve them out, and to this end a small force, strong enough to contain them, was left behind. The rest of the troops joined with the contingents from Verdun, and all of them moved towards Châlons where they soon came to grips with the enemy. At Chaumont, Langres, and Châtillons the combatants were likewise committed to action, and these small engagements soon developed into a hard-fought battle along the entire front. In order to prevent any movement by the French Southern Army, the German Southern Army advanced towards Limoges, Moulin, and Creusot, where they were sent in to attack the entrenchments. Their southern wing was covered by the Italians, who now found themselves on a line to the north—Montpellier, Nîmes, Avignon—and had taken up positions north–west from Digne, Embrun, and Grenoble, although they did not take part in the attack by the German Southern Army.

The gigantic battle that now followed, along a line from Châlons to Limoges, was a murderous struggle fought with heavy loss of life. The effectiveness of the artillery, which could range over distances of several kilometres, made hand-to-hand encounters impossible. The troops could fire only from cover or from trenches at targets that were a barely visible dot on the horizon, so that only a falling off in the enemy response made it possible to estimate the effect they were having. It was easier to establish the accuracy of the shrapnel fire through field-glasses, for a puff of white smoke marked the place where the shell had burst. Often it was possible to observe a commotion in the enemy lines, and a gap became visible when a shell had wiped out a column of infantry and had smashed their position to smithereens. Then there were moments of confusion, whenever soldiers appeared outside their fox-holes and every gun opened up. Every speck on the horizon was as welcome a target as an animal to a hunting party, and fire would be brought to bear immediately. Behind the front line captive balloons rose to vertiginous heights; and from them observers telephoned down or signalled the regimental commanders the success of an attack and the changes or movements in the enemy positions.

The combatants leap-frog forward; they dig new fox-holes, then an hour or more of sustained fire; they leap forward again like kangaroos, moving like lightning before an enemy bullet finds its target. Some are not fast enough, and then right and left they see their comrades fall as fate has decided. What does it matter? The power of the will and love of the Fatherland are far stronger than all the terrors of Death who has command over the battle-field and bears the heroes without pain or suffering to their eternal rest. On! On! Nearer and nearer to the enemy. Now a fatal step, now a death leap, perhaps the last, and then the longed-for attack on the enemy trenches that is the promise of final victory. Like hailstones flung down by the tempest, the myriad bullets from the machine-guns sweep the battle-field. The guns thunder out their fearful battle-songs, spreading death and destruction, hurling fire and brimstone at the distant horizon where the enemy in his final moments fights on with his last breath for a handful of soil. But still there is no end. The sun sinks in a blood-red cloud, its last rays mingling with the blood of heroes until night shrouds the dead in her dark cloak as she prays for an end to the raging conflict. Trumpets sound, drums beat, occasional shots ring out—and then all is quiet.

A few hours pass, and the battle begins again. The soldiers, still half asleep and shivering in the morning dew, rouse themselves. They snatch a few mouthfuls of food and hasten to their battle positions. The first rounds from the guns send their greetings to the enemy, and soon along the whole front the battle rages more fiercely than the day before. The September sun blazes down on the trenches, hiding the battle-field in a glowing haze where millions of frantic insects fill the air with their humming. Midday comes, and only half a day has passed. Suddenly distant trumpet calls thrill the columns of infantry. Forward! Forward to the attack! With flags flying, their bayonets fixed, they race on over meadow and ploughland, up hill and down dale. Hurrah! Hurrah! They are getting near. Over there, clearly visible, are the enemy trenches piled high with corpses. Rifles, tents, and all sorts of gear are scattered everywhere, and further on a enormous cloud of dust rises up as the enemy take to their heels. The cavalry—Uhlans, Cuirassiers, Dragoons—speed after them at full gallop. 'Hurrah!' shout the infantry, as they disappear into the dust cloud of the retreating enemy. Prisoners are led past from all directions. They are French, and when they come face to face with their enemies they show no signs of hostility, but courteously and like good comrades they surrender. A thanksgiving service, and then the victorious army can fall out and rest—and prepare for more battles.

Whilst it had taken a day and a half of hard fighting to overcome the French Northern Army, the German Southern Army managed to defeat the enemy in a single day, with the result that the two French army corps met as they both retreated towards Orléans. The fear of a sudden enemy flank attack threw them into total panic. The French reserves in Châteauroux and Nevers, too weak to make much of a stand, were ordered to abandon their positions and fall back south of Orléans. The two sides now prepared for the final decisive battle which would be fought in the Orléans area, the headquarters of the French General Staff and the collecting point for all available troops. So, the united German armies had time to distribute their forces as the situation required. For the next four weeks, activities were limited to the small-scale engagements that occurred when the German troops encountered stragglers, guerilla fighters, or mad peasants who wanted to make war on their own.

That year winter came early, and when the German troops took up their positions round Orléans at the beginning of November, the weather was bitterly cold. The French troops in Orléans were hardly affected by the severity of the winter, but it was misery for the French colonial militia and especially for the famous black Senegalese infantry. The cold was the only thing that could affect these simple creatures, who wanted nothing more than to live their lives as they had always done. If their wives became pregnant, if their children grew taller, if the African sun warmed them, then they would never have dreamed of changing their place in the sun with the wealthiest White in Europe. But a single snowfall or a little frost, and the lively spirits of the Blacks were frozen solid. Overnight, the snow-white carpet of northern latitudes buried the courage and the endurance of the African auxiliaries; and it *cancelled out those hopes that had supported the French for years and had encouraged their eagerness for war.*

* * *

The huge semi-circle, which the Allied armies had established on the eastern and southern borders, had now become a small iron ring round Orléans save for a gap to the north that gave the French a link with Paris. Now the area round Orléans is hilly, and the heights surrounding the town are separated by small valleys which fan outwards to end in the surrounding upland. On these heights, or clustered on their gently falling spurs, there are a number of towns. East of Orléans there are Troyes, Auxerre, Clamecy; to the south there are Bourges, Vierzon, Blois; and to the west, Tours, Vendôme, Le Mans, and Chartres. Here the German line ran as far as Le Mans. Chartres to the north-west and Fontainebleau to the north, however, were not held by the Germans.

The order came that the advanced troops at the northern end of the German line were to move from Châlons towards Fontainebleau, and from there to Chartres they were to take up positions in order to block the retreat of the French troops to Paris. They were only to attack them, however, if the enemy were in disarray or if they appeared to be concentrating about Paris.

Comic German allusion to the British naval exercises of 1912, which were clearly directed against a German naval force

The heights round Orléans literally bristled with German guns which were all directed at the various valleys or on the town itself. Within this unbreakable ring of iron a fearful battle began; and despite the reckless bravery of the French troops there was no way of getting through the encirclement, even though thousands hurled themselves at the gun-covered hills only to have their skulls smashed in. Within less than a fortnight, the Germans had cleared the valleys between Orléans and Troyes, Auxerres, Clamecy, Bourges, and Vierzon. In consequence, the remnants of the defeated French army had to pull back east and north of Orléans and concentrate in the great valley between Tours, Vendôme, Le Mans, and Chartres, where the wreckage of their Northern and Southern Armies had already assembled. The Germans drew the ring round Orléans ever tighter; they threw a bridge across the Loire at Blois and penetrated the valley from the south. Then they began a turning movement to east and west, and, with the support of the artillery on the heights, they launched a general attack on all the French forces. For three entire days, the French made every possible effort to prevent the destruction of their army and the inevitable defeat of the nation; but all in vain.

The battle even went on in the skies, aeroplane against airship, but without any remarkable results. For example, the French had no success in their attempt to create a diversion by dropping bombs from their planes on the airships; for so few were killed or wounded in this way that the results were negligible. Two Zeppelins, however, were more successful during a night raid. In place of their heavy bombs, they carried bags of explosive. A special device beneath the gondola shot the explosive into the bivouac fires of the enemy so that whole camps went up in flames. Panic followed, and that allowed a squadron of German planes to come in low and drop their bombs on the terrified troops. However, in comparison to the mass slaughter and immense losses of the French forces, these air attacks were more like fireworks than real warfare, for only whole fleets of aeroplanes could have done any damage.

Day by day, the French regiments melted away: two-thirds of their officers had fallen and the entire army, with the exception of some optimists in the General Staff, had lost heart. After many councils of war, the French Commander-in-Chief decided to retreat towards Paris by stealth and in small divisions, so that the way would be clear when the day came to make a stand before the gates of the capital. For some time the leading columns had been slowly moving on their way, whilst the main body continued the struggle with the enemy in order to secure the retreat so that by nightfall the regiments to the north had the opportunity to move off. In silence, without songs or bands playing, creeping rather than marching, the regiments stole like shadows through the ice-cold night. The only sound came from the snow as it crackled beneath the wheels of the baggage-waggons and the gun-carriages. Along the road, the willow trees stood out like ghosts, whilst the bare branches of the birches and the beech-trees, the snow-covered villages in the background, and the all-embracing sepulchral silence—all completed the desolate picture of a beaten army in full retreat. Hour by hour, they moved in files along the lonely way to the north, and many a soldier thought of those in the capital—a son or a brother, perhaps—who had no idea that their kith and kin were so near. With such hopes and dreams, the retreat could seem like a happy home-coming for some. The mass of the troops were, however, quite cast-down and anxious; they were fearful and confused as though afflicted by evil forebodings.

Their fears were soon realized. Before sunrise the leading troops came in contact with the outposts of the German forces that had closed the road to Paris. The first shots caused chaos in the French ranks. They did not stand and face the Germans, but made off as fast as they could back to Orléans and back upon the troops following behind them. Everything halted in fearful confusion—an enormous mass of troops, baggage-waggons, and guns—that brought death to many soldiers. No sooner had some show of order been restored than the bullets and the shrapnel of the advancing German units took the retreating enemy in the rear. At that, the French fled in all directions. The whole army fell apart, and as for those who did not join in the mass rush to Orléans, they ended up as prisoners. The German ring had closed around the French army; but the French General Staff had not yet lost their wits, although it was evident that a miracle alone could save France from her fate. The French cavalry went racing up the hills to winkle out the German gunners; and horses and riders rolled back dead down the slopes. Whole squadrons lay there as though mown down by a vast scythe. The last of the French Guard regiments, with fixed bayonets and with the courage of despair, sought to break through the enemy ranks. Infantry fire and machine-guns soon brought them to a halt, and they stood waiting for the final mercy of death. Mountains of corpses covered the vast combat zone, the most terrible of all battlefields in world history. From the dark sides the snowflakes fell slowly down, falling ever thicker and thicker, until the pure white snow covered the victims of war in one vast winding sheet. Dark clouds hid the sun as it sank behind the hills, as though Nature had put on mourning clothes for the inhuman slaughter of her sons. The watch-fires flamed in the encircling heights and in the camps down in the valleys. The exhausted warriors were sunk in deepest sleep.

In Orléans the streets were deserted. The fires started by incendiary shells during the day had burnt themselves out and left the city in total darkness like a medieval ruin. No one could tell what was going on within the houses. No doubt, fear of the coming day had prevented most of the inhabitants from sleeping. In a small room on the ground floor of the town hall there burnt a solitary lamp, and round the half-lit table, with troubled faces and furrowed brows, sat the officers of the General Staff, bent on finding some way out of their hopeless situation and failing to reach any decision. In the end, they decided to surrender Orléans to the German army provided that the French troops could depart freely. At once the Chief of the General Staff dictated a suitable letter that was to be delivered to the German GHQ before dawn.

As soon as the German sentries informed the Commander-in-Chief's aide de camp that two French horsemen had appeared under cover of the white flag, the entire headquarters staff were summoned from their beds for a council of war. The intention of the French note was self-evident, and in spite of the seriousness of the situation it touched off gales of laughter. The courteous answer from the German commander pointed out the impossibility of granting free passage out of the city, since all the French troops were in effect already prisoners. However, in order to avoid further bloodshed, the Germans would grant a truce until ten o'clock that morning.

The German *Heeresleitung* made it clear that the French were required to surrender unconditionally; otherwise, when the truce ended, the battle would begin again along the entire front and the artillery would hammer away at Orléans. This answer from the German General Staff did not surprise the French. As things were, escape was impossible, and the German stipulation—unconditional surrender—although harsh, was natural. Given the ineluctable circumstances of their situation, there was nothing to be done but watch with breaking hearts as the flower of the French defence forces marched off to captivity. The discussions went on into the forenoon, and they finally decided to capitulate, even though a small number of the staff argued that the annihilation of the entire army was preferable to a shameful surrender. The town hall clock struck nine o'clock, and then half-past nine; and still the statement of capitulation lay on the table, for no one wished to be the first to put his name to the document. A gun boomed in the distance. Slowly the tower clock sounded the tenth hour, and suddenly the officers leapt up and one after the other they signed a document that surrendered a whole army of close on 200,000 men. Then they sank back in their seats, sobbing and lamenting the ruin of their country. Five minutes later, a white flag was raised on the tower of the town hall. It signalled the surrender of Orléans. Shortly after that, out came the French emissaries with the document that announced the capitulation of the French forces.

It took a whole week for the French troops to hand over their weapons, and there was no end to the long lines of waggons that took the prisoners to Germany. Ever since that day, a second Sedan has had a place in the history books—a second Sedan, but also the last.[5]

The Last Battle

Once again there were revolutionary tremors in Paris, as the whole city succumbed to the incitements of the rabble-rousing anarchists and extreme socialists. The mob seized power; and the universal confusion and senselessness grew into a wild outburst of the most violent passions. The latest slogans went the rounds—'The Army Betrayed', 'Corruption of the Army Command'—and they did not fail to have an effect. Hundreds of gangs roamed the streets, armed with cudgels, rifles, and revolvers, seeking to seize and lynch 'the Guilty' and 'the Betrayers of their Country'. Instant flight alone saved the lives of the garrison officers, the ministers of state, and senior members of the administration.

The President of the Republic, old Barrère, only managed to escape a violent death by taking off at once for London in an aeroplane. His fate would probably have been even worse, had not Providence chosen him to survive the ruin of his country. It happened that his aeroplane ran out of petrol and fell into the Channel. There he was fished out of the water by a herring-smack that happened to be passing *en route* for Bremen. Thus, the President of France ended his flight as a prisoner in Germany, where he found lodgings hastily prepared for him in the Stadthaus in Bremen. He was not to stay long there, for the general animosity against the eminent prisoner was steadily growing. In fact, the whole nation had the same feelings, since the attack on the *Schwalbe* was still a painful memory. Once again an aircraft—on this occasion it was German—had to come to the rescue and take the former President to Wilhelmshöhe. There he was given the very rooms Napoleon III had occupied, and he stayed there until all the formalities of the annexation had been completed.

After the military in Paris had given place to a government of 'the people', thousands fell victims to the rage of the mob; and the representatives of the people, even though they were without an army, began to consider what measures they could take to destroy the enemy or at least to drive them out of the country. They discussed and examined the wildest and strangest proposals. Some wanted to dig for miles around the outskirts of Paris, and fill the tunnels with dynamite in order to blow up the German siege troops. Others talked of building vast machines, to be distributed throughout the forts. These would be capable of hitting the enemy every five minutes with a bomb, ten metres in diameter, with a range of up to twenty kilometres. Others took refuge in schemes worthy of crafty Odysseus—letting loose poisoned rats on the German army, or encircling Paris with ancient cannon, packing them with dynamite, and setting them off all together. The most extraordinary of these desperate fantasies was the charming proposition of inoculating 10,000 dogs with rabies and driving them out of the town, as if people who could entertain such notions were not already prime candidates for treatment at the Pasteur Institute.

Fortunately for the good name of France, none of these perversities of military technology got a hearing; and in the end it was agreed that, in place of the captive army, they would send a fleet of aeroplanes against the German troops and against Germany itself. And then, so the proposers of this plan claimed, 'when our air brigades have wiped out the kraut-munchers and the sausage-eaters (which no one doubted), we will fly direct to Berlin and destroy part of that famous potato patch, with the exception of the lunatic asylums at Dalldorf, Herzberge, and Buch. After that the victory will be ours'.

All the aeroplane factories went into full production, feverishly working day and night to construct biplanes of the approved type. In like manner, the munition factories turned out thousands of bombs every day, and thousands of volunteers were trained as pilots. Thus prepared, the Parisians waited for the approach of the enemy, rejoicing at the prospect of the victory to come.

The enemy were not long in coming. Slowly but surely, the Germans deployed their forces around Paris, and then the bombardment began. The French forts returned the fire, and daily a huge amount of ammunition was expended without any apparent results. Airships and aeroplanes were conspicuous by their absence on the French side, but that was only because they had prudently decided to keep them as their weapon of last resort. In consequence, the

German fliers had every opportunity to observe what was going on within the city; and from what they had seen, it was apparent that, in spite of the siege, the Parisians were taking the greatest interest in aeronautical sports.

The German GHQ took the reports in their stride, since they were well prepared for air combat and had a most effective means of defence. An artillery lieutenant called Naglisch, a descendant of the well-known perfume manufacturer of the same name, had invented an asphyxiating bomb which would put an end to air warfare. This contained a chemical preparation in an oblong metal capsule rather like a torpedo in shape. When fired from a launching tube, it would burst in mid-air and fill the surrounding atmosphere with a deadly gas that would instantly kill any aviators in the area. Quite some time passed before this marvel of German inventiveness could be used, since the Parisians were bent on employing their artillery to speed the cursed Germans on their way to the Great Beyond. They could not fail to attain their objective, for the siege and the daily sorties caused many casualties.

Things were far worse, however, for the besieged, and the number of their troops declined ever more rapidly. Again, food was scarce, ammunition in short supply; and there were the fires caused by incendiaries as well as all those attendant disasters that occur in a besieged city. So, the German *Heeresleitung* decided to attack the city from all sides, and early one morning they began a violent cannon-ade of the forts. The ever-weaker fire from the French batteries helped the Germans, and they were supported by the unbroken fire of their own artillery. At midday, then, the German assault groups took up their positions.

Now the French had observed these preparations, and in the opinion of Citizen Army Command the time had come to bring out their fifth weapon that would wipe out the enemy. In the greatest confusion, the drums beat to summon the aviators to their assembly points in all the city squares. There they collected their equipment and waited all ready for take-off. A rocket would give the signal for action. The sun was already getting near the horizon, and the German machine-guns and field artillery were moving ever closer, so that they had already begun to hit the outskirts of the city. To the east, the attack had already gone in, and the most advanced fort was facing so vigorous an assault that it could fall to the enemy at any moment. As twilight fell, the sharp-shooters leap-frogged their way forward close to the walls, and a giant rocket rose into the air. In a moment the sky grew dark as an army of strange black objects went whistling in all directions through the air. They discharged projectiles in the shape of small pellets which burst with a bang in a cloud of gas. These grew ever bigger the nearer they came to the ground, and at the slightest touch they burst like hand-grenades scattering before them a rain of small projectiles. In the first moments hundreds of German soldiers dropped dead, killed by these infernal machines. Although the destructiveness of this new weapon was not catastrophic, nevertheless the effect would have been significant, had not the German gas bombs killed all the pilots in the act of getting out of their planes.

Shouted orders—trumpet calls—and from every section of the besieging army small torpedoes curved up into the sky. From them burst greenish-blue capsules which disappeared into the atmosphere. In seconds there was an extraordinary change: the bombs tore along like maddened horses; the pilots sat rigid, frozen in their seats; and here and there those who had not belted themselves in fell lifeless to earth. The others, still fixed in their machines, went hurtling across the sky, losing their wings or their rudders in collisions, only to drop like flies on the far horizon.

Thus, the most marvellous achievement of French military technology ended in the flaming, flaring lights of a grand fire-work display.

From all the housetops in Paris the inhabitants watched in horror, for the totally unexpected, almost fantastic catastrophe signalled the end of all their hopes. In place of exaltation there was general lamentation, even total indifference. After that, the assault on the forts was more like an evening stroll; and, later on in the night, when the German troops occupied the ramparts long since abandoned by the French, nothing stirred in the great city. Paris lay silent, as silent as any provincial hamlet in time of peace.

The German commander had expected that the plenipotentiaries would arrive next morning with the capitulation document, but no one came, and there was not even a white flag to be seen on the Eiffel Tower. After a brief discussion, the Germans decided to march into the city and, wherever possible, take immediate possession of the government buildings, galleries, and national monuments. The preparations for the entry into Paris took several days, which passed without the slightest disturbance. Then the German troops marched through the gates of Paris as if they were making a ceremonial entry into the French capital. The difference was, however, that for security reasons the troops were in battle order, with the infantry, artillery, and cavalry in their appropriate tactical dispositions. This proved a wise precaution, since the universal quiet was only the calm before the thunder-storm. In the days after the destruction of their air force, the inhabitants had made all the houses along the main streets into strong-points, so that when the German troops appeared, they were met by a storm of shot and shell. They had to fight their way along the pavements, foot by foot and with many casualties; and it took more than a fortnight before they overcame the furious opposition of the inhabitants. Even then, passive resistance continued which the German troops found most disagreeable, especially when it came to requisitioning food supplies; for the Parisians had destroyed all the provisions stored in their houses and in the food depots. They preferred to kill their pet dogs and to starve themselves rather than willingly give the enemy a pound of flour or a tough old hen. Nevertheless proud *Lutetia Parisiorum* had at last fallen. They had to surrender to the mercy—or not—of the conquerors.

The Iron Fist

By reason of the continuing hostilities—both open and clandestine—the German occupation and administration of Paris resembled the most bloody and tyrannical period of the Terror, and that only served to aggravate the situation. Uncertainty and self-interest prevailed in the Paris municipality, which also represented the national government, so that no one rightly knew how the terms of an armistice could be decided on. The animosity on both sides was so great that force alone could make the city fathers hand over anything to the conquerors, whilst these in their turn completely refused to recognize the existence of a French government, let alone a municipality. In the end, however, a deputation appeared, long after the Germans had taken over all government departments, and had consistently refused to have a single word said about their conquest which had cost them so many casualties. This deputation pleaded in the most woe-begone fashion for permission to open the peace negotiations. The answer from the Germans was:

> After the French have broken the peace of the world in so brutal a way, and after all the insidious attacks they have made—in breach of international law—against the German troops, and also with regard to the cowardly killings by the civil population of German soldiers who had been separated from their units, the German government sees no reason why it should show the French the slightest mercy.

The French have always disturbed the peace of Europe. For centuries they have kept the nations in a permanent state of alarm, and their insatiable desire for conquest has often enough involved Germany in conflicts with her neighbours. Germans have not forgotten that France has always sought to diminish the prestige of the German Empire, and to isolate Germany by alliances with other countries in order to bring about the complete destruction of the Reich. Providence, however, has arranged things differently. Today the mailed foot of Germany presses on the neck of a defeated enemy, and Germany metes out to France the same fate that France has for centuries tried to impose on Germany.

There can be no clemency—that has been forfeited, not simply because of Germany alone but rather to tame the disturber of European peace and render her for ever powerless. If the French provisional government wish to avoid further bloodshed and even more repressive regulations, then they should see to it that all remaining weapons are handed over to the victor.

The immediate effect this answer had on the excitable French hotheads is easier to imagine than to describe. It had never occurred to anyone in France that the plain, honest Germans, who had been content with the paltry sum of five milliard francs in 1871, would decades later be able to employ the skill and the intransigence of a Napoleon. At this moment, however, there is no point in cursing the memory of former statesmen. The sufferings of the children make expiation for the sins of the fathers.

All the ablest and the most intelligent people in Paris joined the municipal council, and in continuous sittings they laboured night and day to find ways that might, in spite of everything, bring about the liberation of France. And France did not hold back from the sacrifices she was prepared to make. Fifteen milliards, payable within one month, were offered as a war indemnity; and at the same time, the French offered to surrender their African colonies. But all in vain. They then raised their offers: twenty milliards, all their territories outside Europe, and the disbandment of their army and navy. At this stage, the German government terminated all negotiations and demanded that the French should surrender all their weapons within a week. The proud French would not endure any further humiliation. Instead of laying down their arms, they once more rose against the German troops, and in their towns and villages, as if by a

The competition between a Zeppelin and a U-Boat for a cargo of List sparkling wine

common arrangement, they flung themselves upon the enemy. A second war began that doubled the casualties of the first, so that prudence obliged the Germans to draw reserves from the Fatherland, and in consequence the frontier-defence forces had to be reduced.

This guerilla warfare lasted for three months. Germany had already proclaimed the annexation of France and had introduced martial law, with the consequence that every day hundreds of rebels were shot. Even women and children took part in the desperate struggle to shake off the foreign yoke; and, since it was not possible to shoot women and minors who defended their native soil, they were deported in their thousands to Cayenne and other penal settlements.

* * *

In the end, France bled to death. The country was depopulated, the crops destroyed. There was hunger and misery in the land, and everywhere the results of the long and bloody war were visible. There was not a Frenchman left who could raise his head. The museums, the galleries, and the science centres opened again; the empty barracks filled with German troops; and all Frenchmen were exempted from military service. There were no longer any French soldiers and sailors.

* * *

Hardly had the mailed fist of Germany restored order in France than the former Entente partners began their cautious diplomatic manoeuvres. The name of their game was: 'What can you give me?' It was clear that Germany had no right to keep all the booty for herself, and besides, the Allied central powers had to agree between themselves on the division of the spoils. Russia could not get over the fact that British neutrality had robbed her of the legendary wealth of India, and their traditional commercial instincts persuaded the British that there was every reason to expect that their neutrality would not go unrewarded. So, all the European powers decided on a Congress in Zurich, which would settle the French question once and for all.

Russia and England sent their most important diplomats, and from the very beginning of the Congress they maintained an unbroken opposition to all suggestions and occasionally made a point with a rattling of their sabres. Spain and Portugal joined willingly with the Triple Alliance; Norway and Sweden remained indifferent to the negotiations so that their representatives merely added to the pomp of the proceedings. The envoys from the Balkans kept a close eye on all transactions and resolutions; and Turkey, represented by two fat pashas, had the courage to defend her interests from the hungry lions that sought to devour her. There were no representatives from

Belgium and the Netherlands, and the Greek Minister left early after he had come to an understanding with his Russian colleague.

The conference dragged on in the customary way, with festivities and other entertainments. However, since all things must have an end, so this conference of European diplomats—which many would have had continue for a long time—did not last for ever. Late one evening there was a final communication which was sent by wireless around the world.

According to the Treaty of Zurich, and in recognition of her sacrifices in the cause of the Triple Alliance, Italy received Tunis and Algiers, and in addition the southern provinces of France: Gascony, Guyenne, Dauphiné, Languedoc, and Provence. England swallowed up Artois and Picardie, as well as the French colonies in India. Russia was satisfied with Persia and Afghanistan. Spain secured Morocco on condition that all the other powers enjoyed freedom of trade there. Austria became a colonial power and inaugurated her overseas empire by taking possession of Madagascar, the Camorran Islands, Réunion; and so on. Besides this, the conference gave the Austro-Hungarian monarchy permission to march on Novi-Bazar and to occupy all the territory as far as Salonika. Greece finally secured possession of Crete; and Montenegro obtained Albania and Epirus. These 'presents' came to Greece and Montenegro at the special instance of Russia, and they now formed an Eastern European Confederation together with Serbia, Greater Montenegro, Bulgaria, and Romania.

When the discussions reached this point, the two Turkish pashas suddenly disappeared, no doubt to make sure that Stamboul had not been evacuated. Germany obtained what was left of France and of the French colonial territories in Africa and Asia. The islands of Cayenne, Martinique, New Caledonia, and Haiti were divided between the European powers for use as penal colonies. England then joined the Triple Alliance, which became the Quadruple Alliance. Thus, the Congress of Zurich had made the central powers into a powerful, unconquerable union of states which guaranteed lasting peace for all Europe and was strong enough to impose its will on every other nation in the world.

Once Upon A Time

For several generations, the France-that-used-to-be groaned under the foreign yoke. In the south, however, the French rapidly interbred with the Italians, so that within twenty years they were all celebrating the great achievements and the Italian origin of the Emperor Napoleon; and the one-time republicans were happy to find their place in the new democracy. As for the English territory in France, a flood of settlers rapidly absorbed the original French inhabitants. But there were difficulties with the Germanization of the vast lands that had come under the rule of the Reich. The Fatherland had supplied the new German territories with such a large labour force from its surplus population that almost half their entire population was German. It was impossible, however, to make a perfect fusion of the two peoples, since French loyalty to their language and to their traditional customs made them keep themselves to themselves, and for a long time they formed a state within a state. In these circumstances, the strict discipline of German government chafed like iron manacles; and there were occasional 'Saviours of *La Patrie*' who were ready to defy the German authorities and start uprisings that were always followed by ever more severe regulations and the withdrawal of all privileges.

In other words: France had had her day. For many decades signs of racial decline had been apparent, and this decadence increased greatly from the time when the French lost the right to bear arms. After service with the *Tricoleur* had ceased to turn the young into robust and skilled men, all their latent vices took over. The birth-rate declined, absinthe became the national drink, and here again another strange phenomenon began to manifest itself. This had already been observed amongst the Poles: namely, that after the collapse of a nation, the entire population goes into a decline and tuberculosis begins to increase. The yearly figure for Poles who contract tuberculosis is enormous; and, strangely enough, after the collapse of France, the same disease carried off the French in great numbers.

Slowly but surely, the bourgeoisie faded away; only the intellectuals and the proletariat remained. The latter dragged out a miserable existence as labourers, whereas the French intellectuals, free from all political feuding, were able to give their entire attention to the arts and sciences, and thus they continued to enrich the world with their achievements. The might of Germany grew steadily greater by land and sea; for no Reichstag in these times-to-come ever hesitated to provide the means that the mailed fist required. The great life-and-death struggle for national survival had shown that the only nations capable of defending their soil are those that are well-armed and have a well-supplied army. As the power of a nation grows, so too does its wealth.

Our great merchant ships steam off across the high seas to far-away places, which we have made a new homeland, and they return heavily laden to fill our warehouses and homes with all good things. That should make us reflect on the fact that in this world nothing is gained without sacrifice. We have a duty to contribute what we can to the construction of a mighty fortress so that our grandchildren in time-to-come may never tremble at the superior power of an enemy and may never fear for the collapse of their Fatherland. War is undoubtedly terrible, but the fear of war is worse. Hence, all citizens must be for ever on their guard; they must surround their nation-fortress with cannon. They must arm, and arm for war—not for self-defence alone, but to bring the traditional enemy to a final battle and destroy him for ever. We know full well that human ingenuity has not yet put an end to hate, revenge, envy, and greed.

> I consider that even a victorious war is essentially evil, that statesmanship must strive to save the nations from war.
>
> v. Bismarck, June 29, 1870

It had been a frightful night, for a nightmare vision of a terrible war had troubled me. Then I woke with an aching head, drops of sweat covered my forehead, and the sound of gunfire still thundered in my ears. My first act was to feel my limbs to see if any bits of me were missing. Thank God! I had returned safe and sound from the battle. Only I could still smell something. Was it gun-powder, or was it cheese? In fact, it was cheese, a really mature Roquefort—a French cheese. That gave me a clue to the origin and course of my terrifying dream. Is cheese bad for me? What a question! As though indigestion could never occur! No, this French cheese lay heavy on my stomach, because—But it is better that I should begin at the beginning again.

One evening I was sitting in my usual haunt where I am accustomed to have a combined lunch-and-supper. When the Roquefort came along, the *Tägliche Rundschau* caught my eye and I read a review from the admirable Litzmann of a recent publication:

> Major de Civrieux, *Der Untergang des Deutschen Reiches—* Die Schlacht auf dem Birkenfeld in Westfalen.[6]

I could hardly believe my eyes. But there it was in clear print:

A French officer has made use of an old prophecy which relates that, one and a half generations after the foundation of the German Empire, the grandeur and the glory would come to an end in a birch forest in Westphalia. Convinced that the fulfilment of this prophecy was imminent, this admirable French officer has now described the Battle of Birkenfeld and has celebrated the French–English–Belgian victory.

The whole of Germany together with its Kaiser had been swept away—that was how the dreadful war of the enemy alliance against the German Reich was to end. I almost had a nervous collapse, but I came to my senses, thanks to a glass of the best Schnapps and to Litzmann's last sentence: 'Let us wait and see!'

I turned things over in my mind, and I thought how I would have to take myself off to another country after the destruction of my beloved Fatherland. 'Let us wait and see!' That was my only hope of escaping the catastrophe. In the meantime, I have asked various firms of carriers to let me have an estimate of the cost for transporting a fifteen-metre vehicle to a place that is about 7,500 kilometres from Birkenfelde. Originally I had wanted to buy Civrieux's prophecy in order to learn the whole text by heart; but I did not have enough cash—and it would be twenty years before my mortgage was paid off. So, I had to face the inevitable and abandon all hope of finding more information about my future as a one-time German; and now I have not the slightest notion what that French officer was blethering about.

Was it that French publication in conjunction with the Roquefort, or was it just the smell of the cheese that caused me to foresee the future? It is enough to say that during the night I mounted the Apollonian tripod, and, what with midnight shudderings and noises like thunder—quite usual when the gods deign to reveal themselves—I had my fearful vision of the final war and the fall of France. Proudly I present myself to my French colleagues—in the prophesying business—as a worthy opponent in the hope that I will not be accused of dishonest competition.

Which of us is right? That is the question! For my part, I have to say in all truth that the gods had their reasons for giving me a sleepless night. They told me the truth, and the gods never lie! Moreover, my revelation is original and more recent than the enemy prophecy ever was. That forecast about 'one and half generations and so on', that was in the dim and distant past. Therefore, probability is on my side. Prophets are without honour in their own countries; and for this reason my brother in Apollo, Major de Civrieux, appears in Germany as a prophet of doom. And that is fortunate, since we would not have otherwise known what we have to expect.

If the same thing happened to me, and the French were to receive my own prophecy that comes straight from the sacred springs of Delphi, then that would undoubtedly be a good thing; for Europe would have the hope that my prophecy—God forbid!—would not be fulfilled.

In other words—*Dear Fatherland, no danger thine* . . .[7]

And . . . we shall see.

Bibliographical Notes

The Battle of Dorking: Reminiscences of a Volunteer

Anonymous (Lieut. Colonel, later General Sir George Tomkyns, Chesney), 'The Battle of Dorking: Reminiscences of a Volunteer'. First published in *Blackwood's Edinburgh Magazine*, May 1871, pp. 539–72. There were literal errors in the magazine version. The text used here is the corrected copy of the pamphlet edition of 1871. For the various counter-blasts, overseas editions, and translations, see I. F. Clarke, *Voices Prophesying War* (1992).

1. Louis Napoleon seriously underestimated Bismarck and, in common with the French army, failed to appreciate the capacity of the Prussian forces. The Franco-Prussian War began on 19 July 1870. After a succession of brilliant Prussian victories, the main fighting ended on 1 September with the surrender of the Emperor, 84,000 troops, 2,700 officers, and 39 generals. Chesney echoed the general opinion when he wrote: 'Such a defeat had never happened before in the world's history.'

2. When Gladstone became prime minister for the first time in 1868, he started on an extensive programme of reform. The Secretary for War, Edward Cardwell, set out to enlarge and to reform the Army. He abolished flogging and the purchase of commissions, reorganized the War Department, subordinated the Commander-in-Chief to the Secretary for War, and reduced service to six years with the colours. Because all these changes cost money, there was considerable opposition from the more radical members of the Government.

3. In the late 1860s there had been friction between the United States and both the United Kingdom and Canada. The dispute with the British followed from the American demand for compensation for the shipping losses caused by the Confederate raider *Alabama*, which had been built in Birkenhead in 1862. An international tribunal, agreed by the two governments, began arbitration proceedings in Geneva in December 1871, and in June 1872 they delivered their judgment. One difference between Canada and the United States derived from the Canadian claim for compensation for fishing rights conceded to the Americans. This matter of the fisheries is central to the Anglo-American war described in *The Stricken Nation* (see pp. 164–92). Another claim for compensation followed from the damage done in Fenian raids across the border. The Fenian Brotherhood was an Irish-American secret society, most active in the 1860s. In 1866 there was a Fenian raid, some 1,500 strong, into Canada near Niagara where the village

of Fort Erie was seized. In 1870 there was another raid from across the Vermont border.

4. Up to 1860, the ships of the Royal Navy were built of wood with broad-side guns as they had been in Nelson's time. In 1859 the French finished converting the two-decker *Napoleon* into *La Gloire*, the first sea-going ironclad. The British answer came two years later when the *Warrior* came into service: a part-armoured vessel which had wrought iron plates covering about half her length. In 1866 the first iron turret ships were introduced.

5. Chesney here invents a variation on the old-style torpedo: a container filled with an explosive charge. One form was the spar-torpedo—the charge was carried on a boom after the fashion of the Confederate submarine, *HL Hunley*, which sank the Federal frigate, *Housatonic*, off Charleston in 1864. Another form was the towing-torpedo, which the Russians used in the Russo-Turkish War of 1877–78, but this was generally abandoned in the late 1870s. On occasions the old-style torpedo operated like a mine—the device was anchored, or left to drift towards the enemy. Presumably Chesney had the latter use in mind.

6. The Militia began as the Anglo-Saxon *Fyrd*; it developed as a national levy, based on counties and restricted to service in the county, save that the whole country was called out whenever there was a danger of invasion. By the late seventeenth century the Militia had emerged as a state army, separate from the king's standing army, each militia force directed by the lord-lieutenant of the county and officered by the gentry. In 1757 the Militia was reorganized: counties to supply a quota drawn from the parishes, with militiamen, aged between 18 and 45, chosen by lot for three years' service with the option of providing a substitute for £10. Cardwell's army reforms in 1870–71 transferred control of the Militia from the lords-lieutenant to the Crown. The army reforms of 1908 incorporated the Militia in the new Territorial Army.

7. After they had sunk the British fleet, the enemy were free to land wherever they chose. Worthing was Chesney's choice for them; and it made good sense. Some 32 miles due east of the naval base at Portsmouth and 26 miles south of Dorking—it offered the shortest approach to London. Chesney's account shows clear evidence that he must have examined the Dorking area with great care, walking on foot to note distances and views. That would not have been a problem, since his post as commandant of the Royal Indian Civil Engineering College at Staines put him about 22 miles from Dorking.

8. The description shows close observation. Chesney chose the obvious defensive position along the line of the North Downs which run eastward from the Guildford area. The high ground falls away in the gap at Dorking, where the River Mole turns northward towards Leatherhead. Box Hill, at a height of 400 feet, was both a major strong-point and a commanding narrative location from which the author could survey the imagined scene.

9. The fog of battle was normal military experience until the French invented smokeless powder, *Poudre B*, in the 1880s.

The Battle of Dorking

Anonymous, 'The Battle of Dorking', *Punch*, 20 May 1871, p. 207. The identity of the author of these verses is unknown.

1. *Blackwood's Magazine* was known familiarly as *Maga* (from *Magazine*) and as *Ebony*, the hard blackwood. This most influential and enterprising magazine represented the Tory interest in Scotland. The editor in 1871 was John Blackwood, son of the founder, William Blackwood.

2. William Ewart Gladstone led the newly formed Liberal Party to electoral victory in 1868. In the House of Commons the long-running duel between Gladstone and Benjamin Disraeli (Dizzy), leader of the Conservative Party, attracted intense national interest. The verse implies that 'The Dorking' was an exercise in party politics—'A Tory alarmist article'.

Der Ruhm

'Der Ruhm, or The Wreck of German Unity: The Narrative of a Brandenburger *Hauptmann*', *Macmillan's Magazine*, July 1871, pp. 230–40. The story never appeared in a pamphlet edition, although it is one of the best counter-blasts to *The Dorking*. The author remains unknown.

1. The old hero was one of the Brandenburgers of the 3rd corps. They distinguished themselves in their repeated attacks on the French in the battle of Vionville–Mars–la Tour.

2. The Iron Cross was instituted in 1813 as a decoration for distinguished service in the War of Liberation.

3. On 18 January 1871, in the Galerie des Glaces at Versailles, the King of Prussia was proclaimed Emperor of the new Reich. The famous painting by Anton von Werner, *Proclamation of Kaiser Wilhelm*, shows the historic occasion with Bismarck centre-right at the foot of the dais.

4. *Ruhm*: glory, fame. The author echoes a view, frequently expressed in the 1870s, that the astonishing victories in the War of 1870 had given Germania a swollen head.

5. The Austro-Prussian War of 1866 began on 7 June and ended effectively with the total defeat of the Austrians at Königgrätz on 3 July. The peace terms were mild: Austria paid an indemnity and ceded Venetia to Italy. The author's mention of the 'Germans in Cisleithan Austria' refers to

the Austrian province of Burgenland: the Seegau area in the north drops down from the Leitha Mountains to Lake Neusiedl. Burgenland is a frontier area of mixed populations—German, Croat, Magyar.

6. In 1871 Russia denounced the Black Sea clauses in the treaty of Paris of 1865. A conference of the major European powers met in London and revised the treaty in keeping with Russian interests.

7. Count Friedrich Ferdinand von Beust was an Austrian statesman and Chancellor of the Austro-Hungarian Empire in 1868–71. August Karl von Goeben was a general of infantry and close friend of Moltke, noted for his decisive victory at St Quentin in 1871 which ended the war in northern France.

La Guerre au Vingtième Siècle

Albert Robida, *La Guerre au vingtième siècle*, George Decaux, Paris, 1887. As the editor of *La Caricature*, Robida gave his readers fully illustrated and generally comic accounts of life in the twentieth century. He devoted the special number of 25 October 1883 to *La Guerre au vingtième siècle*: a war between Australia and Mozambique in 1975, fought with every conceivable weapon. The 48-page album of the same title, published in 1887 and reproduced here, was different in several important ways: here, the French are the principal combatants and are everywhere triumphant in the world war of 1945; and the hectic adventures of the hero allow Robida to display all the possibilities of mechanized warfare in the air, on land, and beneath the seas. Robida was thinking ahead of his age in the Vernian light fantastic. He was not writing a military textbook. As the round-the-world adventures of *mon ami Fabius Molinas* demonstrate, Robida was always true to his trade as a draughtsman. He began with his anticipatory images and then he added the text, which could never be more than second-best to the illustrations. Unlike Jules Verne, from whom he borrowed, his inventions did not start from engineering calculations. His flying machines, submarines, fighting vehicles and the rest have no regard for technological requirements; they are what Robida makes them.

1. Robida here has his fun with the contemporary vogue for Mesmerism. The theories of the Austrian physician Franz Anton Mesmer (1734–1815) held that the stars influence the health and the general state of human beings. All possess a magnetic, healing power which Mesmer called 'animal magnetism'. Those who have great power, the *médiums*, serve as intermediaries between humanity and the universal force.

2. Mesmer believed that the stars acted on the universe by means of an invisible fluid. Robida makes this idea the basis of his humorous account of the *médiums* as demolition experts.

3. Robida clearly has the old-style torpedo in mind.

The Taking of Dover

Horace Francis Lester, *The Taking of Dover*, J. W. Arrowsmith, 1888.

1. Count Nicholas Pavlovich Ignatiev (1832–1908) began his diplomatic career in the negotiations at the Congress of Paris after the Crimean War. Later he was the Russian envoy in Peking, and then ambassador at Constantinople from 1864 to 1877. He worked to end the Turkish control of Bulgaria in order to bring that country into the Russian sphere of influence. These activities led to the Russo-Turkish War of 1877–78.

2. The narrative follows the Chesney precedent: the lamentable history of a rapid decline and sudden fall, all told in a slightly Gallic style in keeping with the alleged translation from the French. The author had rightly concluded that the European situation of 1888 would lead to a rupture between Germany and Russia. The many Russian actions against the new nation of Bulgaria and the attempt to turn Bulgaria into a vassal state were a danger to the peace of Europe. When the Tsar tried to prevent Ferdinand of Saxe-Coburg-Gotha from accepting the offer of the Bulgarian throne, Bismarck intervened to prevent an Austro-Russian war. He published the secret Austro-German treaty of 1879 which promised German support in the event of a Russian attack on Austria. That was the beginning of a series of events that brought Russia and France ever closer together in an *entente* which became a treaty when the Tsar signed the Dual Alliance between the two countries in December 1893. That event provided motives and material for a new flood of future war stories—France and Russia against the United Kingdom.

3. The author plays roulette with contemporary history: an Emperor of France in 1892 was the invention of a reckless imagination; and there is a similar rashness in the unusually rapid succession of Russian autocrats: in 1888 Alexander III was still tsar.

4. An early example of the enemy agent at work. Following on the success of Erskine Childers's *Riddle of the Sands* (1903), the spy story became a popular sub-genre of the future war story.

In a Conning Tower

Anonymous (Hugh Oakley Arnold-Forster), 'In a Conning Tower: How I took HMS *Majestic* into Action', *Murray's Magazine*, July 1888, pp. 59–78. The story is an essay on the rate of change in naval armaments, as the narrator makes clear in his opening remark about 'the total want of any experience to guide me in the enterprise which it was now my duty to undertake'. The story was most popular: an indication of the general interest in these forecasts of the war at sea. There were eight subsequent pamphlet editions, and there were translations into Danish, French, Italian, Spanish, and Swedish. The eighth edition, in 1898 (Cassell & Co.), was illustrated and had two prefaces. The first was the original preface to the sixth edition of 1893. In the second preface Arnold-Forster commented on developments in naval warfare since 1888. He somewhat imprudently remarked: ' . . . it seems impossible that anything can occur which will seriously modify or contradict the propositions laid down in this book'.

1. The Victoria Cross, instituted in 1856, is the supreme decoration for acts of bravery in the presence of the enemy.

2. Arnold-Forster's *Majestic* is modelled on the then latest type of the new 'Admiral' class of ironclad battleships: a broadside battery of six 6-inch guns, at either end a pear-shaped barbette with two 45-ton breechloaders, 18-inch armour at the water line, a powerful ram, torpedo tubes, and a speed of 17 knots. Arnold-Forster could not have foreseen that these vessels would be the last built for ramming in fleet actions. The self-propelled Whitehead torpedo, or automotive torpedo driven by compressed air, was invented by the British engineer Robert Whitehead. The first satisfactory model appeared in 1868, and an improved design came out in 1877.

3. The Warner Light marks the entrance to Portsmouth Harbour.

4. The Lizard Peninsula in Cornwall meets the sea at Lizard Point, the southernmost promontory in the British Isles and the location of an important lighthouse. The *Shannon* was one of three cruisers built between 1877 and 1880, all of them failures: too slow, too large, too costly.

5. There was rapid change in naval projectiles: the old round shot gave way, first, to the iron Palliser shell—unfused, with a chilled head, designed to explode on impact; forged steel shot followed, and then armour-piercing nickel steel.

6. The Whitehead torpedo then had a range of about 600 yards.

7. The ramming action is undoubtedly based on the Battle of Lissa during the Austro-Italian War of 1866. On 20 July an Italian squadron of 12 ironclads and 22 wooden vessels began an assault on Lissa, the outermost island of the Dalmatian archipelago, when an Austrian force of seven ironclads, under the command of Admiral Tegetthoff, arrived to engage the enemy. He found the Italian vessels formed in a single line ahead (about 2 miles), and at once attacked with his ironclads formed in three divisions. The Austrians held their fire until they were about 300 yards from the Italians; and in like manner HMS *Majestic* fired her forward guns—'the last discharge from our turret guns, at three hundred yards, had gone home'. In the mêlée the Austrian flagship *Ferdinand Max* rammed and sank the *Re d'Italia*. This incident was taken as proof that the ram would be a principal weapon in future naval engagements.

The Stricken Nation

Stochastic (Henry Grattan Donnelly), *The Stricken Nation*, Chas. T. Baker, New York, 1890.

1. Benjamin Harrison, a Republican, replaced the Democrat Grover Cleveland in the White House in 1889. During the last quarter of the nineteenth century there was a succession of undistinguished presidents.

2. James Gillespie Blaine (1830–1893) was Secretary of State, first in the Garfield administration, and later under President Harrison. He organized the first Pan-American Congress which met in Washington in 1889. He sought American support for common measures: copyright and trademark agreements, uniformity in custom dues, weights and measures, and the arbitration of all international questions between American nations. He prepared the ground for the successful arbitration of the Bering Sea seal-fishing dispute between the United Kingdom and the United States.

3. Like any good propagandist, Donnelly selects his points with care. The mention of *The Times* probably refers to William Howard Russell, special correspondent of *The Times* during the period of the War between the States. Russell was one of the most distinguished war correspondents of that time. His reports on the shortcomings of the British Army in the Crimea led to the downfall of the Aberdeen ministry in the United Kingdom; but his accurate account of the federal rout at Bull Run was so greatly resented that he was forced to leave the United States.

4. Chester Alan Arthur was president of the United States from 1881 to 1885. Frederick Theodore Frelinghuysen (1817–1885) was a successful lawyer and senator; in 1881 he became secretary of state in succession to James G. Blaine. Thomas Francis Bayard (1828–1898) came from a long line of distinguished lawyers. He was secretary of state during the first Cleveland administration and was the first American envoy to hold diplomatic rank as the US ambassador to Great Britain, 1893–97.

5. Halifax, Nova Scotia, the summer station of the British North American squadron until 1905, was one of the strongest naval bases in the British Empire; it had major dockyard facilities. The Canadian government took over the base in 1906 together with the main base of the British Pacific squadron. This was at Esquimault, some three miles west of Victoria, a fine harbour with graving and dry docks and fortifications.

6. The rich fishing areas of the Grand Bank and off Nova Scotia and Newfoundland were the source of a long-running dispute between Canada and the United States. This began with the limitation of US catches by the convention of 1818. The Reciprocity Treaty of 1854 allowed US vessels to fish in Canadian waters. Later, the Treaty of Washington in 1871 established a fisheries commission, based in Halifax, which introduced an agreed formula for calculating the amount the United States should pay for the

advantage of fishing in Canadian waters. Renewed friction followed when the treaty expired in 1885; but a *modus vivendi* was agreed in 1888.

The Raid of Le Vengeur

George Griffith, 'The Raid of *Le Vengeur*', *Pearson's Magazine*, February 1901, pp. 158–68.

1. The probability of a war—the United Kingdom versus France and Russia—dominated political thinking at the time. The Dual Alliance between France and Russia was signed in December 1893, and in that year there was great friction between the United Kingdom and France when the French attacked Siam. In 1898 there was the Fashoda incident, a crisis that almost brought the two countries into conflict.

2. Verne took some of his ideas for *Twenty Thousand Leagues under the Sea* from the first mechanically driven submarine, the French *Plongeur*, launched in 1863. Other science fiction writers followed. Griffith undoubtedly modelled *Le Vengeur* (including the crew of five) on the *Holland VI*, which the inventor John P. Holland delivered to the US Navy in 1900. The future of the submarine, then in the first stage of development, was much debated. Wells could not 'see any sort of submarine doing anything but suffocate its crew and founder at sea' (*Anticipations*, 1902, p. 200).

3. The action takes place in the Solent Channel, which separates the Portsmouth area from the Isle of Wight, some three miles to the south. Cowes is at the north-western end of the island; Foreland at the north-eastern end; the Needles is another point at the south-western end of the island.

The Green Curve

Ole-Luk-Oie (Major, later Major-General, Sir Ernest Swinton), 'The Green Curve', *Blackwood's Magazine*, June 1907, pp. 733–51. William Blackwood made it a matter of editorial policy to devote part of *Blackwood's Magazine* to military and naval affairs. The Letter Books in the Blackwood Papers, National Library of Scotland, show that from 1903 onwards Blackwood sought out senior officers for their views on defence matters. He kept in close touch with soldiers like Swinton and Vickers, no doubt in the hope that there might be another success like *The Battle of Dorking*. In January 1907 he noted the collaboration between Swinton and Vickers in 'The Joint in the Harness'. On 27 March he sent Swinton a cheque for 20 guineas for 'An Eddy of War'; and in a postscript he added: 'Your green curve will do all right, but more when we meet.' On 3 December he explained to Vickers why he had postponed the publication of 'The Trenches': ' . . . after further consideration I thought it would suit me best to use your striking sketch in my New Year number . . . The story reads capitally in proof and I hope No. 105 will excite as much attention as Ole-Luk-Oie and be as highly thought of by your soldier friends as well as Maga's general readers' (Blackwood Papers, MS 30, p. 395).

The Trenches

105 (Captain C. E. Vickers, RE), 'The Trenches', *Blackwood's Magazine*, January 1908, pp. 39–52. Although naval writers had no doubt that the new warships and the new armaments had changed the conduct of war at sea, it was unusual to find the military expecting any great change in land warfare. Perhaps it could only have been an Engineer officer like Captain Vickers who had the specialist knowledge that told him: 'The machine has begun to dominate war.' The situation he describes in his story is comparable to the trench warfare that began along the Western Front in October 1914. The answer to the tactical problem Vickers set himself in 1908 was to invent a machine, 'to evolve a machine that shall dig trenches, that shall be able to move unconcernedly across open ground where no man can show himself scatheless, secure under its turtleback of steel'. When Colonel Swinton considered the stalemate on the Aisne in 1914, he thought that the best way of dealing with machine-guns and barbed wire was to invent a land-crossing armoured fighting vehicle. So, on 20 October he went to see his old friend Lieutenant-Colonel Hankey, Secretary to the Committee of Imperial Defence, and from that meeting came the Landships Committee and a new means of warfare. Swinton would undoubtedly have read *The Trenches*: did that story give him the idea for the tank?

1. Although Vickers does not say that his trenching machine was a tracked vehicle, that was the only means of obtaining the cross-country mechanical movement he describes. Again, it is tempting to think that the American is modelled on Benjamin Holt of the Holt Caterpillar Company of New York. The company had obtained the patent rights of the Hornsby tractor, a British invention, and had developed it into a tracked petrol-driven machine. The War Office had sanctioned the purchase of a Hornsby tractor in 1905. Nothing came of it, and there was no interest in the Holt vehicle, although there had been demonstrations of the machine at Aldershot. It was, however, the fore-runner of the tank.

The Secret of the Army Aeroplane

A.A.M. (A. A. Milne), 'The Secret of the Army Aeroplane', *Punch*, 26 May 1908, p. 366. Alan Alexander Milne is best known as the author of *Winnie-the-Pooh* and other well-known stories for children. He began his career as a freelance writer, and from 1906 to 1914 he was assistant editor of *Punch*. One of his targets was the frantic chauvinism of journalists like William Le Queux in *The Invasion of 1910* (1906) and in *The Spies of the Kaiser* (1909). In *Punch* (3 February 1908, p. 88) he had earlier attacked the effusive patriotism he observed in Guy du Maurier's very popular play about a German invasion, *An Englishman's Home*: 'To wish to distinguish yourself from your fellows as a man who loves his fatherland; to wish to talk about your love for your fatherland to anybody—I cannot understand it. Has the man no secret places in his heart?'

The Unparalleled Invasion

Jack London, 'The Unparalleled Invasion: Excerpt from Walt. Nervin's "Certain Essays in History"', with illustrations by André Castaigne, *McClure's Magazine*, July 1910, pp. 308–14.

1. The nightmare scenario is a recurrent feature in science fiction: the *what-if* fear that is the source of many disaster stories. One of the early terrors was the Yellow Peril: the fear that the vast populations of China or Japan might acquire the technology that would make them masters of the world. An early instance appears in William Delisle Hay's *Three Hundred Years Hence* (1881), where the United Brotherhood of Mankind (all-white) exterminates the Chinese and Japanese. By the 1890s, tales about Chinese or Japanese invasions began to appear in Europe and the United States. The most notorious was *The Yellow Danger* (1898) by the British writer M. P. Shiel. The most extraordinary was *The Recovered Continent: A Tale of the Chinese Invasion* (1898) by the American writer Oto Mundo. There is an interesting discussion of the Yellow Peril stories in H. Bruce Franklin, *War Stars* (1988).

2. The long sleep of China, a journalistic cliché of the nineteenth century, began to end after the Boxer Uprising of 1900. In 1905 the abolition of the traditional civil service examination was a major advance in the drive for the westernization of the country; the system of public instruction was radically changed, western subjects introduced, and government schools increased in numbers every year. In 1911 a nationwide uprising against the Manchus led to the establishment of a republican government with Sun Yat-Sen as president. On 12 February 1912 the Manchu dynasty came to an end, when the boy emperor was made to abdicate the Dragon Throne.

A Vision of the Future

Gustaf Janson, 'A Vision of the Future', in *Pride of War* (translated from the Swedish), Sidgwick & Jackson, 1912. (This edition was also published in the United States in 1912.) The original, *Lögnerna; berättelser om Kriget*, was also published in 1912.

1. Air warfare is one of the oldest themes in futuristic fiction. It began with the balloon fantasies that followed on the Montgolfier ascents in the 1780s; and it became a favourite theme with science fiction writers after the Wright brothers had demonstrated the possibility of heavier-than-air flight. For a thorough study of the facts and the fiction, see Michael Paris, *Winged Warfare: The Literature and Theory of Aerial Warfare in Britain, 1859–1917* (1992).

2. The background of the story is the Italo-Turkish War of 1911, which opened with the bombardment of Tripoli on 23 October 1911. Italy secured Libya, Cyrenaica, and the Dodecanese Islands.

' 'Planes!'

F. Britten Austin, ' 'Planes!', in *In Action: Studies in War*, Nelson, 1913.

1. Austin put together a series of stories in *In Action* all devoted to examining aspects of modern warfare, especially the employment of new weapons. Speculation about the future use of the aeroplane increased with every advance. As early as 1901, H. G. Wells had predicted the use of aircraft, 'very probably before 1950'. In an original phrase, which became operational doctrine in the First World War, Wells introduced the idea of the mastery of the air: 'Once the command of the air is obtained by one of the contending armies, the war must become a conflict between a seeing host and one that is blind' (*Anticipations*, 1902, p. 195).

Danger!

Sir Arthur Conan Doyle, 'Danger!' (illustrated), *Strand Magazine*, July 1914, pp. 1–22.

1. Doyle wrote the story in order to put the case for the Channel Tunnel, then a matter of controversy. The editor sent *Danger* round the naval experts of the day. He printed their opinions at the end of the story under

the heading 'What the Naval Experts Think'. Not much, they thought: interesting, fantastic, 'most improbable and more like one of Jules Verne's stories'. Admiral Penrose Fitzgerald did not think 'that any civilized nation will torpedo unarmed and defenceless merchant ships'. Ten months later, the Cunard liner *Lusitania* was torpedoed off the south coast of Ireland.

2. The Director of the Royal Navy Submarine Museum, Gosport, commends the far-sightedness shown by Conan Doyle. He considers that Doyle's figures 'were almost accurate for the later submarine that had emerged by the end of WW1. The length to beam ratio (186/24) was awry, since in big handfuls this ratio is 10 : 1; but the rest (endurance, etc.) were certainly in sight' (Commander J. J. Tall, OBE, RN, private letter).

Frankreichs Ende im Jahre 19??

Adolf Sommerfeld, *Frankreichs Ende im Jahre 19?? Ein Zukunftsbild von Adolf Sommerfeld*, first published by Verlag Continent in 1912. The text is taken from the revised edition of 1914. There was a French translation, *Le Partage de la France* (1912), and an English translation, *How Germany Crushed France*, with Preface by L. G. Redmond-Howard, Everett & Co., 1915. This English translation omits the last four pages, from the Bismarck quotation to the end. No doubt Redmond-Howard did not want readers to know that Sommerfeld was giving as good as he thought the Germans had got in the French end-of-Germany story by Commandant de Civrieux, *La Fin de l'Empire d'Allemagne*.

1. This artless projection of the most violent nationalistic ambitions came hot from the Agadir crisis of 1911. That began in June 1911, when the German Foreign Secretary sent the gunboat *Panther* to seize the Moroccan port of Agadir in order, it was said, 'to protect German firms in the South of Morocco'. This aggressive manoeuvre, clearly designed to separate France from Britain and Russia, set Europe against Germany. By September a war with Germany seemed likely; and then the Germans became conciliatory. There were treaties, and the *Panther* was withdrawn. The Imperial Chancellor, addressing the Reichstag in November, felt it necessary to placate the many Germans so vehemently opposed to any conciliation. 'It was most lamentable', he said, 'that the attribution to Germany of intentions which she had never had was used, even by the German Press, in the unpatriotic attempt to show that the German Government had drawn back and that the country had been humiliated.' The Social Democrats laughed (*Annual Register*, 1911, p. 341).

The contemporary desire for German domination, the drive for colonial territories, the rage at France and the Entente—these are the ruling passions of the Sommerfeld scenario. His wish-fulfilment fantasy arranges the future to the eternal advantage of Germany, even to the point of expecting Britain and Russia to give Germany a free hand against France. The language—by turns contemptuous, derisive, aggressive—is the combative patriot-talk of a closed mind dedicated to the proposition of *Deutschland über Alles*. The narrative has little to do with the realities of warfare. An army destroyed here, a fleet annihilated there, well-directed shots, appalling bloodshed, instant destruction, killing them by hundreds—all the phrases reveal a desire for absolute supremacy.

Frankreichs Ende is a good example of the future-war story at its worst. It belongs to the chauvinistic fiction that grew steadily more violent from 1903 onwards, as international relations went from bad to worse. Readers will find great similarities in theme and language between Sommerfeld's *Zukunftsbild* and comparable tales such as William Le Queux, *The Invasion of 1910* (1906), Col. Arthur Boucher, *La France victorieuse dans la guerre de demain* (1911), and Franc Gaulois, *La Fin de la Prusse et le démembrement de l'Allemagne* (1913).

2. The author expected that the Triple Alliance—Germany, Austro-Hungary, and Italy—would act in concert. The Alliance had been renewed in 1912. However, when the Austrians declared war on Serbia in 1914, Italy did not join her allies, but announced her neutrality.

The Italo-Turkish War was the beginning of the end for the Ottoman Empire. There were military mutinies, and the Albanians rose against the Turkish regime. In 1912 the four Balkan allies—Bulgaria, Greece, Montenegro, and Serbia—declared war on Turkey and won rapid victories. King Nicholas I was the autocratic ruler of Montenegro (1860–1918), nephew of Danilo II who was assassinated in 1860.

3. Olivier Émile Ollivier (1825–1913), a French statesman appointed by Napoleon III to form a ministry in January 1870, was out-manoeuvred by Bismarck in the matter of the Ems telegram. Went to war 'with a light heart', he said; but when the first military disasters came, he was driven from office and fled to Italy.

4. The cornflower is the national emblem of Germany.

5. The Battle of Sedan was the first and greatest military disaster in the disastrous War of 1870. Four French army corps, some 100,000 troops in all, were encircled by the German forces in the small fortress town of Sedan. The consequent surrender of Napoleon III and his troops brought on the collapse of all the French forces and the downfall of the Second Empire.

6. The French original was published in 1912: Commandant de Civrieux, *La Fin de l'Empire de l'Allemagne. La Bataille du 'Champs des Bouleaux'*, 191. *Histoire éditée en 193 . . . Avec préface du Commandant Driant.*

7. '*Lieb Vaterland magst ruhig sein*! The first line of the chorus for *Die Wacht am Rhein* (The Watch on the Rhine), a popular and most patriotic song similar in sentiment to the British *Land of Hope and Glory*. Composed in 1840 by Max Schneckenburger (1819–1849), and sung throughout Germany in 1870.

Biographical Notes

HUGH OAKELEY ARNOLD-FORSTER (1855–1909) was the son of William Delafield Arnold, grandson of Thomas Arnold, and nephew of Matthew Arnold. His parents died early—his mother in 1858, and father in 1859. The four children of the marriage were adopted by Jane Martha Arnold, their father's sister, and her husband, William Edward Forster. In 1877 they all took the name of Arnold-Forster in token of their regard for their adoptive parents.

Arnold-Forster had a short, very successful, career in administration and in politics: first, as private secretary to William Edward Forster when he was chief secretary for Ireland; next, as an enterprising partner in the publishing firm of Cassell & Co. He was elected member of Parliament for West Belfast in 1892, was Secretary of the Admiralty in 1900–03, and Secretary for War in 1903–05. He wrote frequently on army and naval matters.

FREDERICK BRITTEN AUSTIN (1885–1941) served throughout the First World War: he enlisted in the London Rifle Brigade in 1914, was commissioned later that year, and was discharged with the rank of captain in January 1919. He wrote frequently for the *Strand Magazine* and the *Saturday Evening Post*; and he had several successful plays. He had a particular interest in the possibilities of future warfare, and in 1926 he returned to the subject with another collection of eight short stories, *The War-God Walks Again*. These dealt with various aspects of coming wars—gas warfare, civil populations, aircraft—all presented as warnings against military complacency.

GEORGE TOMKYNS CHESNEY (1803–1895), the youngest of the four sons of Captain Charles Cornwallis Chesney of the Bengal Artillery, came from a distinguished army family. His brother, Colonel Charles Chesney, was a well-known military writer. His uncle, General Francis Rawdon Chesney, presented a report in 1830 on the feasibility of constructing the Suez Canal—information on which De Lesseps based his plans for the successful undertaking of 1869.

The young Chesney gained a commission in the Bengal Engineers and arrived in India in December 1850. During the Indian Mutiny he was Brigade Major of Engineers throughout the siege of Delhi, where he distinguished himself in several actions and was severely wounded in the final assault. In 1860 he was appointed director of the new Public Works Department. His book on *Indian Polity* (1868), which dealt with the administrative arrangements of the Indian Government, became a standard textbook.

In 1870 he was recalled to England and charged with the foundation of the Royal Indian Civil Engineering College at Staines in Middlesex. The institution provided India with the engineers who built the roads, railways, canals, and telegraph systems of the old Raj. In May 1871 *Blackwood's Magazine* published, as the first entry, his anonymous tale of *The Battle of Dorking: Reminiscences of a Volunteer*. Thereafter, Chesney went from one important post to another. In 1880 he returned to India as Secretary to the Military Department; in 1886 he was made the Military Member of the Governor-General's Council. He left India in 1892, and in the election of that year was returned as the Conservative member for Oxford. He died suddenly on 31 March 1895.

Chesney was held in such esteem that in 1899 the Council of the Royal United Service Institution established the Sir George Chesney Gold Medal, to be awarded to the author of 'an original literary work treating of Naval or Military Science, and which has a bearing on the welfare of the British Empire'. The first award, in May 1900, was to Captain A. T. Mahan, US Navy, in recognition of his outstanding studies on the influence of seapower.

HUGH GRATTAN DONNELLY (1850–1931) began his career as a political writer, and occasionally successful playwright, in 1880 when he published a futuristic satire, *The Coming Crown*. This was an ingenious tale for that time, since Donnelly told his story in a series of press cuttings supposed to be taken from the American newspapers of 1882, using them to give his projected views of 'the doings of his Imperial Majesty the Emperor Ulysses I', or General Grant. The following year he published *'84: A Political Revelation*, in which he reported on the imagined 'proceedings of the Democratic and Republican Conventions, culminating in the nomination of J. G. Blaine and B. F. Butler respectively'.

From 1888 onwards Donnelly published a succession of plays. Two of them won the attention of the critics: *Darkest Russia*, produced at the 14th Street Theatre, New York, in 1894; and *The American Girl*, produced at the Third Avenue Theatre, New York, in 1900. Donnelly does not seem to have had any success with *The Stricken Nation*. It was not republished and there is no reference to reviews of the story in any of the periodicals for which there is CD Rom indexing access. His death was recorded briefly in the *New York Times* (25 July 1931, p. 13). Apart from two years in Scotland with an unnamed Glasgow newspaper, Donnelly is reported to have held positions on American newspapers as a city editor and dramatic critic.

ARTHUR CONAN DOYLE (1859–1930), whose name has been the guarantee of ingenious and exciting stories ever since *The Adventures of Sherlock Holmes* appeared in the *Strand Magazine* in 1891, was educated at Stonyhurst College and studied medicine at Edinburgh University, where the professor of surgery, Joseph Bell, taught his students the close observation of particulars that became the characteristic of Sherlock Holmes.

Doyle was a prolific and original writer. After a series of short stories and the first appearance of Sherlock Holmes in *A Study in Scarlet* (1887), he took to the historical novel (*Micah Clarke* in 1889, *The White Company* in 1890). Fame came with the first of the Sherlock Holmes stories which began in the July number of *Strand Magazine* in 1891. He wrote much fiction and a number of plays. In 1912 he turned his attention to science fiction in *The Lost World*, where Professor Challenger made his first appearance; he reappears in *The Poison Belt* in 1913.

The origins of Doyle's short story about submarine warfare, *Danger*, go back to the Agadir Crisis of 1911, when Doyle was convinced that there would be a war with Germany. He wrote an article on 'Great Britain and the Next War' for the *Fortnightly Review*, where he argued in favour of a Channel Tunnel. This argument is further developed in *Danger*.

GEORGE GRIFFITH (1857–1906), or George Chetwynd Griffith-Jones, was born into a clerical family, the second son of George Alfred Jones, latterly vicar of Mossley, Manchester. Shortly after his father's death in 1871, he signed on as a deck-hand with a Melbourne-bound sailing vessel; and, after a period in the Australian outback and several years before the mast, he returned to England, not yet 20, in 1877. Seven years of hard work followed, teaching by day and studying by night.

Griffith's luck began to change when he obtained a menial position (addressing envelopes) with the new popular weekly, *Pearson's Magazine*, which had started in 1890. From envelopes he graduated to answering readers' questions, and from that he went on to writing science fiction stories. The success of Admiral Colomb's serial story, *The Great War of 189–*, which began in *Black and White* on 2 January 1892, had shown the entrepreneurs of the new mass press that futuristic fiction, especially future war fiction, would sell well. That led Pearson to launch into serialized stories. Griffith volunteered to write the first, and in 1893 he turned out *The Angel of the Revolution*—Russian anarchists, advanced flying machines, compressed air-guns.

The increased circulation figures impressed Pearson so much that he engaged Griffith to write exclusively for his publications. A long series of stories followed—future wars, space travel, lost race adventures, world catastrophes, historical fantasies. They were very much of their day, and for that reason George Griffith is no longer remembered today. There is an excellent account of the life and publications of Griffith in Sam Moskowitz, 'The Warrior of If', in *The Raid of 'Le Vengeur' and Other Stories by George Griffith* (1974).

JOHAN GUSTAF ADOLF JANSON (1866–1913) was born in Stockholm, a man of many talents—painting, the stage, fiction. For a time he was a journalist and contributed to the *Stockholms-Tidningen*. He began to write novels in 1895, and soon gained a reputation for his historical romances and his social themes. The Italo-Turkish War of 1911 led him to write a series of short stories on war themes. These were published in *Lögnerna: berättelser om Krieget* in 1912. Janson is little known outside Sweden; *Lögnerna* was one of the few works by him to be translated into English.

HORACE FRANCIS LESTER (1853–1896) was a barrister and a worthy of the Western Circuit who failed to make a reputation for himself in the law. He published various works: several romantic tales (*Queen of the Hamlet*, 1894; *Hartas Maturin*, 1888); some satirical verse; and *Lessons in our Laws* (1893), which was 'an attempt to interest boys and girls, incidentally grown-up people as well, in the subject of our English institutions'.

JACK LONDON (1876–1916) was born in San Francisco and grew up in poverty. He left school at 14, and spent the next seven years seeing the world as a sailor, wanderer, and gold prospector in the Klondike. A prison sentence for vagrancy directed him toward socialism and to obtaining an education.

London's wide reading (especially evolutionary theories, economics, and politics) carried over into his writing, which he began with *The Son of the Wolf* in 1900. His experience as a war correspondent in the Russo-Japanese War was the starting-point for *The Unparalleled Invasion*. He wrote two articles on the subject of China's awakening: 'The Yellow Peril', *San Francisco Examiner* (25 September 1904) and 'If Japan Awakens China', *Sunset Magazine* (December 1909). He was much influenced by his readings in the literature of social Darwinism, especially by the doctrine of the survival of the fittest. There is a most informative discussion of London's racism in H. Bruce Franklin, *Star Wars* (1988).

ALAN ALEXANDER MILNE (1882–1956) was the son of teachers who conducted their own school, Henley House, where H. G. Wells was science master for a time. His father, J. V. Milne, has several pages to himself in Wells's *Experiment in Autobiography*; he was, wrote Wells, 'a man who won my unstinted admiration and remained my friend throughout life'.

A. A. Milne went on from his father's school to Cambridge and then to journalism. In 1906 he became assistant editor of *Punch*. He contributed weekly pieces: theatre and book reviews and witty commentaries on contemporary events. He left *Punch* in 1919 to write for the stage and produced some notable comedies. Milne gained an international reputation with his children's stories, especially with the never-to-be-forgotten *Winnie-the-Pooh* in 1922.

ALBERT ROBIDA (1848–1926) had a son, Fréderic, who said that anyone attempting a life of his father would have to describe his biography as 'Six Personalities in Search of the Same Author'. It is an apt way of characterizing the many abilities and varied enterprises of a protean genius: the humorist, the recorder of daily life, the prophet and projector, the illustrator of great works of literature, the historian and presenter of past events.

Robida was born in modest circumstances at Compiègne and at the age of 16 was apprenticed to a local lawyer. He failed, however, to apply himself to the law, but took to making a satirical album, *Le Manuel du parfait notaire*. This so enraged his employer that he was dismissed, or rather set free to make his own way in the world. He departed for Paris, where he learnt his trade as a graphic artist by contributing to most of the illustrated magazines. He spent two years abroad, in Vienna (where he was editor of the *Floh*) and in Hungary, and from that experience there came a succession of illustrated travel books.

From 1880 to 1890 Robida was the *rédacteur en chef* of the French satirical weekly *La Caricature*; and under his genial direction the magazine offered young draughtsmen (Caran d'Ache, Louis Morin, and Ferdinand Bac, among many) an opportunity to make a name for themselves. At his most imaginative, he was the inaugurator of a new art form: the representation of things-to-come in the innovatory images of *La Guerre au XXᵉ Siècle*, *La Vie au XXᵉ Siècle*, *Un Voyage de fiançailles au XXᵉ Siècle*, and *La Vie électrique*. All these books were published by George Decaux, with whom Robida was on the best of terms. As his son said, Albert Robida was obsessed with his premonitions of the effect the sciences would have in transforming the world. At first he chose to laugh at these changes. Later on he came to weep at them. An excellent, brief account of Albert Robida's life and a list of his illustrated work is to be found in: Fred Robida, 'Un artiste protée: Albert Robida', *Bulletin de la Société Le Vieux Papier*, July 1968, pp. 209–24.

ADOLF SOMMERFELD (1870–1931) was a journalist before 1914, who seems to have had an eye for the sensational: a book on the secrets of the Camorra, another that claimed to be the diary of the Chief Eunuch of the Harem, and another on the Italo-Turkish War. His death in 1931 merited a brief mention in *Kürschners Deutscher Literature-Kalendar* for 1932, where he appears as the author of some twenty crime fiction stories published in the 1920s, a film director, and the author of several plays.

ERNEST D. SWINTON (1868–1951) was born in India and commissioned into the Royal Engineers in 1888. After the success of his account of tactics in *The Defence of Duffer's Drift*, which first appeared in the *United Service's Magazine* in 1904, he developed his gift for writing short stories in a succession of future-war tales in *Blackwood's Magazine*, the *Strand Magazine*, and the *Cornhill Magazine*. By 1907 he had become a chief instructor at the Royal Military Academy, Woolwich.

Swinton's chief claim to fame follows from his work in promoting the planning and production of the first modern armoured fighting vehicles. On 23 October 1914, back from a tour of the Western Front, he saw Maurice Hankey, Secretary to the Committee of Imperial Defence, and proposed that the Holt caterpillar tractor should be used in the construction of armoured vehicles. He said later that he had read Wells's *The Land Ironclads* in 1903, 'but had looked upon it as pure fantasy and had entirely forgotten it'. However, Sir Basil Liddell Hart observed in his obituary notice on Swinton (*The Times*, 17 January 1951) that a vestigial recollection probably remained. A more likely reason is that Swinton remembered the remarkable trenching machines in *The Trenches* by his friend Captain C. E. Vickers RE. The fact is, however, that Swinton began to change the conduct of modern warfare in July 1915, when he set down his ideas for a fighting vehicle in a comprehensive memorandum. After the first successful trials of the new machines in January and February 1916, Swinton gave the cover-name of 'tank' to the new vehicles. His version of these developments are the subject of his *Eyewitness* (1932).

After the First World War Swinton went into business as the British director of the Citroën Car Company. He moved into academic life in 1925 when he was appointed Chichele Professor of Military History in the University of Oxford and Fellow of All Souls. He gave his account of his life in *Over My Shoulder* (1951).

CHARLES EDWARD VICKERS (1873–1908) was born in Dublin, the youngest son of Henry Thomas Vickers, barrister-at-law. Educated at Clifton College, he passed direct into the Royal Military Academy, and in 1892 passed out top of his term, having been awarded the Pollock Medal and many prizes. He was commissioned into the Royal Engineers and specialized in railway work. Posted to Malta in 1898, he there became a regular contributor to the *Daily Malta Chronicle*. During the Boer War he served in various posts—traffic superintendent, railhead traffic officer, and finally deputy-assistant director of railways. He returned to home duties in 1902 and served as staff captain until his early and unexpected death of 6 February 1908, a month after his short story *The Trenches* had appeared in *Blackwood's Magazine*.

Had Vickers survived, it is quite possible that Swinton might not be the name associated with the invention of the tank.